ISBN: 978-1-961677-75-3 (Paperback)

Printed in the United States of America

Published by

info@thequippyquill.com
(302) 295-2278

3 BOOKS IN 1

HOBO

SUCCUBUS

BUENO RIO

BY FREDERICK DALPAY

CONTENTS

HOBO

SUCCUBUS

BUENO RIO

HOBO

BY FREDERICK DALPAY

PROLOGUE

The Roosevelt "New Deal" washed over them like a ripple on the surface of a pond. Before the Great War, there were half a million of them, all living like they owned the country. These men and women were partners to the rails.

They represented the basic elements of society at its roots. The extroverts the introverts and the omniverts. They knew each other from the Atlantic to the Pacific, and back again. They could tell by the cut of a man's jib, the stuff from which he was made. Some, used to wear a scarlet bag around their neck, as a badge of honor. It contained their most prized possession, a straight edged razor. The razor was a tool, a grooming aid, and a source of protection.

Everything used to move by rails before "Big oil" and "Big business" dismantled the passenger trains, replacing them with automobiles and highways. After the war, the homeless men who were left, were getting on in age. The means and ways of their livelihood dried up. They started to settle down into little shanty towns, of their own design. The scarlet bags began to disappear, in part because no one wanted to be mistaken for a communist. The bums took to the cities, the tramps took to the suburbs, and the Hobos took to the highroads.

The highroad is a mystical place, where the traveler is in constant motion; between where he is at the present, and where he hopes he will someday arrive.

The Hobos shuned tramps and bums, as if they carry the plague; which some of them do, no doubt. Unlike the tramps and bums, the Hobo, knows when to keep his mouth shut. He knows, when to put a little distance between himself, and any misunderstanding a sheriff might be having. Hobos were the elite; the musicians, the sculptors and the poets. They were the essence of culture and refinement, growing in soil that would bear no fruit. This does not mean I like them, I do not.

Tramps and bums, I have always hated. The tramps were always drunk and friendly. The bums were always poking around for an extra portion of whatever came their way. A hobo I can tolerate for just about as long, as it takes to get myself, up on my feet and out of town. I used to love them all, but that was years ago and I was young.

I thought the life of a Hobo was a romantic sort of thing.

There was always a mouthful of food, for a guest; and a free ride on a boxcar, for a weary hiker. The hobos kept their own counsel; never offering anything more than a helping hand to a close friend.

They always seemed so courteous and thoughtful when I was young and stupid. With food and shelter they saved my life more than once. This does not mean, I have not had to repay them, in kindness and understanding ever after.

If I ever see another hobo; or will be too soon. Of course, as they learn my new address, they will come calling, like they have done for the last few years. Hobos love to spend time with their heroes. I move frequently.

CHAPTER ONE

I had not laid eyes on a real hobo in ten years, when I noticed some strange events around my house. It started with the cards. I first found the extra joker to a deck to Aviator playing cards. I knew instantly someone was on the highroad. Here I would find an Ace. There I would find a King. Somewhere else, I would locate the Jack of Spades and a ten. A good hand if the correct Queen showed up. Queen of spades meant a working man's flush; someone had come into some money. Queen of hearts would tell me; I was being visited by a lonely hobo, who would move on in a few days. It might even be a lady hobo.

The next card never showed up. They were sitting back, keeping track of what I was doing. The hobos do not recognize the fact; that someone has anything better to do, than to be part of their extended family. I knew intuitively; if I was called on to help them, I would have to drop whatever I was doing and lend my support.

I really did not have time for this foolishness. I had a job, a rental house with bills to pay. I had settled into middle class America and put the past behind me.

My employer would never understand the hobos. I liked my job. I had searched all my adult life for a job like this. The work was easy. Show up for a few hours, observe other people working, then write a hasty report before moving on to the next work site. I knew with every fiber of my being; the hobos would screw things up. I had hobo-phobia.

Not wanting to chance offending anyone, I started leaving the back door unlocked whenever I was away. When food started to vanish, I knew I was doing the right thing. To my unseen friends a peach which has been stolen, tastes better, than one which was acquired honestly. They were willing to overlook the fact, that the door was unlocked, which constituted my permission to take whatever they wanted. I even made a special trip to the supermarket for fruit. They love fresh fruit. They love any fruit except Kiwis, which they will use to polish their shoes. The ring around the bathtub did not bother me. They left an empty Ivory soap wrapper stuck to the mirror to remind me which brand they prefer. Ivory soap florals. It is therefore, more practical to someone who has a habit of washing in a river. I purchased a few 99.44/100% pure bars of the stuff. I then apologized by putting a bar in the bottom of a fresh pair of socks. A traveling man likes to keep his foot clean. Clean socks also make for an acceptable wash cloth.

At the same time, I purchased the soap, I stocked up on tissue paper in the box. Hobos would rather not travel with a bulky roll of toilet paper. I placed a box of plastic sandwich bags in plain sight. If they decided to leave, they could keep the tissue paper dry.

In my effort to please, I neglected to attend to the basic need for tobacco. Their unspoken indignation, came in the form of cigar rings, left in obvious places. I hurriedly placed a whole can of Bugler, roll your own, in a convenient place for them to find. If they found it acceptable, I would know I was dealing with one of the thousands of Williamson brothers.

The tobacco was gone the next evening, but I found the empty can shoved up under the porch. No Williamson brother had done this. The can would be placed in a more prominent place, if it was one of them. I could eliminate my guest, from whole herds of hobos, with this little bit of information.

The Williamson's take their pseudo-name from the Williamson tobacco company maker of Bugler. Many times, the address on the package is used, when a man needs to inform a police department of his permanent residence. They love the texture of it and the fact that besides being a good smoke, it can be chewed. Chewed the tobacco is perfect for spitting in a rattlesnake's eye. The blinded reptile thereby, becomes a delicious entre.

They had not used any of my Old Spice aftershave. Nor did they leave me any hint, as to what liquor, I should supply as a good host. I checked my cooking sherry; it was still full. The next evening, I brought home a selection of beverages. Being short of cash I limited myself to a small botte of bourbon, another bottle of white wine, a can of beer and some Aqua Velva. I decided this was enough to flush out the rascal. In the morning I would be out early, on a job site. Upon my return, their choice of libation, would provide me with a new clue.

I came home that night to discover the white wine was now colored pink, with some cranberry cocktail from the refrigerator.

The Land-O-Lakes butter carton had been skillfully altered. The Indian girl was doing a peek-a-boo, with breasts made from the knees on the package. My guest was telling me, I was being a little too nosey. On the counter, an empty Camel cigarette pack had likewise been altered. The dromedary was made to look as if he had a penis. This had been accomplished by shifting one of the minarets from the back to form the appropriate appendage. They were calling me a-prick.

Still, whoever it was offered another clue. An empty Top tobacco rolling papers package, was left where I would be sure to notice it. They were toying with me. Pink wine meant I was enter-raining a lady. I only knew a handful of lady hobos, and the ones 1 knew, were tramps. Top tobacco users, are what we refer to as re-publican. My choices were very limited by this piece of information. A lady republican hobo, would be a rare bird indeed. That night I corrected my mistake. I picked up a bottle of blush wine.

They would know, what I meant.

I was still waiting for the next playing card. I took a long walk. along the nearest set of railroad tracks. Here I found some playing cards, but they were the wrong brand. Bicycle brand was only used by bums. As 1 expected all the Aces were missing from both the red and blue decks. I did not bother to check the rest of the high cards. Some bum was going to a card game with an extra supply of winning hands. If someone plays poker with a bum, they should count the cards every couple of hands. It is not unusual for a deck to contain seventy or more cards depending on how many bums are cheating. I learned this in a game out in Jackson Hole, Wyoming. There were sixty-two cards. When I flipped them face up, it looked like a Pinochle deck.

The next afternoon, I was heading home from the third job of the day, when my pocket telephone pager started to beep. The office wanted me to call them. I was close enough to make a personal appearance, so I swung by, like a good Pavlov pooch. My boss, the co-owner was all smiles and handshakes. This took me off guard. He explained that he knew exactly how I felt and wished me the best of luck with my new employer. I was shocked, this came as a surprise to me. I did not know what to say.

"What new employer?" I stammered.

"Don't be coy with me. The employer that sent their representative by here today. You know, to check into your financial status." the grinning idiot explained.

"What did this representative look like?" I asked smelling essence of rodent in the air.

"Very dignified, sporting a monogrammed jacket with Vuitton briefcase

"What exactly did you tell them about my financial status?"

"Just, that we could not begin to offer you're the type of package they had in mind. I even told her that you would be a fool to stay here a moment longer." he said. He reaches all into his drawer and removed an envelope. "I had your final check drawn up and included a small severance bonus, not that It will look like much, compared to what you will be making at your next job." " And what if I wanted to stay here?" I suddenly felt weak.

"That would be impossible. I hired a new man this afternoon to replace you." he looked momentarily at a loss for words. "Your new employer wanted me to give you this." He held out a second envelope. That poor stupid bastard must have fallen of a turnup truck, on the way to becoming my boss.

I did not open the envelope in his presence. I dumped my pocket pager on his desk, turned in my unfinished reports, and beat a hasty retreat from the office. I did not feel well. The walls were closing in on me. I just knew; that I was going to end up homeless. I looked in the second envelope. There was half of a one hundred dollar inside, and the fifth playing card. I looked at the four of clubs, it was the hand of a looser.

I should have gone right back inside, and begged for my job back. Failing at that, I should have strangled that grinning jerk.

This at least, would provide me with a jail cell to look forward to.

My head was spinning, I went home. The car wobbled from side to side as I drove. I was not aware of anything except the overwhelming sense of doom.

In my mailbox was a few new bills, second notices on some old bills, and another playing card. This time I was holding a Queen of hearts. Someone was screwing with my mind, first a losing hand, now a low winning hand, something had to give. The Queen of hearts I had always looked upon as a personal good luck card. If she was lucky for me, she better start working her magic. The cards had been dealt: Ace of spades, King of spades, Jack of spades, Ten of spades, Four of clubs and Queen of hearts.

It was my turn to discard.

I knew another Quenn of hearts. I cringed, to ta only be one person. If it was that woman, I did not want anything to do with her. That woman has been a thorn in my side from the moment we met. If it was her, I might as well go in and stick a gun to my head. Or I could make it look like an accident, by taking a shower while I was making toast.

I walked into my living room, there she sat. Her monogrammed jacket was folded across the back of a chair, the Louis Vuitton briefcase was opened like a prop, in a staged situation.

Her white pleated linen skirt, spread out in a fan fold pattern. I did not say a word, I just started looking for my bullets. I had sprung upon the perfect plan to pay her back for all those years of pain. I would blow my brains all over the room, then let her explain it to the police.

"That's no way to greet a guest! Come over here and kiss me."

I heard someone say from another dimension.

"No way Countess, I can't afford the penicillin."

"Must you be so vulgar?" she said as she snapped her head back and affected the air of nobility.

"Cut the shit, If I knew it was you, I would have laced to wine with rat poison." I quipped coldly. I watched her, as she seemed to cower at this provocation. I noticed her eyes turn moist and sad.

She had tried this on it before. Next would be the piety pout, with the lower lip quivering. At all cost I wanted to stop her before she got into the wailing lamentation.

"What is it you need?" I swiftly interjected.

The perfunctory hanky appeared and dabbed her nose. I could not believe it; she was actually trying to convince me that this was not some melodrama she had cooked up. I looked at her again for the first time. She did look good, well healed, as they say. Her clothes fit for once, instead of hanging on her loosely like someone else had cast them off. Her hair was clean, shinning and well groomed.

Even from across the room I could tell her cologne was expensive.

I told myself; she probably had visited a sample counter on the way to my apartment.

I snapped back to reality, this was the countess, she was a rough and tumble as anyone else, whoever rode the rails. She may have been even tougher than some of the men. Her attempt to gain my sympathy was not going to work, I decided. I was not like one of those mid-western farmers in Nebraska. Years ago, she used the same tactics, to convince them, to give us free meals. Food in trade for some of her ample expertise in promiscuity.

"I thought after all this time you might have remembered me fondly." she finally offered, still dabbing at her nose.

"I remember the early days fondly. The latter days I don't remember at all." I counseled, wondering if I was doing the right thing. What harm could it do to listen?

I pulled the wine out of the refrigerator and offered it to her, with a dirty glass. Rather than share the wine, I popped the tab on a can of beer, then took a slug of the bourbon. The "boiler maker" would provide me with what I wanted; a clean break from reality.

Momentarily I would listen to what she had to say, then I would I resume looking for the bullets. They should be in the desk drawer.

What was I thinking? I was not going to shoot myself. I was going to go groveling to my idiot boss, and try to get my old job back. I would explain that it was all a charade perpetrated by a lad- hobo. A dead lady hobo, who I had dispatched, myself. She got up, found a clean wine glass, and poured herself a moderate volume of the liquid. I was impressed to see that she had changed her drinking babies. She continued with the pout and dabbed at her nose. I fought to control myself, but I was beginning to soften in my opinion of her. She really was an attractive creature. Green eves with red tinged, auburn hair. I could not see them at the moment, but I remembered she would have freckled breasts.

"You've got to help me; I don't mean me I mean us." she volunteered.

"What us are you talking about?" I grimaced.

"NO... not even us... you've got to help them."

"What them?"

"The old gang," she erupted into a cascade of tears.

"My old gang was me and you, and you got lost!" I advised.

"I didn't get lost, asshole. I got established." she rationalized.

"You must have got established really good, because I looked for you for six months and never found a trace."

"I was pregnant, what do you expect?"

"You pregnant? I thought you were sterile!"

"So did I, sugar. By the time I found out I was pregnant, I was sitting pretty, down in El Paso. I was with a wonderful man. One who thought; I was the next best thing to sliced bread."

"No wonder I never found you. I was never crazy enough to ride the rails in El Paso. What happened?

"He was a good man and I eventually married him, end of story."

"May I volunteer the question, where he is now?" I amused myself by asking.

"In El Paso, where do you think?"

"Why can't he help you?"

"He's a lite busy with the ranch and whatever."

"You don't mean to tell me, you found yourself in high cotton, after you abandoned me in the middle of nowhere."

"I didn't abandon you, sweetheart, we had a misunderstanding." she corrected, glaring at me with the air of an aristocrat. The same courtly mannerism which cared her the title Countess.

This conversation was going nowhere. She would never admit that she took off one evening and never came back. I was an impressionable seventeen years old; I think she was a trifle older. I never even realized; the reason everyone treated me so well, was only because I escorted the countess. I surely did not know, her highness, was sharing her goodies with them.

I snapped back to the present. Let's get down to basics. You had me fired today, what was the big idea?" I asked.

"Will you forget about that piss ant job; I want to hire you."

"Hire me? What do you plan to pay me?"

"One hundred dollars a day plus expenses."

"That about fifty dollars less than what I was already making.

And, I had a 401 K retirement plan with insurance!" I fumed, not believing the way, she had manipulated the facts, she had presented to my idiot boss.

I decided to listen to her proposal. First, she had gone through a lot of trouble to make sure I was unemployed. Second, I could not expect her to just go away, until she got what she wanted. She was a master manipulator of long standing. I also felt myself being drawn into a genuine desire to catch up on all the years that had gone by.

From the looks of her, she had fared well after we split up. I I could not tell the difference; between the woman in front of mc, and the promise a little girl had made; that one day she would be treated like royalty.

CHAPTER TWO

I preferred to think back to the days when we first met, although I do not know why. I was working my way through Louisiana and around the Gulf of Mexico, picking up whatever work could be found to keep myself alive. Because of my shoulder length blonde hair, I had not found much work in the south. The warm summer evening found me leaning up against a sea wall in New Orleans. I glanced over and noticed the girl with those remarkable green eyes.

I knew at once, she too, was on the bum. We were drawn like a magnet, into each other's arms. We stood there, two kindred souls.

Each enjoying the little comfort the other could provide.

The next thing I knew; there was a gunny sack being forced down over my head and the dull thud of a black jack crushing against the back of my skull. I pretended to be knocked out cold.

There were voices shouting; "Don't let the other one get away!". I could feel the gunny sack being drawn down over my feet. It was tied shut, like they were taking me to a Cock fight. The gunny sack landed in the back of a pickup truck. I later found the truck was headed for Slydel.

Sometimes I could make out dim light coming into the bag from street lamps. There I was, curled up in the fetal position, bouncing down the road listening to the pickup truck noises. It did not take me long, to learn the different noises, the truck made.

It rattled when it slowed down. Wobbled speeding up, or making a turn it shimmied. I listed my scant options. Then decided to roll off the side of the truck bed when I got a chance. I perched myself as close as I dared to going over the side. When the truck slowed to make a left turn the added momentum sent me flying. I was careening, into a steep downward grade, away from the roadway. I could hear the truck continuing on its way, without stopping.

My feet were sticking straight up. The fingers of both hands still interlocked around my neck, my elbows making contact with my knees. My out of body vision told me I looked pretty ridiculous. I heard new voices as I struggled to get comfortable inside the bag.

"Hit it with this stick, then we'll have something to eat." I heard a voice say. I felt a thunderous snap land on the bottom of my feet. My out of body vision, was now telling me; I looked like a big ham hock.

"Hey..." I screamed, "Let me out of here."

"Oh shit, we got ourselves a Woo-Doo. Hit em again" the drunken voice instructed.". Another thunderous womp landed on the bottom of my feet.

"I'm gonna Woo-Doo yer ass, as soon as I'm out of this bag."

I announced.

"Is you an evil spirit, or a good spirit?" the drunken voice explored.

"I'll show you what kind of spirit I am as soon as you release me." I yelled, outraged at the stupidity of the drunk.

"Hit 'em again, I's Jesus knows it's one of Satan's broods come to temp us. Someone stuck em in the bag, to drown 'em in the river but the demon was too slick for 'em.". The drunk instructed.

The stick came slamming down across the bottom of my feet.

I lay with my shoulders pinned to the ground trying to free my pocket knife.

"You know why you haven't hurt me stupid? I's because you keep whacking me on the end of my willie." I said in an effort to confuse the valedictory of this group of scholars. "You keep whacking it and I'm liable to fall in love."

"Hit em again!"

"Go ahead, it'll just get me more excited. The only reason I'm staying in this bag is because when I come our I'll be about ten feet call with hair all over." I cautioned.

They were not listening, another thunderous crack of the stick landed on the bottoms of my feet. I pumped my legs up and down to give them some kind of show to watch, but also to try and work the knife free from my pocket.

"How did you like that, Demon?"

"I like it just fine., spade, whack me again." I said, starting in on a chorus to the tune of; I've been working on the railroad, but instead sang. "I've been whacking on my willie, all the live long day.

The stick crashed down on my feet, one blow after another.

The knife was finally free. I sunk it into the bag near my forehead with the blade pointing toward my feet. "That's it baby, I'm in love. I'm coming out of this bag and I'm going to have sex with the fire dozen folks I can find."

To add drama to the effect I made the bag sway back and forth, I pumped the bag up and down. "You see as long as I'm in this bag. I/m just one big penis. As soon as I'm out of this bag. I know arms and legs. Do me a favor and whack me again, but this time whack my willie sideways.

The force of the blow sent me reeling sideways in the dark.

My timing was perfect. The gunny sack, pulled taunt by the combine action of my back and legs, opened like a pea pod. The group around me, jumped back at the sound of the ripping bag.

I lunged in the dark, at the one holding the stick. I grabbed the thing and started swinging the end of it, like a track and field hammer. Luckily, I was able to pound a couple of them pretty painfully, before they all took flight. I stood there, with this shredded gunny sack around my ankles.

Taking one painful step, I shook the bag off the other foot. In the moon filled night I noticed, the only things that showed, were the whites of a few eyes and my blond hair. Not a word was spoken. Using the stick as a crutch, I headed in the direction I knew to be south. Hopefully, I could reach someplace safe to soak my feet before they swelled.

Slydel, has a railroad bridge. I took it back toward New Orleans.

During this whole incident, I kept wondering about the girl with the green eyes. Something led me back to the exact same spot where I had been dumped into the gunny sack. My hair was shoved up under a baseball cap and I tried to look as much like a redneck as I possibly could. Here I cautiously spent the day. It had taken the whole night to walk back from Slydel on my bruised and swollen feet. By midday my stomach was growling and I was quickly losing interest in the girl.

In cities like New Orleans a hungry man can look for the nearest fish market. By wandering the river front and asking a minimum of questions, you will eventually find someone who will allow you to help him load or unload the days catch. When you explain that you are willing to work for a fish, they usually slip you a couple of dollars. The fish, you wrap in newspaper. Then you keep your eyes open for vegetables, that someone is throwing away.

If you work hard, you will eat well at the end of the day. I always worked as hard as I could.

In Louisiana from March until October the weather is fair unless it rains. It does not have to rain in the local arca. It can rain as far north as St. Louis, and those bayous fill up plenty quick. All types of insects, come around to nibble at you, as you try to feed yourself. Most of them can be persuaded to stay away, after you lather your exposed meat, with tobacco juice. The juice also relieves any bites already suffered.

The next problem is to find somewhere to cook the fish. usually looked for railroad trestles. When you are on the bum, this is where you have to cook and eat your meal. These bridges provide some sheer from tin but also take advantage of the evening breeze. A man wants to be close enough to water to drink, bur high enough above the river's edge to avoid any alligators. At the very least you hope to avoid any alligators larger, than you can finish in one meal. They taste just like chicken. I imagine; to the really large ones. so do we!

Out of water, an alligator can do thirty miles an hour. I applaud anyone, who was able to provoke any of these reptiles to run for an hour, or who has followed one for thirty miles. My own observations are limited. I remember watching an alligator lunge three of four fact with lightning speed and snap up a poodle. The dog in this case probably had it coming. One does not stand motionless, barking at eyeballs floating on the water. A pom-pom shaved coat with pink toenail polish, is of small discouragement to a hungry prehistoric relic. It was all over by the time it registered in my mind what had happened. The only evidence which remained of poodle and predator, was a bubble on the surface of the water. The bubble yelped when it burst.

The meal was almost cooked to perfection, as I dug into my pack for some Louisiana hot sauce. In another few moments, the fish propped over the open flames, would be finished. The Okra and potatoes were already soft and succulent. I turned back around from my pack, and found the girl sitting beside the fire. She gawked at my fish. Those green eyes seemed to explore me.

"What happened to you last night?" I asked, not wanting to seem too startled.

I ran like hell, what happened to you?

"Someone shoved me in a gunny sack and tried to take me somewhere. Took me all day to walk back"

"They thought you were a girl. They were going to put you to work as a whore down in Mexico." she said without taking her eyes off the fish.

"How do you know that?"

"I hear things! They wait and find run away girls then pick them up. They didn't stick you with anything did they?"

"Naw, not that I know of. Why?" I asked.

"Aw they're supposed to get the girl strung out on Heroin. then they sell them to white slavers.' tell she was starving by the way she bit down on her lower lip. She made no effort to invite herself to eat.

"Here have some of this..." I offered her a newspaper plate of some of the meal I had prepared.

We were both silent for a while as we devoured the food. I stared at her now. A different appetite, started to present itself. She did not return my glances. Her entire concentration was on the meal.

It must have been a few days from the last time she had eaten. The huge Red Snapper I had cooked filled both of our stomachs.

"Tell me about the white slavers." I introduced into conversation pretending to be interested.

"What do you want to know?"

"Well, what do they do with the women they take down to Mexico?"

"Shit, how would I know!"

"It sounded like you knew what you were talking about. You said you hear things." I countered.

"The blonde ones like you, they take down there and get pregnant. They bring the babies back up here to the States and sell them on the black market." she said, acting as if this was common knowledge.

"Wonder what they would have done with me?" I grinned like a fool.

"What do you think they do with queer bait? Ya,jerk off." My face must have contorted because she began to laugh. Her wheezing laugh caused me to speculate that even though she was a youngster, the years were not kind to her. She walked off into the bushes and came back with her contribution to our meal, a borde of cheap wine. She must have been evaluating; whether she would share it, to have waited this long to bring it out. We drank the nasty concoction and curled up together next to the fire that night.

CHAPTER THREE

"What do you say, Do you want the job?" the woman on my couch asked.

"Explain what it is, that you want from me." my mind snapped back to the present. The little stroll down memory lane, had the effect, making me more susceptible to her offer.

"Muskrat Pete came to me a while back and said he needed my help. I told him; that, because of my husband, I could not get personally involved. He said that, that was OK but wondered if I knew how he could get in touch with you. I told him; that, I would check into it, and see what I could come up with. I also told him; he could count on my husband's financial support."

"You still haven't told me what kind of help you need..."

Her head made that familiar chin high motion, "We want you to help us find out, who's fucking with the Hobos and why." I tried to explain to her; the hobos we knew where getting pretty old. She would not listen to my logic. I told her, it was perfectly normal for a aging hobo, to slip off the bottom of a railway car and get himself cut in half. It was the way they lived. It was a romantic way to die.

".. And the railways have gotten a whole lot faster with fancy new systems and computers." I said.

She closed her eyes and waited for me to stop rambling " Hey listen, those hobos have gotten a lot more sophisticated too. I heard about one who convinced a Hollywood producer to sponsor him in a trip to Japan so he could ride the bottom of a bullet train." she interjected.

"The bullet train rides on an electro-magnetic field! It is not a real train." I corrected.

"I didn't say it was going to be easy. I just told you, what I had heard." she mocked me; "From what I understand, it seems he had the sensation, of all his hair standing on end."

"I'll bet..." I deferred from calling her a liar.

We seemed to wander around the subject of the hobos, for more than half the night. I gave her a set of sheets and told her to make herself comfortable. She started to refuse my hospitality, saying that she was already booked into a hotel. But, then she decided it might be fun to camp out on my couch. I was wondering; if it would be a good idea to lock my bedroom door when I noticed, she was already aside.

In the morning. I found her curled up next to me, just like old times. She was just as virginal, as she had ever been. Forever chaste when she was with me. I believed then, exactly what I believe now.

A stiff penis has a mind of its own. It clouds the mind, it warps reality. If someone is hungry, they must eat. If someone is tired, they must sleep. If someone's penis screams out for a partner, they must find it one. But, the partner of my choice, had always refused to satisfy my basic needs. Instead, she chose to run away.

Now I found, it was to El Paso. I remembered; I was so young, way back then.

She had always shared her sexuality, with other people, and never with me. This was the reason I held such hostile feelings toward her. I remembered this was exactly what, our frequent flights were about. She wanted to travel with me, eat with me, sleep with me, but never have sex with me. Sex was a tool she used, to get us what we needed to survive. I never pretended to understand the logic that she used.

She somehow believed; because we had never shared ourselves sexually, we had a special relationship. I now had the advantage of years, spent contemplating this subject. She may have been incapable of separating physical contact, from being violated. Our relationship was pristine, because I had never violated her. Seeing her like this, after all these years, it seemed to make sense. I could understand why she never wanted to spoil, our special relationship.

Loving her, and being separated from her, had been a living hell of personal introspection and doubt. I also thought; time had caused me to go soft. Here I was only inches away from biblical, carnal knowledge. Yet, I would not press my hand. I was already worried; I would lose her again. This was why I have always been so exasperated with her. I slid my arm, out from under her head, and went to make coffee. While waiting for the percolator, some spicy Italian sausage found it's was into the frying pan. Slabs of rye bread landed in the toaster. The oils from the sausage, cooked half a dozen eggs, sunny side up. The odor filled the house, as I knew it would. My guest, came drifting into the kitchen, following the aroma. I pressed a mug of coffee into her hand, then divided the meal into two plates. She inspected her share, and smiled.

Instead of sitting. she let herself out the back door onto the porch without saying a word. It seemed she had already made arrangements for breakfast. She ambled back into the room, carrying a brown paper bag from the bag she produced a box of Familia Swiss cereal, and a huge container of yoghurt. Poking around in the cupboards, I produced a large bowl. She filled it with flakes and the lumpy milk product. I haphazardly tossed her a tablespoon, then removed her portion of the meal I had prepared.

"Sorry, but my doctor has me on a strict low-fat diet. I'm not supposed to have more than; twenty-five grams of fat, a day." she explained. " He doesn't want me to develop cancer!"

"Is that just you, or is that everybody?"

"Naw thar's just women, active men can have up to fifty grams of fat."

"How much fat do you think I've got in front of me?" I asked, I trying to sound interested.

"Enough, for about six days. Six more, if you eat the other portion." she raised one eyebrow. I rook her share and made a sandwich for lunch, placing the eggs and sausage, between the thick buttered rye bread. I stood with my back to her, to conceal with my body, what I was doing. With it safely stored in a zip-lock bag, I returned to my breakfast. She wrinkled her nose at me, as 1 gulped it down.

"How's the coffee?" I asked, to take her mind away from being so critical of my eating habits.

"Wonderful, if you limit yourself to one cup."

I grimaced at my blunder, pouring my second cup into the largest mug I could find. " Does the same thing go for the wine? I couldn't help noticing it was hardly touched."

"Moderation in all chings, darling."

"How about a moderate slice of cheese cake?" I asked, slipping a giant piece onto my dirty breakfast plate. I slopped it around, soaking up the rest of the egg yolk.

"That makes; seven days of fat. When was the last time you had your cholesterol checked?" she pondered out loud.

"I don't know that I have ever checked it." I answered. "Your blood pressure?"

"Ditto!"

"Let me check your pulse." she said grabbing my wrist. I submitted to her probing fingertips. She seemed to be ill at case, as the second hand swept around the face of her watch. " One hundred twenty beats a minute." she gasped.

"Hey that's nothing. I can get it up to a hundred eighty by running a couple miles! * I announced proudly.

"Lucky, I got here before you had a stroke. You wouldn't do me much good if you have a heart attack."

At this point. I tried to explain to her; that I would not do her much good, anyway. If she was finished with breakfast, I had work to do. I pushed away from the table and washed the dirty dishes, then trotted upstairs to shave and get dressed. She followed me around, until I forced the bathroom door closed. "What do you think you're doing?" she asked through the closed door.

"I've got to get out and find a new job, while I've still got a good reputation in town. I's impossible to get work around here, as soon as people stop talking about you!" I shouted. The Hobo's?"

"You've got a JOB, you jerk!" she tried to suggest. "What about

"No sweetheart, you have an opening of dubious interest to me." I tried to impress upon her. " You burnt me the last time.

You'll burn me again." I said tapping the razor against the sink.

"I'm not going to burn you, darling." she cooed at the closed door.

"Maybe not on purpose, but I know from experience you'll light me up, like a house on fire. And, forget to call 911 at the same time. You can't help it, there is just something wrong with your brain." I pontificated. That shut her up, for the moment.

I continued to prepare myself to go looking for a job. I have always hated this part of the employment racket. When you have a job, you only have to look presentable. When you are looking for a job, you have to look dynamic and stylish. You have to shave closer, smell better, in short; put on airs. The only way to predict, the correct tie and shoes to wear, was either; watch primetime television, or subscribe to Gentleman's Quarterly. Both of which, 1 had neglected lately, not knowing I would be searching for a new job. I did the best I could, considering the season, in each choice I made. To cover up the fact that I needed a haircut, I plastered my scalp with gel. To freshen it up, without running to the dry cleaner I used baking soda inside my sport coat. For cologne, I would choose something fashionable, stopping at a drugstore then using their testers.

The countess, was the last thing on my mind, as I emerged from the preparations. I glanced in the full-length mirror, my chances were about fifty-fifty, against me finding a new job.

Shoving a handful of resumes into a leather brief case, I headed for the door. The countess sat on the edge of the sofa, puffing on a hand-rolled cigarette. " Hey those things cause cancer too!" I advised.

"Please allow me some discretionary vice, asshole." she commented. She gave me one of those looks that could castrate.

"Well, make yourself at home..! Mi casa su casa! I shouldn't be too long. It could not take longer than, a couple of weeks to arrange for some interviews." I said trying to sound light hearted, which was anything but the truth.

I blew her a kiss and headed out the door. I started for the bus stop leaving my car at home. I could pop in and out of more buildings downtown, if I did not have to worry, about where I parked. Mid-way to the bus I discovered I was being followed. A brand-new, silver-grey Mercedes was keeping pace with me. It was annoying to know: someone not only, could afford the fifty-thousand-dollar euro, but also, had enough time on their hands to drive it at a walking pace. I tried to peer into the darkened windows, the window rolled down, it was the countess.

"Need a lift?" she asked.

I dibbed into the plush interior, inhaling deeply the luxuriant leathers and woods. The ice-cold atmosphere instantly absorbed the moisture left on my clothing, from the exercise of walking.

"Where to sailor?" she smiled.

"Turn left at the end of the block, then right on Wisconsin avenue."

She followed my directions. I noticed as she passed a couple of parked cars, she came painfully close to grazing the side of the Mercedes. I said nothing, being a firm believer in letting the driver of the car fend for themselves. I glanced up at one point to notice the Mercedes would not clear the next obstacle. Without thinking, I reached out and grabbed the wheel.

We cleared the parked car by mere molecules.

"What, are you blind!" I screamed.

She fumbled in her purse, producing a pair of Coke bottle chick glasses. " Their only for reading." she explained, perching them on the end of her nose. I was horrified to think, that we had almost become a statistic, for the sake of her vanity.

"Probably don't get enough far in your diet." I offered,

"Your blood pressure is so low, your eyes can't focus on their own, any longer."

She ignored my self-serving rebuke. At least, with her glasses again, as we drove downtown. She dropped me off where I asked, then offered to pick me up later. I told her; I did not know how long I would be in the building, and that she should not wait for me. Which building? I could see no harm in telling her. She disappeared into the traffic as I went inside.

The interview was remarkable. I walked in, cold off the street, and was speaking with the president of the company after a brief delay.

I liked him from the start. By his manner of speech, I could tell he liked my style. I did not have to look any further. He would be calling with an offer, by the end of the day, I knew instinctively. I thanked him for his time, then moseyed off, to check the employee parking in the sub-terrain basement. It was only one, of the employee perks, he had mentioned. I would have my 401K retirement package, insurance, plus employee parking. Hog heaven for an old ex-hobo.

The basement elevator was clogged with passengers. I walked up the steep incline of the multi-level garage. Over in the pay parking area was a familiar silver-grey Mercedes. Texas tags, with the name of a El Paso dealership on the license cover. I panicked, running out of the parking area, back into the building and toward the office of my future employer. I hoped I could get there in time.

In the elevator I decided; the worst possible thing I could do at the moment, would be to reenter the office. The countess, could not have any idea, which office to go to. I lurked around the third floor, perusing anyone who entered or exited. As luck would have it, I was preoccupied with a curvaceous receptionist, when a security guard caught me by the back of the collar.

She pulled me into my prospective employer's office. She hoped to determine if I was telling the truth, about my business in the building. It is sufficient to say, I came away from this second meeting with less than hopeful feelings of future employment. As I was escorted out of the building, I mentioned to the security person, some creative endeavors with which to occupy her time. She was not amused, stating that she already practiced this particular form of self-gratification. This, I found interesting in kinky sort of way.

No, she did not wish the help of a partner. She refused to discuss it any further.

Back on the street, I was accosted by a vagrant pan handler.

He was the lowest form of tramp, demanding tribute for simply existing on the planet. These beings have a second sense about; who is a... sympathetic soul. I reached into my coat pocket and produced a handful of pennies. This tactic had been my routine for years. It separated the truly needy, from the repulsive sort; who make fifty thousand dollars a year; pretending to be homeless.

One caustic remark and I would demand my money back.

"Hey man, what am I gonna do with this?" he asked.

"Didn't you just ask me for money?" I asked, acting like a concerned citizen.

I sized him up. His bulging front pockets told me everything. He was the type of bum, who spent all day shoving dollars into them. I stared for a moment at his practiced, pathetic looking face. Spontaneously, I knew I could take him.

"Man, I'm hungry. This won't buy shit!"

That comment was all it took. " Hey watch yourself!" said I, as I moved him out of the way of some workmen, carrying a plank.

While shoving the bum aside, I reached into one of his bulging pockets, removing a wad of bills with the polished art of a professional. I slipped the bills into my own coat, without him noticing. Reaching into my trouser pocket, I produced three quarters which were presented to the bum. His face beamed with phony gratitude.

"Now I can buy a hot dog, bless you sir!" he smiled his most endearing smile and clicked his heels.

His empty claims were lost on me, as I wandered down the street. I rounded a corner and counted the booty. Forty-seven dollars, checking his other pocket.

I am not a thief, or a mugger, but I do have a warped sense of justice. Entering the MacDonalds on sixteenth street, I ordered twenty burgers. In a city the size of Washington DC, it is not hard to find people down on their luck. Within a couple of blocks, I had given away all of the burgers. The Truely needy were given what money was left.

The bum, probably would not even know he was rolled, until he got home to the suburbs. It was there he would notice he was short hours pay. I already decided; I would take him one more time, if I saw him pulling his-Mr. Bo Jangles routine crap again.

Maybe not: the police, would surely not see it my way, if and when I got caught. They would overlook the fact; that the bum did not pay taxes, and therefore was not entitled to the same protection as the rest of the community. A rationalization I made with severe inherent social error.

How would it look, for a white male in a sport-coat and tie, to be caught rolling a member of an ethnic group. Most of the police were members of an ethnic group. I persuaded myself; to reject any notions of a repeat performance.

Checking the inside pocket of my coat for my appointment book, I found it was missing. That son of a bitch! No wonder he did not notice me, picking his pocket. That-Bo Jangles Bum, was too busy lifting, what he thought was my wallet. Thank the Lord, I carried my important possessions, in the brief case. Zipping the case open, everything was safe.

Wait till our paths cross again? Not likely! I set out to find the little bastard. There he was, all grins and graciousness, still in front of the same building. He frowned, as he saw me coming, then started to move down the block. I caught him at the corner. I did not say a word, as he retracted the appointment book from his crotch. The little weasel, had been too busy collecting money, to leave his post. I doubt that he even knew; it was not a wallet.

Handing over the book, he lapsed into an uncle Tom version of indignant.

I was just about to cuff him soundly on his nappy head, when I noticed in the corner of my eye, a silver-grey Mercedes. The driver, a woman wearing Coke bottle glasses, pulled up to the curb. I turned around, the bum was missing.

CHAPTER FOUR

"If you are quite finished, we might have lunch." she said.

Climbing in, I inhaled deeply. "Might as well, can't dance." I quipped. She was looking at me with an amused expression.

"You are a riot. First you roll the guy then you have the nerve to ask for your property back." she laughed.

"Where were you?"

"I was looking at lingerie in one of the shops on the ground level, while I waited for you to come out."

"Then you didn't follow me up to the interview?"

"Heavens no! Why would I do that?" she said smiling at me, "

How much did you get off the little beggar?"

"Forty-seven dollars and some change."

"Got any left?"

"No!"

"You always were a jerk. While you were in buying those burgers to relieve your guilt, all the rift-raft positioned themselves strategically to hit on you, when you came out."

"They all saw, what I did?"

"I don't think so. What they saw, was you give the little bum some money. They all knew you were a soft touch after that. So, what do you do... start handing out burgers!" the countess giggled.

"Hey some of those people were needy!" I countered.

"Who are you? Robin (Bleeding Heart] Hood." she mocked.

"Can we just drop it!" I sneered.

We drove silently for a while, me; enjoying my luxuriant surroundings, her; trying to avoid parked cars along the route.

Without any encouragement, she found her way back to the northwest section of town. Using a bus stop, she backed into a vacant parking spot, then motioned for me to follow her into a restaurant. I dumped a handful of coins into the meter, wondering if she recognized the device must be fed.

She was already seated, as I walked blindly, into the dim lighting. The rude waiter, stood hovering over the table, as I waited for my eyes to adjust. As soon as I sat, he shoved a wine list into my hand and vanished. I tossed it aside, preferring to study the menu first. I do not to pretend to be gourmet, but the menu had me puzzled, even though I was fairly certain it was in English. She smiled at my dilemma.

The waiter materialized; I could swear the fellow was wearing make-up. His perfectly slicked back hair. added to the conclusion that he should be laid out in some funeral, for the viewing. With his elbows pressed tightly together he stood here, pen in one hand, pad in the other. The countess, selected a plethora of delicacies, for both of us.

".and for the wine?" he glanced at me.

"Chablis?" I offered, looking to the countess for support. The pale waiter seemed to roll his eyes and a tremor shook his head. 1 took this to mean he did not approve.

" White Zinfandel!" I guessed, only because the color would march the pink tablecloth. The stiff seemed to melt until his elbows were in his crotch, then his hands folded forward down to his knees still holding the pad and pen. He was perched like this for a moment too long, to be in pain.

"Excellent choice sir." he winked at me with a smile.

I waited for him to leave, before mentioning to the Countess, that he should nor he allowed to handle food. She gave me another of her castrating glances and remained quiet. I glanced over at the next table. There it seemed my comment had been received with humor by three fashionable young women.

"He's serious, you know!" the Countess said to them all.

They immediately ignored us, going back to their conversation.

The meal, when it finally was presented, was skimpy. A delicate variety of color coordinated sauces, which vegetable pate's and all the nutritional content of paste. To use the term portions, would be a generous overstatement. We muddled through a plate of bean curd, after a plate of saucy tofu, while I waited for a meat entre.

Some microscopic shrimp in a hideous green and pink sauce, momentarily presented itself, then vanished with our sissy waiter into the kitchen. My fork marks still visible in the residue. While I was still waiting for the main course, the stiff, placed cups of espresso in front of us. A small tray containing the check, beneath two foil wrapped minty chocolates, served us notice, the meal had ended.

"What was this? I squinted, looking no doubt like someone who had seen a magic trick, without benefit of explanation."

Nouveau Cuisine! What did you think of it? Isn't it marvelous" the Countess clucked.

"I just figured out why the waiter looks so pallid; he probably gets to eat here free!" I mumbled, as quietly as possible. The girls at the next table began to chuckle.

"I still want to talk to you about the job!" said the Countess, as we stood up to leave.

"Only on one condition, ..." said I, " _ first, we have to swing by a burger stand, so I can get something to eat. I'm starving!"* The girls at the next table roared with laughter. Evidently; the house wine, a White Zinfandel, still packed a pretty good wallop.

The women at the next table are just part of the reason, there is no such thing as a secret, in Washington. At any given restaurant in the metropolitan arca, there are snoops and sleuths alike, just waiting to search up and use stray gossip. The more discrete a person tries to be, the more they love it. They could hear a gnat fart at forty paces.

Trying not to get Burger-R-Us crumbs on the bucket seats, I listened as the countess rambled. She talked about tramps, bums and hobos. She talked about Mexico and wet backs, mentioning also several border crossings of a less than legal nature. I went on spilling sesame seeds while I munched the burger. There was some higher stale she was neglecting to discuss. As we circled the same block for the third time, I finished the burgers and rolled up the wrapper.

She pulled into the driveway of the Guest Quarters hotel. A valet immediately opened her door and took the keys. I barely had time to exit before he roared off. Su a headed into the lobby in a regal demeanor. The desk clerk smiled as we boarded the elevator.

It shot up to the fourteenth foot at around two Gs. The burgers slammed down initially, then rose into my throat as the elevator stopped. Producing a card, instead of a key, she slipped it into the door jamb, the room sprung open.

Walking into the room, was another world experience. Fresh cut flowers were used as accents to the furniture. The suite of room included a sunken bath. behind silky translucent drapes in the master bedroom. A kitchenette was well stocked with various brands of imported beers, wines, and miniature liquor bottles. Matching Louis Vuitton bags were stacked at the foot of the bed. She laid her hand bag next to the telephone, then picked up the receiver. "Room 1420, were there any calls for me?" she asked sweetly. She scribbled down a series of numbers and a name then thanked the operator.

"Before I make this call, are you going to help me or not?". She stood with a finger poised on the first digit.

You are asking me, to go back our on the bum! Bake in the heat, freeze in the cold, soak in the rain, starve and wear the same underwear for weeks at a time!" was my honest answer.

She punched in the number, using all her fingers like a typist.

I was impressed. The other party must have picked up on the first ring. I could hear a booming male voice care out of the receiver.

The countess explained the situation. He did not sound pleased.

She turned to me extending the phone, shaking it like a ruler. I swallowed hard knowing I would regret that was about to happen.

This was all I needed, some John Wayne style cowboy, who was going to put my mind right.

"Susan says, you're being a real pain in the ass!" he told me. I had listened to what she said to him, and it did not include the accusation he was making. "I want you to get your wrinkled Hobo butt, on down here to El Paso, PRONTO!"

"Listen bud, I haven't been on the rails for fifteen years maybe twenty. If you have a problem, I suggest you get one of those Lone Star hobos, to help you out!"

"Put this conversation on the speaker phone!" he ordered.

"I'm not sure there is one.

I looked around for the Countesses help.

"No speaker phones? What kind of a dump did she check into?" he boomed. She caught the gests of the dilemma, and pressed a switch mounted on the side of the phone. His redneck voice filled the room. "Susan, I'm gonna give you twenty-four hours to convince this peon to get his butt down here."

"Clyde honey, this is still a free country!" she corrected in those motherly tones I knew so well.

"Maybe you better explain to him, who he is dealing with."

"Let's start all over again, shall we? Clyde Starr you are speaking with one, Mr. James Durado. Mr. Durado, I would like to present my husband, Clyde Starr elected sheriff of El Paso and surrounding county." she was so diplomatic, I felt comfortable listening to her, except for that sheriff part of the introduction.

"OK Du-rad-o, now that were on a more personable level, I want you to get your, no good, Hobo ass down here." he boomed.

"I hear you talking Clyde! Now try it again, with some please Mister, and that sort of thing." I said.

"Hey mister! It's bad enough you left my sweet little Suzy O in the motherly way. I've got to warn you, you are treading on some very serious thin ice."

"Motherly way? " I gasped, " I never left anybody in a Motherly way. Especially not the Countess!"

"Susan, what is he talking about? He's not delusional, is he? I mean, I don't want you traveling with no nut case."

"Clyde, can we talk about this some other time. Here is the deal: If we pay him one hundred fifty dollars a day plus insurance and expenses, I think he'll come around.

"Is that all he is holding out for? Done One hundred fifty and all the rest of that hog wash."

"What about my 401K. " I interjected.

"What about an IRA!" she said, giving me an icy glance.

"That nut case, isn't still trying to up the ante is he! Does he know this involves his own daughter?"

"My daughter. I don't have a daughter!" I fumed.

After continued denials on my part, some stern sermons from Clyde, punctuated by icy glances from the Countess, the conversation finally ended. She switched the speaker phone off, made endearing noises into this end of the line, then hung up. We lugged the Vuitton bags down to the lobby where she checked out, waving a gold card under the nose of the desk clerk. She asked him to forward any calls to my residence. "Very well MRS Start." he offered, with a knowing grin. People in Washington, have such a D jaded estimate of human character.

"Why did you pull all those Hobo tricks on me for the last wreck?" I asked her rhetorically. "You were just seeing, if I still had it in me, weren't you?"

She slipped sideways into a conversation about her child the talented, gifted. adorable Peggy Sue. I closed my cars.

Having never been a parent I hate the; my child this, and my child that, -drivel. Prattle, parents are so fond of spouting. If and when, I carefully listen to the details, I would be shocked to learn; the child is less than a prodigy. They are certainly given all the inducements needed to succeed. OK so they screw up and get involved with drugs, sometimes. Most of the time, they come out the other end of it, to take up with living where they left off.

All my life. I have had to start at the end of the line. and work my way up. Jealous, you are damned right. I am jealous. However, I am not vicious, like so many others who never had anything. I do not lurk in dark places ready to pounce on the innocent and the weak. I do not pander powders, potions, or sex. She pulled up to my rental, which until today I had been proud to claim. Now I could see it for what it really was, a hovel. All the furniture was second hand. No two pieces matched, well maybe the fold up dining room chairs. I had painted the bathroom and kitchen, but they still looked decrepit.

She moved through the rooms, not seeming to notice.

I wanted desperately to know: why old Clyde, thought I was the father of his bastard daughter. The countess traipsed into the room carrying the wine bottle and two glasses. Kicking off her shoes and folding her legs up under the pleated skirt, she poured us each a drink. I gulped mine down and poured another. "Re member when we worked on that Movie set, near Palm Springs?" she asked.

CHAPTER FIVE

It was not likely I would forget the movie set. It was an episode in my life where: I was almost killed by actors, and suffered temporary blindness from being shot in the skull by a tranquilizer dart.

The shoot, as they called it, was six weeks of desert scenes for one of those African adventure stories. One of those lost treasures of some biblical character. It was not anywhere near Palm Springs.

It was somewhere between Twenty-Nine Palms and Las Vegas, which is a big chunk of real estate. As far as I know, the only way to get to the shoot; was helicopter, jeep or boxcar. The Countess and I, had arrived by boxcar.

We noticed the activity from under a railroad trestle, which protected us from the sun, while we waited for the next northern bound freight. We wandered out to check on the commotion. To our good fortune we found ourselves working as extras.

The Countess, being roughly the same size as the leading Bimbo, became a stunt double for the love scenes. She would swap spit with whoever happened to be, the lead Hunk at the moment. It seemed the leading lady, had complaints about the oral hygiene of the male actors. Some of whom were pooches. The Countess had no complaints and would rehearse late into the night.

I, being a bit scrawny, looked like none of the actors. Most of the time I helped the stage bands construct ramps and lay camera track. I promised them, I would join the union, as soon as the shoot was over. It was not an empty promise, until I found a dart in the occipital lobe of my brain. I got along well with the road hands who taught me all sorts of technical garbage. They were fond of pointing out the proper procedures quoting: this or that, would satisfy the standards applied by "Uncle Bob"! I always thought this was Bob Hope, they referred to, although I never asked anyone.

Because; I was nor actually in the union, they did not object when I would wander off, to be in the background of the camera frame. On occasion, I would find myself, shoe polished up to look like a Zulu. In one frame; they needed someone skinny, who would be able to fall off a butte, then land in the middle of some cardboard boxes covered by a tarp.

I did not question the skinny requirements, until the middle of the fall. I noticed myself drifting horizontally; in relationship to the boxes. It was the film crews' good luck, to have chosen me, for the jab. I cocked my head, twisted my hips, and cannonballed for the corner of the tarp. Anyone with greater wind resistance, would have missed the padding altogether, due in no small part to the wind whipping through the ravine. They liked my performance so well, they had me repeat it three more times. The cowardly actor, who was supposed to be doing the stunt, finally tried it. I guess; Guy Baron added some certain authenticity to the footage because it was: cut, wrap, print, after his first attempt. I later found my own efforts, were cutting room floor footage. Not filmed?

In the early 1970s, film crews were a gregarious lot. They shared beer and wine when apropos. A great number of the crew also shared their cigarettes. Being a well-traveled hobo, I have always rolled my own, hording what tobacco I had with me. The fragrance of their tobacco, made me question the humidor they used to store it. Had I been the kind of hobo to lift someone else's supply, I should think a likely place to look, would be up a burro's butt. The odor was raunchy. They savored the nasty supply they had, saving even the ends of the cigarettes. I felt fortunate to have my own tobacco, but shared greedily in whatever ice-cold beer I could round up.

At the time I suppose I was naive. I encountered some of the crew sniffing headache powders. I have often purchased Stanback powder for relief of a hangover, but have never been in such desperate pain, that I would shove it up my nose. They would also rub it on the inside of their gums like chewing tobacco. What purpose they had for this method of oral administration; I did not discover until several years later.

Whenever I was offered this powder or the burro butt tobacco I declined, satisfied instead to slurp on a brew.

Filming would go on until the wee hours of the night. This seemed to be mandated in order to be kind to the animals on the set. If nothing else, the crew always treated the animals humanely.

Animals were only brought on the set the day of the shoot, then housed in air-conditioned cages until they were used. The lions and such, were brought in from Las Vegas, where they were part of casino reviews. Animal trainers treated the big house pets as if they were worth their weight in gold, as I am sure they were.

I did not spend much time around the animals. They were part of the production, so as I snooped around, I became aware of the animals. One young female trainer in particular caught my attention.

Stephanie, at this time in her life, was not much to look at.

She was roughly, the same size and shape, as one of the actresses.

Except that she lacked the notable bosom of the Gwen, people often confused the two, from the teat. The actress, who it seemed had a phobia about large animals. used Stephanie in all the scenes where animals were present. Unlike the others. I saw Stephanie not as she was, but as she would one day look. Being a seventeen-year-old "virgin" hobo, does that to a man.

Most days Stephanie would wander the lot dressed in her cos-rime of safari garb. The Countess, being busy with rehearsals and other peccadillos, did not weigh heavily on my mind. When it was convenient to do so. I would try to engage Stephanie in conversation. She had no idea of the narcotic effect she had on me. She herself, did not believe that she was attractive. She suffered from poor self-esteem. I tried various approaches to spend time alone with her, all of which failed.

She had a head over heels infatuation with some character on the set named Guy. Guy, in the meantime, was doing everything in his power to mount Gwen, the actress, for whom Stephanie was the double. Near lover's quadrangle, except I was still on the outside. I even tried to befriend Guy, whose use of headache powder up his nose, was a powerful handicap to overlook in a friend. His animated behavior after snorting the powder was another obstacle to our continued friendship. Still, I put up with his Hot-to-Trot antics, to be close to Stephanie.

It was toward the end of the shoot and people seemed to be wandering in and out of each other's accommodation. The Countess was missing, as usual. I like the rest of the technicians, was quartered in tents set up long the outside perimeter. The actors, were in a line of air-conditioned trailers right beside us. I was happily sucking down a beer, and about to open another one, when I heard familiar voices outside my tent.

"Oh, there you are Guy. I've been looking for you. I was hoping we could practice for tomorrows' love scene." Stephanie said.

Just a little tongue in cheek; I thought.

"I'll be doing the scene with the real actress!" the fool told her.

I started to offer her my assistance but held back.

"There will be animals present." Stephanie said sweetly.

"What does that mean?" he sniffed.

"She doesn't do animal scenes. Not even love scenes!"

"Stephanie I'd rather kiss the animals." Guv crooned.

That bastard; thought 1. That insensitive bastard. I whipped the tent flap open. All I could see was Stephanie, running away from a jerk, who had snot running down his upper lip. I started out after her, then decided to let her have a few moments to herself before I barged in. By the time I made it to her trailer, the door was locked. Banging on it, I was instructed to; "Go away!"

Having just blown, probably the last chance, I would ever have to consummate a relationship with the divine Stephanie, I ambled back to my tent. The countess had returned. She and Guy were in the middle of more rehearsal. Guy came up for breath long enough to advise me; after she finished sulking, Stephanie would be making her nightly round of the animal cages. He also mentioned, that I should not sneak up on her. She always carried a tranquilizer dart pistol at this time of night. It was one of several kept on the lot. Not wanting to intrude on the countess in the perfection of her rehearsal, I wandered away.

This evening, they were filming the part of the movie where the intrepid explorers reached their goal of discovering the buried treasure. We had worked building an enclosure for the camera, in front of which the bogus riches were piled. A real enough looking cave composed of burlap. plywood, and fiberglass, had been created to surround the wealth. The actors were to shinny down into the egg like set, to be filmed. An embankment of loose stone, from the camera's angle looked like the inside of an entrance to a cave. To encounter the culmination of their ordeal, the actors were to draw closer into the frame, with each new treasure they uncovered.

I am proud of the set. I had done most of the labor, while the union people, -medicated themselves with headache powders.

Whenever my work was below union standards, they were helpful in pointing out my short comings. I would diligently correct the deficiency, while trying to say down wind of the odor of their tobacco. Another of the unions on sight engaged me to help construct a pit for the camera. Partially buried in the pit, behind a plexiglass protection, the camera pointed up at the actors. The camera man in the meantime, a member of yet another union. was left sitting in the great outdoors.

While watching this foolishness, I kept an eye focused in the distance at the animal trailers. A couple hundred yards in the other direction I noticed a commotion. Being an curios individual, I wandered over to see what the devil was happening. The good folk fam a nearby town. had traveled all the way out here. to warn the movie people about a rogue cougar. It seems the cougar had playing hell with the local livestock in recent days. They thought it could be heading in our direction. Their mission accomplished, the townsfolk saddled up in their four wheelers and moseyed back to town.

A few of the movie people elected themselves to the task of cougar patrol. Everyone else was supposed to stay as close to the tents and trailers as possible. To a hobo this sounded like a reasonable request. To movie people, who like to wander around the open desert drinking tequila, hooting like coyotes, it as a farce.

Number one; only half the troop had heard the news. Number two; the other half were our wandering in the desert. To avoid any unpleasantness, a stalwart group of rescuers were assembled. We were to go out into the moonlight and locate the others. Picture the blind, leading blind drunks.

I had no idea that a peaceful group of thespians carried as much firepower, as I soon found was available. With instructions to fire into the air in case of any trouble, I like the other was given my choice of firearm. Fire one shot into the air and the others would come running. My choice; a hand-held cannon in the 357-magnum arena. Six shots, without chance of jamming. They repeated the instructions: fire only into the air. I could not wait, to get a bead, on that cougar.

In the first hour, I rounded up a dozen tequila swilling, fornicators, without incident. The next hour I stumbled around in the dark looking for the cougar. The desert was beginning to cool off so I decided it was time to check in. Slurp down another beer.

That cougar was probably half way to Mexico, -now that he heard I was our here. As I approached the animal cages, I slid the pistol into the small of my back. Stephanic, in all her sweet glory, was making her rounds. I decided not to bother her, until I got another beer. I brought two.

Did she care for a beer? Would she like to walk over and see how the scene was coming along? Did I have my Mojo working)

She did, she would, and maybe.

We positioned ourselves behind the camera man. From this vantage point we could see the sweaty actors, hamming it up for the camera. They were shoving stacks of jewels and phony precious coins into bags, then tying the bags shut. Gwen was stunning, as she worked her cleavage for the camera angle. Not too many male viewers, would be aware thar this scene, had to do with treasure.

It occurred to me; the reason Guy was able to help the Countess rehearse, was because Gwen was busy up here working. With sweet Stephanie on my mind, I overlooked the inordinate amount of rehearsal, the Countess was involved with. The countess not only rehearsed with the other actors, she rehearsed carpenters and electricians, one of the producers, and the odd grip here and there.

What can be said about someone, who gives so much to their craft.

The corner of my eye caught a shadow plane, moving toward the rear of the enclosed area. Leaving Stephanie to view the theatrics', I moved to follow the shadow. Without pulling the pistol from my back, I caught the shadow as it was making for the design country side. The cougar, turned in its own body length and charged me. Pulling myself out of the way of its teeth and claws, I was able to grasp it around its throat and sinewy shoulders. Lunging forward, to escape the wart of a human on its back, the damned cougar came crashing through the rear of the enclosure. Both the cougar and I, rumbled down onto the startled actors. The egg-shaped stage, did not seem to accommodate the impromptu film debut, of myself or my new friend the cougar.

The cougar, being much wiser than myself, was able to work itself free, while I tumbled headlong onto Gwen. She having seen the beast, fainted dead away. I landing on top of her, unaware of her zoo phobic condition. I thought; we had killed the poor girl.

With tears streaming from my eyes, I embraced the poor dying actress, and planted the deepest weirdest kiss on her lips, my tender years could muster. The cougar slipped out the back of the enclosure.

The camera, behind its plexiglass protection, continued to roll.

From what I understand; it captured one of the most touching pieces of film-work, to ever hit the cutting room floor.

Gwen, beginning to revive shrieked at the lip chat pressed against hers. I dropped her against the plexiglass and attempted to imitate my friend the cougar. The pistol in the course of the struggle had shifted uncomfortably deeper into my trousers. I yanked it out as I emerged from the rear of the enclosure. Holding the pistol in the both hands, still hoping to ger a bead on the cougar, I bust out of the rear of the enclosure. I came face to face with dear sweet Stephanie. She had the drop on me. I was lined up in her sights, like I had hoped to have the cougar. I wondered how long she had been there.

"That's far enough buddy!" she announced.

"Yes mam!" I conceded. Holding my hands extended, as if it were a stick up. The 357 dangled from my finger by the trigger guard. I was a most agreeable hostage.

"Tell me I'm beautiful"

'STEPHANIE, this isn't the time..." said I, watching her stand there in her safari garb, khaki shorts and blouse, knee high sox with construction workers boots.

"Tell me. she ordered

"You are!"

"Are what"

"You are beautiful, you are just about the most beautiful...". ho I was telling the truth

"You're just saying that, because I have a gun pointed at you.

"I saw you with Gwen."

"No mam, I have a gun, and I'm still telling you, you are beautiful. Gwen's just one of those things, I thought I killed her!"

"A little necrophilia, huh. Besides that's not a real gun." she pontificated.

"Yes mam, it's a real gun. The gun you've got isn't real. It fires tranquilizers.

"Then you wouldn't mind, if I shot you with it?" she held the muzzle dead on my midsection.

"I guess that would depend, on where I was shot said I smiling. I still had my hands raised.

"How about if I shoot you in the foot. Will you still chink I am beautiful."

"Yes mam, I believe I would."

"Would you shoot me back" she joked.

"No mam, not with his gun, I wouldn't!"

I could hear this little puny pop like somebody opening a warm beer can. I looked down and noticed a dart sticking out of my shoe. She must have hit me between the toes because I did not feel a thing. I reached down and pulled it out. She was already slipping another round into the chamber. I am watching her reload the dart pistol, and I still thought she is beautiful.

"I think I made my point. I let you shoot me with your gun. I still think you're lovely." I was surprised to say.

"What happened to Beautiful?" she asked.

"Too redundant!"

"Oh!"

"Before you get any other fine ideas, I want you to listen to my gun." I spoke, peering through the rarified moonlight to see if she was listening. She had the drop on me again.

"First listen to mine again." she said.

"Hold id Let us be a little more scientific about this. "

She seemed a little to trigger happy.

"I'm going to come over there, and stand really close to you. Would you please hold the dart gun up in the air like I'm doing."

"Sounds fair." she agreed. She struck a pose like she was using a dueling pistol. I approached her, standing toe to toe.

A fraction of an inch closer and I could feel her potent breath against my face. We were standing within each other's aura. The warmth of her body, traveled to me, in the cool desert night air.

I reached out with my free arm, drawing her closer. Our mouths touched. A sensation of the sublime, rippled through my body.

Ecstasy. She quoted; an old Mae West line, something about a pistol in a pocket. I could smell her hair, taste her salty skin. All my senses were fully engaged.

The pistol exploded, sending a cannonade of cordite, into the night sky. She practically jumped out of her skin. I do not know what possessed me to pull the trigger. When she recovered, we were two hungry animals, intent on swallowing each ocher whole.

We groped and pawed at each other. Oblivious to time, place, even the fact thar we were holding lethal weapons.

Or, the remainder of the cougar patrol, bearing down on us.

At the head of the pack came that clown, Guy. "Where is Gwen?" He shouted.

"She's up here!" I called back, meaning inside the enclosure. I went back to trying to ingest Stephanie.

A hand grabbed me by the shoulder, ripping me out of the arms of my partner. A fist cold cocked me in the center of my face.

A body interjected itself into my formerly occupied position. I lay on the ground in a time warp, still clutching the pistol. Mr. former partner seemed unable to make the connection; she was now kissing Guy, not the guy who shed been dancing with. I rose dejected, struggling to regain my feet, if not my partner. The pistol hung limply at my side, in silent testimony to my near conquest, and now my rejection.

"OK, but when it's all over, just remember; Stephanie is my girl." I turned, starting to trod off into the gloom of the desert night.

My statement must have alerted Guy to his fall. He reached up expecting to encounter a handful of womanly chests.

"WHAT THE F...." I could hear Guy snort, as he pushed away from Stephanie, "Where's Gwen?"

"She's still inside the set, lover boy!" she laughed.

Good for her; I thought. Give that bastard some of his own medicine. He pushed away from her, climbing down into the enclosure. I continued to stumble off into the dark. I knew in my heart of hearts; she would rather be kissing him instead of some dumb hobo. I was being a consummate jerk.

I could hear the pop of a beer can being opened. Something struck me squarely in the back of the head. All the lights began to dim. I could feel my body pitch forward like a caper toss. Whatever they put in those tranquilizer darts, surely goes to work in a hurry. With the last ounce of energy, I turned to catch a glimpse of my sweet Stephanie.

She was biting her lip. Her eyebrows were raised in an expression of a child at the scene of a broken window. This is the way I will always remember her, along with the point, she was holding a smoking dart gun.

CHAPTER SIX

"Do you remember what happened next?" asked the Countess.

"That was almost twenty years ago!" I whined

"Do you remember what happened next?"

"Yeah, I woke up in a motel room in Beatty, Nevada with round the clock nurses. At least they called themselves nurses."

"You still don't know, do you?" she smiled.

"All I know is the cheap ass movie producer put me in a motel, because he did not want any flack with the unions or the insurance companies."

"He was trying to avoid being sued by a hobo. He didn't want any of the adverse publicity that medical reports would cause. she added.

"Right, he was a business man." I scoffed. "So, he put me in a motel. Then Stephanie, Gwen and you, took turns for the first few days, playing nurse."

"I didn't hear any complaints at the time!"

"Except for the fact I was blind, and wearing a turban across the bridge of my nose, I was in hog heaven. Of course, I did have to listen to the men in the motel, refer to you three as triplets." I laughed; thinking back at it all.

"We did kind of favor one another." she smiled.

"I conned you girls, into three bed baths a day."

"You never conned anyone!" she reproached.

She can say that now. At the time, they were so afraid I was going to die, they would do anything to make my passing less difficult. In a few days, when they were sure I was out of danger, the bed baths came less frequently. Only one of them would stay in the room at a time. The other two would tour Beatty's gambling parlors, while they were off duty.

I lost my virginity in Beatty, Nevada, it happened during one of the change of shifts. It started out as just another bed bath and ended with one of them straddling the bed. Because of my cursed blindness I never knew which one it was. I sort of always imagined it was Stephanie.

Whoever she was, she kept my hands pinned down so they would not wander. This would have provided me with a valuable clue. No breasts would be Stephanie. Great big bountiful breasts, Gwen. I did not even consider the Countess given our past history.

The next day brought a change in medical personnel. Gwen had to get back to the movie production. Stephanie was returning to her parent's ranch in Oklahoma. The Countess lingered around for a while, then vanished into thin air, or more correctly to El Paso. Three other women took over, feeding me and making me feel comfortable until my sight returned. I was still waiting for the Countess to return, when Stephanie's brother came to check on me a few weeks later. When he found I was still blind, he hauled me back to Oklahoma. Beatty, was the last time I heard from the Countess.

"That's where you met Clyde, isn't It?" I asked.

"Yep, met him playing Black Jack." she spoke stilly. " He was up at least a grand when he started calling me his little good luck charm."

"Where did the production company get the other nurses?"

"They weren't nurses, they were.

"Hookers?" I interrupted. I guess I always knew that they were.

They were real professional the way they handed our pills and spoon fed me. I never questioned their training because the movie producer was paying the bills. Bach time, should have suggested something to me! It became a festive occasion of all sorts of earthly delights. It was never as good as that first encounter, with the one, I always thought to be Stephanie. And looking back now, I know it could not have been her.

"All right I just figured out why you took me on this little walk down memory lane."

She smiled. Then you will reconsider helping your daughter.

Still crying to avoid responsibility for the child, I questioned her, as to how she could pinpoint me, as the waifs dad. The day I was shot, was what she called; one of her red flag days. She said she knew; she had defiantly not been pregnant, before we all checked into the motel in Beatty.

"What about Guy?" I grasped at straws.

You remember all his attempts to impress everyone, with what a big stud he was?" she giggled.

"Yeah, when he wasn't snorting nose candy!" I countered.

"Well, that nose candy left him an old softy, if you get my drift." she smiled as she winked at me. " He had the will, but he did not have the means."

"Who would have ever thought it. Guy had the persona of some rooster strutting around a hen house!". Then it occurred to me there was an even more likely candidate. "What about Clyde?" I asked. "I mean if the bee was buzzing around the honey pot!"

"The poor boy had a little accident with a mechanical bull the night we met. He was a little tender for a good six weeks."

She went on to explain; during Clyde's recovery she suspected her condition. Being the darling man that he was, he decided to make an honest woman out of the Countess.

"This started out hobo's, what's with this daughter thing?"

"It is a complicated story." the Countess grinned. Her daughter was a superior student. For Biology homework, she started asking her parents questions, about their blood type. Somehow little Peggy Sue, had worked out that; Clyde could not be her natural parent. Confronted with the information, the parents admitted, the child's true father had been a hobo. They had known the truth for quite some time.

Peggy Sue, got in her head, to find her true father. She started rounding up hobos like stray dog's. The parents kept waiting for the child to outgrow this obsession, but it only became worse.

She would drag home tramps and bums, old hippies and young homeless people. The ranch became a 200 of humanity. Anything that was nor nailed down, began to turn up missing. The parents put an end to it, promising to locate the missing parent. Clyde emptied the ranch by strutting around with his Smich & Wesson strapped to his thigh.

"And, that's when you decided to contact me?" I asked. " Oh heavens no. We hired Muskrat Pete to pretend to be you. Both Clyde and I, knew Pete. We felt we could control the influence he would project on Peggy Sue."

"Yeah, I always liked Pete myself." I said, a little shaken by the knowledge that I was a second choice.

Muskrat Pere, was a gentleman Hobo. He was proficient in a craft known as Hobo Art. The idea behind it, is to produce an object which can be traded for a few meals, some tobacco, money, or anything else of value.

Originally it was a bit of a scam. The art form itself, embraces many deceptions, including stone carving and furniture reproductions. Artfully done pieces of forgery, that had at one time commanded the same price as originals. To become a master of this stylized endeavor, it was important to build tables out of matchsticks and carve intricate oriental patterns into soft soapstone.

Musical instruments are another favorite pastime. Given the time and a minimum of tools a master can fashion banjos, Dobos, and funny little square guitars. Each instrument has its own rare sound.

Many examples still exist, shrouded in myths.

Around the run of the century some flim-flam man, noticing a piece of oriental stoneware in the window of an antiquities shop. made an inquiry as to its price. He was flabbergasted to find the Jade object, was worth more money; than every penny he had earned in his life. He studied it carefully, knowing a place on the California coast, where he could obtain similar stone.

During the Fourth of July parade, the shops window was smashed. Missing was the Jade sculpture.

Roughly four weeks later the film-fam man walked into the shop asking to see the owner. He had come into possession of a number of Jade objects. He would require authentication of their craftsmanship. Among the art objects was the stolen piece. The shop owner, recognizing his property, immediately informed his new client, the one piece was stolen. In a remarkable stroke of generosity, the client returned the statue, to its rightful owner.

The new client, pretended he was shocked. How could he have purchased stolen goods; from some charlatan. The shop owner, still swooning from his lucky recovery, offered to help his new friend in any way possible.

The next day the flim-flam client offered to sell the remainder of his objects to the store keeper. e client simply wished to divest himself of the whole dreadful business. How long would it take, to ensure the other Jade objects were not likewise corrupt?

The selling price would be exceptionally low, to facilitate liquidation.

The wise but greedy shop owner, consoled his new friend. He seemed to think a week would be sufficient to appraise the other objects. At the end of the week, the shop keeper had not received any reports which would indicate the items were stolen.

The shop keeper agreed to pay a fair price for each of the other six Jade sculptures. The two businessmen acknowledge a fair price.

The client would be paid, one quarter of the value of the original stolen piece, for each item.

Tucking the money into a belt, given to him by the grateful shop owner, the client left San Fransisco. En route to the civilized East, where law and order prevails. Also tucked into the duffel the man carried, was a remarkable duplicate of the original Jade piece.

The newly wealthy Flim-Flam man set his course for Tennessee, where he knew of a whole mountain of soapstone, waiting for any industrious stone carver.

Less precious than Jade, the soapstone could be offered to all interested buyers. He eventually even offered bathtubs and sinks to those who could afford his product. This particular myth should have ended here, it does not. Months after the stolen Jade piece was recovered, it was sold. One of the ocher statues was polished to be displayed in its place.

Dusting the sculpture, the semi-honest store owner made a startling discovery. Before the piece was stolen, he had affixed an inscription to the bottom of the original, with pen, paper, and glue. The cipher identified the piece as having come from: China.

The flim-flam man lacking the experience to know better, had carved into the base of each statue: China. Horrified by this discovery, the shop owner did the only thing he could do under the circumstance. He kept his mouth shut. When he died years later, the six sculptures were still part of his legacy if and when, they could not convince the prop tire but selling the bogus Jade as genuine Hobo Art.

"So, what got screwed up on the deal with Muskrat Pete?" I asked the Countess.

"You know how proud he is to be a Hobo! He started teaching Peggy Sue all about the lore of the Highroad." she said.

"Correct me if I'm wrong..." I cook a sideways glance at her with one eye shut, " like mother like daughter?"

"She is supposed to be in college." the countess offered.

"Then she's old enough to make her own decisions." I said.

"That was before all this spooky shit with the Mexicans and the border, and missing hobos, and a dozen other things, I hate to mention." she explained trying to look worried.

I convinced her, if I was going to go on the bum, she would have to pay up my rent, for a few months in advance. If things got screwed up, as I was sure they would, I wanted some place to come back to. I also mentioned; I would feel a whole lot better, if someone was house sitting. She picked up the phone and asked for: the Fisher of Men, Mission in Fall Church, Virginia. She asked for M.D. Donovan. She gave him directions, instructing whoever it was to take a cab. Sure, she would pay for it.

An hour later a cab pulled up in front of my house. An immaculately dean yet shaggy faced man got out carrying a gym bag. As he set the duffel down on the floor, it clanked like a load of bricks. Old Muskrat Pete, had brought along a load of soapstone to keep him occupied. His only other possession was a frayed and torn Bible.

I knew to make myself busy before he whipped the Bible open.

Old Pete had been trying to save my soul for the last twenty years.

If I allowed him to get started, we would be up all night, exploring the significance of long-gone Jewish prophets.

The only way I could avert a Bible study session, was to make sure he kept the book closed. I was not, that I did not, appreciate his proficiency in theology. I never developed the ability to quote; passage, page, and verse, the way he did. I hate the feeling of being embroiled in a biblical argument. I hate where the other guy expects me to trump his; John 14:13, with a; Phil 2:12, because he cannot wait to use a; Luke 11:9, uppercut.

CHAPTER SEVEN

"As long as I am on the payroll I might as well help you drive the Mercedes." I offered, hopefully.

"Not likely sucker. We're caking the Auto-Train, at least as far as Atlanta."

In Alanta she unloaded some paraphernalia from the trunk. A police bubble for unmarked cars was slipped under the driver's seat. She strapped an emblem onto the rear of the car, which identified us as law enforcement in the state of Texas. A radar detector was mounted onto the dashboard. Her police band scanner/radio slipped neatly into a slot under the dash board. When I asked about a cellular phone she said; she preferred to keep it in the trunk unless she was in Texas. Handcuffs hung from the rear-view mirror. Within minutes we were pointed west, doing eighty miles per hour, on Interstate 20.

Outside Birmingham we were stopped. The countess tossed the bubble onto the dashboard and kept driving. The State Trooper was not convinced. He followed us for a few miles, finally using his public address speaker to order us off the road. The countess, slapped the handcuffs around my wrists, as we slowed down. She handled the veteran officer, like a politician handles a congressional page. It seemed her story included; I was a hostile witness in transit to Texas to testify. He radioed ahead to confirm her story.

Everything checked the way she had described it, he let us slide back onto the highway.

As we pulled up to the ranch house it rained. Drops the size of Hershey Kiss candy smacked the ground. Dust rolled around the outside of the raindrops making miniature globes. A few seconds later, the globes would rupture under their internal density gradient, leaving tiny mud pancakes. Rain dollops, hitting the waxed finish of the Mercedes, would curl up into dust-colored marbles which rolled wherever gravity pushed them. The round liquid marbles would pick up whatever dust they rolled across leaving little trails on the finish. A drunken spider's web formed on the hood of the car.

We had driven into the courtyard through the open wooden gates. On three sides we were surrounded by single story red rile roofs behind which a balcony was constructed for the second story.

It was the type of place you would expect to encounter Zorro.

Gravel crunched under the tires as we pulled in. The Countess, in her vanity, was not wearing her glasses again. She almost creamed the fountain in the center of the courtyard. It looked like a wonderful place to water a horse. Large hunks of missing brick did not detract from the beauty of the courtyard fountain.

The Countess dashed out of the storm, into the safety of the veranda of the Spanish style home. Roughhewn timbers formed columns to support the weight of the verandas red tile roof. The clay tiles were suspended at an angle, to eliminate the summer sunlight, but allow amply access to the winter's light. Large patio sliding glass doors were bunted into adobe walls behind wrought iron bars.

I chose to stroll, embracing the meteorological event. The air was alive with the tension of nature. Cool above, hot below, discharge electrical particles were lining up along the front of the storm. Any moment now lightning should sizzle across the sky, sending a peal of thunder in all directions. The sheer power of the lightning exploding, would determine if a cyclone would hit some nameless Texas town, making it instantly eligible for the evening news.

As I gazed out across the landscape, a thunderhead with its drenching rain moved in my direction. An ancient white pickup truck seemed to be trying to outrace the rainfall. Judging by the shape and age of the truck it must belong to the gardener or some Feld-hand from the ranch. It was interesting to watch this classic struggle of man against nature. The thunderhead moved at a constant rate, drenching everything behind it in a sheet of rain. As the pickup lurched along it was forced to adjust its speed for the hills, gullies and curves in the road. I found myself cheering for the driver, hoping he would find himself adequate to the task.

Twice the truck vanished behind the wall of water. Both times he reappeared from the watery veil at the next straight section of road. With almost fifty feet to spare, the driver skidded to a stop.

I shouted my admiration as he parked the truck outside the gates to the ranch house. We both dashed for the veranda, just in time to escape a torrent of water. It was one of those minor victories that usually go unnoticed. I felt proud to be a part of it. I slapped him on the back as a hearty congratulation.

Being an instant comrade in the victory over the storm, he was friendly. In the back of my mind I reserved space for final judgment, until I got to know him better. It seemed to me he could be dangerous when angry. The man in front of me. looked as if his skin was a size too large for his bone structure. I do not mean he was thin, in fact just the opposite, the man was bulky but short.

He had a size forty hyde, hung on a size thirty-six frame. Under his Redman Tobacco ball-cap, grey flecks stuck out at his temples. The same grey washed throughout his moustache, beard and chest hair sticking out of his shirt top.

We stood there out of the rain, reliving the race against the storm. He was able to vividly reconstruct the events as they un-folded. He dwelled especially on the instances where the storm overtook him and he was forced to blindly drive by the seat of his pants. Not an undue amount of respect was heaped upon the abilities of the ancient pickup truck. The American workmanship chat went into the truck, allowed it to charge right through some of the gully washes, he had encountered.

He motioned me to follow him over to the patio table. Out of sight behind the table, a cooler produced two cold long-neck beers.

I judged, these were placed us here for the field hands to share, whenever they were finished working. The shape of the bottle allows the contents to slide down plenty quick. He produced two more beers without blinking. We finished four each, as the worst of the thunderhead rolled on past us. Fast friends now, we had not even exchanged names.

"Yeah, Chevrolet used to crank our one sweet piece of steel, back before they tried to compete with the Nipponese." I offered.

He chuckled at chat. "We should never have Nuked them!" I added.

"I know what you mean..." he added, "It was like putting
Sugar Ray Leonard in the ring with Richard Simmons!"

"That's one I would pay to see!" I laughed, inadvertently changing the subject.

"Don't ever bet on the white guy!" we both said in unison.

He somehow worked the conversation around, to what I was doing in these parts. Without mentioning exactly my purpose for being here, I explained how I was under retainer by the owners to locate their missing hobos. His expression did not change as he fished another salvo of beers out of the cooler.

Noticing the Countess approach, he fished up one more. She sat comfortably, in the padded cabana style chair, as my new friend asked me some leading questions. He seemed interested to know; what sort of experience I had, locating missing persons. Adjusting my seat so that I struck a conspirator's pose, I admitted I had very little to offer. I glanced at the Countess, informing him, it was her idea to have me involved. I suggested that her husband was the type of man that would provide her with anything her heart desired.

The countess let out a gasp that she immediately blamed on the beer. I pounded on her back, to ensure that none of the beer which had shot out her nose, would be lodged in her windpipe.

I continued my story; stating in no uncertain terms, how I would rather bring any of God's creatures back alive, excluding men.

"By men I mean mankind; including womankind." I continued, "Since were on the subject of womankind let me just say that I would rather collect rattlesnakes-bare handed, then chase down a woman!". The beer was doing a good deal of the talking.

The countess protested. My new friend commiserated. All in all, the conversation was going well. I being the guest speaker took every advantage of my position to expound doctrine and decree.

The countess stormed into the house which brought a grin from my friend.

"By the time you two are finished maligning women, dinner will be ready." she shouted over her shoulder.

This should have raised my suspicions about my new friend. I was so self-involved in conversation, due to my state of intoxication, that I did not question the countess offering to serve dinner to a mere field hand. I rambled on questioning the innate ability of women to make sensible decisions. My friend was behind me one thousand percent. Would I like another long neck beer? Sure, I would. How about you partner?

"Clyde, get your lazy ass out of chose dirty work clothes, and get ready for supper!" commanded the Countess.

I cocked my head back and gave him the old one eye stare.

"Why you old dog! You were just going to let me keep digging my hole deeper, weren't you?" I grinned.

"Didn't seem like I had any choice the way you love to calk!" he said recurring my one-eyed glance.

We looked like Black Jacks from a deck of cards.

"So, then you know why I'm here?" I asked.

"Haven't got the foggiest idea!" he countered.

"Well, you do know it's going to cost you. Don't you?" I asked, trying to seem as business like as any drunk could, under similar circumstances.

"Sure, I know it'll cost me ya Varmint. Just between me and you, you were absolutely right about Suzy Q. She gets whatever she wants." he mentioned, as he made an indifferent sniff of the shirt he was wearing. "Maybe after we sober up and have some supper, we can figure out what it is you were brought here for."

CHAPTER EIGHT

Clyde Starr looked neat as a pin as he sashayed into the dining room. He was shaved, sporting a can linen suit, with his hair combed back and plastered down with tonic. He smelled good too. He was unmistakably a country squire in every respect.

The countess was equally handsome in a low-cut linen jumper.

It seemed to be cut from the same bolt of cloth as Clyde's suit. Her freckled breast was demure but visible. I often wonder why some wives dress modestly, at all times, -except when their husband is present. The wives seem to enlist the aid of a neutral third party, to remind their husband, just how desirable they really are.

I felt slightly out of place being dressed in a perm-a-press shirt with wash and wear slacks. Making a pass through the dining area, I slipped quietly away to my duffle, throwing a bolo tie around my neck. Looking down at my boots, I polished them on the rear of my trouser legs. Lacking any cosmetics I soaked my head in the bathroom sink, thereby slicking down my coiffeur. None of the tricks of hobo life were lost on me.

A round Mexican woman treated us as elegantly as if we were dining in the finest restaurant anywhere in the world. We were entertained by a fruit course, with wine. A salad course followed by water. A fish course of Trout Almandine was served. Refills of the wine came at each interval, the color of which varied to compliment the entre'. A succulent cut of Prime rib was followed by sherbet smothered in candied cherries. More wine was served. I had serious doubles about my host's earlier proposition; that we would sober up during dinner.

By the time an after-dinner cognac was served, I could not avoid leering at the round Mexican woman. She wore rings on every finger with the conspicuous absence of a wedding band.

During the meal she had brushed against me repeatedly. My assumption of the situation; she either was lonely, or hunting for a North of the border husband. Probably both!

Her obvious charms were not lost on me.

Many Anglo men, perish the thought of becoming involved with a Mexican woman. Mexican women, who at the moment are voluptuous, are guaranteed to be voluminous later. I am not one of these cowardly cretins. I appreciate a sturdy woman. I use my minds eye to visualize her attractiveness, nor as she is at the moment, but as she was when in her prime.

To actually partake of her bounty at it's prime, is a criminal act known in most States as statutory rape. An unfortunate situation, that results in the more attractive ones being married at an early age. Elaborate ceremonies involving twenty-one-gun salutes take place. Lacking twenty-one guns, a single shotgun is often sufficient encouragement to induce a bashful bridegroom to come to a timely decision.

Soon after reaching the age of consent, these women quickly bloat into a form that requires subtle intoxication to be found attractive. In fairness to the women there is no infatuation, that will overcome the humiliation, of going to bod with an intoxicated lover. The task requires an equal debauchery on the part of both participants. He drinks so she also must drink.

Alcohol being one of nature's perfect beverages, it is almost pure calories. The woman being required to participate in a sedentary lifestyle becomes even larger, while the man labors and sweats away the empty calories. A chain of events takes place where the male becomes even more dependent on the alcohol to find his mate appealing. The wife becomes even larger. It gets to the point where both parties would suffer brain damage if they ingested enough alcohol to find one another attractive.

I should mention; this observation has been handed down to me by other Hobo's, who were able to confirm and validate all the important assumptions. I would hate to be hoisted up a Mexican flagpole for defaming its sovereign people and their habits.

As she refilled my cognac, I realized, I was in the perfect predisposition to begin making advances toward the maid. She was nor guiltless herself, I noticed, as she brushed her size eight bottom against me. For just an instant, she rested a size D cup across my shoulder. She could not be, more than twice the age she had been, when she was in her prime. By my calculations she was only half as plump, as she would be, at maximum capacity. The Countess, catching me in mid-leer, spat a salvo of Spanish at the maid. My lechery would remain unabated, as she waddled from the room. I grinned at her hungrily despite of my tight gut.

"Nice caboose on that one!" grinned Clyde, suddenly aware of the altercation that was giving his wife fits.

"That's right, just go on and encourage him." she rebuked.

"Pretty fine set of headlights, too!" I said to Clyde ignoring the Countess who immediately became apoplectic.

"You sober enough to get down to business?" asked Clyde.

"Sober as I'm going to get tonight." I countered, pretending that I was not three sheets to the wind.

"What do you know about Guadalupe?" asked Clyde.

"Which one? There are places all over the south named Guadalupe." I answered, allowing the alcohol to do most of my thinking.

"There is the Guadalupe River in San Jose. The Guadalupe in.

"The Guadalupe Mountains ye moron!" Clyde interrupted.

"Never heard of em!"

He explained that an hour's drive north-east would put me down in the middle of some mountains as pretty as any I would ever come across. The Guadalupe Mountain range forms a common border with New Mexico.

"How do you feel about UFO'?" Clyde asked.

"Flying saucers? They don't exist."

"How do you know they don't exist? You ever think about how large the solar system is, and how small the Earth is, in comparison to the solar system."

"OK they do exist."

"Wrong!" Clyde made one of those buzzers sounds from TV.

Look Clyde, make up your mind! You are the one paying my salary. If you say they exist they do. If you say they, don't they don't!"

"You're missing the point, Hobo!" Clyde corrected, a little ticked off at my fogginess. "If I send you out to count three legged dogs, I don't expect you to carve up any perfectly good mutts just to make me happy."

" You want the distribution of events to adhere to a common sigmoid bell shaped curve." I said. Alcohol surely makes the tongue wag. He looked across the table to his wife, gesturing that he was lost in the Greek translation.

"Just humor him darling." the Countess said to Clyde.

"You don't want me to substitute phony observations into my reports." I translated.

"Now you've got it!" He smiled endearingly. "I send you out after little green men, you don't come back with primer coat under your fingernails."

I could not help myself when I said, "OK Clyde so far I'm with you. You've got me looking for your runaway hobo daughter in the Guadalupe mountains which are inhabited by UFO's?"

"No!"

"You've got me looking for your UFO daughter in the Guadalupe mountains which are inhabited by runaway hobos."

"No!"

"Come on Clyde, give me a hint?" I finally begged.

The suggestion was made that some fresh air would do me good. My own interest was along the lines of some fresh air and another beer. I did not realize how much of a sadist Clyde was, until he escorted me to the edge of the pool, and laughed when I was unable to prevent myself from stumbling into it. What should have been warm water, was plenty cold after the rain. I was plenty sober when Clyde fished me out.

You want me to go to the Guadalupe Mountains enlist the aid of local hobos and find your daughter. As a cover story you want me to tell everyone that I'm searching for UFO's "Correct!" he smiled, waving for the plump maid to show me to my room. I wrapped a wet arm around her shoulder as she half carried me upstairs. Our rendezvous was short lived because I was asleep as soon as my head the pillow. The lovely creature helped s strip me down to my shorts, as I lay there in a self-induced coma.

Morning found me staring at a plate of sunny side up eggs with sausage links, positioned in a smiling face. The cook had positioned a pear half to form a nose. Fresh parsley was used to con struct eyebrows and a Groucho moustache. My pounding head caused me to stare at the plate without interest. The addition of a Bloody Mary to the meal, brought me around. A couple of sips of the cocktail saw the end to mister smiling face.

After breakfast, Clyde loaded me in the truck for a ranch tour.

He was one of those farmers who was paid by the government to keep his fields out of production. Looking at the parched appearance of the fields I commented, that the government must have a good sense of humor. He seemed annoyed at my statement.

"Hobo, what do you see right over there?"

"Looks like some sort of ditch."

"Ditch, my ass. That's the Rio Grande. All I have to do is crank up an old water pump, and I can flood these fields as far as the eye can see." he announced proudly.

"Pardon me Sheriff, but the old Rio Grande looks a little empty from where I sit."

He ignored me, "Labor is damn cheap around here too. If I put these fields into production, I could bring fem in by the bus load from Juarez."

"Or they could just walk across El Grande ditch! " I said, not willing to be ignored.

He let this comment go the way of the first," Besides, I have political aspirations, I've got a good reputation as sheriff. There is no reason why I shouldn't be able to throw my hat in the ring for Governor."

"So, it is politically astute to keep the fields out of production. You are able to invest time in other endeavors."

"You know, for a Hobo, you sure talk pretty sometimes! If I do give it a go, I might just let you work on my campaign." he smiled.

I could not tell if he was joking. The ranch was certainly large, and he did keep a modest sized drove of cattle.

I do not know what compensation the government withheld, because of the cattle production, but Clyde did not appear to be anywhere close to financial ruin "Texas sure is a big chunk of land." I offered to keep the conversation rolling.

"Big enough to become another country!" he proudly darned.

"Well, I wouldn't go that far!" I interjected.

"Let me tell you how big and important Texas is; Texas is so important thar God has a special branch of guardian angel just for Texas. Texas is so big, that the angels spend all their time, eyes dropping on prayers from people who are just passing through I was feeling a little spirited, so I encouraged him by asking: What do the people pray about?"

"They say; Oh Lord please make Texas just a little smaller so I can make it home to my family a tad sooner." he winked, while driving along a parched stretch of highway. I let it drop thinking that as the end of the fable.

"That's why they have Earthquakes in California!" he added after a moment's hesitation. I smiled to myself, wondering how angels had anything to do with earthquakes. I noticed the ranch house in the distance, figuring on a short dissertation. He slowed the pickup truck down.

Now the angels listen very carefully to the prayers waiting for the traveler to start bargaining.'

"Why bargaining?" I interjected.

They can't leave themselves in a negative mirage situation. he grinned.

"Oh." I said, knowing he was making this up on the spot.

"They listen until, some especially good Christian, starts to bargain: They'll give up some pretty nasty habits, if the Lord will just make Texas a tiny bit smaller. The angels put their haloes together and agree that the spiritual world would be a whole lot better off, if this guy would stop chasing after fallen women or some such nonsense "

"And, they grant him his prayer." I included.

"Not till he gets up close to the border, he isn't that good a Christian!" Clyde grinned, slowing the pickup down to a crawl.

Who Is, I wondered silently, hoping he would cut to the chase.

His story was causing my hangover to return.

"He gets right up dose to the border and all the angels cause the land to pucker up, to grant him his wish."

"What about the earthquakes? Clyde!"

"Well while they pucker up the land in Texas, it takes pressure off the tectonic plates in California and causes an earthquake." he laughed aloud, beating on the steering wheel.

"CLYDE! That sure was a long way to go to amuse yourself?" He stomped on the gas and sped the truck on down the road. I sat there silently trying some way to avenge myself for having to endure his stupid tale. I struck upon an idea and bounced it off him.

"Then, why don't they have earthquakes in Florida?"

Without a moment's hesitation he quipped, " Too damn sandy!" I wandered upstairs and collected my duffel. The ranch house was divided into three separate living quarters. The downstairs was a common area which began on one end as a kitchen. Beside the kitchen was a spacious dining room. It continued into a living room, which terminated in a den. Off the kitchen was a modest stairway leading to the maids' quarters. Above the den was the guest quarters. A grand staircase encompassed the living room leading to the master's suite.

I noticed the house was actually much older than it first appeared. The electricity and plumbing had been installed after its construction. Everything had been so tastefully added that only a trained eye would notice how ancient the structure really A was. The house was horseshoe shaped, with those massive wooden gates enclosing the courtyard. The ground floor on the outside perimeter contained no windows, but went directly up to the second floor. My mind conjured up images of Clyde's saintly mother giving birth to him in this very house. As I brought my duffle down to lunch, I asked my host If this was true.

"Hell, no hobo, My mother's in a convalescent home in El Paso. I picked this place up from the government about fifteen years ago. Before it was seized, it used to belong to a bunch of Mescalito bandits. My family already owned the rest of the land and I picked this place up for a song!"

I encouraged him to continue. This might have been a mistake. He enjoyed telling me the tale of the stake out and seizure of the property. The gun battle and description of the bloody arrest occupied a great portion of the story. The lunch would have been a lot more pleasant, if he had omitted certain details. I barely managed to swallow my burrito, before being informed; what a fat man smells like, after being cut in two by a shotgun blast. An ice-cold beer helped to settle my already queasy stomach and the burrito stayed where it belonged.

"A week after we moved in, a cargo plane dropped a bale of Marijuana smack dab in the middle of the courtyard." Clyde announced.

"We fed it to the cattle!" interjected the Countess.

"Well, most of it anyway..." grinned Clyde.

"Some of these Mao cows gave cream for a month." he laughed.

I thought this would be a good time to announce I was leaving. " Look I don't mean to sound ungrateful. but I thought I'd get a move on. Are you going to drive me to the Guadalupe, or am I going to have to find some other transportation?

"When I hire a man, I let him work out the details. You tell me what you need and I'll see if I can provide it."

"OK, how about lending me your truck for about a month?" He laughed, "No can do Hombre, no one drives Lucille but me. I have always wondered about people who give their voices names. I rather preferred hombre to being called hobo.

"What about one of the old squad cars, asked the Countess, …. they're just sitting around collecting dust?".

Clyde got a contemplative look on his face and agreed. "Shoot, we could just swear him in as an undercover deputy and I could defray some of the expenses as an ongoing investigation."

At this point I started to bargain with the-angels, but soon realized; I did not possess anything that would interest them. If I gave up fat women, I would have to go through life oclibare. If I gave up drinking, the same thing would happen. Besides, I'm not that good of a Christian. I did not want responsibility for any earthquakes either.

CHAPTER NINE

Skeeter Johnson was not a hitchhiker that was likely to get picked up by just anyone. As a matter of fact, Skeeter is the kind of hitchhiker the police warn you to avoid. I was on my second outbound journey to the Guadalupe mountains when I rounded the Dead Man's curve on Interstate 20. I had a full tank of gas, compliments of the El Paso Sheriff's Department. Up under the seat I had a service revolver where I could get at it plenty quick. I was felling generous.

The Dead Man's curve is a section of the highway where the shoulder is so narrow a man can hardly walk beside the guard-rail with our being hit by a truck. If the trucks do happen to miss someone walking on the road, rocks and debris are thrown at a terrific velocity. Avoiding the trucks and the rocks a walker is still liable to be shot in the back by some psycho-killer driving on the highway. Owing to its closeness to Mexico only a handful of the bodies from Dead Man's curve are ever identified.

I was feeling generous, when I saw a figure dressed in black leather, walking beside the highway going into the curve. I pulled over, slipped the service revolver into the small of my back. I then ran back to encourage the dolt, to get into my car. My vision became blurry from walking into the high velocity sand blowing off the trucks. We both were being pelted with rocks and old tire treads. As I guided the stranger back to the auto, I noticed a distinctive feminine lilt to the way they walked. I reminded myself; charity is it's own reward. I surely hoped so! Skeeter was lucky enough to be wearing leather when a Peter built truck sprayed us with gravel.

To prevent the hitchhiker from discovering I was momentarily blinded, I introduced myself while brushing the grit out of my face. A soft melodic voice returned to my ears. The stranger introduced their self, as I fumbled with my shoulder harness. My mind raced through a series of probable sexual scenarios, as my vision returned. Acting as nonchalant as possible, I started the engine and pulled out into traffic. This required my full attention and every cubie inch of acceleration the old squad car could muster.

"Where ya heading!" I asked.

"California." the rider answered demurely.

"It's a little out of my way, but I can sure get you up the road a way!" I guarded the fact that I was actually heading in the oppo-sire direction. Charity is its own reward. I was feeling generous.

Upon closer inspection I discovered that Skeeter was not what she seemed to be. She wasn't even a she. Skeeter was a remarkable example of deceptive packaging. Later in the trip I would learn;

Skeeter could switch between alter ego and reality at will. My mental images of sexual scenario's burst like a balloon at a dart tournament. I chastised myself, for even entering into speculation, about a-_roadside romance. I criticized myself for feeling generous.

1 reminded myself; No good deed goes unpunished!

I quickly rationalized: my original decision to pick up this stranger was to prevent, -whoever it may be, from walking into Dead Man's curve. This had been accomplished. I had already missed my turn and the next large town was Las Cruces, New Mexico. After a cloverleaf we were headed back in the right direction. He did not notice the change in travel plans.

I pulled over at the first rest stop. Could I-divest myself of the unwelcome passenger? Either he was playing possum, or he was pretty damn tired. It was impossible for me to wake him up. Like it or not, I was stuck with a rider who suffered from a gender crisis.

It would be inhumane to drop someone out in the middle of nowhere. Especially, someone like Skeeter.

His dirty hair and clothing told me he had been sleeping in drain pipes. I wondered what circumstance had put him on the bum. No one with any brains would sleep in a drain pipe except as a last resort. It being the rainy season, I wondered, if old Skeeter had learned this lesson the hard way. He must have. He was cleaner than he would have been, if he had not been shot out of the pipe by a sudden burst of water.

I strapped him into the seat belt, then headed in the direction of the Guadalupe. At each rest area I tried to wake the guy but he was too far gone. Finally, some life returned to the rider as I pulled into the third or fourth rest area. The sign said: Next rest area forty miles. I could live with that.

I laid out a bed of blankets in the rear seat and deposited his exhausted body on top of them. He was out like a light again as soon as he slumped down.

In the Navy, I had a little experience with people as they give up the ghost. There is this peculiar odor that announces the end of life. As the bowels relax and gas escapes this odor fills the air. I was nearing the next rest area, when this very distinctive odor started to radiate from the rear seat. I reached my hand back groping for the man's wrist. There was no pulse. I checked again still nothing.

Skeeter was dead. I rolled the windows down to get rid of the stench.

Panic washed over me. There would be a Coroner's inquest. I was the last person, to spend time with a Flammer, while he was still alive. Oh God, I would be branded for life. I comped on the accelerator. Find a town with an Emergency Room, while the body was still warm. Dump the guy on a gurney and split. Slow down, do not risk being stopped by the State Patrol. They would be certain to take names!

I slid into a slot between two trucks. We were doing fifteen miles an hour over the speed limit. They had radios. I knew it was a safe way to insure against being pulled over by a state trooper. As we got closer to a town large enough to provide an emergency room, I peeled off from the convoy. We were still pushing the speed limit at the exit ramp.

Just as I was approaching the hospital, I noticed some red and blue lights in my rear-view mirror. Some local authority was urging to pull us over for speeding. I decided to try for the emergency room. As I was pulling into the ramp leading to the hospital, I heard a groan from the rear seat. Skeeter Johnson was not dead after all. I looked in the rear-view mirror. The lights were still flashing.

Br this time both cars had come to a stop. The police officer got out of his cruiser, as a couple of emergency room orderlies looked on. When he saw a head popped up in the back seat, he drew his service revolver. I pounded my head on the steering wheel, then opened my door to get out.

"Damn it Skeeter, this is not a good time for you to still be alive." I grumbled, pulling my wallet out of my pocket.

Moments later I was presented with a brand-new speeding citation. The officer was even courteous enough to give me an envelope to mail the hundred dollars to the courthouse. He laughed at my story, about how I thought my passenger was dead.

Me mentioned; this was the first time he had heard the story cold, with such so much sincerity, nice try!

"Sheeter You were doing a pretty good job of acting masculine back there. What gives?" I asked, as we pulled back onto the main highway out of town.

"He was a cop! One doesn't act Gay around cops.

"Skeeter explained, sounding like a big sissy.

"You can turn it off and on at any time?" I asked, while considering whether to show him my police paperwork. I wondered if he would give it a rest, if he knew; I was a duly sworn deputy back in El Paso.

"Sure, we all can, that's how so many of us stay in the closet, Skeeter answered.

"Well, would you please turn it off Skeeter, because, you scare me boy."

"You're only scared of me, because, you feel you may be attracted to me!" said Skeeter still in his alter ego.

"THAT AIN'T ITI. You're a little funny, that scares me." I was still trying to figure out how he did it. How did he sound like a woman one minute and a man the next? He clearly preferred to use his feminine gender, but this as a conscious choice.

I watched his lips. They seemed to pucker up when he was in his lady like voice. When he was in his masculine persona, his lips were slack, normal.

I instructed him to be a good passenger and put a little bass in his voice. I would just forget all about his sexual orientation, if he would quit reminding me. He entertained himself by waiting until I was comfortable with the way the conversation was going, then he would switch to his alter ego. My skin would crawl, when one minute I was traveling with Indiana Jones and the next moment I was with Madonna. I imagine; he thought my reaction was funny.

In the standard line, used by all homosexuals at one time or another, he asked me; " How do you know you aren't Gay, if you never tried it"

"Did you ever stand on your head in the middle of a pond with your butt feathers sticking up in the air?" I asked.

"No!" he answered looking confused.

"Well then how do you know you're a queen, and nor a duck?" I asked giving him the old one-eyed glance.

The sun was coming up as we approached the Guadalupe. I cautioned Skeeter, to stay in his masculine role, while we picked up something to eat at a local diner. I did not want him to embarrass me, in front of the local townspeople, some of whom knew me from my previous trip out here.

I caught a glimpse of Skeeter in the reflection of front window.

He was skipping behind my back. I opened the door for him, then planted a boor where "the sun don't shine as he passed. The wait. less smiled when she saw us fooling around. She took us for a normal pair of roughnecks, who always like to cut up in public.

"Don't make me handcuff you to rear bumper of the car Skeeter!

I might just forget you're there." I instructed.

Raising one eyebrow bur remaining in his masculine role he said, "I find it interesting that you carry handcuffs, James."

"Maybe there is a kinky side to you after all.", he added as if threatening to start embarrassing me.

"You know what I consider Kinky sucker?" I asked with one eye shut.

"I probably could." he upheld his end of the argument.

"OK, mister smart guy, what is it?"

"Fat women!" he tossed his head triumphantly.

I was dumbfounded, how did he know that. The waitress grinned ear to ear, she herself qualified as a little plump. She stood there with her note pad and pen, trying to look a little lonely. I knew; if I asked, she would be getting off work in another hour. If it wasn't for Skeeter, I might have even been tempted to stick around a little while.

'Just got out of a mental hospital." I said to her as I noddy my head in his direction.

"Whatever you say!" she answered. I knew; she probably heard the same line thirty times a day.

"I did not" said Skeeter, just barely cracking through the thin veneer of heterosexuality.

"Say you're not one of those sissy fellahs are you?" asked the plump waitress with a smile. " The boys took the last one out back this morning, and hung him!" she winked at me.

"Sorry I missed it." said Skeeter, in a booming baritone voice.

I shot coffee out of my nose, laughing. His subsequent antics while we ate, were limited to normal conversation.

When it came time to pay the check, I was a little irritated to find he made no effort to contribute. We walked out to the car with him seeming to lead the way. I offered to pull around back, to see how his common gender was making out. Ile was not preoccupied in anything, except getting on the road. "Relax, Skeeter, It's only an old joke!" I grinned.

To Skeeter's credit, I was surprised when he asked me; why the sun was in our face in the morning, if we were heading toward California. I explained about the change in plans. How, after Dead Man's Curve, I found myself stuck with him, until I could drop him at someplace safe. He was told; I did not want to just dump him out in the middle of nowhere. Besides, after receiving the ticket, I had not gone past anyplace where I could drop him. He agreed that his survival in the open desert was not too good. He certainly did not like the idea of hitch-hiking from the diner.

"Not too many truckers going to give you a ride, with you acting like a Queen for a day." I added.

"Where the hell are we? I haven't seen a Seven-Eleven or a Burger King all morning." Skeeter pulled off a reasonable Eddie Murphy impression.

Right on the border of Texas and New Mexico. That's the Guadalupe on that side. Carlsbad Caverns, is over there some-place, but you can't see them from here." I said acting as tour guide.

"What's a nice boy like you, doing in a dreadful place like this?" He Flip-flopped into a Bete Midler impression.

I stiffened, first; he could not fill out a blouse the way Bete could, second; I was not sure I should use Clyde's cover story.

Skeeter was not the kind of guy to tell, I was our here hunting down UFO's. It might encourage him to stick around. Everybody else I told the UFO story to, just looked at me like I was crazy, and went about their business. That was what Clyde had planned.

Skeeter was a special case.

"I'm doing environmental research on the transient population?" I explained. It was a deception I was sure I could pull off without encouraging Skeeter to stick around.

"Transients?" Skeeter suddenly started using what I later decided was his normal voice. The voice of a pleasant kid.

"Hobos, Tramps, you know the rural homeless People live our here?"

Sure! The last time I was out here, there were about thirty people coming and going. They were working a fork in the railroad a few miles off the main track. "

"Doesn't the railroad run them off?"

"Hell no! Not way our here, where they too often need a couple strong backs, to keep the rail straight." I said, beginning Skeeters education. " They used to do everything but shoot hobos, but not anymore! "

Skeeter stayed in his excited little kid persona, while I had him engrossed in my cale; of how the desert rats survived. I overlooked his less desirable tendencies, as long as he remained the healthy strapping youth, he looked like he was.

I stopped the car several times to show him aspects of the railroad he would have missed otherwise. Where the tracks crossed the main roadway, I pointed out a stack of old tires that would be burned. The burning tires would war truckers of the position of the tracks the next time fog rolled through. Some old desert rat, lived out here all year long, waiting for the evenings he was needed to burn those tires.

"Fascinating! So, he's hired by the railroad to light the tires?" asked Skeeter.

"Not exactly, but, every once in a while, some unclaimed freight just happens to fall off a boxcar. It keeps them in beans and other stuff they can use. The rest of the time they live off rabbit and wild seed they collect." I instructed, gathering some likely plant shoots to show to Skeeter. * Those desert rats are what you call hermits. They seldom congregate with the transient hobos."

"Where do the transient hobos pass the time?" he asked.

"You ever hear of Hobo Jungles?"

"No!"

"Somewhere out here, close to some source of fresh water, probably under a railroad trestle, there is a place where they wait for the trains. If they are tired, they rest until they feel like traveling wherever the highroad takes them. They swap whatever they have, for whatever they need, while they wait on a slow-moving train."

My first trip out I had worked my way down the freight lines looking for all the hobo jungles. I never came across any young women actually living out there. I did not really expect that I would. Life on the highroad is rough. The men are rough. This far away from cities, it is not easy to panhandle loose change or slip by the local Mission for a meal as a last resort. Even the gentleman hobo disregard most cultural refinements our here.

Women need little personal creature comforts, which are not generally available. Every once in a while, some down on her luck old alcoholic, is escorted by a hobo guide as she makes her way across country. They do not stay long We one place. Having nothing to barter, the ladies of the rail are treated as guests. Scrounging a little supper and an occasional sip from a dregs cask they are encouraged to move on. Only the first meal is ever free. The next meal will require a donation. Of course, some of these grand dames would like to barter their obvious wares.

During the Summer of love in San Francisco quite a few young ladies gave the rails a go. I was still a youngster and did not participate in any of the trading of these wenches. It was probably a good time to be a hobo back then. The women still out on the rails twenty years later, were not something to become excited about.

They were just as leathery as their male counterparts. I am sure: there is still some sympathy sex being traded. It would be a tough call to decide, who was being generous, and who was being sympathetic.

I do not want to limit the contributions a woman can make to the Jungle. She can provide, all the same services, the men use to barter. She can be a cooper who works in a bar carefully filling the dregs casks. She can be a tailor or a tinker or a stone cutter. She can be a rabbit snare hunter or especially a cookery. Women just do not have the heart for dealing with the climate and the dirt; the blistered skin and tuberculosis. Whatever would make them a good hobo, would also make them a good house maid or even a wife. It does not take long for them to figure this out. Even if they were to fail at more productive tasks, women who stay closer into towns have better chances of finding themselves in high cotton.

I knew all this before my first trip out. The chances of me finding Clyde's precious Peggy Sue, were as close to zero as winning the Florida lottery. I was amazed on the previous trip, when some of the hobos told me; there was a young woman traveling with some character, who was trying to contact his-mother ship.

He had handed our flashlights. The hobos had agreed to shine the flashlights up at the mother ship when it arrived.

A trading post in a nearby community had done a brisk business, trading flashlights for tobacco, when the mother ship failed to arrive in the first two weeks. Where had the man and woman gone? No one seemed to know. It was thought; they had made contact on their own and we now streaking across the universe toward Alpha Centauri. If I wanted to examine any of the flashlights, they could be purchased, for five dollars each at the trading post. Leaving nothing to chance, I did just that.

Hobos and UFO's, I shuttered to think, if Earth were contacted by extraterrestrials, they would choose the homeless as an example of the human race. I examined the flashlights; they were similar to the kind used by law enforcement. The aluminum case was shock resistant and could be used as a nightstick. This guy must have pulled a robbery on a military reserve depot. He had to be a thief. No one else in their right mind would hand out the twenty-dollar item. Not to a bunch of hobos, who in turn, would trade it for a dollars' worth of tobacco.

I bought four of them to show to Clyde. The store clerks net profit; five hundred percent each. My savings would have been seventy-five percent each, except Clyde confiscated them. I cannot complain. He did get me a good deal on some hooch, which I planned to use as barter to the hobos on my return. When I made the mistake of picking up Skeeter, my instructions were to get back out there, and track down Peggy Sue.

I was wondering about the coincidence; of Clyde's cover story, matching the Modis Operandi of the fellow traveling with the woman. Clyde knew something chat he was not telling me. He had purposely baited me to go out on a wild goose chase. In the last ten hours, I had been more concerned with trying to get rid of my passenger, then in figuring out what it was Clyde could have known.

I pulled up to a Greyhound bus stop at a rundown store front. According to the schedule the next bus was in an hour.

"This is where you get oud" I announced to Skeeter.

"What are you talking about?" he countered.

"Didn't you tell the cop at the emergency room you had a bus ticket?" I asked.

I told him; my grandmother sent me a ticket."

"Then this is where you get out.

"I repeated.

"I don't have the ticket anymore." he looked absently out the window. "It was stolen by someone I met in Dallas"

"How did that happen?" I asked

"He said he was going my way. He said he would give me a ride to California. He seemed like a very nice man."

"Ill" just bet." I sneered, " He was probably the same son of a bitch thar dropped you at that curve coming out of El Paso, was it he? Do you know how dangerous that section of road is?" "How could 1 nor know? That's all you've been talking since I woke up! Besides that, is not where he dropped me.

"Spare me the details. Have you got any money.

What am I saying. of course, you don't. When did you leave Dallas?"

"Three days ago. "

"Three days to go five hundred miles."

"No one would give me a ride." Skeeter said in his own defense.

"I had to walk most of the way!"

Six miles an hour is about average, he looked like he could do better than most, I figured maybe seven MPH. I ran the numbers around in my head, five hundred miles, seventy-two hours. I reck-owned; he had probably walked most of the way. No wonder he was so tired when he got in my car. "Any food or water?" I asked.

"Just a little water." he answered.

The man had been doubly blessed when I picked him up. He may have been closer to death, than I thought, when I tried to make it to the emergency room. I should have left him there.

"What am I supposed to do with you?" I asked rhetorically.

"You're supposed to get me to California." he mentioned bluntly.

I cursed my damn luck, and at the same time, I felt guilty about dragging him so far off course. If he was able to maintain masculine affectation, maybe I could use him to help locate Peggy Sue. I would deal which trying to get him pointed toward the coast, after I finished my work in the local area. Fate, had delt me a dirty hand, I had a partner. A big dumb gay partner.

CHAPTER TEN

The shopkeeper at the trading post recognized me from the last time I came in. He was all out of flashlights. The Hobos had come back after them, when they saw strange aircraft in the sky for three nights in a row. I knew the store clerk would not just turn over the flashlights without profit. He was a businessman. I asked, what the hobos could possibly have to trade. Very proudly he pointed me in the direction of a display case. A hand printed card read:

Genuine Aztec Miniatures, $20-$50

"How do you know they're genuine?" I asked the proud clerk.

"They look just like the ones in this free tourist travel brochure. he answered presenting a copy with Nourish.

The miniatures were not only exact duplicates of the ones in the brochure they were the exact size and color. The brochure pointed out that although rare, miniatures of this type had been carried north by Indians trying to escape Cortez. Pretending to be more interested than I really was, I asked to examine one of the small sculptures. Unseen by the clerk my fingernail sunk into the soft soapstone. Some clever sculptor had managed to oil the stone to induce the authenticating color.

I did not feel it was my duty to enlighten the clerk. Why ruin the illusion? Somebody with a station wagon full of kids would stop in and purchase one or two. Another traveler, who fancied himself as a bit of a collector, might purchase the lot to resell to his friends back in Baltimore or Newark. The initial investment of a dollars' worth of tobacco, was going to produce a net profit of two-to-five thousand percent.

I returned the miniature to the clerk, "Maybe next time

"They're going like hot cakes!" he pressured, "I may not have any the next time you're in."

"Oh, I've got a feeling you'll be receiving some more of them in trade." I said maintaining a straight face.

For twenty dollars I purchased; a handful of homemade beef jerky, five gallons of water, a dozen empty bottles and a funnel.

The clerk was happy to get rid of the bottles. He threw in some rubber bands and hot wax just to sweeten the deal. He seemed like the kind of a person who was happy just about anything. At the kind or profit ratio he was receiving, he could afford to be happy.

Another twenty dollars, rented the use of a shack down a dirt road, to hide the car.

As soon as we arrived at the shack, I started force feeding jerky and water to old Skeeter. When he was fully satisfied, I had him help me. I had already soaked the tax labels off the liquor bottles while he ate. We dumped half the liquor into the empty bottles purchased from the trading post. The liquor bottles were then refilled to the top with the fresh water.

"Why are we doing this?" asked Skeeter.

"We can't walk into a hobo jungle without something to trade, it wouldn't be friendly!" I explained as I started loading the bottles into a back pack.

"No, I mean why are we watering down the booze?" he asked.

"Skeeter, I'm doing them a favor! If they were to drink this eight-six proof stuff, in the desert hear, it would cause them all kinds of discomfort. At forty-three proof this stuff is pretty harmless." I explained, while I hot waxed the tax stamps back onto the bottles.

I wrapped a rubber band around the neck of each bottle to hold the tax label in place.

"Why don't you just bring them some beer? "

"Because beer is only three percent alcohol."

"So!" he argued.

"So, that's only about six proofs. We would have to carry seven or eight cases of beer to be as effective as this one case of hooch!"

I carefully instructed, " Besides, have you ever tasted warm flat bottled beer?"

"Ugh, yes! That's what I was drinking in Dallas when I got my wallet and bus ticket stolen."

"I don' think I want to hear any more thank you!"

Skeeter looked at me like he was bursting to tell the tale. I ignored him. I really was not interested in hearing how the other fellow was able to get that close to Skeeter's wallet.

The afternoon was still too warm to get started. Breathing, out in the sun, was like inhaling a blast furnace. We sat in the shade of the shack watching little dirt devils' whirl around picking up dust and straw. Skeeter had found the remnants of a pack of cards and we amused ourselves by flipping them into the miniature cyclones. The object was, to try to send the card up the funnel shaped cloud of dust. I noticed him limping as he retrieved one of the cards.

"What's the matter with your foot?"

"Nothing!"

"Take off your shoes.

" I ordered. "

Just as I suspected, the great prancing pooches had developed foot rot from not keeping his feet clean. I was beginning to feel like I had adopted the big kid. I dug a hole out in the sun, close enough to the shack that he could keep the rest of his body shaded. I lined the inside of the hole with plastic, then filled it with water.

In no time the water was tepid. When he had soaked his feet to the point, they looked wrinkled, we poured some of my hooch over them, then let them air dry for an hour. I even had to donate a fresh pair of socks to the guy. Before he slipped the clean sox on, I examined his feet.

"What's the problem?" he had the nerve to ask.

"Frost bite!"

"I haven't been in any snow!"

"Well, it's the same thing as frost bite. Jesus, did I ever screw up when I gave you that ride." I cursed my rotten luck. "Don't worry though, we got to it in time. Keep your feet clean, and they'll be as good as new in a couple of days." We washed his dirty son in the tepid water of the make shift puddle. They were dry in no time from the arid climate. I avoided telling him, what jackass he was, saying instead that he could attend to chis simple chore without me in the future. I wondered; what he would do for friends, in my absence.

While he was still soaking his feet, I had dug a hole in the corner of the shack. Whatever valuables we did not take with us, was buried in the hole. This included the rest of the unadulterated liquor. Over the hole I sprinkled Cayenne pepper, just in case any animals came snooping around. I left the car trunk unlocked, knowing from experience; a crow bar would be used to open it, if anyone was curious about what was inside.

An hour before dark we set out. He carried the lighter of the two backpacks, the one with our food. I ended up carrying the hooch, a couple bottles of water and my revolver. We made the first hobo camp just as the moon came out. It was as refreshing a sight as the first time I laid eyes on one of these places. Some long-forgotten railroad mishap had deposited a group of boxcars at the bottom of a ravine. They stood there rusting where they landed, still coupled together.

Evening cook fires dotted the area on both sides of the box-cars. Men huddled around each fire, savoring the aroma of cooked rabbit, armadillo or gofer. They watched Skeeter and myself suspiciously, as we made our way along the line, waiting to be invited to join in with one of the groups. There are dozens of ways to get invited over to a campfire. All of which, I had forgotten at the moment. During the hike I explained to Skeeter what I expected out of him. He knew exactly what was meant when I told him to go to "Plan B'. He hurriedly collected enough sticks to build our own campfire. He laughed, when I referred to his bundle of sticks, as a fagot.

We set out some freeze-dried food, to cook over the campfire.

While we waited for it to rehydrate, I pulled a deck of cards from the bottom of the food pack. There is nothing like a little game of chance, to pick the interest of men living under the stars. Skeeter and I used match sticks as currency. Having already agreed, the match sticks could be redeemed for a bottle of our stash, we played a few hands. Skeeter was a vicious player, who had no interest in cashing his winnings. The energy he put into the game was not lost on the other campers. Before long, I was turning players away, temporarily. First examining whatever they planned to use to secure the match stick currency: The idea was to learn who everyone was, without barging into every campsite. Match sticks were fifty cents apiece. Five hand rolled cigarettes, was one match stick. A shot of hooch, two match sticks. Skeeter traded ten match sticks for a flashlight. I picked up a genuine Aztec miniature, for five matches and a shot of hooch. Beef jerky, one match. A clean pair of saxes, three marches. A wise little Hobo Cooker offered to prepare our dinner for three march sticks, COD. He spent two on a shot of liquor and gambled away the other one.

They were trading whatever they could spare to ger into the game, hoping to drink for free. I made a big show of chasing Skeeter off, to start his own game. He was too vicious to allow anybody to win a couple hands; unless the fellow really worked for it. Skeeter was doing just fine.

I kept my eye on the Cooker. These guys have extremely fast hands. Cooker's travel around with a couple of old dented pots and a basket full of spices, pretending to be gourmet chefs. What they do well is find someone who has fresh game, then offer to cook it, for a share of the meal. Or, they may barter their services for some other animate object. They are usually friendly, as their trade depends on being able to ger along with just about anyone.

If one does not keep a close eye on them, the food duffel empties itself plenty quick. Women-Cookers are the worst, they have to know every item in your food duffel, to decide how they will prepare the meal. Then, they try to cheat you out of the left overs.

They will not skin a rabbit, scale a fish or even pluck the occasional wild quail or pilfered chicken. Most Cookers can work magic with a skillet. The meals almost always consist entirely of the meat course. If some local corn, kale, or spinach is available there may be a vegetable. Dried beans are also a natural plate for them to serve up, if someone is around for the time it takes for them to soften. Down in Louisiana there might be some poke salad, rice even gumbo with crayfish. But; we were in the part of Texas where the game was rabbit, armadillo, and snake. These were Chili fixings. Where a gourmet chef, would learn to cook rattlesnake or armadillo, I have no clue. Lizards and road kills were even sometimes used by the truly desperate, birches is nor something to be presented to a cooker, -except to piss him off. Trading was brisk and we were soon in possession of all sorts of trash, that we had no use for. I kept cheating to a minimum, making sure everyone was pleasantly inebriated and therefore more talkative than normal.

Working around the flashlights, I started trying to pry some of the UFO sightings, out of the good old boys. The ones who had something to report started winning, the others started losing, At the end of an hour, I was cashing in match sticks for shots of hooch, to a select group of night sky watchers. Most flamboyant of the group was a smallish figure of a man called Frenchy. Sure, he had seen the lights.

It turned out Frenchy, a Canadian from Montreal, had been trying to contact the mother ship. He hoped, they would pick him up and take him to their planet.

"Would you like me to show you where the lights will come from?" Frenchy asked.

"Sure, but were right in the middle of a poker game here. Maybe later." I answered.

A short time later Frenchy began to experience a winning streak of epic proportions. The others could not match his luck and dropped out. I likewise folded having had enough poker for one evening. Pulling a fresh boule from my pack I struck a bargain with Frenchy to settle my accounts. "Where did you say those lights were coming from?"

Skeeter was still working the pigeons at the other game.

I pulled him aside to tell him where I was going, mentioning how the neighborly thing to do would be to lose big for the next hour then close down the game. He looked at me sheepishly trying to figure some other way to end the game. Noticing he was still as sober as a preacher, I told him to start drinking, that way loosing would come naturally and be a whole lot less painfully. He When another bottle out of the backpack then went back to the game.

"Just don't forget where you are!" I added.

"Well, it sure aren't CALIFORNIA!" he fumed. I did not blame him, for being annoyed one iota.

I followed Frenchy out to where he said the lights came from.

He was adamant that they always came from the same direction.

The lights always blinked at him, when he would shine the flashlight beam up at them. They were obviously trying to make con-tact. I was skeptical, holding to the concept that it was some kind of aircraft.

The moonlit night made for a perfect silhouette of the mountain range. Our past the mountains was El Paso. In the opposite direction lay the town of Carlsbad. To the left Pecos, Texas slept soundly. Alamogordo lay to the right, due north by northwest.

This far out in the country the only light besides the moon was the stars. Millions of stars, dots of light that are not visible in even a small crown. It was spooky how small we both felt looking up at the night sky.

"Here they come!" shouted Frenchy. He pointed at a dot visible against the backdrop of the mountains. I rubbed my eyes in a futile attempt to wipe away the liquors. I checked my watch; it was One O'clock in the morning.

CHAPTER ELEVEN

"Clyde, I do not know what it was I saw last night" I stammered into the receiver of the pay phone.

"Listen hombre, if you saw something I want you to describe it" the sheriff instructed, "Hold on a minute while I get out my recorder."

I waited, nervously tapping my boot against the post that held the egg-shaped phone booth. He came back on the line and told me to go ahead. "It was silent, quiet as a whisper. Shaped like a diamond that rotated. The lights flickered on and off, when this guy I was with signaled it. He used one of those flashlights you confiscated."

"Oh yeah, one of those Texas National Guard flashlights, interesting." Clyde said.

"What? You tracked them down to the National Guard?"

"Sure, did Home Boy! What else did you see?"

"Nothing, it came in from the south and traveled north like it was following some sort of predetermined path. It seemed to lose altitude as it got closer. Then, after it passed us by a few miles, it looked like it gained altitude again. I saw it blinking again a short time later."

"What sort of a blink did you see?"

"You know a blink. Something between a strobe light and a police car." I described to the best of my recollection.

"Were the lights on or off when it looked like a diamond?"

"They were on, I couldn't see the damn thing when the lights were off."

"Good work, keep me informed which whatever else you find."

"What, that's it!" I asked, surprised he did not ask about Peggy Sue.

"That's it for now, call me tomorrow."

The camps were separated from each other by thirty miles of rugged desert. Using the car, Skeeter and I moved on to the next camp, and the one after that, and another one after that. For the next three nights we repeated the ritual from the first evening. The faces of the hobos changed, but the game remained the same. The story was the same too, they all remembered seeing a young woman trying to live like a hobo. She was traveling with some stranger who was always talking about the UFO's. They liked her, but could pass on the other outsider.

Each evening found me staring up at the sky, wondering if I would be contacted by creatures from another planet. I saw the lights on the second and forth nights. On the night in between a freak cold wind blew down out of the north, and I missed sighting the object. I was convinced, we were defiantly onto something important.

We were running out of hooch by the fourth night. Our next stop would have to be the trading post. If we planned to keep going, we would have to resupply our backpacks. Making a map of the likely locations of the camps, I discovered we had Madd him arc.

It was putting us real close to the town of Artesia. That was a good thing to know. If Clyde wanted us to keep going, it would be more convenient to use the highway. Either way it was still going to be a hundred-mile drive back to the trading post. I kicked myself for not digging up the box of liquor we had sashed there. I kicked myself again when I realized most of my money as with the booze.

Skeeter almost kicked me, when the squad car ran out of gas, a thousand yards short of the only station for twenty-five miles in both directions. I almost kicked Skeeter, when he would not trade his flashlight for five dollars' worth of gas.

We both wanted to kick the pimple faced station attendant, when he refused to trust me with his leaky gas can. I had to leave Skeeter as a deposit, while I walked back alone, a thousand yards to the car. Returning his can and reclaiming Skeeter, the attendant was nor satisfied with toy last ninety-seven cents for the dollars' worth of gas. The attendant at this precise moment had locked the station and was in the bathroom ignoring us. He knew we could not leave without more gas. I was still trying to work out a deal with the kid, for the other four gallons I needed. It dawned on me to use my service revolver.

"Skeeter, when he comes back tell him to stick around. I'm going after my gun."

When I rounded the corner of the building the pimple faced boy had returned. He was blubbering, tears were rolling down his face. As soon as he saw me, his bladder emptied, and he slumped down onto his knees. " Please!" he seemed to beg.

"Give me a hand here, Skeeter." I asked, reaching down with my free hand, lifting the lad to his feet. His legs were made out of rubber. We moved him onto a bench in the front of the store. He was still blubbering. A huge wet spot showed on the front of his pants.

"Skeeter what's the matter with him?"

"I have no Idea."

"What's the problem?" we both asked at once.

"I don't want to die!" the kid bawled, tears streaming down his face. I looked at Skeeter, he stared back at me shrugging his shoulders. The kid started to sniffle.

"Hey nobody does." Skeeter offered light-heartily:

I squatted down holding the pistol in both my hands like a

Praying Mantis. "He's right, nobody does." I agreed.

"You mean you're not going to shoot me?" he sniffled.

"Shoot you?" I laughed, realizing what was going on.

"Skeeter what did you tell the boy?"

"I told him to hang loose, while you got your gun, just like you told me to."

Look kid, all I wanted to do, was let you hold part of this pistol as collateral until I come back and pay you for the gas. See it comes right apart." I said as I removed the chamber. " It's worth, oh I'd say about four hundred bucks, easy. Of course, you cart fire it unless you have the whole thing, and I'm not going to leave the whole gun. But at least you know I will come back and pay you.

What d'ya say do we have a deal?

"You bastards make me piss my pants and you want to make deals?" the kid started to scream. "You have me bawling my eyes out and you want to make DEALS. I'll show you a deal mister." He started through the door to the office. Skeeter tackled him before he was all the way inside. The kid had one of those pizza and TV-flabby bodies. He was no match for Skeeter's bulk.

"Bet you'll find a loaded shotgun in the office!" said Skeeter, indicating I should go take a look. He kept the kid pinned down, adding, "True me."

I stepped over the two of them. There was a pump twelve gauge in the office alright. Along with, an over-under .006, a 22 rifle, a pellet pistol, a BB rifle and a sling shot. Every one of them loaded and ready to go. It took me the better part of five minutes to unload them all. When I was finished, we let the kid up and shoved him into the office. "What was it you were going to show me?" I grunted, flipping through a stack of porno magazines. The kid had stacks of them.

"Let me talk to him?" Skeeter begged.

"No, you just go find something to do, while I get this all straightened out."

We had a long serious discussion inside the sweltering office. I pulled out my paperwork from Texas and scared the piss out of the poor kid again. I explained how he was interfering with official business.

"B-B-B-Bur this is New Mexico!" he started to argue.

"B-b-b-b-NOTHING, Porky." I did my best Dirty Harry routine. " You were going to fire a shotgun at a law enforcement of fixer that is a federal offence. So why don't you just lock up this gas station, and climb in the back of my car, so we can go talk to the local Sheriff. And, if you don't want to push the car, in all this heat, I'm going to need a tankful of fuel."

The kid was sobbing again, big mama's boy tears. I would have felt sorry for him, if I did not already have him pegged as a weirdo. He was just waiting for me to turn my back, to stick out his tongue, he was that type of kook. I made him pump the gas himself, the good stuff. The whole time he was sniffling and crying. When the tank was topped off, I had him check the oil and water. He did such a good job at that, I had him check all four tires and do the windows.

"Think you learned your lesson son, or do you want to take that little ride we were talking about?" I asked.

"I learned my lesson sir." he whined like a little girl.

"What do you think Skeeter should we let him off with just a warning?"

"How the hell should I know? Let's just get out of here!"

"Consider yourself lucky young man." I grumbled stepping into the car and starting the engine.

I had gone all of fifty feet when I looked in the rear-view mirror and noticed the kid extending both middle fingers in our direction. I slammed on my brakes; he ran inside the station. There was no way in hell I was going back. Skeeter just laughed.

We got back to the trading post late. Instead of stumbling around in the dark we decided to spend the night in the shack. I got up at half past midnight, then climbed to the top of a ridge, looking for the mysterious lights in the sky. There was nothing to be seen. Clyde had told me in our last conversation, no radar reports had been turned in for this area. We were dealing with a completely unconfirmed sighting. I felt special to be on to something so spooky. Around one-thirty in the morning I was making my way back to the shack when I detected a humming sensation.

It sounded like a mosquito buzzing around my head and ears. I brushed both sides of my head bur the sound only got stronger.

When it was as loud as it would get, it sounded like someone was pushing a lawn mower through the Sage brush. I followed the sound as I ran back up the ridge hoping to see the lights. The noise faded again rather quickly. What the devil did this mean? I stared in the direction of the Guadalupe. In which direction did the noise travel, I had no clue.

"Sleeter, wake up man. Did you just hear anything? "

"Yeah, I hear a dufus disturbing my rest." he answered as he rolled over, going back to sleep.

I reported the new event during the next telephone call to Clyde. He was not amused. He actually did not want to be in-formed; there were any true sightings in this part of the desert. He was still holding something back. Something sinister was going on, and he was not sharing a speck of what he knew.

To weasel it out of him, I mentioned, I had been told by a few of the homeless people that a woman and man were traveling out here.

"Was it Peggy Sue?" he gasped.

"I couldn't tell from their descriptions."

"Show them the pictures? That's why I gave em to you!"

"Yea, sure did! Nobody remembers seeing a cheer leader with pom-poms or a Debutante' or...Alright wise ass, I get the idea." Clyde drawled, "Keep on top of it. Let me know how things are coming along."

"Might have to have you wire me more money." I pleaded; the phone was silent for a few moments. I could tell he was holding his hand over the receiver. He was talking to somebody on the other end. He was chuckling when he came back on the line.

"Che, I think we can spot you a little cash, how much do you need?" Clyde laughed.

"Just a couple hundred."

"What about the rest of the months' pay you've got coming!"

"Hang on to it, I'm going to need money when I finish this job. My Washington DC palace should need a lot of work after Muskrat Pete is finished with it." I answered coldly.

"When you're finished, I might just have you to give my little Suzy O a few lessons, about saving money." he said as he hung up the phone. I could still hear him chuckling.

Now it dawned on me, why he was laughing. In the month I had been working for him, I had only spent four hundred dollars, out of the forty-five hundred he owed me. If I was still living in the city, I would have already been forced to spend the money on expenses. It occurred to me, that if this job took a couple of months, it would be the first time in years I was out of debt. I would even have a few dollars set aside for an emergency.

I was not really worried about Muskrat Pete Donovan, except 1 knew he had a habit of picking up stray people, then inviting them home. His habits were gentle, but some of the people he came in contact with, were anything but sanitary.

Once, when we were camping in Georgia together, Pete picked up some old tramp who desperately needed a meal. Muskrat Pete's only request; was that the man wash, before coming to break bread The tramp was so filthy, he left a ring around the stream he bathed in. Having failed the initial scrutiny of Pere's inspection, he was ordered to bathe again, this time removing all his clothes. When it came time to remove his socks, the man was unable f3 pull them off. He had been wearing them for so long, they had grown into his feet. We had to cut them off with a pair of scissors. I refuse to even describe the odors that accompanied this event.

Another time, years ago, Pete had secured the use of a cabin, by doing odd jobs for the elderly widow who owned it. True to his kindly ways, he invited other homeless waifs to join him, so they might be out of the weather for a few hours. As the storm raged for the next three days, I watched the quaint little cabin floors being splattered by tobacco juice. The final straw came when I caught one of the bums, starting to relieve himself in the corner of the room. All three of them took flight when I gave them the choice: deal with the storm, or deal with me. When I produced a broom stick handle, they chose the storm.

There was no reason to expect Pete would have changed his ways in all these years. He was too much of a good Christian.

Since I was thinking about it, I decided to phone home just to check. I dumped a handful of quarters into the pay phone, waiting for the operator to connect the call. A voice came on the other end.

"Hello, you are in contact with M P Donovan, dealer in fine stoneware antiquities. We are unable to come to the phone at this time.

At the beep; please leave your name, number and a description of the piece of sculpture you are interested in braining. We will return your call. Thank You."

I did not leave a message. I was too steamed for that. I began to question why; good Christians, always made such good con artists. I told myself it could be worse; he could be running some evangelist scam out of my place. Muskrat Pete's work was in a class by itself, I reminded myself. The chances, of him implicating me in fraud, was so insignificant that they did not exist. I wondered; what was happening to my phone messages.

I drove back up the shack where I had left Skeeter sleeping.

When I got there, he was awake, talking with French.

They seemed to be getting along quite well. Too well in fact. I hoped I had not barged in to a romantic interlude. Skeeter was still in his masculine gender. I put any thought of he and Frenchy, disappearing into the bushes, out of my mind.

"Did you see the lights last night, Mon Ami?" asked Frenchy.

"There weren't any lights!" I answered.

"Que ces se, you did not see them! I thought they were coming for me last night!" he argued.

"There were no lights!" I repeated. " We were right here and there were no lights."

I pulled out the crude map I had drawn up, asking Frenchy to show me where he was, when he saw, whatever it was he had been looking at. He informed me the map was all wrong. The shack was at an angle, not in line, with the Hobo camps. It was located on one side of a swale in the rolling countryside. The nearest camp was on the other side of the swale. His finger plunked down at the position he thought to be correct. Another finger plotted the correct location of the camp.

"They will not be back until the next full moon." He advised,

"It is a shame you missed them last night."

"What does the full moon have to do with this?"

"Sac re blu, how should I know? I have only been trying to contact them for a short time." he shook his head, "When you find the woman and her partner, maybe they will be able to tell you."

"Yeah, if I ever catch up with them!"

He looked at the car and back at me. "Maybe there is a way we can help each other."

CHAPTER TWELVE

We waited until noon, for Western Union to release my money.

During this time, we got to know each other. Jacque St Ive better known as Frenchy, had been an investment banker in New York.

Before he turned his back on his career, he had managed to become a citizen. He had also slipped a few dollars into the bank for a rainy day. He must have burned out on Wall Street, because he refused to talk about that, except to say he preferred the quiet of the open countryside.

Frenchy had a post office box in Pecos, Texas. His bank sent monthly dividend checks to the post office. When he was nor watching the night sky, he made a monthly excursion to collect his mail and cash his checks. He stuck up a bargain; if we would give him a ride to Pecos, he would pay for the fuel.

I agreed for two reasons, first; Pecos was on Interstate 20, a few miles south of Pecos was Interstate 10, which Leads all the way to California. Second; To sweeten the deal, Frenchy offered to tell us whatever he knew; about the strangers. How else would I learn anything about the man and woman, who were trying to gain the trust of the hobos.

This way, I could do right, by my hitch-hiker. I never in- Do tended to adopt the man so Interstate 20 was a satisfactory place to put him out of the car. Skeeter had ceased to disturb me, but I still planned to point him in the right direction, then set him loose. He had started to grow on me, the way people do whenever someone is placed in a position of close contact over long periods of time. The truth was, I had grown fond of the big kid in a fraternal way. He learned things plenty quick. He had also gone out of his way, to maintain the mannerisms of his male ego. After his swift action at the gas station, I had started trusting his instincts and listening to his opinions, Skeeter made blunders like everybody else. Because I was hypercritical, he probably made fewer than most people, but they just seemed like more. The only real mistake he made, while we were in the camps, was to urinate in a burn barrel where they were trying to collect ashes. I had to say something to him about it, before the others caught him.

"How would you like it if someone were to pee in your soap?" I asked him.

"Soap? I don't see anything but ashes!".

It took a while but I was finally able to explain to him how to make soap from the burn barrel. The men would burn in one barrel until it was full of ashes, this might take a few months. They would pour water over the hot ashes to leach out the Soda Lime residue. The soda-lime water would be poured off into a smaller half barrel, containing hot liquified animal fat. A chemical reaction between the oils and soda-lime would render a solid block of soap upon cooling.

It might contain animal hair and insects but the stuff would clean just about anything. They would cut it up into smaller bars at their leisure. It was another item used to barter at places like the trading post. The card on the table in the trading post would read:

Genuine Frontier Castile Soap $2 each.

Frenchy was no fool. As soon as he came out of the bank he started acting strangely. He was friendly and our going on the way to the post office. He was friendly before he went into the bank. When he came out of the bank, he started acting suspicious. I knew the look well. While standing in line to cash the check, he had decided he did not know us properly. I told him; we had filled our side of the bargain; it was time for him to reciprocate. I had mentioned it so casually that the merchant inside him took control, he became congenial again.

He started yammering about the two strange travelers he had mentioned earlier. The woman was a quiet, cute lite thing with big emerald green eyes. She seemed to be searching for someone.

She let the man do all the talking. The male was a self-serving sort of fellow, similar to the Wall Street types, Frenchy used to deal with. "They were an oddly matched pair." Frenchy said.

"How did they travel?" I asked.

"Same as you, they parked their car and walked into the camp! They didn't pretend to be homeless though."

"What did they use as an excuse to be hanging around?"

"I already told you. they were looking for UFO's!"

Skeeter came awake just then, his head popped up in my rear-view mirror, "UFO's! Whose looking for UFO's?"

I had forgotten to tell the boy about the extraterrestrials.

It was partly because I wanted to encourage him to continue to California. Partly because I just plain overlooked the subject.

The way it was introduced into the conversation, was to my ad-vantage. He would never know; I had lied to him, about being on an environmental study. By the look in his eyes, I knew he was fully attuning to the UFO's. Just when I was so close, to putting him on the road again, damn!

"Skeeter, isn't your grandmother going to get worried about you?" I asked, in a desperate attempt to dampen his curiosity.

"Oh now, I called her collect from that gas station, while you went back after the car." he answered with childlike enthusiasm.

"What about the UFO's?"

They're just a bunch of lights in the sky." I said in a monotone, playing down the importance of the encounter.

"I've been watching them for the last six months. "Frenchy interrupted. "They're just as regular as clockwork."

"What do you mean?" asked Skeeter.

"Twenty-one days from the time I saw the last one, they always return. It's always during a full moon, ALWAYS!"

Skeeter was now absorbed in the discussion. It was all I could do to hold up my end of the conversation. The two of them rambled on, about little green men and all chat nonsense.

'Getting back to the original subject..." I interrupted, *When was it that the two strangers came into camp?"

"Just before I spotted the UFO the first time." said Frenchy, after a moment of contemplation.

"Did you say, before?"

"That's right, I never noticed a thing, until I saw that stranger swinging a flashlight at some lights in the sky. I asked him what he was doing, that's when he showed me the UFO."

A dull pain formed itself in my brain. My frontal cerebral cortex was active. There was an unbalanced equation bouncing between brain hemispheres. The logical side of my mind, was asking for information from the creative side. Centered, just behind my forehead, was a crashing spasm of chemical reaction and agony:

Lights, Guadalupe-hobos-watching lawn mowers in the sage-brush-didn't; Lights, Lawn mowers-watching-Hobo-lights; Lights, dim painful_-lights.

The pain was unbearable. I shook my head fighting off the sensation which clouded my vision. My mind came back from the delusion. The pain cased, grew less potent, then disappeared.

"Is he the same stranger that gave away all those flashlights to the hobos? I asked.

"Yeah! Well not for a while. He came back several times before he decided to hand out flashlights."

Frenchy went on to explain thar the stranger was really jumpy when he started passing the flashlights.

"He asked a lot of questions, sort of got to know the men first."

"Did he know they traded the flashlights for tobacco?"

"Yeah, he was really jumpy about that too." said Frenchy. "But, what could he do, the flashlights were gone."

Frenchy and Skeeter soon found they had another thing in common. The last trip into Pecos, Frenchy had lost his wallet.

Lucky for him, he kept his passbook for the bank in his shoe. They commiserated about the losses. They had both last their wallets to the same type of characters. I pretended not to listen to their stories, just in case Jacque St Ive, proved to be a little light in the loafers.

From the sound of it, whoever cook the wallets was interested more in the identification than any money. A thief does not take more than a split second, to determine if a wallet contains any money The only difference between the two stories, was that Skeeter did loose cash and a bus ticket.

Frenchy, cook his time explaining to Skeeter, places a traveler should conceal valuables while on the highroad.

"Where you got yours hidden?" I joked when he finished.

Frenchy did not appreciate my wisecrack. He paid for a rank of fuel, then bought us a meal, explaining he wished to "spend some time in town. It would be another three weeks before the UFO's returned. He was going to catch up on some news, maybe purchase some paperback books to take back to camp with him. I grumbled about the drive being worth more than one tank of fuel.

He pitched in a few extra dollars.

"Was the information worth anything?" he asked.

"Too soon to tell." I answered.

I normally like to work alone. However, because of Frenchy's big mouth, it looked like I would be stuck with Skeeter. We rolled down the highway listening to the country music station.

I wondered; if people had enough misery in their personal lives. The popularity of country music, would seem to indicate, they did not. Most of the singers play tangy doodle tunes about; cheating lovers, or dead lovers, or dead cheating lovers. They play tunes about pickup trucks, mothers, trains, and jail cells. I like country music, but I have to be objective.

Except for Willie Nelson, the themes never varied. I switched channels hoping for his happy-go-lucky serenade. Maybe Willie is the troubadour, with whom all chose ocher singers' wives have affairs.

How else would he be happy all the time?

Skeeter reached up and twisted the radio tuner. He was looking for some head banging heavy metal music. I slapped his hand away, tuning back to Willie. He reached over and turned the radio off. Then he pulled the knob loose and stuck it in his pocket.

Normally I would have taken offence. Such rude behavior deserves a pop in the mouth, at the very minimum a strong verbal reproach.

Instead, I decided a more fitting punishment.

He would have to listen to one of my hobo stories, which I would fill with mundane detail. I would boorishly force him to return the radio knob. "Did I ever tell you about the time I almost met Tanya Tucker?" I began to prattle.

"It was a true story. Years ago, an acquaintance had driven up to Birmingham Alabama with me in tow. He said he had a job working behind the stage and needed someone to help him. It meant a few dollars in my pocket, so I went along. We got there a day in advance, to inspect the arrangements. When I discovered some of the carpenters had not shown up, I pitched in to help construct the stage.

We got down to a few hours before the electrical equipment was to be brought out, and we still needed a roof. I looked around to see what lumber was available. There was not too much. There was a just a few four-by-four uprights; someone by eights, fourteen feet long; some furring strips; and a roll of plastic. I made a list of the lumber, then drew up a crude design that I thought would work. I showed it to the stage manager. He said to go ahead and build the thing."

"Is this story going to take long? I have to go to the bathroom. said Skeeter, looking a tad anxious.

"GOOD!" I thought to myself silently, bringing up even more details to include.

"We built the outside frame for a canopy, just before the crowds started to arrive. People were spreading out blankets and passing around beer. I laid the furring strips across the flat structure. The roof was supposed to have an angle but the other carpenters failed to follow my exact design. The roof was flat.

When it came time to cover it with plastic, we found chat we would have to hurl the roll from one end to the other, in one shot.

We only had one ladder. It was an aluminum extension ladder.

We could not lean it anywhere, in the center of the roof. We could only lean the ladder against the sides."

"What about Tanya Tucker?" he asked in an effort to hurry the story along.

"Hold on... I'm coming to that." I lied.

"I hurled the black plastic, one toss, clearing the other side of the roof with inches to spare. Then we had to staple gun all the sides. This made it as right as a drum. The roof was as strong as a waterbed frame. The whole time the crowd was watching. They roared with delight, when they saw the plastic, clear the other side. This skinny little blonde came out of one of the trailers to see what was going on."

"And it was Tanya Tucker... Now pull over." he begged.

"You know, I just might have been Tanya. I never thought about it before, but I believe you're right." I said hitting the occasional pot hole, still continuing down the highway.

"Anyway. "

"The plastic began to stretch in the Alabama heat. It remained sturdy and kept the musicians protected from the fierce sunshine so we left it up. Hank Williams Jr played a few sets. I was right up front when Willie Nelson played. I shouted for him to play: Make Room for A Better Man, but he never did. I did not even know who she was at the time, because she was so young, but just across the roped off area was this blue eyed blond. She looked into my eyes, and I looked into her eyes, there was chemistry in the air. Love at first sight."

"It was Tanya!" he whispered through clenched teeth. "Correct!"

I agreed.

"Will you pull over now?" he pleaded.

"Wait for the end of the story.

"Nobody expected it to rain. The far roof filled up with cool clear water. Water weighs a lot, almost eight pounds per gallon.

This water did not undermine the strength of my design until the next day when the sun heated it up and it began to sag.

The next evening it rained again and the water came bursting through, drenching everything and everyone.

Alright that's it. pull over!" He screamed, holding his crotch with one hand. fumbling to replace the radio knob with the other.

Beads of sweat were dropping from his face "Maybe this'll teach you not to steal the radio knob." I grinned.

I pulled over, ever so gently.

The only time I have seen someone get out of a car faster, is on TV shows, when the car explodes. The color returned to his face, as he evacuated his bladder. He sucked up a few deep breaths of air to regain his equilibrium. Skeeter was one happy camper when he returned to the car. I was laughing so hard I did not notice him stick the radio knob back in his pocket.

"You Bastard...." He fumed, "You want Country Music, I 'll give you country music.", Skeeter started to sing:

"I spent most of this evening, trying to believe in
what I would say, when you walked through that door.
Now that you're here,
all I can do, is stare at the floor
So, take me to the Greyhound and put me on a west bound,
And I won't be back, round here anymore.
Spent most of my life believing, I needed a reason for what I would do, when you loved me no more.
DA da da da da,
You rotten crotch whore.
So, rake me to the Greyhound and put me on a west bound,
And I won't be back, round here any more
You're lying and cheating, have given me reason, why I won't be around, for you anymore.
Frankly, I'm tired of sleeping, with you, cause you snore.

So, take me to the Greyhound and put me on a west bound, And I won't be back, round here anymore.

When Skeeter had finished composing his country music ballad, he fell silent. I must admit, I was somewhat impressed. He even used the nasal action, which made Willie famous. The lyrics were atrocious, but the melody was soothing. He sang really slow, enjoying himself while trying to be entertaining. Change the lyrics a little and all Skeeter needed was the right agent. He could go right up the charts. I wondered; what Nashville would do, with a big homosexual crooner like Skeeter.

It dawned on me that he was not acting like a fairy any longer.

He had for the better part of the last week acted straight. Must be one of those cultural chameleons, I thought. Nashville would never know the difference. It was something to think about.

"So are you going to finish the story" asked Skeeter.

"Well OK. I was a good-looking young buck in those days. I didn't have this paunch. Not that it's chat bad, nothing a few sit-ups wouldn't fix.

" I started to say. "

"A few million sit-ups." corrected Skeeter.

"Hey, you want to tell the story?"

"Sorry." he grinned.

"I was just across the yellow rope, no more than a few feet away from Tanya, waiting on my acquaintance to get me back stage. We were totally unaware there was anything wrong with the stage, until my friend grabbed me. He whisked me away into the night. They were looking for someone to blame for the wet conditions. My name was on the top of their list. The worst part was; the promoter of the event was zapped on the bottom lip, which is wearing microphones, when he tried to address the crowd. We got in my friend's car and did not stop until we got to Mississippi.

"That is a stupid story!"

"Thank you very much!" I said, as I noticed the missing radio knob.

CHAPTER THIRTEEN

I looked in my rear-view mirror, just as I passed the border into New Mexico, A police car was following me with its lights flashing. My speed was good, I was not drinking. There was no reason to try to outrun the state trooper, I pulled over. The officer approached the car cautiously. His service revolver was drawn and he ordered me out of the car with my hands raised in the air. I was in a pair of handcuffs, before I could bat an eye. He asked who the passenger was.

"Just a hitch-hiker, I picked up a while back." I answered.

He ordered me to calm myself, and my passenger, who was likewise now in handcuffs. Being a curious individual, I asked the officer what the charges were. As we were tucked into the back of the police car, he mentioned something about; the armed robbery of a gas station. Before he took us in, I made sure he collected my own service revolver, from under the seat of my car. He was pretty shaken up about the revolver, until I showed him the permit in my glove box.

"Listen, I can explain. This whole thing is a misunderstanding.

" I said hoping to worm my way out of chis jamb.

"Work it out with the magistrate court." he ordered as he slammed the door.

Skeeter and I found ourselves in the local poky, staring at a bunch of Mexicans. They all tried to act tough. They looked about as threatening, as a heard of Easter bunnies. Lunch came and went.

The afternoon dragged on, I demanded to see a lawyer. Legal counsel was only for prisoners, who had actually been charged with a crime.

We were still being held on suspicion. I demanded to make a phone call. Clyde was not amused when he answered the phone.

His hands were tied unless we were extradited to Texas.

We could be held in jail, up to twenty-four hours, without being charged with a crime. If I was correct, that little pimple faced station attendant, was going to wait until the last minute to show up. When he did show up, the little wimp would refuse to press charges. He would wait out in front of the jail, until after our release, to tell us how fortunate we were, that he was so generous.

What the doofus did not suspect was, he had given me twenty-four hours to plot my revenge. I thought about a plan involving his stack of pornography, and any local minister.

I had already spent the better part of an hour scheming, when a deputy showed up at the cell door. The deputy called out a name. One of the Mexican prisoners rose, smiling like a cocker spaniel in heat. The deputy repeated the name, the prisoner nodded his head. The captive was released. Skeeter came over and interrupted my day dream.

"Guess what that guy's name was?" asked Skeeter.

"I don't know what?"

"Jacque St Ive, that's what!"

"So, what!" I grunted.

"No stupid, Jacque St Ive. You know as in Frenchy's real name!

That guy must have Frenchy's identification!" Skeeter gasped.

"Guard, Guard!" we both shouted. A dumpy looking cell matron shuffled slowly back to our cell.

What happened to the guy who just left here?"

"He was released."

"There has been a mistake! He is not the man he claims to be. You've got to get him back."

She waddled out the door. A few moments later the original deputy returned. The deputy reveals to us, they had only held the Mexican, to check his immigration and nationalization status. According to their records the man was clean. We patiently told the deputy; we knew the real Jacque Sr Ive. That man was nor him.

The deputy rushed out of the lock up, in the direction of the front office. Returning a few minutes later, the deputy informed us, he had just missed catching up with the Mexican fellow. We were taken to an interrogation room.

"How can we get in touch with the real Jacque St Ive?" asked the deputy.

"That's going to be a bit of a problem." Skeeter cold him.

"Yeah, right now he's in Pecos. I can tell you which bank he does business with." I added.

The conference went nowhere from there. The New Mexico police, were not to please to find, that Frenchy lived in a hobo camp, on the Texas side of the stare border. They were not pleased he had never reported his wallet missing. We found ourselves back in the tank, having served no purpose coward salving any real crime.

While it may have been a waste of time for our host, it was an enlightening experience for me. The only thing chat separates a United States citizen from an illegal alien, is a handful of plastic identification. The countess wanted to know; what was happening to the Hobos. I felt confident, I was closer to solving that riddle.

Take a man who has no record of residence, but like every other American has a Social Security Number. Substitute an illegal alien, and what have you got? Forget the census figures, there could be an illegal alien for every homeless person in the country.

What would happen, when there was one to many of someone. I shuttered to think about it. We had to go back after Frenchy. His life could depend on it.

Twenty-three- and one-half hours, after we were taken into custody we were released. The pimple faced kid was waiting out front, just where I knew he would be. We ignored him, as he dashed into his car and stand away. Our own auto was impounded at the towing company. It cost one hundred dollars for the cow. plus, seven dollars a day to be stored. The fee came out of my own pocket. Demanding a receipt, from the privateer behind the counter, we wandered out to scrutinize the tow truck damage.

As I waited to turn at a light, the pimple faced kid pulled up from the other direction. His face was turned the other way as his arm signaled for a left band turn. His wrist watch became an irresistible target. Without thinking my hand flashed out. My finger slipped under his watch band. When my hand returned, it was holding his watch. He glanced over in my direction. He did not even notice the timepiece was missing. We sat there for an eternity glaring at each other, then he went his way and I went mine. For one hundred and seven dollars, it was a nice timepiece.

I checked the back; it was made in the USA.

We drove for an hour during which time Skeeter practiced his country music. I finally told him to put a sock in it. We were back in Pecos, driving up and down the main drag. looking for Frenchy.

Half a dozen times we thought we saw him but it always turned out to be some teenager. We were about to give up when we saw a short wiry figure come slipping out of a topless bar with a girl on his arm. He was grinning from ear to ear. We decided to sit back and observe, so as not to disturb the lonely old man. They went into a fast-food place. Skeeter was starving so we followed. Sitting in a corner booth, we overheard everything they were saying to each other. It was the same old banter repeated a thousand times a day, in a thousand different cities.

Beautiful topless dancer, talking about her career. Lonely old man who wishes he could take her away from all this. He wants to make an honest woman out of her, whatever thar means.

Personally, I do not know, how much more honest a woman can get, than to dance naked. By exposing herself to God and everyone else who cares to watch, she is saying: this is the real me take it or leave it.

She got up to go to the bathroom. I made my move.

"Frenchy, we have to talk."

"Not now, I'm a little busy!" he fidgeted in his seat.

"Yeah, I can see that! I've got my car parked outside. As soon as you can get free, come out there and see me." I begged.

After a three hours nap, there was still no sign of Frenchy.

We had seen him leave the restaurant. He had gone back into the topless saloon, but we thought he was coming right out. I turned to Skeeter telling him to wait.

'I'd better go get him." said Skeeter. I thought about that for a moment, "We'll both go!".

Frenchy was sitting at a table surrounded by six dancers. I slipped into the middle of them, while Skeeter took a seat near the door. I could see why Frenchy was having such a hard time leaving. A dozen heavenly orbs adjure hovered at face level. The girls were shamelessly woman-handling Frenchy and myself. It took total concentration on my part, to remember what I was doing there. "Could I please talk with Frenchy privately?" I asked. "Ignore him ladies... "He responded. Turning to me he added with a wink, "Were the only men going to be in here until dark."

At five o'clock the regulars started to wandered in from work.

By eight o'clock the girls were all busy with other clients. I dragged Frenchy out to the car, for a chat. He came kicking and screaming.

Spring over my shoulder, I noticed Skeeter was still inside. What the hell, it would probably straighten the boy out, no pun intended.

I only wished; I had warned him, not to buy the girls any watered-down drinks. The girls charged the customer five dollars apiece for a glass of soda. Nor chat I would want to see any woman drink forty cocktails a night. I am not even sure that is possible.

Every drink they sold, they received a token, to be redeemed at the end of the night. For each exchanged token they were paid between one to three dollars. I suddenly realized; I was worried about nothing. Skeeter, did not have any money.

"I thought you were going to buy a few books and return to the camp?" I asked Frenchy.

"Who are you, my mother?" Frenchy answered. 'If you must know, I already bought the books."

He produced a small satchel containing a few second-hand volumes. He pulled out a book, waving it in my face. It looked like an old textbook on Astronomy.

"Pretty heady stuff for a hobo. "I announced.

"You think so.. just look at this!". Frenchy flipped the pages open to a passage he had marked. The jest of the passage was concerned with the rotation of the Earth. The author was describing the power needed to enter and escape the gravitational force of the planet. An object traveling west, would be required to travel six tenths of a mile-per-second faster, than a object traveling east, to cover the same distance in the same amount of time.

"Yeah, I think that makes sense." I said nodding my head.

"Well then look at this!" declared Frenchy.

The author offered the proposal; that an object to be launched into orbit, should travel in a North-easterly direction. This would enable the object to take advantage of the rotational dynamics of the Earth. The object traveling west, would have to achieve five point three miles-per-second, to escape into orbit. Another object traveling cast, at only four point seven miles-per-second, would be just as effective.

"There must be some reason you are showing me this." I said to Frenchy. He looked at me with those big saggy eyes and shook his head. He made me feel like I should be wearing a dunce cap.

"Let me see that map, you showed me at the shack."

While I groped around looking for the map, he produced a flimsy little book: The Prospectors Guide to The Southwest. The book contained hand drawn maps, including old railroad lines.

We compared the two maps. "Ya see char: The lights travel in a westerly direction then turn north." said French.

"OK, so what does that mean? "

"It means they are landing. Those UFOs are landing!" He grinned; his face scrunched up into a whiskered dolls head.

"They were going pretty slow when I saw them.

"That's right, I thought about that and figure they must be landing someplace close by." Frenchy agreed.

"Wait hold it let's just back up a minute. At five miles a sec-and there is nothing close by. That's ... THREE THOUSAND MILES A MINUTE." I gasped. I did not believe it myself.

"Relax, they were not doing anywhere near that speed.

That's how I know they were landing." He grinned, " They were doing about cherry miles an hour if my calculations are correct."

"What calculations?"

He took out a square piece of wood. It had a notch in one end that he explained was for the bridge of his nose. He said he lined the opposite cop corner of the board up on the top of the Guadalupe Mountain. He marked the board once when he first saw the object, then he wrote down the time. He wrote the time again when it passed over head. He said he could determine the distance the object traveled, based on the height of the mountain. He knew the time it took for the object to travel the given distance. He said the object was traveling thirty miles an hour. I was not going to argue with him.

I switched the subject. I told him about the Mexican in the lockup. He was interested, but not to the point he was willing to ignore the other subject. I listened to him rambling for thirty minutes. I was still wondering what happened to Skeeter.

Leaving Frenchy to watch the car, I went back in the topless saloon. Up on stage, surrounded by buxom dancers, Skeeter was singing his country song. I was truly shocked. I had created a monster. The girls were weaving in and around the boy, making it the kind of show that would be a hit in Las Vegas. The crowd cheered when he left the stage. I motioned for him to follow me. It was all we could do to drag himself away from his fans.

"OK mister big shot, get in the car." I ordered. He followed me like a puppy. I stomped on the accelerator, Pecos disappeared in our rear-view mirror. Later I decided; I should have left him there.

Early the following morning we were back to the radix post.

Frenchy was still discussing his theories concerning the UFO's. I was ignoring him by now, concentrating on the types of aircraft who flew less than thirty miles an hour. Nothing came to mind.

Just to stay airborne a plane would have to exceed seventy miles an hour. The whole thing did not make sense.

I was finally able to convince the cantankerous old man to report his wallet missing. He did not seem to mind the Mexicans were using it. As a final plea, I supported my argument by saying; his own citizenship was on the line. This brought him around. As a matter of fact, he then agreed to help us question the other hobos.

I wanted to see if any of them had a similar experience.

My inquiries landed a mother-load of information. Hobos do not like to discuss their real names. They have turned their back on organized society. They all use nick names, and yet still choose to remember a man's face instead of his name. This way if a police officer asks; "Have You seen so-and-so?", they can honestly say:

No.

The rich harvest of information came, not from learning everyone's real name, but from something minor. The hobos had already given all this same information to someone else. The woman who had green eyes. She had entered the information into one of those dinky little computers the size of a checker board. There was just something about the girl that made the hobos trust her. I did not like the sound of the whole deal. Something was fishy. The couple had discussed the reason for their inquiry with each of the hobos. They had told the homeless men; it was because of the UFO's. The couple, wanted to be able to state caragorically, who had seen the lights and who had not. It was a slick bit of conniving.

Believe me, I should know.

There might be a good reason to call Clyde again. I made a point of pulling Skeeter and Frenchy over to one side.

"Are you two in or out? I need to know right now.

"What's this all about?" asked Skeeter.

"There are a few things thar add up wrong and I need to know who I can count on."

"I'm in!" said Skeeter without hesitation.

"In or out of what? Mon Ami!" asked Frenchy.

"We're going to be doing some serious traveling for the next twenty days. I want to pinpoint where those lights are first noticed and where they disappear. If some kind of craft is landing out here, I want to know what it is, and where it came from "How are you going to do that!" asked the whiskered old man.

"Follow the path the strangers left. You said yourself, you never noticed the lights until the stranger mentioned them."

"You can count me in, if I can stay right here. I am too old to run around in the desert. Besides, those strangers will be back here before the next sighting."

"OK that's fine. You stay here, Skeeter and I will do all the leg work."

CHAPTER FOURTEEN

Using the same routine from before we visited hobo camps to the south. A few drinks to loosen tongues, a few hands of poker just to keep things friendly, we moved from camp to camp. Each camp we came to told us they had been visited by the strangers. This went on for a week. We turned our attention to the north. I once worked for an old lineman who hated to climb telephone poles.

He taught me a trick that saves a lot of time. What he would do is to split the difference every time he climbed a pole. If he climbed one pole that was good, he would run on down the lines looking for an easy pole to climb that he thought was bad. He would count the poles as he drove back toward the good end of the lines. Half way back he would climb a pole. If it was bad he kept on going. If it was good, he would turn around and head on back splitting the difference again. He never had to climb more than five poles to fix the problem. I decide to use his method, to locate the end of the line on this UFO business.

We already knew the town of Artesia, New Mexico, was in line with the direction the mysterious lights had traveled. We shot past the town, landing in the middle of a hobo jungle a few miles north. The tramps here had not seen any lights. They had never been visited by strangers besides us. There were only a handful of them in camp. I could tell right away; they all had seen better days. If they had met anyone, who could do them any kindness, they would certainly remember and appreciate it. I wished them a brotherly Via Con Dios, then slipped them a bottle of liquor. We had one end of the mystery lights located.

It did not take long to find where the strangers would turn up next. After five stops, I knew where they had been, and where they had not. That night we camped by ourselves, in the middle of nowhere. All those stars shone brightly in the moonless night. For a moment a hundred streaks lighted the sky where some meteorite entered the atmosphere, brake apart and caught fire.

I almost had to gag Skeeter, to ger him to quit singing that stupid song of his. He had, greatly improved the lyrics over the last few days. At the moment he was trying to find which key he should sing it in. He tied a booming bass, then a baritone, next a tenor, it was here I complained about the noise. He had not spooked me in days with his little falsetto feminine voice. I was not going to give him a chance to use it, while we were sleeping out in the bush.

He seemed to have something on his mind. I listened as he started to tell me about himself. I cautioned him, that I may not be the best person to discuss some things with. He said chat it was just this type of honesty, which prompted him to want to talk. I could tell where the conversation was headed, and started to petrify. There are certain subjects which I prefer to ignore. Again, I cautioned him to not disturb any of my prejudices. Then I re-canted, if he wanted to continue on a purely psychological level, I would try to accommodate him.

"You know I am attracted to you." Skeeter said.

"Skeeter! You could try beating around the bush a little bit!" I said stiffening in my bed roll.

"I don't mean like a lover; I mean like a brother or something." he quickly corrected. "You didn't think I meant

"Well, I damn sure hope not!" I interrupted.

It's just that it has been a long time since I had a male friend who was not... he started again.

"A homosexual!" again I interrupted. I was not fully ready to enter into the type of discussion, which had presented itself.

"Is it so hard for you to say; Gay?"

"Is it so hard for you to call a spade a spade. You don't mean frivolously happy; you mean attracted to your own sex. I don't know where you people get off perverting the English language." I became livid, out of nothing but self-righteousness.

"What were you doing out here in the first place? People like you belong in big cities, where you can be surrounded by your own kind. Why aren't you in New York, or San Francisco."

"You jackass. "

"He started to say,". I was trying to tell you "How I thought about you."

"Well make it short. Just remember what a walk it'll be to California, if I leave your butt out here." I snorted.

"You have changed my life. You have made me see a whole new world." he stammered.

I cocked my head around to see his face. He was laid back with his hands folded behind his head, staring up at the star filled night.

He looked like some overgrown cub scout on his first camping trip. I could not help feeling a tiny bit guilty for chastising him.

The campfire crackled away; I tossed another piece of wood onto its glowing embers. I was willing to forget the conversation in progress and go to sleep.

"Do you know when I knew I was gay?" he asked chronically,

"My father came home drunk one night and threw me out of the house. I didn't have anywhere to go, until this friendly man asked me if I needed a place to stay."

"And you went with him."

"Yes." Skeeter answered.

"How old were you at the time?"

"Thirteen."

I thought about that one for a minute, trying to remember something from a psych class I had taken. That was the age when some boys explore various sexual tendencies. "You know what Skeeter if that was all there was to turning into a homosexual everyone would be one!" I said.

"What are you trying to say?"

"I don't think you are gay." I reasoned, "How did you feel when you were surrounded by those topless dancers?"

"I felt like a bisexual!" he said staring up at the stars. I glanced in his direction again. He had a big grin on his face, like he was having fun with me. I shook my head. He was a lost cause. I rolled over trying to ignore the entire event. I wondered; how much a bus ticker would cost me.

A freak howling wind came up around four o'clock in the morning. The temperature went from a comfortable fifty-five degrees to somewhere in the neighborhood of zero. The wind chill factor had my teeth chattering, Skeeter was curled up in a fetal position beside the dying embers of the fire. I shook him awake, then scurried to the car. The wind made it impossible to breath without burring your face inside a jacket. This was the kind of weather thar could kill the unsuspecting traveler.

Even inside the car it felt like a refrigerator. I cranked over the engine and warmed the interior. At daybreak the wind calmed down. The temperature rose slowly as sunlight refracted through the crisp morning air. A blanket of frost covered everything. If we were not in the car, we could have been freeze dried, like beef jerky.

My teeth were still chattering as I checked the liquid in the radiator. It was thick but not frozen. Ice had formed in the windshield washer fluid. Nothing to worry about. The old squad car engine groaned as I turned over the ignition. We sat inside munching a breakfast of canned fish as the cab warmed itself. The thick ice covering the windows started to melt.

We started off the morning bouncing up and down dirt roads between hobo camps looking for tractor sheds and shacks. If some. thing was landing out here; they would need a place to hide the craft. Skeeter was bored and began singing again, until I warned him, I would leave him out here in the middle of nowhere.

This was the seventh year of a drought. Any buildings had inside them, exactly what I expected them to have, a big empty space. No one was going to maintain equipment unless they planned to use it. Only a few livestock sheds had less than a years' worth of dust inside.

The hear rose steadily throughout the day. By noon it was one hundred degrees in the shade. We chanced into a shallow pond formed in a low section of stone, on the bank of a trickling stream.

The water looked inviting, when you consider we had been in the same clothes for a week. Skeeter stripped down and plunged in. I waded in clothes and all, knowing they would soon dry in chis arid climate.

"Aren't you going to take your clothes off?" asked Skeeter.

You'd like that wouldn't you." I grinned.

"Hey man, I told you I'm not attracted to you in that way." answered Skeeter.

"'Let's just say I have my own reasons for staying dressed."

"Suit yourself." he chided.

By one o'clock the temperature was at least a hundred and ten. I was drip drying in the shade of a Yucca bush. Skeeter was sunning on a rock, nude as the day he was born. Every so often he would dip back into the water to cool off. I noticed he was starting to turn red and told him to get dressed before he blistered. For one part of his anatomy, the warning came a little too late. I heard him make a grunting sound as he slipped into his jeans.

I knew there should be some Aloe Vera cacti, someplace close by. I started scrounging around in the underbrush looking for it.

What would this tender foot do without me. I could hear Skeeter yelling insults in my direction as I located a clump of the soothing succulent plant.

"You son of a bitch! You knew this would happen." he screamed as I tossed him the Aloe plant.

"Hey, everybody knows these streams are saturated with lime.

It does a real good job cleaning clothes."

"Cleaning clothes my ass. It feels like my penis is going to melt off." he said, sending glances in my direction, that he hoped would kill.

"Just trot behind chose bushes over there, and rub some of that plant juice on it. It'll take the tang out of the sunburn." I instructed.

"If you're lying to me, you are a dead man. " Warned Skeeter.

"Well suit yourself" I mocked, returning to the shade of the Yucca bush. I noticed my clothes were already dry. Must have been caused by the zero humidity. I slipped back into the water to cool off again. A greatly relieved Skeeter came hobbling back over to the water's edge. I warned him not to come back in, unless he wanted to reapply the Aloe juice.

"Hey what do you make of this?" he asked, holding up a sooty black sphere with a wick on top.

"They used to use those as lanterns to mark bad sections of road. It's probably been out here thirty years." I said completely uninterested in his find.

"What do you want me to do with it?"

"Just an old piece of junk. Get rid of it."

He picked it up like a shot put and hurled it as far as he could.

Instead of clattering it made a dull thud against the ground. "Thirty years and it's still full!" he commented.

"No way, that thing could not possibly be full out here in this heat." I argued pulling myself out of the water.

I went over and picked it up, sure enough it was still full. I poured a little of the liquid out onto a stone. It was crystal clear.

Someone had refilled that lantern in the last month. Whoever it was it was not some little green man.

Skeeter showed me exactly where he found the lantern. There is a common law chat states; whenever something happens once, it will and does happen again. If someone finds one kerosine lantern with fresh fuel in it, they will be able to locate another. The search called for a plan. The first object was found near a stream. The next one should also be found, near sore other easy to locate land-mark.

The lanterns would be easier to find from the roof of the squad car. I strapped a rope from the front to the rear of the car and put Skeeter the top. I cautioned him it would take a while to adjust to the ride. He was a big baby about it. We switched places, after the first dozen bumps. We found a second lantern, where he almost fell from the roof.

To the south lay the hobo camps which I knew had been visited by the strangers. We focused the search to the north. We found another lantern, approximately the same interval away from the second, as it had been found from the first. I predicted; they would be laid out in a straight line. We set the odometer to calculate when we would reach the next one. Every four tenths of a mile we found another lantern. Following the lanterns, we were led directly up to a sheet metal shed hidden in the bottom of a gully.

The shed was shaped like a big mail box. It was painted desert camouflage, with patches of brown, tan, and khaki. Soft sand stretched in both directions from the sides of the building. I had a premonition about going inside. I was not sure I even wanted to know what purpose the building served.

What if we went inside the building and found little green men? We back tracked a mile or two, to put the car out of danger of being discovered. It would be dusk in another hour, we decided to wait it out. Skeeter started singing again, for once I did not bother the kid.

He was proving to be quite a trooper. He had his faults, but he was starting to grow on me. I did wish he would use his head a little more often. He was ready to storm right into the building in broad daylight. It would not be the smartest thing to do, but I sort of had to admire his courage. Chances were; we would get down there and find just another empty building. It would not hurt my feelings if we did. Something told me this was not going to be the case.

We started our little two-mile stroll while evening was setting.

Skeeter brought his flashlight but I made him keep it turned off until we needed it. I wondered, if he had ever been to summer camp. He surely did not act like it. One and three-quarters mile later I started listening to the night sounds. Two hundred yards in front of us lay the shed. Light was shining from one end of the Quonset hut; the end chat was open. One hundred yards out, we squared down to view the scene through a pair of binoculars. A noise came from the building. It was the sound of a lawn mower.

There were no little green men. Men were working, loading something into four-wheel drive trucks. I followed their movements, but this did not tell me anything. We were going to have to get in closer. I thought about it, no way in hell; I decided. We would sit tight wait a while see what happens.

"Skeeter, wake me if anything happens!" I ordered.

About three hours later, it was starting to get cold. I turned over and found Skeeter curled up next to me, asleep. I was worried about the freak wind from the night before. If it returned tonight, we would be caught out in it, without shelter. I woke Skeeter. We raced down to the building to see what protection it would provide. It was locked up tighter than a bank vault. The back of the building had no opening of any kind. Both sides were curved up like someone had cut a drum in half and laid it on its side. If we were going to get inside, we would have to go in through the front.

The only window in front of the shed was installed about ten feet off the ground. Skeeter boosted me up on his shoulders, as I limbed hand over hand, clinging to the curved roof. Dangling from one hand, I focused the flashlight beam into the building.

Just as much light reflected back at me from the window, as entered the enclosed area. I hoped we were alone.

I could barely make out the shape of one of those large hang glider kites against the back wall. A dealer's banner hung from the ceiling, proudly announcing this was a ROTEC hang glider. My finger grip slipped and I came crashing earthward. The soft sand cushioned the fall. I picked myself up, dusted myself off, then asked Skeeter if he wanted to take a look. He did, so he climbed up on my shoulders and peeked into the building. I left him hanging there by one arm, as repayment for letting me fall. He dropped down unfettered, none the worst for my sneaky trick. We fell into a trot, running back to the car. The exercise warmed our bodies as we ran, "What do you think they use that building for? asked Skeeter.

"Probably just a bunch of hang glider enthusiasts!" I answered, playing down the importance of the find.

I was mulling the thought around in my mind. I remembered tiling I and it sound of a long an ek coming out of the shack. Lawn mowers and hang gliders; I wondered. An Ultralight hang glider? Maybe! It was certainly an aircraft that would stay airborne, at less than seventy miles an hour. This was going to require a little research.

CHAPTER FIFTEEN

I telephone CIyde from the Trading Post. While we were there, I noticed the owner had just obtained a new shipment of Aztec miniatures. He had been doing a fair job of selling the remarkable little statues. It seemed like every tourist who saw them, had to have one. He had done so well with them, in fact, chat he was now giving the hobos five dollars in trade for each one. As the price went up, the supply had also increased, a factor at the smooth salesman never questioned.

"Look hombre, if they're in New Mexico there is nothing I can do!" grumbled Clyde, "I've got to have a whole lot more to work with, before I start sticking my neck out in someone else's jurisdiction."

"Well, I'll warn you right now, if you sit around with your thumb up your butt too long, this whole thing is going to vanish into thin air." I pontificated.

"Just bring back Peggy Sue and well worry about the rest of this nonsense later, comprendae amiro."

"While we're on the subject of Peggy Sue, does she own a lap top computer?"

"Hold on a moment..." he ordered. Clyde must have held the receiver against his chest, because I could hear him repeat the question to someone else in the room.... ten-four, hobo. She's got one of those Nipponese jobs. It's supposed to be the size of a Sunday newspaper."

"Good, that just about confirms what I've learned about the kid who is our here asking the cramps questions.

"Fine grab her, hog rise her if you have to, then ger her silly prep-school ass home."

'It may not be thar simple. Everything seems to hinge around those UFO sightings." I interjected.

"For the last time there aren't no damn UFO's! " Clyde spat.

"No shit Sherlock, you must have been paying attention. The thing is; we can't let anyone else know, that we know, it is a hoax or we'll trip our hand."

"OK I follow what you're saying. What's your point!"

"Get out a note card, you and I are going to construct a little problem-solving diagram."

I instructed Clyde to draw a triangle on the card. Within the base line I told him to write the word hobo. On the right-hand side of the triangle, I told him to write Mexicans. On the left-hand side, I told him to write Peggy Sue. In the corner between Peggy Sue and hobo, he should write: UFO. In the corner between hobo and Mexican, he should write: identification papers.

"What about the top corner?" He asked.

"That's what we don't know. We solve that and we are home free!" I answered with a certain amount of conceit.

"Quit fooling around. JUST GRAB THE GIRL! " He groaned.

People like Clyde should live simple lives. He refused to under-stand; that if I just grabbed Peggy Sue there was no insurance, she would be out to the cycle permanently. Her escort had some kind of power over her, or she would not continue to travel with him. I wanted to know what it was. Maybe the Countess could help. I redialed the number.

She seemed tired and detached like she needed decompression. I started asking personal questions about her daughter. She squirmed at the nature of the derails that I thought would shed some light on her activities. Peggy Sue was a cop's kid. Was she rebellious? The countess did not seem to think so. Of course, the countess was not an individual, qualified, to make such general assumptions. She herself was what could be considered a- wild child.

According to the countess; Peggy Sue was simply normal. Did the girl drink, sleep around, use drugs?

"How the fuck should I know? I'm her mother. "

"She snapped."

"Surely you should have some idea!"

"OK, she drinks moderately, she hates drugs because a friend of hers committed suicide while on LSD. She does not sleep around, but she is too pretty to be a virgin. Satisfied?"

"Good enough!" I ran through the normal salutations and hung up the phone.

CHAPTER SIXTEEN

Skeeter had located Frenchy, and started up a poker game which the old man was losing with abandon. We had come full circle, searching for Peggy Sue. The moon had been waxing for the last seven days, going from a thin slit, to three quarter full. Tomorrow night was the beginning of the full moon phase which should last another seven days. According to Frenchy the strangers shrilled pass through the camp this evening or the following morning.

I was still attempting to decide how to handle the awkward chore of greeting a daughter I had never met. Not that I had swallowed the story the Countess and Clyde had tried to feed me. I still held onto the belief; they had made a mistake. Durado women have a particular look to them, my mother had it, my grandmother had it, my great grandmother had the look. From the pictures I was given, Peggy Sue did not have it. It was not something remarkable like a nose or eyes, it was a combination of attributes, an ethereal quality. Who knows, maybe it was just my imagination. I had a difficult time, raking responsibility for the conception of a twenty-year-old woman, whom I had never known as a child. It would have been easier to swallow if her mother were not the Countess.

The evening dragged on. I was the only one in camp who knew that I was interested in the woman as anything besides an oddity in the Hobo Jungle. I played a few hands of poker to take my mind off the intrigue of meeting the girl. It was like waiting for Santa, when I was a child. Not knowing what to expect when she finally arrived. I was excited but reserved when the strangers approached. Suddenly I decided to allow them to make the first move. I would pretend to be just another homeless man, in camp for a brief period before catching a box car. I watched her carefully trying to not be noticed. She glanced in my direction but looked right through me. I was just another Hobo!

"Say missy, aren't you going to register me in that computer do-dad of yours?" I asked the woman.

"Did I put you in, the last time I was our hers" she asked sweetly.

"Naw, Skeeter and me, weren't our here the last time you came by. We just got in last night!"

"I suppose I had better get you on the list then hadn't I° She fumbled around in her backpack until she was able to dislodge the small plastic case. The top popped open revealing a keyboard and tiny electronic screen. "I need your name, nickname and your age.

Also have you seen the lights!

"Oh of course you haven't... if you only got here last night."

"I saw them last month! "I offered. She got a strange look on her face then asked, "Last month!"

"Yeah, we move around a lot." I picked up the fumble.

"You mentioned a friend?"

"Yeah Skeeter, he should be around here someplace. Do you want me to go find him?"

"Not right now, what did you say your name was?"

"James. . . Burlap... Bag "I lied, making the bogus information up on the spot. "Burlap is my nickname.

"Spell the last name please."

"B-A-G-G just like it sounds."

"Age?"

Thirty-eight, I be thirty-nine the end of December."

"And you've seen the lights?"

"Yes mam."

"That's everything Mr. Bagg, chank you!" she said folding up the lap top computer. I was still watching her, looking for any trait that would identify her as a Durado female. "When you find your friend, you can tell him to come over." She added.

Where was Skeeter? He had been playing poker with the boys.
Now, he was nowhere to be found. I felt nature calling and trotted off to a nearby clump of trees to relieve the pressure. Before I could get my zipper down, a hand reached out of the darkness and grabbed me by my collar. I went soaring into the bushes, with a hand covering my mouth. I started to struggle, got in one good lick, then found myself in a headlock.

It was Skeeter. He had seen the stranger's approach with just enough time to make himself absent. He recognized the man accompanying Peggy Sue. It was the fellow who had lifted his wallet and bus ticket. I immediately took a dislike for the male stranger.

It was his fault I had been stuck taking care of the Skeeter for the last three weeks. As much as I had come to admire the kid's good qualities, it still would have been better if our paths had never crossed.

"Are you sure it was him?" I asked

"As sure as Rock Hudson was gay."

"Rock Hudson was gay?" I gasped.

"Skip it..." He grimaced

"Yeah, I'm sure."

Skeeter had turned out to be a fly in the ointment. I had to go back to Peggy Sue and explain that I could not find him. I could work with that; I thought. Devise some fictitious tale; about him being too timid to present himself. That was perfect, use it to pry information out of her. Maybe it was not so bad having Skeeter around.

"By the way, just how did he get your wallet?" I asked.

Skinny dipping! Want to know more?" Skeeter smiled.

"'No clinical derails, if you please."

"We were headed down the highway, when he asked if I wanted to go skinny dipping. I said I'd love to. While I was still in the water, he grabbed my wallet and bus ticker."

But he knows you're the words failed me so I made a limp wrist motion with my arm.

"You can safely say he knows. "Skeeter snickered.

"Then by all means, stay out of sight!" I begged.

I finished, what I had gone to the bushes to do. I then returned to where Peggy Sue had stretched out her sleeping bag.

There was no doubt she was the Countesses daughter. She had that shade of brunette hair which glows red when the light hies it just right. Her eyes were florescent emerald green. A petite aquiline nose was set off by skin so soft it was translucent. Not a dab of make-up, her lips were cherry red. The only thing which could distinguish her as a Durado female were her breasts. She did not have any. But neither do a lot of women, so this observation did not count.

"Where is your friend?" she asked, when I returned alone.

"He's a little bashful, says he doesn't want to be in your computer unless he knows what you will do with the information.

"That's fair." she shrugged, offering nothing more.

"So, what are you doing with the information?" I pried.

"Keeping a record of everyone who has seen the UFO."

"BULLSHIT I grunted, trying to put her on the defensive.

"I beg your pardon?" she countered checking my attempt with a proper offensive tactic. Must run in the family.

"You aren't out here keeping track of a bunch of old hobos, who if even a million of them swear they've seen a UFO, nobody will believe anyway.

"Clermont... eh... Charles doesn't see is that way, he thinks people will have to listen."

"Who's Clermont, your boyfriend?" I baited. Hey, she brought it up.

"I do declare sir; I think you're jealous?" she mimicked Scarlet O'Hara.

"Personally, my dear, you don't have enough meat on your bones." my best Rett Butler came bursting forth. " You didn't exactly answer my question." I added.

"Clermont is not my boyfriend. He is a serious psychic, trying to prove the UFOs exist. He says sexual contact will diminish his psychic abilities." she explained, tossing her head back and inhaling deeply.

I remembered the way Skeeter snickered, when I inquired if Clermont knew he was swishy. Something told me old Clermont was a man's sort of man. The revelation momentarily tossed my timing off, I forgot the thrust of my interrogation. I needed something to use to pry more information out of Peggy Sue.

"Then you spend a lot of time with Clermont?"

"Only when were out in the field. The rest of the time I work out of his office making print outs from the information I collect."

"And he pays you?

"Of course, why else would someone wander around our here!"

"Who pays him?"

"I don't know. He has some private research grant or something. He's got a lot of research projects."

I was on a roll. I could not think up questions fast enough to glean tiny bits from Peggy Sue's story. I noticed her glance up over my shoulder with a smile. A very suspicious Charles Clermont glared down at me. Peggy Sue instantly introduced him in an air of respect. She made a big show of consulting her computer to remember my name. It lent a positive business-like quality to the introduction. I cook advantage of the moment, asking if I could take a look at the device. Clermont gloomily nodded his permission, as if it would be time wasted.

Compared to my personal computer back in Washington DC, this thing looked like a toy. Now that I had my hands on it, I found it was a nasty piece of Japanese technology. It was as solid as a Yamaha dirt bike. I had her kick start the thing for me, then show me how it worked. If I wanted to pull up a name, all I had to do was press this and that, wait a nanosecond for the screen to clear, punch in the name and it appeared on the screen. I did not even have to put in the whole name. I pretended to be toying with the thing entering J-O-H-N, then pressing enter. Three John's, six Johns, and eight Johnson's appeared on the screen. As I scrolled down, the John and Johns vanished off the top of the screen. I innocently stopped at Johnson, Steven.

"What do I do now?" I asked Peggy Sue.

"Press this function key." she reached over and capped a button. The screen instantly changed to a profile of the individual.

Johnson, Steven: Roanoke VA.; Citizen USA; No fixed address; Occupation NONE, Entry status OTHER; Age 21.

"What's that mean?" I asked pointing to the entry status.

"Here let me show you on your own file." she took the com-purer and entered B-A-G-G. The screen revealed I had an entry status as Witness.

"What's it means when it says: other?"

"That's just someone Clermont had me keep on file."

"Do some of the D's, I'm looking for a friend of mine." I asked turning on the charm.

Clermont reached over and closed the lid on the computer.

He made a pointed speech about the data base, being privileged information. Peggy Sue obeyed him at once. It was clear he was a demanding tyrant of a boss. I looked past his veneer of L.L. Bean safari garb, and saw a tight ass corporate raider mentality. He instantly struck me as the anal-retentive type, who loathed pension funds, unless they could be plundered.

"Don't you have someplace you are supposed to be? A poker game perhaps." insinuated Clermont.

"I suppose I should be moving on." I agreed, not wanting to let on, I knew from his statement; he had been checking up on me.

Back at the latrine bush, I asked Skeeter if his real name was Steven. It was, and he was also from Roanoke before his sexual tendencies came into question, on the heels of the HIV epidemic.

We decided it would be a good thing for him to remain out of sight. I made a couple of trips back and forth to the bushes, bringing him a bed roll and food. When he wanted me to tell him a bedtime story, I warned him not to press his luck. He acted a lot younger than twenty-one.

Playing poker when one is distracted, is like shaving with a hangover. It is a painful experience. Only slightly less painful than the ballyhoo of people offering well intentioned advice on how to control the damage. These fellows had been practicing. They were so good; I barely got a chance to drink any of my own hooch.

I do not mind losing when I want to lose but this was terrible.

They were taking no prisoners. I was forced to turn in early in order to retain my self-respect.

I tossed my bed roll out onto a knoll overlooking Peggy Sue and Clermont. The plan was to wake early enough to follow them as they left camp, maybe get them alone out on the trail. There were still a few tricks to be tried to separate them one from the other. The hard part would be to convince Peggy Sue to return home. I could tell from the brief encounter that Clermont had some sort of unhealthy control over her.

We were still barely inside the Texas border. The next Camp was in New Mexico. If I was going to grab the girl, like Clyde suggested, I wanted to do it without crossing any federally enforced boundaries. Parents or no parents, the Starr's were asking me to kidnap Peggy Sue, bringing her back against her will. I was confident I could find some way to shmooze her into going back.

When I could get my hands on her computer, I was sure it would give me a valuable clue. If she was actually looking for her father, as the Countess had suggested, there should be an insightful entry for the name Durado. Providing of course; Muskrat Pere had given the girl a name to search for. The girl's mother could have fabricated the whole tale, to foster a sense of loyalty in an old flunky.

My head hit the pillow and I was out like a light. I was driving past the Orlando International Jetport when I stopped to pick up a hitch hiker. She said her name was Marielle Hemmingway. She was running away from home, because she was angry with her boyfriend. I took her to my apartment where she spent the night with my brother, my girlfriend, and myself. I told her not to tell anyone who she was, but she did not obey, she told my girlfriend.

When she went in to take a shower the curtain was pulled back and a flashbulb popped. Someone had taken her picture. It was my ultra-tiny girlfriend. We tried to ger the picture back, but my girlfriend slipped under the crack in the door and sold it to her ultra-tiny brother. I told Marielle not to worry, I would get the picture back. While I was gone my brother tried to have sex with her, but she told him she was pregnant. I finally got the picture back and gave it to her as I drove her back to the airport. While she was in the car, I ordered her to show me her breasts. If anyone asked where she had been, she was supposed to say she had been with me. If they asked what we had done, she should tell them; all she had done was show me her breasts. Best breasts I had ever seen.

CHAPTER SEVENTEEN

"Wake up hombre!" ordered Skeeter, trying to sound like a Texan, while shaking me roughly.

"Wow what a dream, leave me alone I've got to see what happens next." I begged.

"Come on, they have a half hour head start on us!"

This was not good. If they made the border before we caught them, I was going to have to come up with a better plan to convince Peggy Sue to abandon Clermont. I might even have to use the honest approach. That would be as foreign to my nature as hunting ducks with hand grenades. Perish the thought, that I should be honest. Loyal and brave maybe, but not honest.

"Which way did they go?"

'Down toward the shack where we hide the car." answered

Skeeter. As he ran along side of me, he added, " Hey you should have seen, what I saw last night!"

"A big golden diamond shaped light, traveling north?"

"Exactly, how'd you know:" he innocently asked.

"Skeeter are you for real? I mean, are you with the program?" I grumbled while stopping to pulled on my boots. "What do you think we're doing our here in the desert?"

"Looking for UFO's?"

"Exactly!"

"But you said we were working on environmental issues that concern transient populations." he gasped, "You lied to me!"

"No, I did not lie to you, were doing that too!" I sheepishly explained, feeling humbled by his faith in me. God, must have a plan for the boy or he would never have made it outgo Virginia with that wallet.

The squad car was not going anywhere. Someone had unloaded a shot gun into the radiator. Not a scratch anywhere on the car, except a fist sized hole in the cooling system. I tuned the radio into a Willie Nelson song, and prepared to remove the damaged radiator. Judging by the tire tracks, it was someone in a four-wheel drive vehicle. Pointing to a blemish on one of the treads, I asked Skeeter to find some way to make a copy of the tire marks for future reference.

Why is it, whenever something simple like a radiator has to be removed, you can never find the correct tools on hand? You can purchase cheap Taiwanese socket sets and wrenches for about ten dollars to be kept in the trunk of the car in case of an emergency.

When the emergency arises, you have lost or broken the exact ones you need. I wish I had a dollar for every time, I have had to use channel lock pliers, and a pair of vice grips, to do something like this. The channel lock pliers, never lock, neither do the vice grips.

Instead, they both crush your fingers against sharp places on the frame of the car. If you are lucky the screw heads match the screwdriver present, but as a rule of thumb, screws are standard while the driver is a Philip-head.

Any job done at home, with beer and a toilet handy, always takes an hour The job done in an emergency cakes three times as long. Filers of skin are scalped off the knuckles. Puncture wounds form in the meaty parts of the fingers and hand. You tell yourself it could be worse, but this actually is not true. You promise yourself to buy a new set of cheap sockets. By the time the next emergency arises, you have two sets in the trunk and not a single cool you can use. The demon possessed channel lock pliers and a pair of vice grips are always there in the trunk waiting. At least I also had a couple pairs of overalls in the trunk. They would make a good place to wipe my bloody knuckles.

The radiator wrestled me to the ground. I was flat on my back, under the front end of the car, crying to bribe the last bolt loose. When it finally came, the only thing that saved me from being decapitated, was the hoses to the water pump.

By some miracle the screw driver-matched the application. I wiped large hunks of road dirt out of my eyes and scrambled to my feet.

"How's it coming over there Skeeter?" I asked looking over my shoulder.

"Just about done!"

I made one final grunt, the last hose flopped loose. Holding the radiator like it was a priceless oil painting I walked over to see how Skeeter was doing. He had made a beautifully scaled drawing of the tire treads with an arrow pointing to the notch in the tire tread.

"No! You blockhead, I need something full sized that I can put up against the real thing when we find it."

His face turned bright red, his fists shot up to this hip, "Oh, that's right. It's my fault you can't communicate with other people. he screeched.

"Calm down Skeeter! Jesus Christ, you sound like were married or something." I snorted, beginning to explain exactly what I wanted. "Skip it, we'll get it when we come back."

Down at the trading post the proprietor offered he sympathy but nothing more. If I needed a radiator, I would have to run up to Carlsbad. I looked at the radiator and cussed. I looked at it again counting the damaged fins. If I could seal the broken fins, it would be roughly sixty percent as efficient as it was before. The shopkeeper agreed to rent a gas welder for twenty dollars an hour. Ten minutes later Skeeter and I were climbing the hill leading back to the shack. The radiator looked like a bagel but would work just fine.

While I put it back into the car, he fooled around making a plaster cast of the tire tracks. Filling the empty radiator from a five-gallon jug of water I asked him where he got the plaster. He said there was big pile of it around the corner of the building. I went to investigate. He was using bird droppings from some wild fowl. which roosted in the eyes of the roof. I smiled, shook my head and asked if he had washed his hands.

"Skeeter, let me ask you something. Do you like the wide-open spaces?" I grinned.

"I love it, why?"

"Oh nothing, just thought I would ask." I answered, thinking what fun you could have with a guy like Skeeter up in someplace really wild. Someplace like Alaska where there a wolves and bears.

Where do you want me to put the plaster cast" he asked.

"Why don't we just leave it here. Well come back and get it if we need it. I'll just use your drawings, OKS" I winked.

We caught up with the four-wheel drive vehicle at the next camp. The camp was twenty miles inside the New Mexico border.

It turned out we did not need the plaster cast to recognize the tire tracks. The tracks came from a bright shiny brand-new Jeep. It would not be hard to keep track of a vehicle like that, out here in the desert. Whatever Clermont did for a living, it probably paid very well. If this belonged to Clermont. Which I was sure it did. It had all the anal-retentive extras.

Being a red-blooded American, I believe in fair play. Turn the other cheek and all that nonsense. However, it was all I could do to talk myself out of revenge. Something inside myself cold me; an eye for an eye, a radiator for a radiator. I mused while we waited, revenge was from the Old Testament, modern Christians should rely on justice. Damn that Muskrat Pete for trying to save my immortal soul.

Skeeter pulled out a cigar, lit it, then started puffing away. In a few minutes his face turned the pale green shade of a cadaver. He kept smoking the thing regardless of the hacking and coughing he was doing. His mouth filled up with saliva and his eves started to tear.

"How long you been a smoker?" I asked

"Just started?" he hacked.

"Let me see that thing I ordered, plucking the cherry of ash from the end and grinding it out in such a way it could be saved.

"Here put this in your pocket, in your mouth it looks like you're chomping on a turd."

"Thanks?" he mumbled through a mouthful of spit.

"Just out of curiosity, where did you get the stogy?"

"Won it, poker game with Frenchy. He had a whole box."

"Those are the kinds of things you're supposed to put in the next pot, then loose the poker hand." I instructed.

It struck me as funny that Frenchy was running around with a box of cigars. Hobos will usually cake one cigar and cur it into four pieces, or they will crush it down to roll cigarettes. The name of the game with tobacco products is to hoard them. Nobody risks such a precious commodity in a poker game, well maybe if you do not use tobacco. I had bigger fish to fry than to worry about Frenchy.

"Here try this on." I told Skeeter throwing him a pair of cover-all's. It fit him snugly. He still had those stupid basketball shoes on. His shoes were the kind street punks wear, white, unlaced and padded like clown shoes. They were not the kind of footwear for what I had in mind. I wanted both of us to look as unremarkable as possible. He would have to go barefoot. A couple bandannas over our hair and covering our faces, presto instant outlaws.

I predicted they would not spend the night at the camp because their gear was still in the Jeep. We would surprise them as they returned. I would grab Peggy Sue and explain everything to her, on our way back to Texas. Enough of this running around in the desert. If all went well, I would even cover the cost of a ticket to send Skeeter to California.

Around about dusk, Skeeter located the two of the them in the binoculars. They were strolling single file, Clermont was leading the way, like the big Bwana in a Tarzan movie. Even at this distance he looked arrogant. We waited until they got half way to the Jeep before lunging out of the underbrush, pistol in hand.

Clermont immediately pulled Peggy Sue in front of him like a shield. The tactic threw my timing off.

"OK hold it and nobody gets hurt." I ordered having heard this line used a thousand times on TV. "Get the girl!" I told my accomplice.

Skeeter swiftly moved forward holding Peggy Sue by both arms as he struggled to free her from the clutches of Clermont. Clermont likewise was holding the girl rudely keeping her positioned between himself and the gun. The girl in the meantime was being jostled back and forth to the point where her head looked like one of those dog figures you see in the rear window of a car.

Looking at it from the perspective of hind-sight the bare feet were a bad idea. That feisty Peggy Sue stomped down on Skeeter's bare instep, at the same time landing a knee just below his rib cage. He toppled over like it was his first childhood steps. His voice was making little gurgling noises. His butt was in the air, his face in the dirt. Clermont used the distraction to plant a roundhouse kick on the side of my head. He executed it, not as a martial artist, but instead in ballet form. The net effect was the sire. My skull whipped around my neck, like a tether ball on a pole. I did not see it coming, and had not cocked the pistol. Then to add insult to injury, they ran off without looking under our bandannas.

As soon as my vision returned, I grabbed Skeeter and hurried him away from the location. Just in case Clermont returned with the shotgun. I heard the shogun being fired but it was way off in the distance. It was sort of a warning shot. The exact kind of symbolic gesture one would expect from an MBA dressed in safari garb.

I could not wait, to catch him the next time. Especially after he tried to use Peggy Sue as a shield.

We got back to our own vehicle, uncovered the tumble weed and replaced the coveralls in the trunk. Skeeter was not really hurt more surprised than anything. I reserved any comment on my condition, until I could get a second opinion. It felt like there were tiny fragments of bone floating around where there were supposed to be spinal vertebrae.

You sure don't seem like you're in any hurry. Are you sure you're OK." asked Skeeter.

Don't you worry about that. I've got a feeling they won't be getting too far without this!" I commented reaching into my pocket.

I showed Skeeter, the drain plugs to the cooling system of the Jeep.
I always was what Muskrat Pete called, a back-slider.

CHAPTER EIGHTEEN

I had a sort of second sense about this Clermont fellow. He was too much of a tight ass, to really be a psychic. He was more like one of those evangelists who put up a good front. The kind that gets people all worked up, then empties their bank accounts. I had to remember; I pegged him as a phony, even before I laid eyes on him. Whatever scam, he was running, was working on Peggy Sue.

I was shocked when he tied to use her as a shield. He could not know; I meant no one any harm. Even more amazing. Peggy Sue allowed him, to use her as a shield. She had an unhealthy faith in this guy. It would make it difficult for us to kidnap her if she was so intent on protecting Clermont.

As I drove past the Jeep, Skeeter followed my instructions and ducked. He was my ace in the hole. While I was helping to repair the overheated Jeep, he was supposed to circle around and keep me covered. If I could separate the two of them, by taking Clermont to get water, Skeeter was to approach Peggy Sue and to try to acquire her confidence. I let him out of our car over the next rise in the highway then headed back. It was a loose plan, but I was sure we could work something out. Even if Skeeter could get a peek at the computer, it might be valuable.

"Why its mister Baggs." beamed Peggy Sue when she saw me

"Why so it is." agreed Clermont. He seemed surprised he would come across anyone he knew. His surprise seemed increased by the sight of the old squad car. I could see immediately; Peggy Sue knew nothing of the shot gun blast to my radiator.

Clermont was skeptical of my intentions. He strutted around like a wet hen, while I crawled up under the Jeep to try and locate the problem. I slipped the drain plug out of my pocket and back into the bottom of the radiator without him noticing. It was obvious he was the kind of motorist who never learned his way around an internal combustion engine. He must have just taken a wild guess when he pointed his shotgun under the hood of my car back at the shack.

He was fuming about his own vehicle being broke down, with-our any clue as to what was wrong with it. I tolerated his critical insults to American workmanship, until he mentioned; this would never have happened if he had purchased some Japanese four-wheel vehicle. At this point I interjected, how it was not a vehicular problem, but was a driver deficiency. He absorbed the insult, shifting from anger, into the patronizing attitude of the well-educated but socially inept.

And I suppose this would have never happened to you?" He blathered, shaking his well-groomed head.

"Hey it could happen to anyone!" I commented fighting the urge to mention my own misfortune.

"If you will be so kind as to inform Triple A that I am out here

I would be ever so grateful." he continued to patronize.

"What for? I already found your problem! All we have to do is run up the road and get you some water to fill up the cooling system.

Clermont smiled one of his most endearing smiles then said, "You are a most clever fellow, aren't you?". What a phony this bastard was.

"Peggy darling, will you bring water for the portable shower?" he ordered.

He watched as she struggled to ger the forty-pound container out from under the seat. He continued to watch, as she hauled it over the rail-gate, around to the front of the Jeep. He ignored Peggy Sue, who was breathing hard. from digging the container out from under a pile of gear. When she set it down, he made a show of moving it six inches closer to where I was standing. "Here you are my good man, I hope this will be enough." he motioned for me to fill the cooling system.

Where was Skeeter? He should have showed up by now, I had told him to use plan B, if I never left to go after water. Plan B, called for him to wander up and offer his assistance. By the time he showed, the Jeep was ready to travel again. There was nothing I could do to prevent them from going.

Almost nothing. There is little tool I always carry. It is a jack knife, a bottle opener and a file. Ir also has a fold up pair of needle nose pliers. I bent down like I was tying my shoe and grasped the valve stem of one of his tires with the pliers. With a swift twist the valve stem came unsealed, I walked away. Moments later someone mentioned they heard a hissing sound.

I allowed Clermont to locate the hissing sound for himself.

While Charles went into his criticism of American workmanship again, I winked for Skeeter to begin talking to Peggy Sue.

"Let's just see what the owner's manual says about leaky tires, shall we?" I offered trying to distract the pompous ass.

"It's a flat tire! I already know what to do with flat tires. Peggy darling get the spare tire!" ordered Clermont.

I noticed Peggy had the computer out, and was asking Skeeter some questions. "Leave them alone. Can't you see they'll working!" I said. "I've got a can of tire sealer in my trunk, hold on while I read the instructions."

The leaky valve stem quieted as soon as I connected the can to the tire. Once more they were ready to shove off. The instructions on the can said to drive for fifteen miles upon inflating the tire.

So, I offered to follow them for a while. Clermont resisted the intrusion, but Peggy Sue convinced him it was a wise thing to do.

Skeeter rode with me while we rambled down the road.

"What did you find out?" I asked.

"Only, chat she is convinced; there are no UFO's our here." What about me. Did she ask any questions about what we were doing out here?"

"No, but she did give me this!" he held up a tiny plastic disk.

It was the type of floppy disk that goes in a computer. "Why did she give it to you?"

"She said she knew we were working together and thought the information should be given to the police. She knows that the guy she is with. is a crook of some kind."

"How did she know that?"

Beats Mel I told her my name she punched it into the computer then asked me how old I was. I told her nineteen. She asked me; if I knew another Steven Johnson from Roanoke who was a Mexican. I told her, there is no such thing as a Mexican Johnson in Roanoke."

"That's when she gave you the disk."

"No, she gave me the disk, after I cold her; I had my Fake ID stolen by her friend outside Dallas. That was why she had the wrong age inside her computer."

I asked Skeeter what she would do if Clermont wanted to use the computer. "Not to worry, the disk she gave to us, was a copy she ran off while we were talking.

The Jeep pulled over to the shoulder of the road, after we had gone about fifteen miles. Clermont climbed out and checked the tire. He walked back to us, to say everything looked alright. He tripped on something besides my right front wheel twice, once when he was coming, once when he was going. It was strange, he should trip twice over the same object. I did not give it any further thought.

We continued to follow them. After a mile I noticed, my car was pulling to the right. I started to blink my high-beams on and off. The Jeep accelerated when it saw my flashing lights. I pulled over to the side of the road. That bastard Clermont had not tripped, he had stepped down on the valve stem of MY TIRE Of all the low. . OK, OK, so he probably got the idea from me but really. He had done a superb job of it. The valve stem was pushed into the tire. We had to unload everything from the trunk to get to the spare. In place of a full-sized tire, there was one of those doughnuts sized, thirty-mile spares. These dinky spare tires might work inside a city bur if someone takes them off road, they go flat plenty quick.

Thanks to Clermont, Skeeter and I were detoured to a truck stop. At least it had a US post office with daily pick up.

"Clyde listen I'm doing the best I can!" I squirmed on my end of the phone.

What's the big deal you just grab the girl and get her back down here to El Paso?" Clyde thundered.

"It is not that simple. She is involved with some Svengali out here who is up to no good. I'm trying to let everything run its course before 1 extricate her from the situation."

"If anything happens to that little girl there will be no place for you to hide. Do you understand?"

"Calm down Clyde! That's not why I called. I'm sending you an Overnight Delivery package in the mail. When you get it, you'll need to have one of your police computer operators put it on line.

I do not have any idea what is in it, we got it from Peggy Sue."

"Just remember what I said about my little girl, HOBO!"

He warned as he ended the conversation.

We bought a couple two-dollar showers, while we waited on the tire. It reminded me of all the comforts of home. I was surprised how quickly I had made the transition back to being on the road.

Wearing the same clothes for a week at a time. Shaving every three days, without shaving foam. Eating meals only when I was hungry, not because it was again time to eat. I had been drinking a lot less too. Sure, I was sharing a spot of hooch with other hobos, bur overall I was drinking less. It felt good, I felt young again, then I looked in the truck stop mirror. What used to be well proportioned shoulders and chest had relocated to become a paunch. What the hell, women still outnumber men, they would just have co-lower their standards. Like most good truck stops this one had a laundry, or rather a couple of old beat-up coin operated machines. You put the clothes in before taking a shower, then move them up to the dryer while you shave. You can be ready to go in thirty minutes.

That is why the good truckers always look so fresh. Even when they were in Los Angles on Monday, Dallas on Wednesday, and Atlanta Thursday night, the better truckers know to look sharp at all times. If you are one of those types who hitchhike on truck routes you know to keep sharp too.

After a sit down home cooked meal, I felt ready to get bad out after the bad guys. Where was Skeeter? He had asked for some quarters and disappeared. I checked the video arcade but he was not there. I checked the laundry room, still no Skeeter. I was about to give up searching for him when a telephone booth popped open.

It seems he had taken matters into his own hands. A phone call to the Rotec ultralight hang glider people had supplied him with some worthwhile information.

'Did you know they have a two-seat model?" he asked.

"Can't say that I did." I answered.

"It will carry a four hundred pound pay load."

"OK, so get to the point."

"The point is, I am getting tired of the way we keep running around in this desert!" said Skeeter.

From the information he had gleaned during the conversation with Rotoc, Skeeter explained he had noticed something peculiar.

The ultralight would be running out of fuel within a one hundred fifty-mile radius of the point where it took off. He walked me over to the road map stuck up on the wall. Using a pencil as a ruler he measured one hundred fifty miles. From the arrow marked: you are here, he dropped the pencil into Chihuahua, Mexico.

"Sort of explains why Pegey Sue keeps coming up with the h wrong man when she checks in her computer, doesn't it?" he added.

"I was way ahead of you on that one!" I scoffed. * She has got herself mixed up in a illegal alien ring. So what!"

"Let's forget about the girl for now and concentrate on the connection between the Hobo's and the UFO's."

"The Hobo's think; they're signaling UFO's." I said.

"Richt, actually what they are doing is guiding an ultralight hang glider to a safe landing near that building we found." Skeeter grinned. "And what does the Hang glider see as he approaches the building?"

"Probably the kerosine lanterns.

"What would happen if someone moved the lanterns?"

"Skeeter you are a GENIUS!" I gasped. "Hey wait a second What difference does it make, if we capture a couple illegals."

"You serve notice to the ring, that their operation has belt compromised. Peggy Sue is out of a job and she goes home.

Damn I sure hope you right. "I wondered aloud.

CHAPTER NINETEEN

Just to be on the safe side, we positioned ourselves to observe the landing of the next ultralight hang glider. It was a beautiful sight.

They had arranged some sort of lights, which gave off a diamond shaped beam, above and below the wings. The hang glider was perfectly silent as it skimmed the top of a ridge. The engine kicked in and I could hear the sound of a lawn mower pushing it aloft for the final approach. It climbed higher and higher into the dark evening sky.

With binoculars we watched it line up on the light given off by the kerosine lanterns. Slowly it leveled off and started to de-scend. All at once a flare was fired into the air. The craft seemed to hesitate it spiraled once and landed. We could make out the figure of a pilot and passenger as it spiraled. Just as it touched down. light flooded the area in front of the building. I was glad we had waited to put Skeeters plan into action. We had worked into the early dusk making bottles filled with kerosine and a wick. They had been placed in a direction leading away from the other lanterns. The flare was something I would have never expected. I was certain the pilot would not land without the signal. The problem was, where could I get a hold of a flare gun, before the next landing. It was a detail we would have to work out in the morning. We still had a good mile hike, to view the activities that went on after the landings. Seven miles if you counted the distance back to the old unmarked squad car, we had hidden under tumble weed.

We had to move extra quietly. The light given off by the nearly full moon made everything stand out in vivid derail. The night landscape looked like a Salvador Dali painting, without the melted watch. You feel like you are in a giant fish bowl as you move across the sterile surroundings. Distance was warped. Things that seemed close were actually miles away. The stars twinkled on and off, just out of reach.

All was quiet as we approached the building- I had Skeeter boost me up as we had done before. The scene inside was un-changed. I tried to force the window open. It swung on two greasy pins, one on either side. The lip of the window caught me squarely under the chin. I abandoned my quest, as I hung limply from the edge of the roof. This type of thing never used to happen to me when I was young. What was wrong with my life?

Is this what it is like, to grow old?

'Cease and desist, Hombre!" ordered Clyde, when I telephoned the next day.

"Hey I've got too much invested in this to back away now."

"Look who's talking!" he corrected. "I'm down almost ten grand and I still don't have my daughter."

"She'll be home in a couple of days, Trust Me." I begged.

"No, she won't. You say she will but she won't" he argued.

"Clyde listens.

"No, you listen! I'm giving you the order to cease and desist.

This doesn't come from me it comes from higher up the totem pole. There is a man named Abernathy headed up to see you. You are going to meet him at the truck stop. You will do whatever he tells you to do. Have I made myself clear?

"Yes, but.

"No butts about it hobo.

"Well, who is this Abernathy character anyway?"

"I can't tell you that. You just meet him at the truck stop. Got grumbled Clyde.

"Yeah, I got it!" I agreed angrily.

We were closer to the hobo jungle than we were to the truck stop. I stopped by on my way to the main road. The men who were in camp were excited about the latest sighting of the UFO's.

Skeeter and I agreed to keep the truth to ourselves. We did not want to start an argument with homeless old men who for once in their lives had something to share besides misery. I figured it would be midafternoon before we would meet Mr. Abernathy whoever he was. Plenty of time to relax with a deck of cards.

Along about noon some familiar guests appeared. Clermont was his usual ill-tempered self, when he saw us. Peggy Sue was trailing behind. She looked like she was carrying the lion's share of the camping supplies. I put on my most endearing smile. In the back of my mind I recalled, we had hidden the car out of the sight of prying eyes.

At once Peggy Sue was surrounded by hobos, all trying to register as witnesses of the flying saucer. She pleasantly attended to each man in turn. Skeeter in the meantime was holding a position at the rear of the line. I could not figure out, what it was, he had up his sleeve. It soon became apparent, he simply wanted to converse with Peggy Sue again, like he had the other night. I had no idea she had made such a profound impression on him. If I did not know better, I would swear he was infatuated with the girl.

When it came time for me to go meet Abernathy he offered to stay behind and keep an eye on Peggy Sue. I thought that was a brilliant idea. We could accomplish much more if we split up our energy. Why had I not thought of such a simple idea. I was prob ably spending too much time thinking up ways to screw with Clermont. Ways that would not endanger Peggy Sue.

"Don't let her out of your sighed!" I ordered. Skeeter just smiled.

I watched the two of them talking together. I thought I saw her using little Durado female mannerisms. It must have been my imagination. I turned my attention to locating Clermont. He was nowhere to be found. Clyde sure picked a fine time to order me to cease and desist. I could be headed down highway 62 with his daughter in half an hour.

Abernathy turned out to be Agent Abernathy, FBI. The big secret Clyde was trying to hide was beyond me. If you have seen one FBI agent, you have seen them all. Gum shoes and a wash and wear suit, no expression when he introduced himself. He drove a plain unmarked light green sedan, government license plate, AM radio. He would have four to five years of college, two children, an adoring wife. He would also have a home in the more expensive suburbs, be a sober protestant who did not smoke. With thirty years of service, he would retire and become a paid consultant. His chances of being killed in the line of duty were about one in thirty-nine thousand, but this figure was slowly increasing because of the war on drug cartels.

The wash and wear suit were important. He would live in the clothes he had on until this assignment was complete. The briefcase, it too was wash and wear. If he was a junior agent, he would prefer a nine-millimeter automatic hand gun to the service revolvers carried by senior field personnel. Again, this preference had to do with the increasingly hazardous criminal climate. He would be a man who was hard to either like or dislike. At least he would get his job done as expeditiously as possible and move on. I felt relieved at knowing that. When Clyde had been so evasive that morning, I was worried; he might be sending some pain in the posterior, private investigator.

Abernathy got right down to business. He showed me his credentials as part of his introduction. What did I know about Charles Clermont?

"Only that if his ass was any tighter you could use it to chalk a pool cue."

"I rake it you are not fond of Mr. Clermont?" he monotoned.

"What can you tell me about the woman who gave you the floppy disk?" Abernathy continued.

"From what I have been able to figure ours she was collecting a computer file of homeless people when she got mixed up with Clermont. He has been using the computer file to move illegal aliens into this country."

"And that is all you know?"

"Hey if you want to know more you can ask her yourself. I have to warn you, you're going to look out of place in that suit. I don't want you spooking any of the old timers. I put a lot of time into building a working relationship with these guys." "How about a pair of coveralls?"

"I don't think so." I answered, thinking about how Skeeter and I were dressed when we tried to abduct Peggy Sue.

I gave him some of my old clothes to wear. Dressed in jeans and a flannel shirt, he looked more like a hobo. I could not replace his gum shoes so we covered them with a pair of socks. Homeless people sometimes do this to protect their foot wear. I decided it would not look too out of place.

The facial pores of homeless people, always have the appearance of being huge. It come from the combination of dirty grit, sunlight and exposure. We tried to duplicate this effect, with moderate success, by rubbing a burnt wine cork into Abernathy's face.

He was still clean shaven, with one of those Dagwood Bumstead haircuts, the FBI insists upon. We would just have to make the best of it.

"Keep your head covered with this ball cap." I recommended.

Arriving at the hobo jungle in the midafternoon, we were immediately scrutinized by the permanent residents. I could still find a bunch of discrepancies in Abernathy's appearance, but there seemed to overlook them all. They had a chance to get to know me, over the last couple of trips. Their head hobo seemed to crust my judgment. It may also have been, they were too busy with UFO lore to pay attention to us. If the mother ship did land, it was going to have to rake all of them.

Peggy Sue and Skeeter were still where they were when I left. I waited a few moments watching the girl, looking for any of those cell tale signs, of her being a Durado woman. They were smiling at each other. I watched her reach our placing her hand on top of his.

The signal was indisputable. Any heterosexual would know, this was the moment to lean forward and kiss her. Skeeter hesitated; he got this panic expression on his face. To his credit he did not leave the girl hanging. His choice of kisses did leave something to be desired.

He gave her one of those kisses, usually reserved for distant relatives.

Peggy Sue corrected the blunder by grabbing him by the back of the neck, giving him a long-wet soap opera kiss. His eyes bulged as his panicked expression returned. A moment later he closed his eyes and surrendered to the sensation.

I have never claimed to be a diplomat. I took this opportunity to announce my presence with a hearty; "HI, how are you two getting along?"

Skeeter blanched; Peggy Sue smiled but kept her hands around his neck. She chuckled, sending air through her nose.

"Skeeter I thought you were a. ..." I started to say.

"Not anymore!" he interrupted. It looked like he was mopping his brow. The boy was resting uncomfortably, on the horns of a personal dilemma.

"Peggy Sue, this is Mr. Abernathy. He's with the FBI and has a few questions he would like to ask you." I explained as a means of introduction.

I left Abernathy alone with Peggy Sue, to sort out whatever business they had. Skeeter and I had some personal business of our own. I skipped the subject of Peggy Sue even though it was a tempting target. I concentrated on learning where Clermont was.

"He leaves Peggy here for a couple nights each trip out!" Skeeter said. "She doesn't expect him back until the day after tomorrow."

"Here's the keys to the car. As soon as she and Abernathy are finished, take her and get into the car. I'll meet you, where the railroad crosses the main road, two miles north of here." I instructed.

"What's with all the sneaky stuff?"

"Let's just say I'm getting tired of all this nonsense! Well run Peggy Sue back down to El Paso and let the sheriff sort out all the details a About this time, I saw Abernathy coming. I motioned to Skeeter to get moving. The FBI agent wandered over to confide in me, he was taking Peggy Sue into custody. Protective custody. I glanced over my shoulder with just enough time to see Skeeter and her disappear in the direction of the car. Unfortunately, I did not have enough time to call them back. All I could do was play stupid, when the man noticed they were gone.

I squirmed, as he mentioned: the consequence of interfering with a federal agent, in the completion of his duties. It was a federal offence, punishable by a ten thousand dollar fine and/or up to five years in prison. I started to joke about it being the same sentence, for every crime at the federal level. Vandalism, sexual harassment, falsifying a government document, were all the same punishment.

Something told me to hold my tongue.

"Protective custody huh? Why protective custody?" I expertly changed the subject.

"You're right about the illegal alien status of the men being shuffled around by Charles Clermont, but you're wrong about their country of origin." Abernathy explained.

It turns our Clermont was mixed up with a slightly more lucrative venture. He was providing assistance to Marialito Cuban exiles. The Marialito Cubans were a concern to the FBI because a great number of them were Communist operatives. Even the Soviet Kremlin had warned the United States; they could not control the activities of this renegade faction. The Marialito used an agenda of anarchy and violence to further their cause of guerilla insurgency against both the cast and the west. If it was allowed to continue unchecked the ramifications to social welfare would persist into the mid twenty-first century.

The floppy disk Peggy Sue had given to Skeeter contained a bounty of information. She had unknowingly recorded a great number of the alias's being used by the Cuban political exiles. The problem was to prevent an all-out witch hunt, where innocent Cuban immigrants were placed into jeopardy. It was the type of volatile information which should be sanitized before too many small-town police agencies were given access to it.

My head started to swim. Here I had been working under the assumption that Clermont was just making a few bucks on the black marker hustling were backs. Now I was forced to admit, there was much more at stake.

I was convinced Peggy Sue must be a Durado, no other female could calmly sit around in the middle of this kind of confusion and act like nothing was happening. I also wondered to myself, if she was too old to spank. How dare she do something like this to her dear old dad. Especially if he did not know she even existed until two months ago.

"Hey look they probably just wandered off to look at the stars or something. I'm sure they'll be back by morning." I lied. "If you want me to, I'll go look for them, while you wait here."

"Mr. Durado, I hope you aren't involved in any shenanigans!"

Abernathy stated bluntly, "I would be required to use the full force of the law against you!"

"Ha, it doesn't worry me a bit" I grinned, "Did you ever see thar Gary Larson cartoon, where the devil is standing outside two doors into hell?

"Can't say that I have." answered Abernathy,

"On one door it says: Damned if you do. The other door says:

Damned if you don't." I snorted merrily slapping my thigh.

"You are one of the strangest people I have ever met Mr. Durado." said Abernathy.

"Thank you very much." I continued to grin, as I drifted off into the afternoon haze. He was probably too confused to follow.

CHAPTER TWENTY

The windows of the car were steamy when I got there. To give you an idea how difficult this would be to accomplish. let me point out, the sun was still up and the temperature in the shade was over ninety degrees.

"Her don't let me bother you Two, but...ch. .. we better get moving." I screamed through the glass. A small rectangle formed in the water vapor on the window. An eye pecked out.

"Come on! Open the door, before the hear gives you brain damage." I bellowed. "Hurry up, there's been another change in plans."

There was only one way I could think of, to throw Abernathy off the trail. We would give him a bigger fish to fry. We had already prepared to side track this evening's phony UFO flight, out into a different section of the desert. We would just follow the same plan, grab the pilot and passenger, then deliver them to the FBI agent. Unable to take charge of the banders and a protective custody case at the same time, Abernathy would be forced to let me take possession of Peggy Sue. Clyde would get his daughter; I would get paid; Skeeter could hop on a bus to California. If only the rest of life could be so simple.

Hiding near the hang glider building, I watched with binoculars as a man set out on a mountain bicycle to light the kerosine lanterns. I waited almost an hour for him to return. After dark, I went down the line putting them out. I hoped the rugged terrain would hide the few real beacons that remained. nearest the real landing zone. I had to skip them to prevent the ground crew from becoming suspicious. Still, I was not sure if they checked on the lanterns, or if they just let them keep burning, until morning.

Skeeter was supposed to drive the squad car across the desert to a position we had already surveyed. He would start from the other end before dark, lighting the bottles we had placed the day before. Everything went according to plan. When I got to where our phony lanterns intersected with the real ones, I stopped extinguishing the lights. I simply followed our bottle lanterns out to a rendezvous with Skeeter and Peggy Sue. I noticed the car windows were foggy again when I got there.

To duplicate what would be visible from the air at night, we located a nice patch of soft white sand. We made this our phony landing spot. It was all part of the master plan Skeeter had come up with. At two o'clock in the morning I started to pay attention to the southern sky. By three o'clock we were all anxiously watching. I knew from experience, the pilot would show up, between now and four o'clock AM.

We spotted the diamond shaped light, heading directly on a course to meet us. I waited until he was close enough to hear the whine of the engine. We fired the red flare pistol. The pilot threw the ultralight craft into a pitched bank. The plane spiraled down to the ground, just as we had seen it do before.

He leveled out a foot off the ground. The glider skimmed the surface of the desert without slowing down.

I knew in thar instant, the pilot was not going to set down, until he saw the lights of the building. Skeeter must have sensed it also. He ran forward at an angle which would collide with the hang glider. He threw himself on the tail of the big kite. At this, the moment of impact, the pilot put everything he had into a rake off. Skeeter's extra weight caused the craft to angle up sharply. The crazy fagot was hanging onto the right rear stabilizer. He was forcing it down, while the pilot was doing everything in his power, to force both stabilizers up. The net result was a barrel roll.

The left-wing tip of the kite bit into the soft sand sending it up on end. Skeeter's grip on the tail of the plane slipped. I stood by horrified, watching him pitch forward toward the spinning propeller shaft. With his other hand Skeeter grabbed the left stabilizer.

The craft started to spin on end, like a giant top, rotating on the wing-rip still buried in the soft sand. It traveled, a full three hundred sixty degrees, then Skeeter was thrown away from the center of rotation. He landed like a rodeo cowboy shaken but not injured.

The pilot, was still forcing the stabilizers in the direction of a take-off. This caused the hang glider to crash down on its wing top. upside down.

If someone should contact the Rotec Company, they would learn; one should never attempt a barrel roll in an ultralight hang glider. The fuel drains away from feeding the motor. The engine sputters and dies.

A very startled pilot, hung upside down by his chest harness.

His passenger did not move. We all stood there motionless for a moment trying to understand the events which had just taken place. The pilot hit a button on his chest and crashed to the ground.

Being upside down, he was surrounded by unfamiliar guy wires, which formed the supports for the wings. I waited for him to become untangled from the spider's web of wires and aircraft aluminum. He tried to make a run for it. With almost no effort on my part, I had him tackled and hog tied.

Abernathy had unknowingly supplied me with a handful of locking nylon bundle ties. He had asked me to watch his equipment while he went to the rest room. I used one for the pilots' hands, one for his feet, and another one between his hands and feet. He was going nowhere.

I turned my attention to the passenger. Skeeter had already climbed into the maze of wires and was checking on the other man.

"Hey, he doesn't look too good!" offered Skeeter. "I think this one is dead."

"That's impossible, let me take a look at him." I commanded, crawling through the mess.

Skeeter was right he did not look too good. He did not look well at all. It was obvious his skull was crushed. We left the poor man strapped in as we flipped the hang glider over. There was no blood. No bodily fluids were seeping from anywhere. I touched his skin; it was stiff as cardboard. He must have been dead all along. I was greatly relieved he had not died as part of the accident. Skeeter brought the flashlight over. I looked into the man's eyes. They stared out at me like the eyes of a painted doll. Which is exactly what he was!

"It's a Pin-ata!" gasped Peggy Sue.

"I thought I told you to stay back?" I thundered, " What's a Pin-ata?"

"You know, it's a hollow toy Spanish people hang at parties for the children to bat at with a stick. It sends a shower of candy in all directions... You know a Pin-ata!" she got an exasperated look on her face.

"So, this thing is supposed to be hollow?" I asked, trying to pick it up.

The seating configuration of the hang glider was side by side.

You could not have, one seat weighed down with one hundred fifty pounds, and the other seat weighing nothing. The hang glider could, however, be flown with the pilot sitting in the center of both seats. The pin-ata had to weigh at least as much as the pilot.

This had to be the case.

"Skeeter, peel open the crushed part of his head and look in-side." I ordered. I already intuitively knew what they were using for ballast.

"Were rich!" shouted Skeeter.

"How do you figure that?" I asked.

"Do you have any idea how much we can get for this?" Skeeter grinned ear to ear.

I made some hasty calculations. One hundred dollars per gram; times, Twenty-eight grams to the ounce; times, Sixteen ounces the pound; times, roughly One hundred fifty pounds.

Carry the zeros.

"Six point seven, Million dollars' worth of Cocaine. " I announced. The thought of it made my knees weak.

"Holy SHIT, we're rich!" shouted Skeeter again.

"Not so fast, ya moron! We've got to turn this over to Abernathy. I recommended.

"Let Abernathy get his own Cocaine."

"How far do you think we'll get before the people who own this stuff come after us?" interjected Peggy Sue.

"Listen to the girl, stupid. We've got to get Abernathy involved for our own good." I prevailed.

Skeeter roared with laughter, "OK, Master-mind start working on a plan, to get us out of your last plan!"

The boy was right of course. They were both right. It looked like I had finally got myself in over my head so deep even a miracle could not save me. Those Marilito Cubans would swoop down on the hobo jungle with a vengeance, as soon as they found this shipment missing. Why do I do this crazy stuff? Why can I not just leave things alone? Everything would be fine, if I had just let the hang glider make the delivery. Wait a second, that was the answer.

The delivery could still be made. All someone would have to do is fly the hang glider back to the original destination. That is, if the thing would still fly.

"Were going to give the cocaine back!" I announced.

"What! Are you nuts?" cried Skeeter. This coming from someone who had just barely avoided becoming Sushi in the propeller a short time earlier.

The fuel tank was empty. The batteries to start the engine were shorting out, from landing upside down. Structurally the craft seemed to be sound. I had a one gallon can of gas in the trunk of the squad car. It was the wrong kind of fuel for the two-cycle engine. The engine would probably run on the stuff but it would burn out the cylinder walls. I decided to chance it, hopefully the cylinder walls would hold up long enough to get me where I was going. I tried the flaps. They moved smoothly. We could spin the propeller to start the engine.

I am no pilot, but, how hard could it be? The theory of flight is straight forward. Vector force A, exerts a positive pressure on one side of a foil, while at the same time creating a negative pressure on the inverse side of the foil, thereby creating lift. Press forward on the foot pedals and the thing should climb. Pull back on the stick should cause it to climb faster. Push the right foot peddle to bank right, left to bank left. Push forward on the stick to descend.

"What are you going to do when it comes time to land?" asked Skeeter.

"It can't be that difficult. If push comes to shove, I'll point the thing at the hangar and jump." I said bravely. I knew when the time came to land the thing. I would be making things up as I went along.

"When the two of you get back to the hobo camp turn yourselves into Abernathy. He wants to put Peggy Sue under protective custody!" I directed.

"Why didn't you mention that before?" asked Peggy Sue.

"It must have slipped my mind." I lied.

The pilot prisoner was loaded into the rear seat of the old squad car. I sent along a one-pound bag of the contraband. They were to use it, to secure a claim of citizens arrest, against the pilot.

It was worth over ten thousand dollars, a factor which fit into my new master plan. I hoped the smugglers would be convinced; the pilot had stolen the missing bag.

"Tell Abernathy, to get some reinforcements our here. The National Guard if he can swing it. IF I don't make it back be tomorrow night, they should raid the landing strip when the next shipment comes in."

"What, are you going to do, when you get there?" Peggy Sue asked sweetly.

"Don't worry I'll think of something!"

I plastered my most determined look onto my face, then yelled.

"CONTACT!". Skeeter swung the prop. The still warm engine caught on the first try. Adrenaline rushed through my system. I gritted my teeth and goosed the throttle. The kite started to lurch forward. The speed slowly increased, faster, just a little faster. I hit a bump the whole ching bounced. I pushed down on the foot pedals and held back on the stick. I was airborne. Hey, this was not bad at all.

I followed our set of phony lanterns to the end, banked right and tried to gain a little altitude. I only hoped I was on the correct angle, to intersect with the hang glider hanger. It was still pitch dark but the hour was getting late. I never did figure out how to turn on the lights to resemble a UFO. As I flew along, experiencing the exhilaration of the moment, I could make out the figure of someone on a mountain bicycle. He was attempting to relight the kerosine lanterns. I buzzed him, causing him to give up the chore, and follow me back in. The flare was fired into the air. I began to panic.

They knew I was close. I needed to disengage from the aircraft with enough time to vanish into the tumble weed. If necessity is the mother of invention, panic is its father. I strapped my harness around the stick to keep the bird level then shoved a one-pound bag of cocaine onto each of the pedals. I took my hands and feet away to see if it would work.

The bags of cocaine ruptured sending a cloud of white powder into my face. As I inhaled the crystals flooded into my lungs. It looked like I was going to be the happiest dead man, to ever fall out of an ultralight hang glider. A sensation swept over me like I was indestructible. I strapped the harness back around myself and prepared for a crash landing. After all, the other pilot had survived.

I banked the craft, heading back in the direction I had come.

I was looking for the man on the mountain bike. He stopped to wave just as I clipped him off his vehicle. When he went tum bling, I knew I was low enough to jump. When I did, the hang glider adjusted to the severe redistribution of ballast, and gained altitude. At the same time, it banked sharply to the right. The throttle died. I watched in amazement as it landed itself without further mishap.

The cyclist, was still groaning where he had landed. I grabbed the mountain bike and headed in the direction of the hobo camp.

Some strange overpowering sensation of absolute control, swept over me as the miles disappeared beneath the wheels of the mountain bicycle.

As I pumped along mile upon mile, I remembered the cocaine. I wondered if I was addicted. No one could afford a twenty thousand dollar a day habit. I kept pumping on the sprocket. adjusting the gears for maximum speed. I would enjoy it, while it lasted.

CHAPTER TWEINTY - ONE

There is an expression called; Dragging it on Home. Most of the time, they use this expression, to denote the way a man feels when he has a hangover. I will admit, I have had a few hangovers in my time, but I have never had to; drag it on home. Not until that morning, when the artificial exhilaration wore off. I felt like the shell of a man, no, the shell of a cockroach. I had gone from one of the most dynamic masters of the universe to a mummified cripple not worthy to share the same sunlight with the rest of humanity. I am not talking about the normal depression of waking up to reality.

This was the sort of depression one might feel, if all civilization came to an end, in fulfillment of biblical prophecy and the only thing that was left was eternal punishment. It was the inverse equation to what I had felt the night before. Last night I was Conan the Barbarian, today I would not even make a good drooling moron.

I had shifted the mountain bike into the easiest combination of gears to peddle and I was still having trouble. Lucky for me I had picked up a set of railroad tracks that kept me away from the main road. My mind kept telling me to continue moving. The truth was, nothing seemed to matter. Even the sun light seemed dimmer. I knew the temperature was in the nineties but I felt cold.

Maybe if I stopped to rest. This was worse, I started to shiver. I kept going, across a bleak empty desert.

I must have traveled twenty-five miles when the hobo jungle popped into view. They had never seen someone as pitiful as me as I wandered into camp. A few drinks of watered down liquor later and I was beginning to revive. I crumbled down into a jumbled uncomfortable sleep, waiting to die. I awoke to the persistent prodding of mister Abernathy. He was one, upset, federal agent.

Peggy Sue and Skeeter had made contact with him and were at present safely sequestered in a motel near the truck stop.

"How dare you release six million dollars' worth of cocaine to the Marialitos! " Fumed Abernathy.

"Would you relax, I have a plan." I countered.

"Did you ger the National Guard?"

"We can't use the National Guard for something like this. " Abernathy explained.

"Well go get something, because tonight is the last time this full moon, they will cry to bring in a shipment." I whined trying to return to the comfort of sleep. "I'll hand you the whole god damn smuggling ring, on a silver platter, but you are going to need help.

I added, passing on into oblivion.

"Wake up!" Abernathy demanded. "I need to have a general idea of your plan, the lay out, WAKE UP!" he demanded.

"The plan is we wait for the next shipment. and nail them!" I generalized.

Produced a scrap of paper with a crude map. Abernathy snatched it from me. I noticed also, he had changed back into his wash and wear suit. This was a sign he was tired of fooling around.

I had seven weeks in on the project, and he was tired of fooling around in less than seventy wo hours. No wonder we were losing the war on drugs.

"That's why I gave them back the contraband." I drooled, "Ther will still be stockpiling the stuff until after the last shipment."

"How much do you believe they've got up there?" asked

"Abernathy. "Just a ball park figure!"

"Let's see; six point seven per night, times six nights.

At least thirty-six million dollars' worth.

" I grumbled " now leave me alone until you've got some back up." I begged, drifting back into an unrelaxed unconsciousness

I heard a grinding of loose gravel as he stormed away. My body was dripping with a fetid perspiration. I wanted to vomit but there was nothing in my stomach. I could feel individual photons of sunlight, burning through the flesh of my face. The rotation of the planet was making me seasick. How could anyone enjoy the effects of this obscene white powder?

I drifted back to sleep. I was slow dancing with a tall beautiful woman, in a room full of beautiful women. It was Candice Bergen.

No other men were present. She told me; if I wanted to be a magician, I should always check my equipment carefully. I squeezed her and said, her equipment was fine.

She wandered away, while I danced with other ladies. Every so often, she would return, to ask me; if I had checked out the equipment. We would both smile and laugh at each other. The dream wore on. 1 danced with one lady who kept her face covered with a veil. Candice appeared, asking: if I had checked my equipment carefully. I lifted the veil. I was dancing with Charlie McCarthy dressed in drag. The sight of the big puppet shocked me awake.

" C'mon, Abernathy wants to see you!" ordered Skeeter, as he pulled me to my feet.

" Skeeter, I don't fool too good!" I complained." I feel like I want to implode and explode at the same time."

" If it's any consolation, you don't look too good either." he offered, wrapping one of my arms over his shoulder. My legs felt like rubber bands. The toes of my boots, left little haul marks along the path, where he carried me by my belt loops. Skeeter was appalled when he heard I had dusted myself with two pounds of the white powder. He thought it was a waste. He informed me;

Most heavy users, never get past a one gram-a-day habit. I did some quick arithmetic. To my horror, I discovered, I had used up a three-year supply.

"You're lucky you're not dead." Skeeter stated bluntly.

" That's easy for you to say!" I slobbered. " You're not the one trapped inside a paralyzed body!" Shut up and start walking?" said Skeeter. " You couldn't have got that much in you or you wouldn't be here.

Now thar he knew what the problem was, he was able to offer some beneficial suggestions. He steadied me by the back pockets of my dungarees. I could feel the crotch rising up to give me an excruciating wedgy. The dream must have been a premonition. I dangled like a marionette from Skeeter's clutches. My legs started to carry their own weight. Soon I was walking on my own. Skeeter slapped me in the face. I could feel the blood rising. He slapped me again, on the other side of my face.

" C'mon, put up your dukes!" ordered Skeeter.

He slapped me again. My rubber band arms rose to fend off his attack. He slapped them aside. My clenched fists rose to protect me. I could feel the life returning to my upper extremities.

Blood started to surge into my arms. He slapped me again. I walked limply forward into the slap, like a scarecrow on a stick. He took a step backward. I lunged at him. He took another cautious step back. I stumbled forward. He kept backing away, with me following him in a ridiculous ridged procession. " Come back here, Skeeter!" I smiled, using the voice reserved for house-breaking little puppies.

" I won't hurt you!"

"You must really think I'm stupid." he taunted.

 "Come and get me sucker!".

The blood was returning to my limbs. I started out, doing a stiff drunken baby shuffle, trying to reach him. He stammered back another few yards. I broke into a slow deliberate trot. Too slow to catch the prancing fagot. My arms and legs began to cooperate. My lungs started to rise and fall in rhythm. We approached the parked squad car; I ran past it. Skeeter pulled up beside me in the car as I continued down the hill toward the highway. Now that I felt alive again, I did not want to chance a relapse.

" I'll meet you at the bottom!" I shouted.

"You're just luck the cocaine was uncut." offered Skeeter as I slipped into the passenger side.

" How so?" I questioned.

"Have you ever heard of Mannite?"

"No, what is it?" I gestured for him to proceed.

"Magnesium Nitrate, It's a baby laxative" confided Skeeter.

They use it to cut cocaine. On the street the coke might be stepped on five or six times with Mannite"

"Wouldn't that…" I started to ask.

"Sure would, diarrhea!" Skeeter smiled.

"Montezuma's revenge." 1 echoed, knowing I had escaped death twice, no make that three times if you count jumping from the ultralight hang glider. Personally, I would rather break my neck than die from the dehydration caused by diarrhea.

"What?"

"What, what?"

"What is Montezuma's revenge?" asked Skeeter.

"Diarrhea! Where did you learn so much about cocaine? "

"Let's just say it's the drug of choice among some of my associates." offered Skeeter.

"Say no more!" I warned him.

The squad car went right past the hotel, continued past the truck stop and angled off the main road. It came to rest among a thicker of tumble weed. Over a gentle rise in the road were three huge container trucks. They were parked end by end forming a mock plaza.

The center truck served as a radar command post, complete with air conditioning. I was ushered into the chaos to verify certain topographical features. A clear dip topped hied neurons. in this plastic wrap was prominently fine detail of the insert to the map. Abernathy explained it was a AWAC photograph taken earlier that morning. It had been telephoned to this location over a facsimile machine.

"You better be right about the volume of contraband Mr. Durado. This equipment is costing the tax pavers plenty!" warned Abernathy.

"Don't try any of that crap on me pal. You didn't run out and purchase this stuff last night. If it wasn't our here right now it would be collecting dust at some armory." I haggled.

The same was true of the personnel but I did not want to be too critical. I hate the logic which is used at the bureaucratic level.

The tax payer, already bought and paid for this equipment before it was even built. What difference does it make if it is used for an actual exercise, or if the exercise is just a training mission. If anything, it looked like we were over prepared for this exercise.

"What's in the other two trucks?" I asked

"Apache Attack Helicopters." answered a radar technician.

"We'll be pulling them out around dark."

"You know what I always thought they should use on drug smugglers?" I asked the technician. He nodded for me to continue.

"They should use those old WWII flying tigers' style of aircraft."

I said being perfectly carnets.

The technician grinned, "Against a hang glider? Get serious!" he laughed.

Like an Apache Attack Helicopter was not overkill. I was trying to qualify my reckoning, by telling the man, I meant against the normal Cessna flying-bush pilots. He was already sharing my blunder of a statement with the other technician present. They both laughed. I went outside and urinated on their parabolic radar receiver. That should keep them busy. A thousand unidentified bleeps danced across the screen inside the trailer.

Two sharps seven-man crews, unsealed the remaining trailers just as dusk was beginning to fall. Extraordinary rear work went into unloading the gunships. Rollers were unloaded to construct a ramp which allowed the Helicopters to be slid from their protective trailers. The blades were unfolded then locked into position. A pilot and co-pilot, from each crew, went through the pre-flight procedure. Now came the period of waiting before the operation went into effect.

Abernathy, approached Skeeter and I, with a small electronic package. It was a radio locator signal. We were to take it out to a position adjacent the hang glider landing site. It would give the helicopter crews a homing beacon.

Well wait until the aircraft lands then we will surround the area." explained Abernathy. "Make sure you are out of the line of fire when we land. We don't want any civilians getting shot up!"

"When can I pick up Peggy Sue?" I asked.

"After the exercise!" recommended Abernathy. "I'°I release her into your custody, after we have a successful mission."

"Fair enough..." I agreed, make sure she's ready to go in the morning.

Sheerer drove, as we bounced along the now familiar desert landscape. We parked and hid the car where we always did. The same tumble weed was used, for this the third night in a row. As the bicycle rider lit up the kerosine lanterns we followed him back to the Quonset hut.

The sky was raven dark as we waited. Lite night creatures skipped and jumped around us. A gentle breeze pitched the fragrant creosote from the tumble weed into the air. Skeeter and I took turns cat-napping, while waiting for the operation to ruled.

There was nothing, either of us could chink to say.

The lights of the hang glider came into view. I mashed down on the control panel of the radio beacon. We dropped it in the dirt and walked away. As we dimmed to the top of a ridge, we could make out the clamor of the helicopter blades churning the thin air. They were headed in; we were headed out. There was a spooky silence that followed. The next sound we heard was the roar of the old squad car engine as we headed for the truck stop.

We were both parts, of what was going on miles away, yet we were detached from the carnage. Men could be dying back there but we would never know anything more about it. It must be the same ghostly sensation as dropping a bomb from an airplane or sending a torpedo against a ship. Sure, we would probably pick up a newspaper to read of the event, or see it on television but we were part of it. It was part of us. I tromped on the accelerator. The squad car rocketed toward the truck stop.

CHAPTER TWENTY - TWO

"What do you mean, I can't take Peggy Sue?" I shouted at the FBI Agent. Abernathy remained calm.

"Our agreement was contingent on a successful mission." He corrected.

"I promised you nine hundred pounds of nose candy and that's what you got!" I fumed.

"This is true, however..." Abernathy began to explain.

"However, nothing, flatfoot!" I slobbered. "I'm taking the girl, and that is that."

Mr. Durado will you please listen to reason, before I am forced to have you detained." continued Abernathy.

"You are, a god damn hero because of me... you jerk!" I exploded.

"Mr. Durado, I am sure you will agree, there is an inherent danger in releasing Peggy Sue until we have Charles Clermont under arrest." Abernathy stated evenly.

He was accurate, and I knew it. I refused to let him dissuade me from my perception of the predicament. We had solved the mystery of the UFO's. The hobos were safe from marauding illegal aliens. I needed one more feather in my cap, to become a big chief. That feather was Peggy Sue. One way or another, I was going to deliver Peggy Sue to her parents and wash my hands of the whole affair.

"What happens when Charles Clermont is in jail?" I surrendered.

"We will be able to relax our protective custody."

"Speak English! Can she go free?" I grumbled.

"Yes." conceded Abernathy.

"Fine!" I smiled, "Skeeter let's go.

"Mr. Durado, I think it is only fair to warn you; people like Charles Clermont sometimes take years for the agency to track down!" explained Abernathy

I was past listening to reason. Clermont was a first-class anal fixated piece of work. He was not going to scurry to cover like any reasonable criminal. He was going to keep going over the failure of his perfect strategy. Right now, he was out in the bush somewhere, trying to correct the error. In many ways he and I were a lot alike.

We both refused to admit defeat.

Knowing this about myself, caused me to consider; what must be going through Clermont's mind at the moment. He would be concerned about his timing. He was orchestrating an event which hinged around a lunar cycle. He was not concerned with the present fiasco. He was worried about resuming operations as soon as possible. Abernathy was right, it was not finished until Clemont was tucked away in prison.

The hobos were an oversight. Clermont had made a significant blunder there. He had invested too much of his energy in soliciting their unknowing support. Here may be the answer to my dilemma. He would return to the hobo camps. He had to! The whole operation pivoted on timing. Clermont had twenty-one days to pure his smugglers back to work. The hobos were the ones, who could put him back on track somewhere else.

I had already studied the finer details of his scheme. He needed someplace obscure as a landing zone. I would wager, Clermont would consulting some old hobo, to suggest just such a field. A gregarious hobo would be a first choice for a man in a hurry. The most outgoing man, I had met, was Frenchy. I made a beeline for the trading post.

We pitched up the hill, to the weather-beaten lad shack. I flung open the doors. The Jeep was already inside. This was going to be too easy. We parked the squad car a fair distance away, under some tumble weed. I did not want to scorch my paint job, as we burned the shack to the ground. My only pang of guilt came from the Jeep-being an American made product. I reconsidered at the last moment. Too bad it was not a Suzuki. Skeeter taunted me, calling me a sissy. Coming from him, it was quite an insult. We let the air out of all the tires. Her, it was a symbolic gesture.

The boxcars were as quiet as a tomb when we approached.

There should have been men scattered around, resting in the noon day sun. I went up one side of the derelict railroad, as Skeeter passed up the other. There was not even a flea bit hound dog present. Something of major importance would have to be brewing for this particular camp to be empty. It was the country club of

Hobo Jungles. Convenient to the trading post, the highway, a freshwater stream. It was not a place likely to be abandoned.

I heard a blast from a shotgun. We ran cautiously in the direction of the clamor. Stopping to rest in a wide section of the patch with our heads ducked, a stone skipped out of the thicker beside the trail. "Hey over here!" a voice whispered loudly: It was Frenchy.

"What is going on?" I demanded.

"It's that damn fool stranger. He's been out here all night looking for the girl. He went to the other camps, came back, left, carne back again.

'What else has he been doing?" we asked.

"The last time he came back, he tried to convince some of the old boys; to help him look for the girl." offered Frenchy.

"Big folly, huh." said Skeeter,

Frenchy grinned his whiskered smile, "We aren't exactly a bunch of nurse maids." he laughed. "We told him; she would show up when she felt like it. That got him real upset, if you know what I mean.

"I can imagine! When did he start firing the shotgun?".

"After half a bottle of hooch. We shared it with him, hoping he would take us, to go buy some more." Frenchy explained.

"What, the liquor I brought our here?"

"Naw, that stuff was too weak, we were drinking moonshine from our still. It's a little strong but.

"A little strong! Moonshine is one hundred eight proofs." I interrupted.

"Yeah, but we were almost out of hooch anyway, so continued the whiskered old man.

"So, you all deliberately forced the last of the moonshine on him, to make him an easy touch." I gathered.

"Hey, nobody expected him to start dancing around like a fool, firing the shotgun." gasped Frenchy.

"Has he shot anyone yet?" we asked

"Nope! The moonshine has him so blinded, everyone has a chance to scamper away, before he gets the shell in the chamber.

"Jesus Christ! Why hasn't someone just taken the damned fool thing away from him?"

"Be my guest." grinned the wise little hobo. "TIl tell you one thing though, he sure is irritated with someone."

It did not take a psychic to figure out who that would be, not for Skeeter and I. " When did he start firing the shotgun?"

"Oh, I'd say about an hour ago. Weve just been trying to stay out of his way ever since."

This was a significant revelation. He had not had time to sober up. Maybe we could get in close enough to take him down before he did become sober. We heard another shotgun blast back near the boxcars. I went one way Skeeter the other. I kept checking under the cars to make certain, I knew, where Skeeter was located.

I was ready with my service revolver, to put a round through Clermont, but I did not want to accidentally hit my own man.

Suddenly on the other side of the boxcars there were two pairs of legs. One wore jeans, the other khaki. The dungarees lunged at the khaki-colored legs. I heard the blast of a shogun at point blank range. The denim-colored legs rocketed backward. I immediately scrambled under the cars to the other side behind the Khaki colored legs. Clermont turned, with the shotgun leveled on my mid-section. He pulled the trigger. The gun made a harmless dicking noise.

"Don't move!" I demanded, holding my service revolver on his chest. This is where police training is ambiguous. If you order a perpetrator; not to move, and they do move, I really believe you should be able to shoot them. A suspect should stand as still as a statue. They should literally freeze. If they breath, cough, fart, anything: they are in motion, and the officer should fire.

A little voice in the back of my mind kept saying; I was not a bonafide officer of the law. I hoped, the expression on my face, did not give away my indecision. Time solidifies, there was this moment, nothing else existed. Another voice in my subconscious mind told me; to wait for the ballet move.

Clermont rose up into a round house kick. I caught his ankle with my free hand. My other hand, the one holding the gun, twisted down forming a trustworthy fist. I unloaded my full arm's length into the small area between his wide spread legs. His khaki clad body, folded up into a withering mass, that resembled a crumpled grocery bag. Lite whimpering suck sounds came from his excruciatingly curled lips

I slipped a nylon bundle tie around his neck and connected him to a section of abandoned railroad track. Another of the self-locking straps went around his hands. I left him like that, kicking and cussing.

Skeeter flashed into my mind. My last vision of him. was like that of a rag doll, being tossed from a moving train. I ran over to him and picked up his head in my arms. His eyes were rolled back in his head, but he was still breathing. When I checked his eyes, his pupils were declared. It looked like his vision was beginning too dear. He started to speak.

"Come closer..." he groaned "He got me in.

"Your OK Skeeter.

" I interrupted. My emotions were unchecked. I glanced at his jacket; it was in shreds.

"Closer..." Skeeter beckoned. "He got me in the.

"Skeeter, don't talk save your strength." I begged.

He got me in the co. . .the co. . Skeeter paused, He was trying to gulp down breathes of air. His color returned to his face.

He got this mischievous grin on his face. "Just a little closer.. he begged.

I was holding him so close our faces were almost touching.

He move his lips to whisper in my ear. "He shot me in the computer sucker." he smiled, then he kissed me on the lips.

I dropped him in the dirt like a foul odor. My face withered up resembling an allergic reaction to a lemon. the only thing I could think of to say was; "Ugh!". Then I tried to spit the kiss off my lips. "Skeeter you sick puppy!"

I reached down to where his jacket was shredded and checked inside. There was no blood. Sure, enough he had been making the computer around his neck inside his jacker. He was laughing, coughing and laughing. Lying on his back like a stoned cockroach he was laughing at me. I pulled him to his feet. He started to pass out.

The retort of the shotguns, had only knocked the wind out of him.

"Where did you get the computer?" I asked the grinning jerk.

He still seemed to think something was funny.

"Peggy Sue gave it to me."

"What for?"

"So, I would have something to pawn to buy a ticket to

California." he tried to explain.

"YOU STOLE IT! Didn't you?" I corrected as I went over to check on Clermont. I checked his pockets and found his car keys.

I was sorry now that I let the air out of the tires. I always wanted to test drive the new Jeepster.

"No I didn't You can ask her yourself."

"Don't think I won't." I warned.

EPILOGUE

A telephone call to my residence in Washington led me to believe there was nothing to return to there. Besides becoming quiet, the merchant in stone sculptures, he had also opened up a bible study studio for the homeless in my apartment. My personal belongings had been placed into storage with the exception of my telephone answering machine. This he found to be most effective in keeping his social register in order.

Skeeter never did make it to California. He and Peggy Sue fell into love, over the fact, her computer had saved his life. They re-marked; how this was proof, they were soul mates. I had to keep the air conditioner running all the way to El Paso to eliminate the window fog from the back seat. The steam was one thing, the grunts, groans, and other noises, were abominable. I was glad it was only a two-hour drive.

"What do you think they'll do with Charles?" she asked, on one of the rare occasions she came up for air.

"Clermont will end up in one of those federal prisons. I wouldn't worry about him though. Federal prisons are as nice as any private club. He'll probably write a book and come out in ten years with a small fortune." I answered, breaking two of the seven deadly sins; covetousness and envy.

"What are you going to tell your parents about your experiences?" I asked trying to interrupt the love-making award.

"I don't know, I'll decide when I finally get to see them.

She stated exhaling deeply.

"Your parents are in El Paso. Aren't they?" Mr. full attention was focused on how she would answer this question.

"Oh, you mean the Starr's!" she giggled. "They are not my real parents you know.

I prepared myself for the father- daughter significance, we were both going to share, in a few moments. It made me feel a little dizzy. It is funny how emotions overwhelm a person, just before they know they will share a moment of tenderness. A tear started to form in my eye. I pulled the car over on the shoulder.

Without explanation, I pulled back onto the pavement. Now, El Paso was only an hour away.

When the Starrs, saw Peggy Sue, it was hugs and kisses all around. Clyde was about to burst with pride. The Countess nuzzled the girl affectionately, as we made our way to the comfort of the veranda. Skeeter almost looked jealous. Beer? Why sure.

Now I decided to bring up the subject of paternity. The Countess was in an uncustomary loss of composure.

Peggy Sue offered," Clyde here gets paid a hundred thousand dollars a year, to be my guardian, till I turn twenty-one. Wait till they find out The Stars haven't known where I was for the last six months! BOY HOWDY. Mom and dad will sure be pissed when they get back from Europe."

The Countess turned pale. Her rational mind however was as quick as ever. She has always been able to our run me. She was across the Grand Dirch before I could catch up to her. As long as she stays on her side of the border, she should be safe. I have this funny thing about Mexico. But that's another story.

END

SUCCUBUS

BY FREDERICK DALPAY

FOREWORD

Congress shall make no law respecting an establishment of religion, or prohibiting the free exercise thereof; or abridging the freedom of speech, or of the press; or the right of the people peaceably to assemble, and to petition Government for a redress of grievances.

-First Amendment –

CHAPTER ONE

He told her to hit the bricks. Jake knew if he kept listening, she would keep talking. With the slamming of a door, she went away. He did not want to be right. He just knew he was right. Jake even hoped he was wrong about her, the same way a parent hopes his child is not part of a cult. He reminded himself, he was not her parent, lover or priest. It was too late to be any of those.

Monica was just some bar fly, who showed up on his doorstep. She was looking for a stable environment. First, she stayed a week, then a month, now she'd been underfoot six months. He thought things would eventually work out for the woman. But, if she kept talking, she would only force a warped reality on Jake. A persuasion of perception without evidence to support her claims.

It was not bad enough; she believed her own nonsense. She wanted Jake himself to believe. Ile refused to believe gibberish, and now to even listen. Monica put out a thick musk of sexual tension, without presenting any mechanism for release. It was time for Monica to leave.

Many men would listen to her, hoping a little sympathy would result in getting laid. She would drone on under a full load of alcohol. She could match the suitor drink for drink. This tiny woman drinking at the same speed as a man two or three times her size. No wonder, she would occasionally fall into a stupor, with her legs spread.

The drinkers both knew what was going on, when they started drinking. Her legs akimbo. Her rational mind shut down. It is not rape, when the woman does not protest. She woke up with many strangers.

But not Jake, he wanted something satisfying and personal. He wanted an intertwining of spirits, not just a commingling of body part. He wanted something real and tangible. He wanted an embrace without the element of prostitution. Jake was looking for the type of encounter, that made him feel good about himself, not sponsor self-loathing. He rejected Monica's invitations, which he viewed as a pornographic cartoon.

The clowns would come and go. It was good for a quick tumble in the hay. Monica went out over and over, just like a spider, but she was looking for human prey. She required a patron to provide her chosen lifestyle with its amenities. Smoke a little pot, take a mood enhancing prescription, wash it down with a beer. Spread those legs.

Jake was concerned but he was not stupid. He knew; she would swing by his place to crash, before heading out on her next adventure. Monica would leave, but she would be back. Even when Jake told her, he was well aware of her activities, she would always return. He told her to get out, and stay out, but she was convinced he would take her back. Jake wisely ignored her sexuality, knowing; to sleep with her meant -she would never leave.

Her bar fly lifestyle was the process of many years of self-abuse. It was not his fault, but somehow, she could work her argument to include Jake in her complaints.

She had a simple system. First, she would locate a potential suitor. Second, she would explain how horrible her present lover treated her. Then she would allow the man to beg her to leave, and come with him. Her new lover probably meant for the evening. She would own the bedroom by breakfast, the kitchen by lunch, and the rest of the apartment by dinner time. She would use this tripod action in infinite variations, to the point she did not need a permanent address except for mail.

So, Jake's place was nothing more than a letter drop. Monica's little office of affairs. If he allowed her to talk, Jake would have to listen to the same garbage, with a different twist to the information. The conversations were one sided anyway.

He told Monica to quit. Quit drinking, quit smoking pot, quit using mood altering prescriptions. Quit sleeping around. Quit using him as a pawn for her excursions. The words would rattle around an empty skull with no effect.

No, he did not want to know how this fellow or that fellow, made her do shameful things. "First he made me sit like this. Then he made me touch him. He touched me. He grabbed me..."

Jake knew full well, she was only trying to provoke him to assume those same positions. Besides, she was not ashamed of anything. She liked the rough treatment, or she wouldn't take part.

For the most, she was only describing what people do when they have sex. The same information is available in the letters section of any adult magazine. Her tactic seemed to be centered on a moral compromise, to be turned to her advantage. Monica was only claiming to be remorseful, so Jake would grant her absolution. Her descriptions were calculated to mortify him, mitigate her, and induce his participation in a sick fantasy.

Monica was a creature, not a woman. She was a Succubus, a cleverly disguised demon of seduction. She had learned early; her looks would provide everything she needed and desired. She only had to summons a few tears, while spinning a plausible story. It worked when she was ten years old. She was still using the dramatics as a woman. She nurtured the stories when she fifteen, twenty, twenty-five and thirty. This was her instinctive reaction to how well the subterfuge worked, on those she wished to impress.

As her small town grew larger and larger, she modified and enhanced her performance. Monica would wear out her welcome in one circle of friends, then move on to the next. She was readily accepted into any new group of an expanding community. Introduced to all the most eligible men, regardless of marital status. She never seemed to gravitate to developing friendships with other women. While the ladies clucked away in the kitchen, Monica was prone to entertaining the men in the living room.

She never was without an invitation to dine; lunch, dinner, or especially breakfast.

Of course, lunch and dinner invitations could result in window shopping. Window shopping leads to a new wardrobe. She knew, men could not resist any excuse to impress the damsel in distress, she so convincingly portrayed. Men were such suckers. They deserve to be taken for the advantage. She received rent and transportation, along with any number of nostrums to ease her discomfort. In her wake she left the quivering husks of former men whose lives she had shattered.

Always the innocent maiden, at the whim of an unforgiving universe, she would ensnare a willing participant. The rescuer never realizing the peril of his circumstance until far too late. Just like the rabbit still struggling to survive as the snake's venom is absorbed, such were her victims.

Men would toy with the idea of leaving their present lover for Monica. The last person they wanted to learn of this flirtation was always the first to make the discovery. Monica herself, would inform these women, "I am in, and you are out!" This would force the man to back-peddle, soul search and make promises to the offended lover. If he chose the former relationship over Monica, she would appear in the proximity of the lovers with enough regularity, to call the romance into question. If he chose Monica, she would quickly loose interest.

For sport she may keep him on the hook. She was always able to pit this man against some other man. She liked to think of herself as a trophy.

Monica could have been a direct descendant of the harpies and sirens; her deception was so complete. No mortal woman should be capable of refining such seduction, in a single lifetime, without demonic intervention. Nothing inflames passion like the deflowering of the virtuous. This was her facade. An act she practiced on the world stage. A drama to which she was Queen.

Then there was Jake. He could look within the woman and see the demon. He had made his peace with the insanity of the siren's song. This was not the first succubus he had ever encountered. The phenomenon was very familiar to him. By all outside appearances the creature looked like a normal woman. Within the physique was a cold dark heart, beating pickled poisonous blood, to the ruin of any man. The warmth of her touch was not from a momentary caress, it was from being dissolved in her venom. Her victims pumping life into her, as they pump life away from their own needs. She would gain everything, their money, their reputation, and their vital life force. They would be reduced from a vigorous being, to an animated corpse whose pulverized brain no longer exhibited a free will.

The nature of men, she knew too well. They only wished to possess the object of desire. Once obtained the object could control the man. If a man obtains a pile of gold, he must now protect the gold with all his waking moments. He must surrender his spirit to the protection of his possessions. Gold is an inanimate object, thereby being simply protected.

A woman, especially a succubus, constantly proves any means of defense futile. She will not be treated as an inanimate object. Little by little he surrenders his free will to her dominance, losing his own spirit in the process. The man toils away plunging his flesh into her flesh, in the mistaken belief satisfaction would result. Sex without trust is simply a narcotic. Only later the victim would find the most powerful narcotic is also the most fleeting.

Jake knew he could never trust Monica. Any attempt at sexual liaison was at the risk of becoming dependant on her narcotic effect.

Jake was perceptive enough to understand the equation the she devils presented. His rational mind determined if A is true, and B is true, then A plus B must be true. She had already proven she could not be satisfied. *A: The line procession of former paramours and husbands proved; she ignited passion without cooling the flames of desire. B: Among her entourage were several human puppies, sniffing around, hoping their friendship would be rewarded. A plus B equals she is a she- demon.*

Perhaps it was an underdeveloped brain stem which would not allow this she-devil to accept responsibility for her misadventures. If in fact, she was conscious of her actions, she was a demon of the first order.

There was always the possibility she did the devils bidding without his instructions. As with so many moderns, she denied a spiritual existence, which Beelzebub himself strongly endorsed. Focus on the scientific and reject the unseen spiritual landscape. Forget the ancients, trying desperately to describe in human terms, the consequence of man's actions.

To Jake the equation was very simple. Time is only resolved in one direction. Any random event could be interpreted as time zero. Time zero evolves with a collection of foreseeable results dependant on variables. Time does not stand waiting to mature into a different dimensional representation. Anything starting at a given moment in time will have a probable result. Time zero plus time end, results in a description of a time interval. One description may be a scientific explanation, and another may be a spiritual explanation. Both descriptions may be accurate. The resolution of the convergent methodologies depends upon artificial symbols, or more simply-Art.

For Jake the elements of spiritual and scientific did not always overrule each other. On the contrary they reinforced each other. Noah had his Ark. The geological record proved some ten thousand years ago the icecaps melted, flooding human habitation in the known world. It is unclear if Noah was a Hebrew, however the evidence supports he was a survivor. One man's mystery is another man's history. If people take the time to preserve a record of an event, it is only a question of the language they employ

Therefore, mediaeval man described his relationship to civil realization in terms of spiritual understanding. It would follow that stoning the succubus, was the right thing to do at the time. In the dark ages, transportation was as swift as an ox cart, communication was limited to word of mouth. The virtuous woman was exalted. The succubus got stoned, literally.

Eight hundred years later, rehabilitation of the succubus was the preferred methodology. With better roads and telephones, the non-virtuous could disguise her actions. She could be sixty miles away from discovery before her actions were known. A debutante in Orlando, could be a slut in Miami.

Jake figured the mediaeval method was a bit wasteful, if not practical. This was before he realized the very essence of the succubus was to suspend disbelief. He knew there was a set of numbers termed irrational, but what he did not realize was the dependence of a succubus on this set of integers. Any attempt to communicate was an opportunity to walk away calculating the square root of two, mentally. Jake tried to live in a rational world.

"Jake, tell me how you feel about Homosexuals?" the little Harpy coyly dropped into the middle of a conversation.

"Well, in the strictest sense, anyone who masturbates is by definition Gay. Because, they are having sex with a member of their own sex!" He offered, knowing it would cause a spiraling cascade in her own sexual identity. He responded to all her follow-up questions with silence.

She decided to pull out all the stoppers in the next interrogation. Some way, somehow, she was going to get to this guy. Even if she had to serve him, up like a four-course banquet, he would suffer. She was going to make him sorry, he ever had the nerve, to show her the least molecule of sympathy. She even envisioned leading him around by a bridled scrotum, like some prized quarter horse. Someday Jake would pay.

Jake for his part could see this coming a mile away. He did not wish to become a sexual zombie. He could examine the condition of her former lovers, husbands and children. All of which swirled around a vortex of her abuse and neglect. Nothing was more important than her own hedonistic pursuits. She would continue to generate new problems, for those within her sphere of influence, until someone ended the cycle. Jake saw himself as one of the mechanisms, to end the sequence of events.

He rationalized; she only needed to enter into a period of self-reflection, to bring her misery to an end. But, for her part, Monica lived in an irrational world. She viewed herself as a lightning rod for misfortune. She imagined herself never to be held accountable for the misery she endured. It was the fault of all those factors working against her. Her abuse of alcohol, drugs, and sex were the result of her condition -not the cause of her problems. Her sick little fantasy.

CHAPTER TWO

Jake had his own problems. He was in the middle of negotiations with investors, without the full support of his partners. They kept telling him to continue with the project, while withholding financial support. Somehow, he was using his own monies to push the project along, wondering when they were going to jump in and assist him.

Every project needed at least three people, to put together all the sorted technicalities. Jake was always the one who analyzed the finer details. Elephant boy was the nuts-and-bolts equipment man. Alabama was the deep pockets. Working alone was simply a foolish thing to do.

The clients were always satisfied with the product, small independent theatrical productions. Little church fund raisers. Nondenominational charity affairs, with just enough combined ticket sales to break even, after everyone was paid. The motivation was education and community development. Say no to drugs, work with your neighbors to clean up the neighborhood, give a pint of blood. That sort of thing.

Freewheeling without Elephant Boy and Alabama was a chore. Jake had to spend too much energy, giving the client, - face time. He was just not cut out to carry the whole project on his own. Bama, was the cocktails and dinner business guy. He had a natural grace at this sort of thing, which would always ease the client into a sense of being in good company. Elephant boy on the other hand was like a teenage motor head. He could spew a long list of components in such a torrent, the client did not have time to doubt the need for the equipment being provided. Jake was simply the knuckle buster, who kept the whole thing rolling smoothly.

Jake would always say the wrong thing at the wrong time. He might mention a celebrity by name for -emphasis. It was only a gesture of irrelevant allusion. Later he would realize the client misunderstood the reference to mean they thought the celebrity would be involved. If the topic was film stock, he might mention Alfred Hitchcock or Steven Spielberg, as a reference between black and white compared to color. What he was describing was the limitations of 35 mm photography. What the client heard was Stephen Spielberg was part of the crew.

Bama would never give off an impression like that. Elephant boy would have droned on and on about lighting, camera angle and a thousand other technical details, never once mentioning Mr. Spielberg. So, Jake had to spend as much time on damage control, as he did on presentation to a client.

Another major fault with having Jake as the point man, was his colorful language skills. He would be eloquently describing a course of events, when to emphasize a point, out of nowhere he produced a cursive remark. A singular vulgarity may be overlooked, but Jake did not stop at small inconspicuous utterances. The more excited he became, the more cussing he employed to emphasize his point. Blame it on the Navy.

It really did not matter if the client was a church deacon or a priest, even a nun for that matter. Jake had read the bible cover to cover. He was certain, at one time or another, the book had explored every human condition. For his part, he was just using modern terminology to describe biblical reference. He did not invent the words he just used them. Sure, he knew the terminology was vulgar. He also knew Spanish, French and English were all vulgarities of Latin. Latin was a vulgarity of Greek, Phoenician, and Hebrew. Russian was another language arising from the banality of Latin, Greek, Hebrew and Persian.

Traveling all the way back these spoken languages were in some way influenced by Egyptian, Sanskrit, and Chinese.

In his own way Jake was contributing to the evolution of the spoken word. Vulgarities and Banalities were what kept the process of communication moving toward ultimate perfection.

Jake even knew that once upon a time, India had been a drifting continent, which slammed into Asia. The monks of Tibet had stubbornly stood their ground as the Himalayas rose thirty thousand feet into the sky. He could only imagine all the vulgarities they invented to describe the experience. Warfare and vulgarities were what fueled cultural awareness. Treaties and arguments over terminology promote civil realization.

Each civilization is only looking for a land promising an opportunity to evolve toward Utopia. In the long history of man there has been some other culture, nipping at its heels.

Each culture has always determined its own standards for written documentation, even if the record of a transaction was nothing more than a tattoo. Any conflict of cultural standards has always been used as an excuse for warfare. Without diplomacy the globe has been subdivided innumerable times. So many times, people realized; they would have to agree on a lawful standard of conduct. Even this was not good enough. Now instead of tribal retribution the stage was set for national identity.

Here is where a well-timed profanity is not only handy but also required. Laws within the confines of national borders are always the target of detractors. The truth is the detractor is not willing to follow the law of the land. The supporters of the detractors use every excuse except the truth. Collaboration and rebellion have been going on for thousands of years. It doesn't look like it is going to end any time soon, damn it.

Refinement of laws and cultural affectations has always been the result of post-war strategy. For a thousand years, if the rebels were not put to the sword, they were sold into slavery. And slavery is fertile grounds for propagating colorful language.

With slavery is also the rise of despotic government identity, using any vindication to eliminate opposition. Borders are crossed to escape persecution, with every practical experiment of governance. Even democracy is only experimental.

Eventually the human race ran out of room. In all this time the justification for torment and torture went unsatiated under the pretext of national defense.

First comes language, then comes a border. Sometimes, lawless behavior on one side, was legitimate commerce in the corresponding land. Issues of personal freedom were resolved at the border with a gun. This went on for hundreds of years. War became an apology for the diplomatic process of constitutional government. There was always a race to improve ordinance and ammunition. The population of the planet always seemed to focus on the depravity of its neighbors, without recognizing personal lawlessness. Communications and diplomacy, education and government intervention; slowly ended the mass homicide for political gain. But providing a service on one side of a border, became a business opportunity on the side of a border. Feigning an injustice by the political elite of one nation, advances the migration of the downtrodden. No sooner are they granted asylum; they construct the very device they were ridiculed for in their land of origin. Drugs, sex, hygienic practices, polygamy, predatory behavior toward children; all cultural affectations carried in the baggage of the traveler. The newly established visitors construct an enclave of the behavior they regard normal.

They also carry with them the means toward retribution against their former oppressors. As a means to an end, the new arrival, may seek to service the debauchery of the existing population. Recruiting the support of the existing population is as timeless as warfare itself. It makes for short supply lines.

Complicity on the basis of naive depravity and curiosity, cannot be underestimated. Curiosity alone is enough to compromise an otherwise honest man. There is nothing more curious than sex. Exploration of cultural affectations may lead the initiate to become a devout follower of some obscure sect. Some religious variations even offer sacraments including; vision producing mushrooms, and the opportunity for lots of sex.

A religious anomaly, offered to the unwary and uneducated. Someone unskilled in the approved religious experience is a ready target. There is no wonder the devotee will sometimes sacrifice themselves in a suicide assassination attempt.

He or she is so high with religious fervor, or stoned on mushrooms, it is impossible to distinguish reality. It is impossible to separate a drug induced vision of the Creator, from a normal reliance on Gods will. Having been introduced to devotion under these circumstances, the foolish seek to convert as many possible bystanders, when the bomb explodes.

What started as curiosity, promoted by normal sexual commingling, has a tragic result. The entire event ends up on the cover of a newspaper. Allah, Yahwe, Buddha, even Jesus Christ, it was never a religious question. It was an act of a risk taker under the influence of a political goal.

Risk takers almost always hazard experimentation. Their hormones influence their behavior. The risk takes on an alibi of dependable behavior. If this were not true, there would be no singles bars. But first they have to be recruited.

The target group for recruitment is anyone with pubic hair, who has not yet graduated from college. First, they are influenced to condone small civil discrepancies. Next, they are told to disregard any legal authority, who has reason to disapprove of a singular behavior. The recruiter then should eliminate any lingering suspicion the behavior has any serious consequence.

When a secular atrocity is committed under the guise of religious fervor, steps must be taken to exonerate the clergy. The parishioner must have been acting alone. Mitigating circumstances, are proven to cause an observable wrong.

Jake saw these things for what they were; just another opportunity to trot out a hooker in a party dress and call her a debutante. With minor variations the same could be apply to race, national origin, and sexual orientation. Recruit the weak-willed individual, and pardon the conduct under the title of Freedom. Use the recruit to pester your enemies.

He knew; for the last fifty years, little piss-ant third world nations, had been playing the United States against the Soviet Union. He just could not prove it, until the Communist all went underground, with the collapse of the Soviet Block. The communists were still out there, putting on party dresses.

These same piss-ant countries were now blowing sunshine up the skirt of capitalism. Sometimes attempting to gain entry to the United States solely on the basis of religious persecution, they packed into the only game in town. It was beginning to be easier to track the variables. Jake was getting closer to the truth.

Jake was not in the business of collecting the truth. He was in the business of producing small carnivals as charity events. So, to skip to the short version; he would sometimes blurt out a colorful phrase. When he used the word "Fuck", it was a condensed version for what he observed happening in the nation.

His audience did not always view his speech patterns with the same forgiveness. With each vulgarity the purse strings would draw tighter, until the client decided to look elsewhere for the talent they needed. Damn, lost another one.

The client never seemed to understand all the work it takes. Even to get to the point, where they could discuss the charity drive, took a lot of effort. These things were not simple bake sales in the auditorium. This was building a little tent city for a weekend. Jake would tour the site, take measurements, custom create a carnival atmosphere right down to the Porto-potties.

There were lists of equipment to put on hold; Climbing walls, with moon walks and trampolines. This all needed to be done out front, so Bama could make a presentation. But Bama was not available this time. Jake was on his own and out of pocket. Who knows where Elephant Boy was hiding? He owed Jake money; therefore, he was very hard to reach.

Where the sponsor got Jake's number was a complete mystery. He was always a member of a team, never a freelance. What was more important, he did not feel comfortable carrying the full load. Sure, he knew all the technical and administrative work. These things were simply too complicated for one man working alone. Not that there was much profit. These things were a side job at best. It was something to do when nothing else was happening. Sure, the sponsor could double their money overnight, but for the running crew it was almost minimum wage. Jake still wanted to unravel the mystery how the sponsor got his number.

This neighborhood was in desperate need of a charity event. It was not a neighborhood at all; it was the "Hood". It was a post-Civil war relic, of black emancipation in the rural south. An experiment forced on whites and blacks by the victorious northern carpetbaggers.

This section of town was originally a scarcely inhabited agricultural community. Baptist, Methodist and Catholic missionaries took the notion of supporting a multi-cultural, ethnically integrated social experiment. A rural experiment, that a century later would be a desperate island of poverty, inside a modern city landscape.

Each and every step of the path they collectively considered the needs of the residents; white, black, Hispanic, Greek, French, Indian, English, Yankee and confederate. The law of the land was the United States Constitution. And it worked, at least for some it worked. Explanation for how well it worked, depended on who was responding to the question.

Those who showed up for church on a regular basis, thought it worked pretty good. Those who did not attend meetings, being unaware of their civic obligation, did not think it worked at all. Adding to the confusion was the people who did not attend the meetings but did attend the church socials. They thought it sort of worked, maybe not!

Well, why not? This is where a fellow has to come up with an excuse plenty quick. The invention of the Shuck and Jibe. He really can not mention he was too hung-over to get to the meeting on time. He can't even mention he was not there. The only reason he showed up at the afternoon social, was to avoid cooking at home. Also, there is the element of the fox, visiting the best and the only hen house in town. After a night spent chasing the sporting women on the Orange Blossom Trail, he is looking for something easier to pen down. Given the correct enticement he might consider becoming hen pecked, even if it did mean attending meetings on a regular basis. To make matters worse this is the guy who offers an objective opinion.

The objective opinion of all the various ethnic groups was; "Their kind are being made to feel inferior by members of the other groups represented.". It was a plausible answer. It was a answer all the deacons, priests, rabbis and holy men could endorse.

They never even considered the source. Shuck and Jibe was an easy thing to sell in the carpet bagger era. Perhaps it was taken under recommendation, because they had all been young once. This atoned for anything they may have done, prior to being saved by the grace of God.

Being a spiritual community, the first action was to provide a house of worship for each of the various groups. Then as time went by separate schools appeared. Separate schools led the way for separate housing Separate but equal was never considered. No one ever considered this practice - Segregation.

At that time, this was a rural community with an agricultural economy. A level of truancy was expected, with absolution granted as a demand for the crops. Some took full advantage of the state funded educational opportunity. Some did not. The pleasant conditions of the southern climate proved irresistible to many.

Hooky was met with different measures of disdain in differing segments of the population. Funding from the State was on a per-capita basis. It was in the interest of the various schools to keep students registered, even when the truancy rate reached seventy and eighty percent.

The exception was those damned Catholics, where the church and schools were connected. The poor students did not get a fair shake. The schools always kept the student pinned to a desk, unless they had a damned good excuse, in writing, in triplicate. Failure to comprehend the assignment was not an option. The only way to escape the tutelage of the monks, nuns, and priests was to finish the assignment. They did not make any exception based on race or nationality, because the teachers were a combination of every imaginable cultural identity. They also had no place to run off to; because they all took a vow of chastity, and did not date. Oh, those poor students! From home, to school, to church. Day in and day out, until graduation. A minimum eighteen-year sentence, with the only possible parole; successful completion of the recommended course work to include geometry, physics and Latin. Roman Latin not Latino Spanish. The derivative Latin of *veni vidi vici*. The Latin of every vulgar modern language in Christian countries throughout the globe. At the same time the student was required to base his actions on humility, always serving his common man. Those damn Catholics.

With a segment of the population enjoying a seventy percent truancy rate, and another segment of the population allowed none, there is going to be disparity. The inequality of those equipped to handle life's trials and tribulations was enormous. From an educational level alone, the truant students lost ground from the very first day they skipped school. Troublesome to the successful graduate of the system, was the "service to mankind" clause of the agreement. Even when encountering repeated argumentation by the less qualified individual, the graduate was duty bound to deal fairly and humanely every time.

As if this was not bad enough, the education prohibited suicide, when the task of dealing fairly became overwhelming. What it all boiled down to was; by the end of the century, when complicated machined and engineered stuff became available, some acquired more stuff than others. The trend continued with those who took advantage of education. They were able to acquire more stuff than those who did not.

So, going back to the fellow who suggested segregation in the first place. He was proven wrong. Every child feels inferior to the outside world. This is exactly why they are so small. They learn to be humble, so when they reach their full potential, they will be something besides a pain in the ass.

If someone makes elaborate excuses for their own behavior it is one thing. If they project the excuses onto their young, they retard the full potential of the next generation.

Here, almost five generations later, stood the result of all the excuses. The small town was becoming a big city. A big city with a two square mile slum right in the middle of it. All around prosperity could be seen, but not in the Hood.

Somehow there were still believers in the original experiment. The rate of success was supportive enough, that those who participated were rewarded. Those who did not, made more excuses. Through it all, there were those so Jack Ass stubborn, they refused to allow the dream to die. After a hundred years it looked like it was going to work. At least to the limitations of a small rural agricultural community. But this rural community was growing into an urbanized business center.

The pot would boil for another fifty years, before Jake realized there was something defiantly wrong.

CHAPTER THREE

Jake suddenly understood the production costs were putting a drain on his accounts. If he did not start separating personal funds, from production funds, he would end up broke.

He took his bank account and cut it in half. He then took that money, placing it in an account with the bank who held his mortgage. Now his personal finances were in one bank, and his business finances were in another. Or, so he thought.

What Jake needed was a couple part time employees to help him keep everything moving. This is where the story of Jake, takes a turn for the worse, and becomes the story of Poor Jake.

The proposal was simple. Put together a Halloween Spook house. That is what the client said they wanted: Characters dressed in spooky costumes, rattling chains, fog from dry ice, hidden doorways, spooky music. Jake even had the perfect house. As an investment he had picked up an old farm house in the hood. It was a spare time project, where he had been rebuilding the house for several years. The old farm house had wooden floors and a ransacked exterior. Splash around some ultraviolet paint, and it would be the perfect spook house.

Spook houses are a natural. You just sneak up on little children and scare the be-Jesus out of them. Send them in the front door, and then let them run horrified out the back door. Five minutes alone in a spooky old house for a two-dollar contribution is a thrilling experience for any kid. Adolescents love to pretend they were not frightened. Five bucks for an adult.

The thing could turn a profit after the first week. Let it run three weeks and the sponsor has a hefty profit, with all the bills paid. If all goes well, the spook house is a decent business, and in no time becomes an annual event. At least that is the way these things are supposed to work.

As poor Jake would learn; sometimes people arc unemployable, because they never developed the talents to find a job. Other than the obvious, strippers and exotic dancers are among these unemployable people. The boyfriend of a stripper can sometimes be included in this group.

The boyfriend is even less employable, given the fact he can't even provide a lap dance. Surely, he can sometimes make a good nanny, a service he provides, while his old lady is at the job. This is sometimes the limit of his creativity. Any other talents he possesses is usually limited to procurement of contraband, and therefore not a commercial aptitude. It is the result of playing hooky. Without a girlfriend this guy would be homeless.

A really talented boyfriend may know how to cook up a batch of methyl-amphetamine. Or, break into cars at the strip joint. Also, a few play the cuckold so well, they encourage patrons of a strip club to grope and paw their mate. Dollar after dollar is parked in a garter belt or G-string.

Jake called it the twenty-minute theory. Go into any strip club with twenty dollars, and it will be gone in twenty minutes. Five dollars for a single beer, fifteen dollars in tips. Nobody ever got drunk at a strip club. The dancers hover over the patrons like a bunch of buzzards, each pecking at the corpse, until it is picked clean. That is even without a two-minute lap dance for five dollars. For the amateur anatomy student, the lesson is prohibitively expensive. Better to spend money at a Community College where credits are counted.

Still there are times when a man should be reminded of the appearance of a nude woman. When his wife or girlfriend leaves him for no apparent reason. When he's been in boot camp for six months. When he reads a Dear John letter from back home. Sometimes as a comparison to the woman he will marry in the morning. Even occasionally using the encounter as a morbid remembrance of a long lost loved one. Where better than a strip joint, to choose from living attributes.

When dealing with a stripper, the employment interview is a comical event. On the application, no reference is ever presented to expose the possibility of an elaborate lap dance in progress. Sure, she is nervous and overly friendly with an enthusiasm hard to match. That is her normal occupation! The last thing she is going to mention is needing your pathetic job as a tax dodge for her stripper earnings.

The application shows she earned a degree. What is not apparent is she banged all her professors. They're not going to say anything in order to protect their tenure.

Probably the most important thing to remember about a stripper; her primary mission in life is to get the money from your wallet into her purse. She'll brag, about dragging in four bills in a shift. Even without a degree in economics, this should be plenty of income. A quick check of expenses shows this is not true. Hair, nails, makeup and costumes; half a bill. Mood enhancing prescription, mound of Cocaine, a couple bottles of formula for the kids, the budget is pretty tight. She is back down to the earning potential of the checkout girl at the grocery store. Incidentally, the checkout girl at the grocery will give you correct change from a twenty-dollar bill without being groped.

As an employer you don't know why you hired her, except she makes you feel good about yourself. Isn't that exactly the job description of a stripper. After she is hired, she will only strut around from desk to desk wearing high heel shoes, because that is her true aptitude. She insulates her position with the company by becoming involved with everyone's business.

Where ever she goes she leaves a fragrance in the wake. She accomplishes nothing on her own, taking credit for the hard work of less -ethereal employees.

You Chump! Your first clue should have been when she accidentally brushed her hand against your inner thigh. That never happens, with the homely office girls, wearing sneakers and cheap perfume. If she was actually doing her job for the company, her arms would have been full of documents fresh from the copy room. But, if her arms were full, her hand could not reach crotch level.

Do any of the homely women come into your office crying about how all the other women hate her? You know why! They actually earned their position of employment.

But as egocentric as any employer may be, the moment of truth will arrive. The final reality check comes when an employer walks into a topless joint, and finds his prize employee on the stage. Suddenly, the ability of a four hundred dollar a week employee, to dress in designer fashions becomes a simple equation.

For the good of the company, she may have to clear out her cubical under the boss's desk. Of course, this might just jeopardize his own position with the company, and possibly with his spouse. She no longer makes the boss feel good about himself. What occupies his time now, is visions of booby-traps exploding, when she climbs under his desk. Preferably, while he is at a meeting with plenty of witnesses. However, the rational takes control and the boss worries about her three children. He lets bygone be bygone. She moves to a corner cubicle, is given a normal workload, and quits because it is too much work. Or she takes over the company, runs it into the ground, then bails out; usually in enough time to put it on her new resume.

How was Jake to know, these were the rules? He had never experienced corporate castration. In all his adult life he had never mixed business with pleasure. He had a job to offer; loosely described as copy, fold, collate and staple.

What high school drop-out could not perform these simple tasks? Well, Candy for one, and her stepsister Daytona for another. Then there was Candy's boyfriend to name a third.

Jake knew Candy was a dancer. Jake would only hire her for light housekeeping. Her boyfriend, who just happened to be Daytona's brother, was said to be a decent carpenter. This proved to be untrue. This left Daytona, as the only possible candidate, for the office work Jake required.

All he had to do was keep the client satisfied, until the Spook house was complete and the venture capital was secure. Then he could bring the whole process to a close. He would return to his normal profession as soon as the charity drive was finished. This was the plan. Oh, poor Jake!

First of all, the charity promoter had contacted him. He did not contact them. Jake based his confidence on his own talents, as was supported by the promoter inquiry. Surely, he could provide all the props and fabrication needed for a Spook house.

Permits were no problem. Insurance for a charity affair was not a problem. Before he realized it, he had spent two weeks in the preparatory process. He was entering the time frame, where it would be nice to have Bama and Elephant boy on board. He needed someone to take part of the work load under consideration. They were busy, so the only alternative was to hire -outsiders.

Candy, her boyfriend and stepsister, were looking to earn money. Remember this: Someone looking for money is not necessarily looking for work. Swinging on a pole naked is not work; it is entertainment. Entertainment suggests the money is a discretionary expense. Work suggests labor has a purpose.

First things first, a small amount of carpentry was required. So, Candy's boyfriend Ned was hired. Ill did not have a lot to do except cut a line after it was marked on a piece of wood. He might have to nail two boards together. He might have to glue or chop or paint. The only trouble was, anything he was asked to do was a source for discussion. He always had a better way to get the task done. The task itself was never completed; it was only discussed. Ned could spend hours describing the work, without ever doing the work. Jake suddenly realized; out of all the work in progress, it was the product of his own labor, never the result of his employee.

Ned stormed off in an angry fit when he was handed a broom to clean up the work site. In short order he returned to demand payment for hours of work which he had not done. This was where Jake should have fired the man.

He realized some of the future labor was going to require two people and could not be done alone. He paid Ned and chalked it up to having a bad day.

So, after paying Ned for hours of work he never did, Jake had to hire Candy to clean up the mess. Candy was a dancer, so, it would follow, Ned had to lurk around in the shadows. He did not trust Jake to be alone with Candy.

Jake never did spend too much time in strip joints, so he did not know too much about cuckold relationships. Jake only knew they were a couple, and as such he respected the exclusive nature of their claim, one to the other. Jake was not interested in a relationship with a dancer in any case.

Candy did what was required in a reasonable amount of time. Just like Ned had done, she demanded payment on the barrel head. When Ned showed up the next day he was rehired. As was Candy rehired to clean up the work site, at the end of the day.

This only left the paperwork piling up on Jake's desk. This is where Daytona fit into the scenario. From all outside appearances she was a dutiful mother of three. Jake had never really known her; he had just seen her from time to time. She was attractive in a down home country girl fashion. Jake had once toyed with the idea of asking her out, but decided she was probably too young. Having made this decision, he would never again consider her as a possible romantic interlude.

He had hired one of Daytona's former boyfriends for a project years ago. The man reported she was a Psycho. That was good enough for Jake. He stored this knowledge away in his memory. Take the prettiest girl out there, and there is some man who is happy she is gone.

CHAPTER FOUR

Poor Jake had a fatal flaw, an Achilles heel. If he said he was going to do something, he would do everything in his power to see that it was done. This was the common perception when Jake was a youth. People just did not make promises they did not intend to keep. The modern world was a big problem for Jake.

Now everyone said anything appropriate at the moment, and later denied saying anything at all. Jake never cultivated the need to present a contract to a prospective Client. His was an act of faith. He could never foresee the need to present in court, a binding document, to show he was working under the direction of the client. However, the Spook house would, once and for all, cure him of his fatal flaw.

With months of work and thousands of dollars invested, not to mention hiring the unqualified, and revisiting their mistakes, the client pulled out. He was standing there with specialized printing and tickets. He had costumes, props, performers and personnel to put together this charity affair. And the client decided to go in a different direction.

"Why, at least tell me why?"

"We do not approve of the lifestyle of your employees." was their honest reply. Never trust an evangelist. They go wherever the spirit leads, and take the money with them.

So, there you have it. Point blank, right between the eyes. Jake wasted months he would never get back, to provide a service to a community, toying with an idea. They contacted him, he did not contact them! What a gala foul up!

The only thing to do now was go back to the crew and tell them they were all fired. Werewolves, Frankenstein's, Freddy Kruger's, and Elviras, all fired. Lighting technicians, special effects, some guy playing spooky music, fired.

Poor Jake knew there was an alternative. He had brought it this far alone. He pondered self-promotion of the charity event. It would be more difficult to calculate attendance. He could not count on the congregation to show up.

He would have to carefully pique the curiosity of the community. If he could draw them into a level of participation, with the suggestion of having a good time, he could still break even. This was all he had ever expected. He did not do the nonprofit affairs with the expectation of ever-growing wealthy. His professional work was where his real money came from.

The whole concept of a Church bazar, or a bake sale, was to encourage a community to gain a notion of self-pride. This community needed a severe injection of self-awareness. It takes time for a rural Neighborhood to turn into a inner city "Hood". Over the years, homesteads were converted into cheap rental properties. The good residents retreated inside while illegal activities took control of the streets.

His proposal for a Spook house was in response to the observation children in this community did not know anything about Halloween. A simple harvest festival or All Souls Night for the Christians, the children had nothing to break up the monotony of their pathetic lives. The only tricks were being turned by Hookers. The only treats were distributed by bicycle, illegally.

Jake was a tortured genius who chose to use his mind to solve problems. Before too long he convinced himself to promote the Spook house without the investors. Without Mr. Bama or the Elephant boy, he would go it alone. Many tortured geniuses are rock stars or actors, who sink into a morass of drugs and alcohol. Jake had always taken an opposite approach. He would seize an idea like a pit bull with a chew toy. He would maul the concept until it became real or disappeared on its own.

Sure, he went to college. As a neophyte he had done all the experimentation any other student undertakes, as a rite of passage. The difference with Jake was, he never was convinced a departure from reality, was any more significant than reality itself. He liked to believe he was a careful experimenter, taking each new experiment in stride. Even in high school, he like many others tried alcohol. The swimming spinning distortion was a pleasant experience. He did not wish to spend much time in an uncoordinated diminished capacity. Of course, there are those who do!

That happy little hippy crap of sharing a joint, was something which wore thin in short order. The experience was alright except for the procurement process. A buyer has to meet the unhygienic seller, in some unhygienic location. All for the purpose of buying a bag full of stems and seeds. Then there is the ritual aspect of rolling it into a joint, or stuffing it into a bong. The smell of which, was as offensive as a pipe load of mule dung. This was always followed by more ritual. Specifically, discussion of fantastic probabilities with no basis in fact, the pipe dream.

This is where he began to form his opinions, regarding the women in his life. The quickest way to encourage a relationship with a co-ed, was to ask her to smoke a joint. Because it was such a fool proof means, he cultivated a lingering fascination for the process. However, his motivation was to attract a long-term mate.

The reality of the circumstance was that when he ran out of weed, the woman always seemed to lose interest. A plus B equals C. A: She only finds me interesting when she is stoned. B: She'll leave me if I don't get her stoned. C: See you later you skanky bitch, you're obviously not what I was looking for! A simple act of eliminating the variables.

This was where Jake departed from the rest of the experimentation. He had sufficient information to base an expectation on what such a woman would do for a line of cocaine, a sugar cube of LSD, or a monkey tranquilizer. Most of his contemporaries had to see for themselves what a woman would do to get high. Jake simply calculated the outcome. He was not looking for a relationship based on debauchery and abasement.

Once, after what he thought was a normal sexual interlude between two sober consenting adults, his confidence was assaulted. During the cool down cuddle, woman say they need so much in a relationship, the sweethearts entered into small talk. His lover mentioned in passing "If you can come up with some Coke maybe we can do this again." It suddenly dawned on him; he was being drawn into a pattern of prostitution. Sure, he probably could go out looking for some cocaine in some dark alley. It wasn't like this chick was that great in the sack. Now that he thought about it, the whole session was rather mechanical. Prior to this revelation, he had even entertained the notion, she might be the one. But, if she was already a Coke Whore, it only proved she was not the One.

Little did he know at the time, she was as likely a candidate for rehabilitation, as any other woman on the planet. Her name was Nancy, a name he could never forget. She was a good experience for the future quagmire Monica.

Years later when he was offered a bit of a proposition regarding a unique basket in his collection, he simply stated in no uncertain terms; "That would be an act of Prostitution!"

He spoke without reflection of the impact of the statement, with the full knowledge, that this woman may at long last be the one he was searching to find. Worse yet, he made no attempt to clarify his comment. This was no minor flirtation. They were both busy professionals with extremely complicated schedules. This encounter was the result of many months, of hastily planned lunches and dinners, just to bring it to this point. If ever a relationship deserved to experience abandonment of sexual tension, this certainly qualified. That damn basket.

She dropped her enormous -natural breasts back into her Victoria's secret. She tucked her blouse into her tiny waist band. Then she bolted out the door. Jake just laid back on the bed astonished. He knew full well; he probably needed the service she had offered. Jake also knew, it was never going to be offered again. Subsequently he would discover, she was engaged at the time of the encounter. This made the lost opportunity even more bittersweet, depending on interpretation. Ironically the whole misadventure only served to prove, she too was not the One. Her name was Gloria, another name he would never forget.

Whoever said, "hope springs eternal", should have been censored. Jake was not getting any younger, and the likely hood of ever finding a satisfactory relationship was becoming distant. By the time he reached middle age he had taken on the trappings of a cloistered monk. He was not even looking any more. If he found himself staring at a woman, it was only to calculate how much damage she could do to his life.

To his credit, he always presented himself as adequate, but not extravagant. He gave off the persona of honest, maybe poor. As such he was seldom the target of a gold digger. Jake appealed to the type of woman who was an amateur social worker. The trouble being, he was without too many character flaws. He did not present enough of a challenge, for these women specializing in restoration.

Maybe it was for the best. Maybe one day he would compose the perfect country song. Then Willie Nelson could do the song justice. Something about the sex drive, being a barn dance. That ought to do it.

CHAPTER FIVE

Years before the Spook house, Monica entered Jake's life. How he ever became involved with Monica was another minor mystery. Jake was initially attracted to Monica by her iridescent eyes. Her eyes were the color of a mountain stream. They were the same color as a former lover. A woman whom he had concluded in retrospect, was the One and only soul- mate he would ever have. She was twenty years gone, and he still held out hope. He would see her in large crowds, only to find he was mistaken, it was some other woman. What a sap.

It was only a momentary fascination on his part. The brief encounter put Monica on his trail like a bloodhound. She picked up the essence of a vacuum, surrounding the man. The faint hint there was no woman in his life. He was the prefect soil to plant her succubus seed garden.

The very fact he was content with his life, was an irresistible challenge to the succubus sisterhood. No man could ever be allowed to escape, the full depth of misery in the domain of the she-demon. She would ruminate; it was his own fault, for noticing she had pretty eyes.

Her present husband was almost a withered husk. He had almost exhausted himself, providing her incessant demands for more booze and more drugs. What energy remained was drained by sexual marathons, too strenuous for even the Marquis de Sade. The man was only thirty and appeared sixty. As life was sucked out of the man, Monica took on the disguise of a much younger woman. The ever-expanding universe between her thighs was the only evidence her innocence was only an allusion. Had her present husband been less culpable to her attractions, he would have realized her anatomy was just a snare trap.

Within the final moments of their marriage, the husband gathered just enough strength to fend off her assault. As if in a moment of clarity, he saw her for what she really was; a Succubus. A man, suddenly fighting for his life, is a violent creature. Monica was battered to the point, where she looked like she had been in a car wreck. She instantly attempted to exploit the turn of events.

First, she needed sanctuary. She used her bruises and bandages to entice sympathy from Jake. At the same moment, she plotted her revenge against her former lover. She came to Jake who she knew was an honest man, and therefore, able to be corrupted. He had a property where she could lick her wounds. From the sanctuary of his accommodations, she spent every waking moment rehearsing a drama, where she was an innocent victim.

She ran every rehearsal past the unwitting Jake, to determine how well it would play in court. For his part Jake remained unaware of her dramatic potential. He was too preoccupied with business to realize the plot.

Jake was fortunate enough to always provide enough for his own needs, and a little bit more. He had always worked hard and diligent. He did not mind sharing with others, after meeting his own obligations. He was not a churchgoer, but always looked out for the less fortunate. He probably donated at least ten percent to the downtrodden and dispossessed. He just preferred to do it directly, instead of dropping it in the offering basket.

Perhaps Monica saw him give a bum a handout. This would at least explain why she chose Jake, during her time of tribulation. She zeroed in on him like an arrow to a target. It was his self-confidence, his spirit, she needed to crush. For no other reason than he was a man and all men needed to pay tribute.

She was a chameleon, a shape shifting wench. She used the time needed to recover from her injuries to discover Jake's preferences and prejudice. If he liked simple summer dresses, this is what she would pull out of her wardrobe. If he said he did not approve of drinking, drugs and whores; she knew to limit her activities until he was not around. It wasn't like she was going to give up anything unless she got caught. She was a sly one this self-abused and battered succubus.

She showed up at his doorstep, on a calculated gloomy day. Just like the homeless do, on the occasion of a cold snap. Storm clouds dominated the horizon. It should have been taken as an omen. She had a black eye, a split lip and assorted abrasions and contusions. Her play for sympathy did not end here.

Among her other personal effects, she brought an adolescent daughter. Although he had no way of knowing, the daughter was an orchestrated prop, to gain sympathy from Jake. Sharon was on the cusp of womanhood. Jake was supposed to be confused in his treatment of the daughter. Luckily, Jake had no interest in the mother or her amazon prodigy, outside of human kindness.

With the daughter, Monica brought a human puppy. John was for all practical purposes a witch's familiar. He might as well take on the persona of a lap dog. Jake was a little disturbed at John's treatment by Monica. She could snap her fingers and he would jump through a hoop. There was something strange about their relationship. She had John on a short leash.

Jake could not identify the problem, but there was an element of Harem Eunuch in the manner of John's solicitations. Perhaps the man was her pimp. Perhaps she was other reason than he was a man and all men needed to pay tribute.

She was a chameleon, a shape shifting wench. She used the time needed to recover from her injuries to discover Jake's preferences and prejudice. If he liked simple summer dresses, this is what she would pull out of her wardrobe. If he said he did not approve of drinking, drugs and whores; she knew to limit her activities until he was not around. It wasn't like she was going to give up anything unless she got caught. She was a sly one this self-abused and battered succubus.

She showed up at his doorstep, on a calculated gloomy day. Just like the homeless do, on the occasion of a cold snap. Storm clouds dominated the horizon. It should have been taken as an omen. She had a black eye, a split lip and assorted abrasions and contusions. Her play for sympathy did not end here.

Among her other personal effects, she brought an adolescent daughter. Although he had no way of knowing, the daughter was an orchestrated prop, to gain sympathy from Jake. Sharon was on the cusp of womanhood. Jake was supposed to be confused in his treatment of the daughter. Luckily, Jake had no interest in the mother or her amazon prodigy, outside of human kindness.

With the daughter, Monica brought a human puppy. John was for all practical purposes a witch's familiar. He might as well take on the persona of a lap dog. Jake was a little disturbed at John's treatment by Monica. She could snap her fingers and he would jump through a hoop. There was something strange about their relationship. She had John on a short leash.

Jake could not identify the problem, but there was an element of Harem Eunuch in the manner of John's solicitations. Perhaps the man was her pimp. Perhaps she was the only pony in his stable. It was a disturbing relationship by any measure. He still felt compelled to help even with all his reservations. He only hoped to help mother and daughter in their time of need.

The house was not a permanent residence. Jake purchased it on the market as a weekend project. He did not live there except on those rare occasions, where he was too tired to drive back to his apartment. His work kept him on the road, so he went looking for a location where all the major highways intersected. It did not matter at the time, the house found, was in the seedy section of the city. He even bought into efforts to revitalize the neighborhood.

Jake was not a customer of any of the vice activities being conducted by street walkers and crack dealers. He could care less what went on outside, so long as it did not knock on his door. The constant turf wars by drug dealers were as remote as walking on the moon. Poor demented stupid Jake.

The first improvement made was to install two strong doors to keep out intruders. He then brought the electrical system up to code. He moved in a few odd furnishings, to use in the event he ever wanted to stay overnight. Mostly he kept the house empty so he had a place to work.

First, he finished the kitchen, moving in an old stove and refrigerator. With a place to prepare meals he was able to exit the atrocious rush hour traffic on the way home. He would eat before going to his apartment, while the traffic would subside in the hour, he spent dining. Something he detested was being trapped in an intolerable battle with road rage. After dinner he could travel the same distance in a few minutes as he was able to travel in an hour on the congested highway.

This was nothing new. Jake had always avoided traffic by dining during rush hour. He was tired of fast-food restaurants.

He was tired of theme restaurants. But, most of all, he was tired of restaurants which were really bar-rooms.

The bar-room restaurant was always a molestation of his peace of mind. As soon as he ordered a non-alcoholic beverage, the waitress always ignored him. The patronizing server sized him up as a small tip, and quickly forgot he was there at all. Having been part of the service industry at one time, he always dropped a dollar for every five dollars spent. That was twenty percent in anybody's book, even when the server was a self-involved snot.

By experimentation, he found whenever he ordered a beer the service improved. The same waitress with no beer would give shabby service. If he drank the beer, she might even flirt. Even if he didn't drink the beer, the service improved. It was as if; she could not do her job, until after she cleared the hurdle of taking a beverage order. He stored it in his memory, good to know.

The whole dynamic, of waitress intercourse with customer, is based on the premise of dominance and submission. Jake knew to be polite without being condescending. Condescending would only get the meal seasoned with waitress spit. A customer is only an interloper in the environment of the waitress. She lives here, the customer just wandered in from the street. Therefore, a customer surrenders dominance, to the digression of the waitress.

Eventually, Jake formed the theory; to relinquish dominance put him in the uncomfortable position of being a submissive. Ugly visions of him being hog tied in a corner booth played in his subconscious. He could even picture the waitress flogging him, while forcing him to drink beer. All to squeeze another dollar out of his wallet as a tip.

With a kitchen of his own, he did not have to wait in suicidal traffic, or submit to being part of a sick little restaurant charade. Located just off the major interstate, his kitchen was as convenient as any restaurant. It also served exactly what he was in the mood to have for dinner. With a kitchen of his own, he could unwind and relax, while others were tormented by road rage.

Unfortunately, no man is a lord of a kitchen. He may be lord of all he is able to survey, except a kitchen. The kitchen has and always will be the kingdom of a woman. If there is no woman present, a kitchen is the property of the first woman to discover it exists. A man might think he can control what takes place in this room, but he is only delusional at best.

The kitchen is described by three basic properties; a sink, a stove, and a pantry. Whenever these three elements are in close proximity, one to another, a woman will appear to bend them to her will. As time goes by, these appliances will foster the need for a garbage disposal, a dishwasher, a washer-dryer, a microwave oven, mixers, blenders, pots and pans. In short order, the space needed for all the additions, reaches beyond the original room.

The woman meticulously arranges for a takeover of the remaining domicile. The man unaware of the hostile takeover, stands by as his things, are converted into the currency of "Our" things. Later "Our" things take on the distinction of her things. The very fact a kitchen exists, is enough of an excuse to begin this process.

Men watch, as all their possessions are removed to the Goodwill or Salvation Army, where he can repurchase them at the end of the relationship. Everything is slowly replaced with brand new. Women know, the men didn't want any of this stuff, in the first place. She also knows, she'll get to keep it when he's gone. To be sure, if the relationship does go bad, it will be the male who exits. Women attach themselves to a kitchen like a barnacle. Men should just think of the Goodwill as a storage locker.

No wonder men, do not like small talk, before and after sex. This is when women casually mention, dumping an old sofa and buying a new one. It is always two or three days later, when she brings up the subject again. By this time, the poor fellow is standing in a showroom, with his credit card in her hand.

She knew exactly what to wear to the showroom. This is the reason, so much of the purchase, was feminine furnishings. She knows how to drape her body suggestively over the furniture. She uses an alluring glance to bring him in, to join her. Using a pout from her lower lip, the man is forced into the purchase, by guilt. Once she has made her selection, any hesitancy on his part will result in verbal castration, until the item is in her living room.

The whole scenario is as old as paleolithic man. The women sat around a cozy campfire, tending the pantry. The men went out and trapped game. Everything connected with the kitchen, including the cave, belonged to the women. Everything outside the cave, belonged to the men. As long as he wasn't eaten himself, a man was safe outside the cave. Then as now, if something was cooked outdoors, it was the man's job to cook it. The rational for this is simple; no furniture. No way for a woman, to stake a claim to a man, and make it stick!

Because Jake had a kitchen, he had only himself to blame. When Monica showed up with Sharon in tow, she saw the kitchen. It was as if he had constructed a bomb, hoping it would not explode. Sure, as the sun rises in the east, the habitation took on a feminine touch.

The carnage started in the kitchen, jumped to the bathroom, then started to roam to places in between. Candles, incense, shells on the toilet tank, potpourri, and doilies all began to surface. Hand towels no one was allowed to use. Fluffy window curtains instead of window blinds. This all belied the couple of weeks the intruders said they would stay. Poor stupid Jake.

It was not twenty-four hours before all his tools were piled up in a spare room, too small for anything but storage. Here they would remain, except for the odd occasion they were borrowed without permission. The lapdog John would spirit things away. Paint sprayers would return, uncleaned and unfunctional. The shop vacuum was never emptied of its reeking contents. Saws were dull and useless. While all his tools were ruined, without his knowledge, any of the projects Jake had planned had to wait.

Monica originally indicated the sanctuary was short term. She even offered to pay. Six months later she was still there. In all that time there was never again a mention of money. Even the lapdog John tried to move into the free rent lodgings. Jake sent him packing. This led to the discovery Lapdog John was paying for all the food. Jake was paying all the utilities and mortgage. Monica was paying for nothing. She was working paying a car loan, but that was all she paid.

A bum, a tramp, and a succubus devote their entire existence to making others responsible for their well-being. They force others to provide for their needs. When Monica was confronted by Jake on the issue of "Rent," an argument ensued. The type of argument where the woman runs off, later to return and trade sex for forgiveness. But Jake was not having sex with Monica. There was nothing to trade for forgiveness.

This was the first of many times where Monica would run away. She abandoned Sharon, probably expecting Jake to take care of her. Jake liked Sharon, but he was in no position to be a parent. What was he supposed to do? Turn a fifteen-year-old woman out onto the streets. Jake had seen plenty of teeny-bopper hookers in his time. He did not even want to consider Sharon being subjected to that rough trade. For the present, he could only hope to keep a roof over the child's head. He would furnish Sharon a home, even at the chance it made him look like a child molester.

After a few days he was forced to track down Monica and demand she take Sharon. By tracking the lapdog John, he located Monica. She had set up housekeeping, in a two bedroom with John and a roommate. The house was very small. The roommate wasn't too pleased, sharing his home with two people. He firmly demanded Sharon was not welcome.

In a few days the little love-nest fell apart. John sent Monica out the door kicking and screaming. Because that is what you are supposed to do with a succubus after screwing her blue. You don't let her hang around rearranging the furniture. You send her packing, "Wham" slams the door, "bam" she lands on her ass.

Actually, during the few days Jake and Sharon spent together, he realized she was more mature than her mother. Sharon was thoughtful, kind and even tempered. Sure, she was still a child, but she never tried ridiculous validation to prove a point. They had adult conversations with meaningful exchange. Somehow without Monica it was almost peaceful.

Just about the time thing were going smoothly, came Monica! John the lapdog left her homeless, so she decided to take responsibility for Sharon, under a roof provide by Jake. In the whole time she was gone no one had presented in cat like fashion. The mother always presented, during emotional wrenching dialogue. Tail in the air, begging for strokes, pretending to purr.

Nevertheless, Jake was grateful she was back to care for Sharon.

CHAPTER SIX

He was busy keeping clients happy while time shot by, six months elapsed before Jake caught his breath. Sharon made the adult decision, to move back in with her farther. This was three husbands back on the Monica meter. The woman had more legal aliases than the bulletin board at a post office. John the lapdog was still sniffing the bushes any time Jake was not around.

For the most part Monica and Jake were roommates by this time. Of course, he was still paying all the bills. He spent most of his time at his own apartment. He only used the house downtown when he was too tired to drive any further.

Monica had undergone a transformation. The source of her redemption was the chilly treatment she received from Jake. He was not cruel, only cold. She had entered into a reconciliation of small efforts to please him. She was seeking his approval. It was good for her to make the effort. Monica was still sneaking alcohol and prescriptions and he knew it. He never mentioned what he saw, as a small compromise.

She made her own compromise, by no longer referring to Jake as a Fag. The whole controversy centered around the fact Jake had never attempted to bed down with Monica. She went through a phase where she announced he must be Gay.

For his part, Jake maintained; she would never have a normal relationship with men, unless she stopped sleeping around. Having stated this, he would justify his decision to sleep alone, by not being a hypocrite. He had fallen into the pattern of a therapist. A therapist should never sleep with a client, even if she owes him rent and therapy payments.

Jake had repeatedly fended off inquiries, as to his relationship with Monica. Certainly, it was no one's business.

Everyone wanted to know if he was sleeping with her. Some even suggested this as method of paying rent. He did not want to look ashamed to admit it, if it was true. There are two types of men, those who brag, and those who say nothing. Jake was the silent type. His silence was taken for admonition of guilt.

Jake hated the braggart, who always relived a conquest in the locker room. This sophomoric tactic was below his contempt. According to their infantile fantasies, these men never slept with anything less than a Nine. The reality was, they would sleep with anything moving slow enough to be mounted. Even if this meant, slipping something into a drink, to slow a target to a stumble.

Jake was a different story. He went out of his way never to sleep with anyone he would be ashamed to be seen with in public. The logic of this decision is based on the idea; that a lover may take inopportune moments to express her infatuation. He did not care for public displays of affection, but they are a fact of life. Usually a public display happens, when the present lover, sees some other woman threaten to jump her claim.

Jake was old school. He would never leave a date without the woman he brought. What a sensible idea. It was only a case of cover your ass. When a woman accepts a date, she expects to leave her home and return safely. The trouble with this philosophy was at this stage of his life there were very few available women. The women who were available to go out, all had emotional baggage. It was like picking his way through a mine field, and just a tedious.

If a date wandered away, she was probably a waste of time. Taking her home early was always an option. Leaving her in the company of strangers was only asking for trouble. Women with emotional baggage do strange things. She may even decide to have a one-night stand after her escort leaves. She might also decide to describe it as rape in the morning. If something was placed in her drink, it might be rape.

As her date, the police may have questions unable to be answered. Imagine the questions to be answered if a date disappears. This is the whole premise behind tabloid journalism. After reaching the tabloids, a man has got a problem, even a jury of his peers cannot solve. God forbid, he is an ex-ball player, with a resume including movie credits. Even if a citizen is acquitted of a crime, the innocent is prosecuted ad-infantum in the voice of popular opinion. Prosecution, outside a court of law, by popular opinion is persecution. Conjugate the verb.

The old school worked for Jake, but hardly anyone else. Women travel in packs when they go out on the town. This was a phenomenon of post-war culture. It was also a emerging trend toward a Amazon society. Women no longer needed a date, to go out hunting for a man. As with anything inherently feminine, the more choices available, the more difficulty making a decision.

Some women, under duress of their emotional baggage, give the rest of women a bad reputation. Some women even look at dating like ordering from a Chinese menu. This guy is funny, that guy is generous, and another guy is good in the sack. A regular Moo Goo Guy Pan.

They rationalize; all men are only interested in one thing. The unhealthy generalization. Women only get treated the way they expect to be treated. When they are looking for the old Wham-Bam that is exactly what they will find. They create their own emotional baggage, by always selecting a stud when they are really shopping around for a work horse. Great for the stud, bad for the rest of the men.

Sure, portions of the population of men are predatory. However, they did not learn this practice on their own. They start out knowing they have to cut a heifer out of the herd. Women traveling in drunken merriment, always loose a few members of the herd. A gentleman may eventually escort her home. It is the route and speed of delivery that comes into question. The osmosis of the detail's filters back to the rest of the herd. Just like everything else they only listen to the side they want to hear.

The whole interaction of man and woman is littered with generalizations. Another unhealthy generalization is the question of sexual peek. Men do not reach their sexual peak at nineteen. Nineteen is roughly the age men have their first unspecified urinary tract infection. A man wakes up one morning with fire shooting out his penis. He takes a perfectly natural event and blows it out of proportion. He pledges to God, and the doctor, he'll never do that again. Narrowly dodging a bullet always slows a fellow down in enthusiasm. It is just an example of graduate potty training.

The other falsehood surrounds women, who do not reach a sexual peak in their thirties. They reach it when they reach it. Sex is a derivative function of the frequency of encounters. One good encounter, in a lifetime of mediocre, could be described as a peak. Sobriety probably plays a significant role. For many women, the first sober sexual encounter they can remember happens when they are thirty. Up to this time they only suspected they were having a good time from what they were told. Even with the evidence of children under foot, someone has to remind them how this could have happened.

Still as women took to being independent, traveling in packs for protection, a new influential process took place; the Consortium of popular opinion. It was never the habit of women to make a decision for herself. Historically, she had to consider doing what was right for all those surrounding her. Over the progress of civilization, the role has changed. She now, has to receive approval from all the other women in the immediate environment, to form an opinion. She is only seeking approval.

Unless alcohol is involved, women seek approval. Once the domain of men, Alcohol is an equal opportunity intoxicant. A two-hundred-pound man can catch a glow from one beer. The same beer to a one-hundred-pound woman is a double. Line of cocaine, same thing. Marijuana, same thing. The male has a buzz, and the woman is flying. When someone gets loaded twice as fast, they are likely to become habitual, twice as soon. Habits become addictions. Addictions give way to excuses. Excuses are a poor substitute for planning, and fosters the need to search for advice.

Women do not trust men, because they are only after one thing. Men are not even consulted. By the time men do learn of some irrational decision, the damage has been done.

If a woman gets an answer, she does not want to hear, she simply expands the statistical sample population. By asking more of her peers what she should do, she is able to prove she is doing the right thing. She is still going to do whatever she damn well pleases, but at least she has approval.

Somewhere the dependence on developing a relationship with men, was replaced, by seeking approval from other women. As evidence to this claim is the growing number of single parent households in the developed nations. The demented perception men were only interested in one thing, was contorted into; men were only good for one thing. Men were becoming walking sperm donors, who in some cases may also contribute financial support.

The feminist movement must be very proud. Given their past performance, they are probably meeting in a damage control session somewhere, planning new Amendments to the Constitution.

"Let's see if we modify, amendments XII, XIV, XV, XIX, and XXVI, we might just sneak it under the radar, past congress and onto the President's Desk." Cluck the woman's liberation movement.

Women invent the best excuses, and the rest of them follow suit. Wonder if they imagined this would happen, back in the burn the bra era. Or maybe this was their plan all along. Distract the male population, while the feminists ran a cu-da-ta on America. If this was the case, we may all want to focus on Amendment XIV sections 1 and 4. Those foolish Lesbians.

People like Jake were not born cynical. It took a lifetime of careful detailed observations. He was mesmerized by the woman's movement with their bra burning; symbolic of being unharnessed from men. He was a young buck at the time, and strongly endorsed anything they had to say. Who can argue with two erect nipples on a chilly day. Somehow the Consortium of women picked the wrong vehicle to emphasize their demands. They said they were tired of being treated like sexual objects, then turned right around and provided a walking peep show.

It was only later Jake learned; when their shirts come off, they are angling for something. Usually, it was for a bigger slice of the American Pie. Somehow the slice they always jockeyed toward, came out of the working man's share. The average middle to low-income Joe, that was the slice they were after. Especially the unmarried or divorced, heterosexual - capable of breeding, average Joe. They would portray him as a Dead-beat, even if he was not a dad. This term sprung into the lexicon of national approval, soon after the last slice was taken away from him. Prior to losing the last slice, he made his child support payments.

Men were marginalized by women. Women who now did for other women, that which was once done by men. Equality of the sexes notwithstanding, there should be a limitation to defining roles, without going too far out of the box.

Men are usually competitive up to a point. They learn early when they are being too rough with their horseplay. They don't want to compete with women, over women. But that is exactly what the modern world required. Blame it on labor saving devices.

The entire concept of labor-saving devices built by men, to do work for women, was always intended to be stand-alone appliances. Little did he know the reliant harmonic effect of a woman leaning against a dishwasher, would ultimately relegate him to a sole function of servitude.

Too stupid to avoid competition where the only requirement is an opposable thumb, men were slowly being reduced to a walking repository of a "y" chromosome. That was still better than trying to compete intellectually. Men are equipped to do imagery or they can do logic, not both at the same time. A woman, on the other hand, is capable of arguing over things, that only make sense to herself.

It all starts with the argument by women; "If you won't do it, I'll find someone who will." She uses the complaint once too often, to provide for a harmonious home.

She usually can't see; she has everything she needs to make any queen satisfied. Sometimes she is too bovine to understand her man is working at his full potential, to provide her with luxuries. The war of the sexes goes generation to generation un-resolved.

A certain portion of each generation never seems to strike a balance. The male considers if he worked any harder, it would only result in melt-down. He reconsiders her offer to let someone else; "Do it", whatever her present dilemma may be.

As the immediate supply of available men grows smaller, the woman is forced to rely on the opposable thumbs of other women. Congratulations ladies, you are now an unconfirmed lesbian. Get on your broomstick and ride. "Oh look, it's a U-F- L", an unconfirmed flying lesbian.

To be sure all feminists are not lesbians, it is just hard to distinguish who is whom, whenever a large group assembles and starts chanting; "we're here, we're Queer!"! That is not exactly a Madison Avenue pitch, for a large group. Why this never happens during a Ku Klux Klan meeting is explained by the unified nature of its agenda. Feminists usually function as spokesmen, for some other group who actually have a serviceable domestic problem. As long as the group was not the working man.

All Jake knew was the bras were off again. The woman's movement was up to something sinister. Sinister because they took off their shirts too. Ask any of the women if they planned to be videotaped and the answer may vary. All of them will admit alcohol was involved. Some of them only remember the incident from waking up in a Girls Gone Wild T-shirt.

The feminist movement must be very proud. They were the ones who came up with the concept of bra burning. Every time they tried to attract the attention of the male population; they ran the same scam. Not the original bra burners, that would not get much accomplished, what with the forty years gone by. These were the daughters and granddaughters of the originals. These women were coached by mom and granny, to use the only method that ever seemed to attract attention, in the bygone era.

If the mini skirt came back Jake knew the nation was in deep shit. Productivity would drop as men were unable to concentrate on important work. It's hard to concentrate when being mesmerized. That was the whole plan; to replace men who were not doing their job, and send in a woman.

Not only did the mini-skirt return, but this time the view was improved by thong panties. We're not talking about strippers and hookers; this time it was bank tellers and substitute teachers. The uniform of Rosy the Riveter, had evolved from baggy overalls, to erect nipples and unblemished panty lines.

It wasn't that Jake did not appreciate the view. He just would not allow himself to become aroused. Someone had to watch out for the welfare of the working man. Although the sliver of self-esteem was growing ever smaller.

This thong underwear was an unforeseen event. They were nothing new, just more distracting in the office, classroom and grocery store. If women did not want to be treated as meat, they should not package the product like a ham.

When the thong was first invented, it was real distracting. It was not even a feminine garment. Back then it was known as a "wedgie", and was spotted by the smallest student in a gym class. It was real distracting when suddenly instigated by the class bully.

Jake knew this for a fact having been a bit puny in the seventh grade. But he had a long memory and a fortunate growth spurt the following year. This allowed him to settle the score with the culprit. Still the memory lingered, suggesting the impractical nature of underwear fitting this description.

The whole concept of underwear; was so you can wear the same trousers twice. In the modern world this never happened. From the time the first joker thought he would make a woman's life a little easier, by inventing the washing machine, underwear was obsolete. Tidy-whites, were replaced by under garment fashion sensuality. Little did this inventor know, the gentle harmonic motion of the machine, would eventually replace him in the bedroom. Jake was certain, if the man had taken the time to really research his invention, he would have left her pounding laundry on a rock. A woman with time on her hands, bedevils her man.

He could have left her pounding laundry on a rock. No; this clown has to instigate the whole sexual revolution, by bringing convenience into the home. Unlike the Amish who know to leave a machine out in the yard where it belongs, this guy brought them behind closed doors. He even packaged his new products in dependable forms, replacing the heretofore undependable broom, mop, or anything else with a handle.

Just a little bit of forethought would have told the fellow not to let women forget how to handle, a handle. Start replacing everything with push buttons, and before too long a woman can't find her way in the dark, around a man's pajamas. If the guy had truly wanted to service mankind, he would have improved the butter churn. Now there is a hypnotic, harmonic - motion. Instead, he allowed the ladies to improvise, thereby setting in motion the entire sexual revolution.

The history of the sexual revolution would have to consider the history of lonely women. While men were off providing cannon fodder, in the name of some righteous indignation, women have always waited for them at home. When the troops came back, it was the women who were required to compete for a mate. This had been going on for ten thousand years.

Every time an invention reaches the lives of a portion of the planet's population, discord rises on the other side of the Earth. Some "thing" of dubious value surfaces, and the rest of the world wants to take part.

The whole sorted affair, is a balancing act between religious doctrine, moral conduct and the legitimate use of farming implements. In the early days a woman's lonely existence may cause her to perform an act of immorality. When the Church was still also the keeper of the laws, this could be quite a dilemma. Many old crones were put to the torch, following impropriety with a butter churn handle. With the removal of penalty of being in league with the Devil, civil authorities politely asked the ladies to take their butter churning practices down the road.

This did not happen overnight. American law would wisely separate civil procedure from religious doctrine. Of course, that was after the Salem Witch Trials. Any time you deal with; life, liberty and the ability to pursue happiness, allowance for Freedom of Religion must follow. If an old bitty wants to label her butter churning, as an obscure form of nature worship, that's her business. So now civil procedure, had to install a provision for personal privacy. The intervention of government always follows the introduction of some new labor-saving devise.

CHAPTER SEVEN

Jake was unable to go anywhere, where he was not forced to at least consider temptation. The combined influence was too much for him to ignore. Even at a charity event, some woman would select to "accentuate her assets". If one did it, they all did it, as some form of beauty pageantry. Even if it meant running home to change, the impromptu panorama of women ensued. A plethora of perfumes offered as enticement. Competition between women, is often distracting to men.

He tried to keep his mind on business. Just when Monica could have been an asset, she was out the door again on one of her husbands' searching sorties. It was just as well. He changed the locks. Changing the locks did not insure absolute privacy. At least it would give him enough time to collect his thoughts.

Put a little charity in a questionable neighborhood. That was a simple idea. Well, it was not a charity anymore, because the sponsor pulled out. If Jake was going to be footing the bills, he was going to reap the rewards.

Here was something he never imagined. He could pay the entire mortgage with the profit from each season. Instead of giving the money to the charity, he could keep the money. Normally as the hired man he did not question, the charity being rewarded.

He sat down with his original paperwork:

PROPOSAL:
Halloween Spook house Charity Event.
Halloween Spook house. Characters dressed in spooky costumes, rattling chains, fog from dry ice, hidden doorways, spooky music. Lighting to accent small cameo stage settings.

TIME FRAME:
Event to run from Friday October 10, to Friday October 31, opening at 5:30 PM closing 9:00 PM, Tuesday through Thursday. Special hours on Friday and Saturday. Closed Sunday and Monday. Candy distributed to children at exit on the 31 October.

TICKET SALES:
The Hole Hell Neighborhood encompasses an area of one square mile. This is an (low) approximation of over seven thousand student age residents.
Projecting a fifty percent participation, this is a net revenue of seven thousand dollars, with the following ticket receipt. Two-dollar contribution for any adolescent. Five dollars for an adult.

SITE AND PREPARATION:
The offered location is an old farm house located at the corner of West and 24th street. The Owner is responsible for this proposal.
Install theatrical lighting for various set locations. Introduce localized sound effects and music. Theatrical curiosities such as blowing cobwebs and dry ice fog will be installed. Optional effects to be limited to approval. Any grotesque display will be avoided.

ATTENDANCE FLOW:
Attendees will enter through the front door and exit through back door. The Volunteer crew, in costume, will greet the ticket holder at the door then pass ticket holder to next volunteer. Ticket holder will be supervised at all times, but allowed to explore various vignette acts.

Acts to include but are not limited to the following:
Three witches sitting around a crackling fire in fire place.
One Wolfman. (Jumping out of dark corner.) One Dracula (Sneaking out of a closet.) One Mummy
One Elvira mistress of darkness (comic relief).
One Mermaid (hidden behind bathroom curtain.)
One Voodoo princess
One Zombie (for ticket sales on site).
Local school drama clubs may furnish volunteer students as an extra credit assignment. Children will be given a safety code word to say, if they become too frightened, in case they need out.

PERMITTING AND INSURANCE:

The Office of Community Action located in Option, Florida is in the position to offer assistance to gain permitting for an event of this nature. They may be contacted at (407) 555-1234. A recognized community association may contact County Permits at (407) 555-4321.

Insurance is pending acceptance of proposal. The County Risk Management Division may be used as a resource to secure information regarding special event insurance. Extra-ordinary caution should be used in selecting an insurance carrier for special events. Selection should be made from those underwriters, who will actually pay, in case of an accident.

SPONSORS INVESTMENT:

Given an expected revenue of seven thousand dollars any offer of sponsorship will be entertained.
The building, located at 1000 24th street, Option, Florida is at the moment in the same Spooky condition as it was at the time of purchase. Props are easily assembled from thrift shops and other locations.
The cost to the sponsor will be based on actual spending by the promoter. The actual structure is offered to the Community of Hole Hell with the provision:
It is suggested qualified officers of the Hole Hell Neighborhood Association, tour the site. Take measurements, custom create a carnival atmosphere. Alternative sponsorship may include the following:
Central Florida Blood Bank
Jacks High School Drama Class
Boondoggle High School Drama Class
International Alliance of Stage and
Theatrical Employees.
Option County Sheriff Department.

OPTION COUNTY FIRE RESCUE.

These are only a few of the interested parties who would lend their support to a project of this nature. Acceptance or rejection of this project, needs to be done out front, to make a presentation to secure alternative sponsors. Promoter is willing to enhance this proposal in the event it finds community support.

DISCLAIMER OF INTENTION:
This is to be a nondenominational charity affair. It should produce just enough combined ticket sales, to break even after everyone is paid. The motivation is education and community development. Say no to drugs, work with your neighbors to clean up the neighborhood. Give a pint of blood and get a free ticket.

Advanced planning and community support is needed to institute this worthwhile plan. The promoter wishes to be recognized as member of the team. What is more important, he will assist in all the technical and administrative work.

There is NO guaranteed profit. These things were supposed to be a mechanism to promote community involvement. For the initial offering this may be considered experimental.

If it is successful, it may be used as an example of similar community activities to promote ethnic diversity within Hole Hell. A Spook House was selected because of the universal appeal. Observations made during October of subsequent years showed, residents of Hole Hell did not participate in Trick or Treat activities.
SUBMITTED Jake Dorado

Other members of the community were way ahead of Jake. There was a charity on every block. A tax dodging charity. A bum catering service. Not the normal Salvation Army style, service to mankind charity. This was the take it in, and keep it, charity. The service yourself style of charity. The kind where the man in a suit shows a bunch of photographs to appeal to Christian morals, quoting scripture, seeming to represent the downtrodden.

To Jake, it was just a spin on the panhandler at a train station, with his hand out. He'd seen some panhandling bums pull in fifty thousand a year, tax free.

This was different, this was knocking on the front door. It was going onto a property, making inquiries into the religious affiliation, of the occupants. A violation of the right to privacy, tolerated by moral sensitivity.

Jake always told them he did not discuss his religious affiliation. This only attracted the attention, of those tending to his salvation. These jokers would expect to be invited inside, where they could scan the wall hangings, looking for a religious motif. Even the cops knew better than to invade privacy. Not these clowns, their devotion to their own concept of morality, demanded they see what was inside the home.

Everyone feels compelled to help the homeless. As a society it is a damn good thing we do. However, an unrecognized charity always goes out and recruits the homeless. Jake used to ask the scruffy people why they were homeless. A guy should know why he has no home. If they had a plausible answer, Jake might part with a meager sum of money.

Just because a man shows up with a truck, does not make him an advocate for the homeless. With a little networking, a charity for the collection of day-old pastries, can send a skinny guy to the bakery, and have a fat woman serve as administrator. A shelter for battered women, should never be organized by a pimp. The same applies to an adoption agency.

The local opinion was; these people needed help. The fact a charity existed was never questioned. Instead, the establishment of a vigilance committee was favored to stamp out crime.

Jake always told everyone he did not discuss his views. He was of the minority opinion a vigilance committee was the same thing as a lynch mob without a rope. He did not mind municipal taxation to pay for a police force, who were accountable for their actions. He just could and would not; support a homeowner's association to tackle crime. Jake was always a stickler for the Constitution. Most homeowners' associations think "due process" is collection of membership funds.

The trouble with Jake, and the reason this story revolves around "poor Jake", is the interpretation of fine print in the eye of the reader. The whole reason for a judicial process is to distinguish who interpreted the reading correctly. To his credit he was neither a convicted felon, or a prisoner.

It was not the letter of the law, due process, or anything else but popular opinion to separate the wicked from the righteous.

Not even: guilty by association. It is guilty, by not associating, with the self-righteous. Not marching at the head of the parade, not flying a flapping banner was just as reckless, in the view of the populace. If you are not one of us, you must be one of them.

On one side of the equation were the numerous self-serving charities. On the other side was the vigilance committees. Stuck in the middle were bums taking their breakfast in bed, when they were not out pursuing criminal activities.

Jake owned probably a mile of rope he used for work. He also had a stack of bibles to swear on. He had some other interesting literature scattered about the house. Put it all together and it said "never loan out a piece of rope longer than three feet." Must have been one of the unrecorded commandments. Tied properly a noose is not effective, in a piece of rope shorter than three feet. The righteous assembly would have to conjure up some other accidental scenario to punish the wicked.

As for those banners flapping in the breeze, Jake was a little cautious. Every banner told you something. Mostly it told you some day they are going to cross a property line and start something. The banners Jake would march behind, were few. If he flew any himself, it was always indoors.

Badges were another thing he did not much tolerate. Flashing a badge was to endure scrutiny. He had a proper respect for the man in uniform. Jake had a problem with the badge flasher, the out of jurisdiction, nose in someone else's business clowns. He called them the KGB, because that is exactly what they were, non-government secret police. Anybody can buy a badge to flash around. Just like anyone can buy a currently popular police style weapon. If a man is working undercover, he is surely not going to flash a badge. There is a very fine line between flashing a badge and being an outright criminal.

With attitudes like Jake showed the world, it is no wonder he was going to go broke. Everything would come together to undermine his every energy. All the forces would converge to ruin his planning, expectations, even his very sanity.

CHAPTER EIGHT

He never thought he would wish for the day he could use Monica's help. Daytona was doing a sloppy job of keeping Jake's affairs in order. Considering what he was paying her, she should have been making a hell of a lot more progress paying bills and arranging his schedule.

He handed her a stack of American Express travelers checks and a roll of stamps. Her job was to stuff envelopes with enough checks to cover the bills. Her job was to place a stamp on the envelope and include the correct return address. She could even work out of her home if she so desired. That was the last Jake saw of the bills the stamps or the travelers' checks.

Considering the job taken in good hands he centered his attention on more carpentry. Ned was still helping with what little talent he possessed. The verbal dexterity of the man was the only thing which suppressed Jake's diagnosis of attention deficit disorder. Ned could sure carry on a conversation. Work, he was not too familiar with, but he could talk a blue streak.

Ned was not a fellow to take fishing. He would only criticize the bait, the boat, and the lake. He would also pontificate on what a good fisherman would do in a circumstance like this. Any fish that were not frightened to the other side of the lake, would roll up on shore out of sheer boredom. Largemouth bass would choose suicide, just so they would no longer have to listen to his unending chatter. That would be fine, if they would use a hook as the expedition intended. No, they would just bob to the surface and be taken by a hawk even a racoon.

It would be different if his incessant drivel was the product of some intellectual process. To listen to Ned was like an update of the local television news. It was clear he had probably never even read a book. So mundane were his topics the listener had no choice but to ignore the noise.

Jake was so pleased when his pager rang, he could have kissed the caller. He was even more happy when he learned he would have to go out to receive details on an upcoming project in his professional career.

He secured a promise from Ned, the current work would continue as planned. All the equipment was laid out and only needed assembly. Even Ned should be able to complete the work. A skylight sitting not three feet away from a large hole in the roof was to be installed. The afternoon showers were still hours away. Plenty of time for Ned to finish the job, which he again promised would be done. In the event the rain came early Jake gave him a tarp to cover the hole.

Ned made a reasonable request. He asked Jake to pay him for the day, just in case he finished, before Jake returned. Normally he would have been resistant, to an indulgence such as this, but he did not have much choice with the rain on the horizon. All he cared about was getting the hole plugged.

As with many of his professional engagement, Jake had to sit through tedious detail. It took a few hours. It was still early in the afternoon when he finally got free. The job was going to be a lucrative deal to dwarf any money he spent on the Spook house.

His wallet had been missing for a couple days but he was sure it would turn up eventually. Just in case the wallet never returned, he swung by the license bureau for a duplicate drivers license. It was right on the way home. While he was inside a cloud ripped loose, drenching the local area in two inches of rain. Typical Florida rainstorm. Jake reminded himself to close the windows in his car next time. He settled in for a soggy ride home.

Still raining and almost dark when he arrived home, Jake ran into the house to change clothes. Greeting his arrival was two inches of rain draining from a hole in the roof. The water had soaked through the ceiling and was playing havoc with the electrical system. Delicate electronics and expensive cameras were all flooded with rainwater. The computer in the corner was still sparking, until the circuit breaker finally flipped, making it no longer a lethal condition. The clock radio sat sizzling, waiting for the next circuit breaker to end its misery.

Why change clothes when you have to go out in a torrential downpour with a flashlight? Jake climbed up to the roof to survey the problem. The extent of the work done in his absence was the annoyance. Ned had probably climbed down off the roof, before Jake had time to get around the corner.

Covering the hole with the tarp, Jake used the skylight to hold it in place. When he lifted the skylight he found his missing wallet, dry as a bone. He could distinctly remember checking under the skylight earlier in the day. Odd that he should find it on the roof -dry. Somebody was playing games and it was a short list.

Wet and miserable, livid beyond measure, he went back inside to shower. The bulbs blew when he flipped on the light. Not one bulb, but all three of the lights blew out. Rainwater in a vanity socket does that sort of thing. For a split second, a spark shot out of the light switch. Standing in a two-inch puddle of rainwater with bare feet, does that sort of thing. A spark shot out of the bottom of Jake's foot creating a small hole.

Had Jake not rewired the building, the event would have killed him. Bringing it up to code requirements had saved his life. The old wiring had no grounding wires, meaning he would have been the path of least resistance for the power surge. He showered by candle light, plotting the action to be taken in the morning.

Jake woke up at the crack of dawn in a foul mood. Everything around him was drenched. He painstakingly brought everything into the back yard to dry. Pillows, sheets, electronic gear all the small effects of human habitation. He even put out a soggy old pellet gun hoping to prevent rust. His back yard began to resemble a flea market or garage sale. He would sort through everything after it dried.

Across the street from Jake's place was a two-bedroom house with four adults and six children in residence. This alone seems crowded, even in Appalachian standards. Outside the gate at Ned's place stands a bell on a post, at least there used to be a bell. Just like in Appalachia the fenced yard was full of many freak mutts. The only way to call the family, was to ring a bell, located on a post outside the front gate.

Jake knew all about that bell. The following morning, he picked up the largest hammer he could find, an eight pounder. He walked right up to that bell and rang it. With the second blow from the hammer Jake was holding the bell in his hand.

As Ned sheepishly approached Jake threw the bell. He did not throw the bell at Ned, as was shortly reported to the police.

He threw the bell on the ground at Ned's feet. Jake was too much of a gentleman to actually hit someone with an object. Jake never intended to strike Ned with the bell. He simply wanted Ned to step outside the gate, so he could use his fist like God intended. Vengeance is mine, saith the Lord. But then the Lord was not motivated by standing in two inches of water, with a live fifteen amp, one hundred twenty-volt electrical circuit.

Jake was not going to hurt the man too bad. He was just going to slap that Attention Deficit Disorder out of Ned. Cure the man with the laying on of hands. Ned would be speaking in tongues in a jiffy. Jake could cure him of a few other problems that might be congenital. Lazy, stupid, unmotivated; all gone, replaced with wiser people skills.

That was what was supposed to happen. Ned would come outside the gate; Jake would give him a tutorial. He was going to catch Ned up, on all the course work he missed, while skipping school. There wasn't much Jake could do about Ned being the product of inbreeding. Playing hooky was another matter.

Ned refused to come out. He ran back inside like a little girl. This may explain why he was so good a talking, without saying anything. Jake walked away disappointed. He had no idea how long he could remain pissed off. To offer his tutorial advise, in its proper translation, he needed to be angry.

The Sheriff had a different perspective when he showed up a short time later. He asked Jake why he hit Ned with the bell. Jake replied "he did not hit the man with the bell.". OK, he said "God Damn bell", but we're aware of Jake's speech impediment. The officer let the preposition stand uncorrected. A poor choice of words was not how Jake ended up in the back of a squad car.

Ned was demanding to press charges. But Jake might just as well drive himself to the slammer when he informed the deputy, "Hell, if I was trying to hit the man, I would have used the Pellet Gun in the back yard.". The deputy was supposed to understand the logic of the statement. He did not.

The Sheriff did not require to know the pellet gun was placed outside to dry that same morning. All the deputy heard was the word "Gun". This was enough for Jake to be placed in the back of the squad car.

Ned took advantage of Jake's dilemma. With Jake in the back of the squad car, Ned was running back and forth outside the gate, demanding to press charges. Ned was a strutting rooster defending his home, now that Jake could not reach him. His righteous indignation boiled over into red-neck ranting and raving.

As the squad car pulled away, Jake took solace in the fact he would be out in a few hours, and he would be plenty pissed off.

The actual charges were written up as: Shooting into an occupied dwelling or vehicle, with a bell. No prosecutor would want to touch this case -with a ten-foot pole.

CHAPTER NINE

Just to prove how wrong a man can be, Jake was not out of jail in a few hours. It would be a long time before he had a day when he was not pissed off.

Based on the location of his arrest and his appearance on arrival, he was treated like public enemy Numero Uno. He was picked up in the "Hood". A white man in the "hood" could only mean he was involved in drugs and prostitution. At least that was the perception of the intake officer.

A squat little man took him over to a table to sign a document which still remains a mystery. Jake did not have his glasses, because thirty minutes ago he was tutoring Ned and thought he would not need them. By virtue of inability to read the document, Jake refused to sign. He asked to borrow the glasses worn by the intake guard, who being of Hispanic build, thought Jake was lunging in a threatening manner. It was a small annoyance of bi-lingual communication. The first of many to come.

The guard tried to overpower Jake, who was already trying to cooperate. Even though he felt like a Doberman being attacked by a toy-poodle, he made no attempt to shake off the man. Sure, he could have tossed the guard across the room like a rag doll. That does not prove anything. Out on the street, the little guy always comes back with a gun in any event. Jake was sure there must be a gun somewhere in the jail, this little guy could find in a pinch. Best not make it a question of pride.

Seeing the struggle, a few more uniforms jumped into the fracas. They slammed Jake into the counter, striping him naked. This must where he lost his handcrafted special order Redwing casual boots. He never got them back and would leave the jail barefoot. Had he known the day was going to be like this he would have worn more modest shoes.

Jake stood there naked, hoping he was making a good impression on the female staff standing around. He was glad the lady cops were there. None of these other Yahoos were likely to try a cavity search, with women present. Smack him around, strip him naked, sure why not? Stick a finger up his rectum for no good reason, not likely. Even the hyperactive, English as a second language, toy-poodle guard was not that frisky.

One of the guards who observed the melee told the poodle to take a break. Oh, he took a break, and a two-hundred-dollar pair of boots. Jake and the new guard made eye contact. The guard was not threatening, but he was going to take any crap either. This made Jake feel better about his predicament.

Someone handed him a jumpsuit to wear. Step to the right, step to the left. Take a towel, take a blanket, take this take that. Just like in the Navy. Take a shower, take a nap. Go in here. Squeeze through there. This is your cell, pick a bunk.

Punch in the face, wrong bunk!

"No, I did not see him punch you. I only saw you punch him!" Go to confinement.

Confinement, Jake would find, was a cold place. No blanket and hardly any food. Food would at least fuel the shivering. Hypothermia makes one shiver, and pounds just drop away.

The guy next door was going through withdrawals. He screamed all sorts of bazar unintelligible pleas and curses. He started softly then louder, and louder, then a defining roar and finally softer. The only way to tell the time was to count the frequency of his murmuring. Jake reckoned twelve hours, one baloney sandwich and a juice box.

"If I let you out of there, do you promise to behave yourself?" a pimple faced guard asked, trying to patronize.

"I only made one promise in my life." Jake truthfully replied. He thought it was a rhetorical question. He should have known to choose; yes or no, the way his luck was going. Maybe there was no correct answer. The guard may have been pulling his chain. Twelve more hours scraped by, filled with raving and vomiting from the cell next door.

Another baloney sandwich, and a juice box. Jake was sleep deprived with sore muscles from endless shivering. The place was cool enough to hang meat. The only comfortable position was standing, curled up in a gargoyle crouch. It was the only way to conserve body heat.

This was a good thing to know, when every other day he would spend in confinement. He'd spend one day in population and the next day in solitary. Stupid little things got him there. Someone called to him as a Cracker. Jake called him a Negro, pronouncing it the way the Spanish speak the term. He had only been out of solitary for twenty-four hours; it was time to go back.

Another time he asked the chaplain if he was a chaplain. The man said he was only a chaplain to the Hispanic prisoners. Jake came unglued. "Either you are a man of God or you are not. You must not be, if you pick and choose between sinners who deserve your prayers!"

As he was being led away to the cooler, Jake shouted over his shoulder "Never too late to learn the difference between sanctified and sanctimonious, you Fraud. Hey Zeus told you to love your neighbors as you love yourself. You must live in a damn small neighborhood - Padre."

This experience was turning in Jake like a worm. He was never going to let another holy-man off the hook without a fight. This was a long time coming. He had been to all kinds of Christian charities. He had seen, where they posted a version of the ten commandments in such a form, as to read differently than intended. He had seen ministers, picking up hookers and dope, down in the hood. Counseling is one thing, so why did they need the dope?

He knew one thing for sure, when Jesus does come back, he is going to be plenty pissed off. What with that crucify thing the last time around, and chaplains making it up as they go along. All this from Jake, a man who did not follow any church rank and file.

Sitting in the clink, gives a man time to think. Right now, he was preoccupied with the Hispanic holy-man. Sancto- Sanctorum, that guy was a pothole in the spiritual highway. Jake had not trusted the Spanish tradition from the first time he studied the Inquisition. If they could screw up once, they could do it again.

Sure, it is said the Moors had invaded Spain, using it as a launchpad for the conquest of Europe. The Christian defenders would like everyone to believe, they had to repel the Islamic invaders. It is convenient to swap eleventh century wars with eighth century civil process.

It is said; El Cid saved Spain from siege. The inaccurate legend proposes, only later did the children of the raped women, suffer the humiliation of being ostracized for their mixed heritage. The warfare of the time dictated these children be introduced to Christendom, conscripted into a standing army, and unleashed on their own fathers.

What a load of crap.

Under the guise and intrigue of a Holy War, came the opportunity to eliminate all opposition to the national interest of Spain. Fueled by the fervor of religious might, and a standing army, the stage was set for bloodshed. The only reason the dark ages are so murky is to overlook the contribution of Islam to the Iberian Peninsula. It would be another thousand years before someone would even consider Freedom of Religion and separation of church and state.

The prophet Mohammad died in 632 AD. Strangely he agreed with most of the teachings of the Christians and Jews. Just not enough of the teachings to make Christians and Jews comfortable.

By 636 AD Jerusalem fell to Calif Omar in the name of Islam. Islam continued to establish itself in the seventh century, forcing the Christian churches out of Antioch and Alexandria. By the eight century, spiritual and regal authority was represented by a system of Caliphs. Caliph Haroun-al- Rashid ushered in a golden period of learning. Caliph Al- Mansur established the city of Baghdad.

Outposts of learning were established in Spain by the systems of Caliphs, with Charlemagne upholding the Christian authority. The feudal system exploded across the European landscape with advances in agriculture. By the middle of the ninth century Cordova, was an advanced center of learning for both Moorish and Christian learning.

By the time El Cid conquered Valencia in 1095, the Moors had been in Spain for almost four hundred years. Twelve generations had passed, without being able to communicate. But, at least El Cid, stood up for what he believed. It would take another four hundred years to have a proper Inquisition, going door to door, collecting Jewish heretics. Islamic culture was crushed by the sword, under a collection of small kingdoms.

The Arab Caliph system-built Spain during the fall of the Roman occupation. Rome had allowed itself to become fat and lazy. The Moors originally came in as cabana boys to retired Romans who sat around sipping Sangria. Spain was an important trading center for all of Europe. It was not warfare but commerce that placed Islam in kingdoms and fiefdoms of Iberia.

Find the weakness of your adversary, and drown them in it. Come to harvest crops, stick around to lay claim to real estate. Keep those senoritas busy delivering -Sangria.

This is the whole reason the history books call it the dark ages. They are trying to obscure the fact that the infidel Moslems during the fall of the Roman Empire, were responsible for building Christian Culture.

It was the pro-active Saracens waging war against the Christian world. They too also happened to be Moslem. As Europe invested in the war for the Holy land, they became aware of the similarities of culture in Cordova.

From the first crusade to the last came the defendable evidence; Christianity was challenged at its doorstep. Not the Churches Christianity, but the exploitable Civil Christianity. Not the check the facts carefully, stay in school, punish only the wicked Christian ethics. The playing hooky, fabricate evidence, hold your breath till you turn blue, civil litigating - charlatan style church.

Jake endorsed the faith based Christian pity, as practiced by monks and friars. What he could not tolerate was the tax dodging, make it up as you go, unorthodox, -Clandestine Church. He'd seen a lot of gerrymandered worship hidden in obscure rituals. Sometimes it was done by approval seeking, golden ox toting, impostors; who were only sneaking around religion, trying to see how the other man gets it done.

Throw in some bells and whistles and you have Voodoo, Santeria, or in the first millennium Pro-test-ants. Of course, a protestant in the first millennium was a heretic worth burning. Not that it took very much effort, when the only educated man in town wanted to torch the wicked.

By refusing to establish diplomatic means, like learning the other man's language, there was always profit to be made. It is easy to persuade a third party he has suffered a grievous insult. While redressing the insult, one may manipulate not only the affairs of the third party, but the affairs of the second party as well. Simple cold war politico. It took mankind a thousand years to learn this.

At the close of the second millennium, we take for granted our own frame of reference. We may appreciate something belonging to another individual. This may cause us, to make him, a fair and reasonable offer. If he refuses our offer, we go somewhere else to do business.

At the close of the first millennium things were much different. Due to the feudal influence of the era, certain members of the population had no right to refuse others, ascendancy to ownership. Whenever the pride filled privileged class, found a prized object of desire, they would not take no for an answer. Exactly like a slum-lord after rent.

The feudal lords and ladies would obsess over acquiring the object of desire. They would be obligated to conspire privately, to avoid condemnation, for breaking the tenth commandment. Being well grounded in biblical text, they used the obvious loophole. Civil litigation allowed them to take possession of their obsession by "Surrendering unto Caesar what was Caesars."

Domino Patro, Ahem, so now if a lord wants a duck or a goose or a moment alone with a wife, the serf is obligated to give it to him. If they didn't call it taxes, they called it rent. Chew on that process for a few hundred years and see where it leads.

Generations of fine tuning Civil due-process, leads to a hair-splitting, shuck and jibe nightmare. Each generation would be forced to revisit the short comings of the previous cycle. Only in these days there was a shortage of paper and a surplus of weapons. Anyone unable to read would choose the latter. Because almost no one could read, the courtroom never had a somber library atmosphere. It really did not matter who could read, because the only version of the story recorded, belonged to the last bloody combatant at the scuffle.

If there was ever a time in history to point to, and say there should be a separation of church and state, this would be the time. The only educated men were the clergy. To a lesser degree some of the nobility at the tutelage of the clergy. The clergy had time on their hands too, with the decree of celibacy in 1074 AD. They were the only reliable witnesses, and recorded what they saw for posterity. Nothing was secular, no deed, no contract, not even a license was without the approval of the church.

When presented with a Caesar loophole they may side with the serf, if they were bold enough. When presented with a ligament case it would go to the best argument. When a case involved Mohamad -Vs- Goldberg, all bets were off. The predominate beliefs of Europe, required ignoring Arab and Jewish contributions to architecture, medicine, agriculture and the arts.

The true Knights Templar, set a standard we follow to this day. A treaty of law within the land, with a boundary. This far and no further. Within this border the applicant will be granted sanctuary. The law of this land will extend to its border. Sounds simple enough, for a group returning from the Holy Land. They burned the Knights Templar at the stake in 1312 AD.

So, when the chaplain made the statement; "He was only here for the Hispanics." Jake was mortified. Red flag down, umpire to the call. Every neuron in Jake's brain fired at the same moment. Every scrap of stored memory filled his Cerebrum, cascaded through both Corpus Callosum, activated his Cerebellum and shot down his Medulla Oblongata like a white-hot poker.

Jake did not treadle the preacher, he exercised self-control.

Years spent dealing with anger management, left Jake vibrating under the chemical load of neurotransmitters. He may have even become invisible; he was vibrating so intensely. His mind was searching desperately for a mechanism of release. This crystalline nanosecond spent choosing between allowing his brain to explode, or shunting epinephrine to his motor centers. Hold in his rage and sacrifice a vital organ like a heart valve, or let it out with all the ramifications. A bubble formed between his lips, as he stared directly into the preachers' eyes. When the bubble burst it formed the sound "*Sua tu Asinus!*"

Jake sat there in his tiny dank cell, chewing his baloney sandwich, washing it down with a box of juice. He figured he had lost a pound a day. The truth was, he was down twenty pounds, and he was still in custody.

From the cell next door came ranting and raving. This was a different guy, another crack head stuck in the cell block. This one was screaming in Creole. The other guy was Haitian. The guy before that was Puerto Rican. Jake never saw their faces he only listened to them scream. Glad to see; the Option County Jail was an equal opportunity Gulag.

Halfway through the recent ordeal some big Mulatto came up to the cell with the demand for Jake to strip. "Take off that Jumpsuit, now!"

The corrections officer outweighed Jake by fifty pounds. Behind him stood another equally big, ugly corrections officer. These clowns were dressed as swat team members, right down to their fingerless gloves. Both of them were smiling like a guard at a Mexican shakedown. Over their uniform they wore a black T-shirt with white letters that actually said "Shakedown". Jake had seen them in the population cells searching for any infraction of the Jail rules. They were a couple of sadists who really enjoyed their work.

There was no reason behind the request. The only thing in the solitary confinement cell, was Jake in the jumpsuit. There was no blanket, no mattress, nothing but Jake.

"Back away from the door." came the order.

Jake did not comply. He was ready to die; right here, right now. Fat boy Shake and Fat boy Down, burst through the door. Pile driving Jake into the wall, pinning him under five hundred pounds of flab, he was unable to move. One of them wrestled the jumpsuit from Jake, as the other kept him pinned. Then they were gone. They stood outside the cell grinning like idiots.

"What you Fat Fuckers get off on seeing an old man naked?" Jake spoke slow and deliberate, thankful he was not otherwise violated.

They stood there taunting him with the garment. He remembered the high school wedgie; it was this same mentality. He carefully took pains to remember their faces.

He contemplated the introduction of Mexican prison tactical advantage, in an Option County Jail. Somehow, it was hard for him to merit the system. Surely you have to provide the people with something they can understand. This was one cultural affectation, in serious need of review.

Combining Amendment V and Amendment VII should do the trick. No, that was federal justice. He was in a county jail; they make their own rules. At least he had time on his hands to ponder the problem. No place to go, nothing better to do, naked and all!

It slowly occurred to Jake this was the first time he had a moment of privacy in years. No cell phone, no pager, almost no one barging in unannounced. He was not locked in; the beauty of isolation was everything was locked out. On the one hand all he had to deal with was his nakedness and the cold. On the other hand, he was insulated from all distractions.

Under different circumstances, and never in public, nakedness was a preference. A life spent in the tropics does that. This was different, the inside of the jail was sixty-five degrees. Too warm to cause serious damage. Too cool to be comfortable.

The freedom from distraction was a whole new universe. When he was out in public, he would suffer assault, after assault of unmitigated distraction. Everything from navigating through a maze of suppressed road rage, to constantly averting his view from catching a glimpse of a mini-skirted thong.

Surely, he could appreciate a thong, just not everywhere he went. His work involved integral and differential calculus. It is impossible to accomplish differential calculus, when distracted by a thong. It's a right brain, left brain, thing.

Months later he would discover another location free from the distraction of thongs and unharnessed breasts. The court rooms. When he went to court, he discovered even the nastiest hookers covered up like they were living in Algeria. Only in Algeria the hookers wear coins sewn into their head-dress, to establish fair market value to the client.

So long as he was destined to spend time in isolation, he decided to put his time to good use. Each time a baloney sandwich was delivered it came in a foam carton. Jake used the foam to chart his progress. First keeping track of the day, date and sometimes the time. He made notations with a thumb nail pressed into the foam. In this way he could let his mind wander without spiraling out of control. He could work out a logical progression of ideas the way a musician works on a piece of music.

Each time he was put back into general population he took the foam with him. Each time he was shivering naked in isolation he would start over from scratch. Day, date and time, followed by a hieroglyphic system of notation. The important information was the day and date. He knew he would be become disoriented, without the day of the week, and the date.

Whenever his day and date were recorded, he could allow his mind to wander. Distorting the space time continuum, he would evaluate the fate of mankind. Silently he would sing any old song he remembered. Mostly they were old country tunes he would sing. God bless Johnnie Cash!

The seventh time he landed in isolation, his hieroglyphics produced a defined pattern. The first time he was isolated was for striking a black man, in return for being struck. The second time was for upsetting a Puerto Rican who became enraged at Jake's efforts to explore the use of his limited high school Spanish. The third time was from a similarly unimpressed Mexican. The Mexican complained, Jake's Castellon Spanish was reminiscent of imperial Spain. He tried French on a Haitian who was predisposed to improve Jake's knowledge of the Toto Maku. The thing with the preacher was racial bias. The last couple of times just because he had grown weary of dealing with uppity inmates.

All of his trouble while he was in the slammer was centered on him being a white man in the cell block. All the racial tension from out on the streets was reversed in the Jail. In here Jake was the minority, and the others let him know exactly how they felt about white Americans. Strangely he didn't have much trouble with the black Americans. It was mostly the Hispanic Americans who got bent out of shape. Even the Shakedown crew were part of this third wave rocking the boat.

All those fifteenth century efforts to colonize the New World, sure produced a bumper crop of uppity nationals. Of course, these were all prisoners and not representative of the population at large. Still for every man in jail there were ten waiting to get in. For every illegal alien in jail, waiting to be deported, there were ten black Americans to keep them company. Jake plotted a progression, somehow calculated a normal distribution, and employed the quadratic equation. Something almost impossible to do with a thumbnail hieroglyph, on a foam baloney sandwich box. He would never attempt such a feat, were it not for the sigmoid curve. That, and a lot of time on his hands.

He had just finished when in walked the Shakedown twins. A momentary distraction, he should have expected, seeing he was still wearing a jumpsuit. This time they were not here to molest him. Something he should have picked up on, because they were not grinning like village idiots. They were here to escort him to a holding cell for release.

Fat boy Shake and Fat boy Down, were acting professional. A characteristic Jake was not going to put any faith behind. He preferred to consider them the contemptible scum, he knew them to be. For the moment he would summons up as much decorum as the situation demanded, not one iota more. Foam box in hand he marched to release.

While waiting for his street clothes, there was still time to consider the exercise scratched into the foam. What did it all mean? It meant that America was in some deep shit, that's what it meant. Well, the foam box did not say it directly. Coupled with the theory behind all those ubiquitous thong sightings, factoring in an overall lack of conformity to Constitutional guidelines, there was trouble brewing. Add in, the most common high school graduate was the proud, hooky playing, holder of a GED.

Throw in a few state-of-the-art weapons, it's Cordova all over again. If not Cordova at least Alfonso's Toledo. Toledo, Spain not Toledo, Ohio. Anywhere where the language and customs are thought of as a detriment, instead of an enhancement, can be used as an example. Sometimes it was all about letting the other guy make the move. Call it an atrocity then seek retribution. Deep lingering, thousand-year-old retribution bull-shit!

Marching at the head of the pact, acting as a vanguard is the bra burning succuba. They never met a politician they could not distract. If the efforts of a special interest lobbyist fail, they can always send in a ringer. Some congressional page or White House intern will always volunteer to service an elected official. Usually under a table festooned with special interest documents.

As he dressed in his street clothes, Jake mulled over the observations presented by his two-week vacation in the county Jug.

He went to jail believing; the powers in charge of the process, had everything under control. He came out of the jail without trust for anything he saw.

The only difference between Jake and a homicidal maniac, was he was storing his rage. When the day came, evidence would prove he was acting in self defense. Even his driving habits were going to change. He would no longer slow down for a crack dealer jumping in front of his car. If he didn't drive on the sidewalk, it was not premeditated.

He left the jail walking barefoot. The streets were wet with a chilly late September rain. His two-hundred-dollar boots were missing from his personal property. Just prefect, after losing almost thirty pounds shivering in a cold cell! More fuel for the fire. the slave trades. They were still shipping slaves to America after the colonies had outlawed slavery in 1812.

For three hundred years Espanole bounced around the globe planting flags and claiming real estate. They still did not always know where they were going, because, the friars were still doing their homework for them. As far as they were concerned the whole New World was only five hundred miles wide. This was because they measured the island of Mexico from east to west, with an infantile grasp of geometry.

When they did get around to measuring north and south, they had to do what they did best and burn the earlier inaccuracies. They could not consult the Aztec codex, which was already in ashes. And, they could not communicate with the Aztec astronomers who were likewise burned on a pyre. So, with the limited resources available, the globe was not quite a sphere, but shaped like a rugby ball.

Charts of the early period of exploration show at some definable moment in time, Europeans rediscovered trigonometry. It was not Arabic, like one would use to build a dome on a Mosque. It was not Euclidian like one would use to build a cathedral. It was not even as complicated as an origami paper folding exercise. It was simply drawing three intersecting lines, on a flat piece of paper. This is still known as the Great-circle course. The early explorers even over- valued this navigational tool. Again, it was treason to traffic in charts, between kingdoms.

The Spanish Crown, defender of the Church, was also regal authority in the Netherlands. Dutch ships were used to transport slaves to the New World and Gold back to Spain.

The discovery of a New World to the west, came as no surprise to British sailors. Locked away in dusty archives was a Latin text describing the journey of St. Brendan dating back to 800 A.D. It told of a party of monks who had reached land and returned to the British Isles.

English sailors had to do their own homework after Henry the Heretic pissed off the Vatican. England had its intrigue, being part of the protestant revolution. The first thing Gutenberg cranked off his printing press in 1450 was a copy of the Vulgate bible. Now any old peasant, fighting for something he could not understand, could look it up. Of course, the vulgar tongue was German, which at the time, was close to English.

Holy wars were raging on the continent. Protestants were branded heretics. Englishmen took a very dim view of being burned at the stake. They were not fond of branding -lest they be branded. Suddenly, the new world looked like a good place to escape religious persecution. That must be what God wanted, because when the Spanish Armada tried to bring the holy war to the emerald isles, England blew the armada out of the water.

It would take centuries to clean up the rest of the mess the Spanish Crown made in the New World. The whole time they used the pretext; they were under the authority of the Pope in the Vatican. The original thirteen colonies had to draw up a constitution and mortgage everything they owned, to put an end to the subterfuge.

That is why Jake was so pissed off with the preacher.

CHAPTER ELEVEN

Jake did not need to find reasons to be pissed off. If anything, he needed to find reasons to quit being pissed off. He even considered; he might have to find a quiet cave in the side of a hill as a sanctuary. He'd have to find someplace to be by himself, until the big dirt nap.

He was no stranger to pride. Being one of the deadly sins, he was cautious of its power. Still, he brushed up against pride time and again.

He could remember the day he was sworn in for the first time. The pride he felt for being selected. He could remember the guy who swore him in, why he was sworn in, and the tremendous responsibility. The guy who swore him into the service was killed on an unrelated exercise the following day. This leaves a lasting impression.

Jake could remember the pride he felt the next time he was sworn in years later. The pride of each promotion. The red on his left shoulder gave him pride. The gold on his left shoulder made him prouder. But; proudest of all, putting it all behind with an honorable discharge from service to his country. Being out here, where none of those other things mattered, made him proud.

Pride goes before a fall, they say. Judging from what he saw, Jake knew they were absolutely accurate. The proud country of his birth was an eroding society. Not all of it, just enough of it to make him pissed off. The American pie was getting sliced so thin, you could see the pattern on the plate right through the damn thing. The eagle was getting plucked so regular it was no wonder he was going bald.

What ever happened to moderation? Where was common courtesy? Who were all the demented lobbyists, constantly using legislation to clarify civil rights they already enjoyed?

With an automobile capable of going sixty miles an hour, why would anyone need a strip mall every half mile? Didn't anyone realize, that was one hundred twenty strip malls an hour? If you didn't find what you were looking for, in the first sixty strip malls, it won't be in the next sixty. Sure, you might need such a density of shops, in a pedestrian environment. But Americans don't walk, they want to become entangled in traffic. Traffic snarled around sixty miles of strip malls that used to be main thoroughfare.

Didn't anyone realize every strip mall is an intersection. And one hundred and twenty intersections, in sixty miles, take a hell of a lot longer to negotiate than one hour. As a matter of fact: traffic reduces the efficiency of the machine to twenty miles an hour. So, all the public really needs is a golf cart that can travel twenty miles.

He'd been wasting his time putting together a stupid little carnival for intercity kids. Focusing on a project, brought to his attention by a client who backed out, was a waste. He didn't need this abuse. Now he was walking home from a Jail, where his shoes had been stolen. What kind of a third world shit-hole was this? He was walking home FROM JAIL, barefoot.

He worked it over in his mind. The best thing Jake could do for Ned was kill him. The cruel thing, would be to let that miserable piece of shit continue his pathetic excuse for a life. Jake would choose the cruel thing. No sweat of his back. He did not even consider the reeducation program started fourteen days earlier. Ned would just have to go on living, with a short attention span. Hell, he was too inbred to have much on his mind besides Klan meetings anyway. Not that the Ku Klux clowns wanted him.

Fourteen days and barefoot on a wet highway in late September. Only bright side it was Florida. Another thing to consider was it was only a couple of miles from the jail to his house in the "hood". The convenience of the location was no coincidence just ironic. He had never planned on walking home from jail.

On the corner stood a UFL moonlighting as a hooker. A couple of crack dealers rolled by on bicycles. One of the rides was Jake's old bicycle, stolen a month ago; sixteen days before he went to jail as Jake reckoned. He watched as a slick BMW rolled up to the bicyclers, and delivered more product. He could see the bicyclers sell crack to the driver of a work truck, with a hooker in the passenger seat. He knew they'd pull over in a vacant lot, where she'd smoke the crack then get down to business.

"I don't need this shit!" grumbled Jake to himself, "I don't even know why I put myself in this position. Everyone knows this place is for losers"

Just then a cute black girl was walking home from school with an arm load of books. A car pulled up on the side of the road to proposition the child. Jake kicked the right rear quarter panel of the car putting a barefoot sized dent in it.

"Yer gonna need the money for the dent!" Jake yelled.

The black girl smiled, like it was the funniest thing she ever saw. Jake just kept walking. The car sped away with the driver nervously checking the rear-view mirror. That little girl, her and all the others just like her, that was why Jake did the things he did.

He was almost home when he saw Marcus coming. Marcus was a thief, who just happened to be a black Viet Nam veteran. He was supposed to be on medication for Post Traumatic Stress Disorder. Jake knew he probably wasn't. Marcus would always say he didn't need medication before going to Nam, he sure didn't need it now. He was a good man, for a thief.

They always had long talks. Jake was ready for some company even if it meant something small was later missing. Marcus never stole anything important, most likely another clock radio. Jake could not understand the obsession with clock radios. Last time it was a tiny AM-FM television with a built-in clock. It only cost twenty dollars at a pawn shop. It was no big deal.

Marcus liked Jake because he was the only guy who could actually follow the conversation, when he was off his medication. The funny thing was he would say three sentences and stop. Fifteen minutes later he said another three sentences. It would take hours for Jake to find out what was on Marcus's mind. This guy would make an excellent fishing partner.

From Jake's perspective, whenever the man became aggressive, he only needed to be faced down. He was not going to attack from the side or the back, he only came head on. Jake really wished Marcus would take his medication.

From the perspective of Marcus, the encounters were an opportunity to revisit regimental discipline. "Yes, sir..." "Right away, sir..." "I'll see what I can do sir," followed by fifteen minutes of silence. "No sir...," "Not right now, sir." "You've got to be fucking kidding, sir," followed with a big warm tight-lipped smile. Marcus had a smile that told you; whatever else you knew about him, deep down inside, he was really a good person.

Something Marcus liked about Jake was the way he cooked. Down home country style. Coronary artery blocking, French Creole Su-chef, or biscuits and gravy, it really did not matter. Jake could cook a four course Pot roast dinner in a cast iron skillet, and feed six people. Marcus could never figure out how he did it. Amused by the man's astonishment, Jake kept him guessing with the dexterity of a magician. Quite simply, whenever he used a pan he washed it, allowing everything to eventually collect in the skillet.

Someone else who enjoyed Jake's cooking was a moth- eaten ex-Panamanian by the name of Manuel Cartagena. He had found his way Norte, after the fall of Noriega. With a name like Cartagena, Jake was forced to question his references. Sure, enough he was a former resident of Panama, although it was inconclusive if this was his country of origin. When he arrived in the United States, he was studying Medicine. All he had to do was finish his residency. To do this he needed a sponsor, and this was something he did not have. He was not likely to find a sponsor looking like an unfed sewer rat.

Jake found Manuel wandering the streets in a disillusioned status, talking to himself. This was months ago, pre-jail to Jake. The singular act of kindness, which cemented their friendship, was the offer of a glass of Agua and a cheap cigar. The fact he spoke Castellon Spanish, instead of some variant dialect, didn't hurt either.

It was comical whenever the three of them were in the same room, sharing from the common pot of grub. Marcus smiling with his mouth full of meat, Manuel shoveling down rice and beans, Jake dishing it out. All three of them looked like poster boys for a Grateful Dead concert, now that Jake was down thirty pounds. Marcus with his three sentences and silence. Manuel filling in the silence with polite dinner time rambling. Jake constantly telling Marcus "That's not what he said! He said..."

"He did not say Niger, Mary. He said Ninfa marina. He was talking about my mermaid painting. You really got to get your ears checked," Jake explained.

"That's good. Don't want to kill him without a good reason. Too hard to hide the body." Marcus shoved more food into his mouth, with a big grin. He was set for another fifteen minutes.

The conversations would move along like a piston motor. Marcus would build up steam. Manuel would push it to the limit. Jake vented the accumulated pressure. Bing-bang-boom, La-de-da, rock-paper-scissors, the whole thing was comical. It wasn't as much fun as before he went to the slammer, just interesting.

They threw some logs into the fire place and put a video into the machine. None of them were watching the news these days. Ever since the bombings in New York and Washington it was just safer to watch videos. The media coverage was too emotionally exploitive. Everyone in the room had spent some time defending freedom. Everyone at one time or another had lived at a probable Ground Zero. The whole cold war was an exercise in predicting, what would take place at a given location, when an ICBM landed. Everyone in the room knew exactly why it happened. It happened because some religious fanatic was willing to twist their views to suit their purpose. Holy war for the purpose of taking some stuff, belonging to someone else.

Americas wake up call. Maybe for the armchair quarter back sticking their face in the camera looking for a photo opportunity. What about Oklahoma City, Ruby ridges the branch Davidians? What about Jim Jones? Remember the Alamo, Southern secession, the rough riders, Crown prince Ferdinand and Pearl Harbor. The very nature of mankind, is to be dissatisfied with peace when a charismatic leader appears. Hitler, Stalin, Saddam Hussein, they are all cut from the same cloth. Despotic tyrants manipulating the fragile minds of gullible people with promises of ridding the land of undesirables.

What happened in New York was predictable. They tried twice before to bomb the Twin Towers. If America was this fat stupid and lazy; it had to happen. The only question was how fat stupid and lazy were Americans. Stupid enough to complain about the lowest gasoline prices in the world, and at the same time purchase bottled water for a dollar, when the community water supply sells it at nine cents a gallon. Lazy enough to need sixty miles of strip malls, in a sixty mile an hour vehicle.

Maybe it was distraction instead of fat, lazy or stupid. Americans were lulled into submission by media analysts. Every wakeup call worked to the point it was irrelevant. The mono-toned consultant putting a spin on the information, punctuated by sales pitch for cars, beer and feminine hygiene products. The only unbiased coverage was the weather report, which anyone could gather from going outdoors.

Jake and the others preferred to watch videos. No commercials, and no hysterical coverage of things they had no control over. As the video dragged on they sat around smoking cigars. Monte Cristo Habana 2000 cigars. Habana 2000 was a trademark to suggest the cigars were Cuban, but they were really Dominican. Jake tried to slip Marcus a cheaper brand, and was caught in the deception. Marcus gave him one of those smiles. Manuel was beyond trickery, to him Monte Cristo was a cheap cigar. He once lived a life of privilege with the finest of everything.

To finish Jake poured them each a snifter of a mixture he enjoyed. One part Drambuie, one-part Bushmills Irish Whiskey. He was all out of Cointreau and Mezcal, a mixture he called the conquistador. His liquor supply, like his bank supply was almost drained. Big deal, four bottles of spirits was a two-year supply. He was only drinking now as a home coming.

Manuel showed Marcus to dip the cigar into the snifter. Introduce the liquor onto the tongue slowly savor it's presence. Everything must be accomplished with a direction of purpose, enjoying the combination of elements. Consider the soil and the harvest of grains and fruits. The fermentation and the curing of the tobacco must be considered. Identify with the patience of the distillation of the liquor and hand rolling of the cigar.

Marcus, who would have been happy with a beer, suddenly gulped down the contents of the snifter. Manuel rolled his eyes, jumping to his feet in the pose of an instructor, correcting a pugnacious student. Marcus pretended that he was concentrating on the TV screen, ignoring Manuel. Jake could see from his vantage point; Marcus was using his peripheral vision to keep the offended party in view.

"Sit down Manuel, I'm trying to watch the show." Jake suggested. Marcus attempted to pass the snifter to Jake for a refill. "Oh no pal, bar is closed, you should have listened to Manuel!"

This is where he expected them to claim "He started it." Both men shot condescending glances at each other. Now each of them were pretending to watch TV, while also using peripheral vision to focus aggression. The tension mounted like refraction on a pond. Jake let it go for just so long before saying, "If you guys don't stop it you're both out of here."

It sounded just like a parent. They all started laughing. Marcus called Jake "Mom", while Manuel used the term "Popie."

They both started in on their host, goading him. He gave first one, then the other, his one-eyed stare. Now, Marcus was calling him "Popeye," joined immediately by Manuel adding the song.

"Marcus, I've got a Hood and a rope in the next room." deadpanned Jake. Manuel exploded with laughter.

"What are you laughing at wet-back." same dead pan "I've got immigration and naturalization on speed dial."

Pointing to the TV, Marcus gasped. Elvira mistress of the dark, was whirling a pair of tassels like propellers. It was suddenly silent enough to hear a pin drop. They had to rewind it and watch it again, not the whole movie just the tassel twirl scene.

The Elvira movie was a classic. After rewinding it for the last time, he took it out and replaced it in the jacket. It was the only national movie premier he had ever attended. Every time he had a copy stolen, he had to go through hell, to get another. He locked it in an old footlocker with the rest of his spooky movies.

Jake finally kicked his visitors out. He was grateful for some company after what he'd been through. It was good to know he still had some friends. On the other side of the scale was a pending court case. He was innocent until proven guilty in a court of law. The attitude of the vigilance committee in the hood, was he was on release, until convicted.

CHAPTER TWELVE

With sixty miles of strip malls, in sixty miles of travel there should be no problem finding any product. Some strip malls cater to the upscale clients, some don't. So, some strip malls take on a seedy appearance, which lowers their sales. Jake didn't care if it was shabby or not. Every once in a while, he would pull into a place with a distinct border town appearance.

He would be out of his car, before being presented with a reason to question his safety. Out of the shadows would come a character or two projecting gang pride. Gang pride and the possibility; the shop keeper was suffering extortion. Protection payments to the gang was a third world business practice. If the shopkeeper did not tolerate, a taste, a little bite, the gang would loiter on his doorstep threatening potential customers. Here in the United States with no loitering ordinances, it takes a big gang. They just work in shifts, and accomplish the same Embargo.

A standard practice is to bum a cigarette, followed by a bumming a quarter. In this way a customer was not going to slip through the gauntlet. Just because a customer did not smoke, was no excuse. He must have at least a quarter, or why would he go inside a store. Coming out of the store there would be two bums to contend with. One to bum a cigarette, the other to borrow a quarter. Grade school, lunch money, gang tactics.

The overall effect of the procedure was to convince the customer to never come back. The shopkeeper was forced to cater to a select membership of customers. The strip mall gets rundown and shabby. Eventually sixty miles of strip malls exist, catering to all travelers. Segregation practiced on an socioeconomic level, forcing local government to step up practices and procedures to insure integration. Every new gang, needs a new sheriff. So, the law enforcement of a community, suffers segregation.

Snowballs in the sub tropics.

Jake was used to the subterfuge. He pulled into any old place he pleased. If he was approached, he used a sidestep action to avoid the confrontation. He picked up whatever he was after, and a box of "Top" cigarette rolling tobacco, in a bright yellow package. The choreography of the gang was always thrown off step by the bright yellow package. If they attempted to bum a cigarette, they might have to roll the damn thing. Why bother a man too poor to buy cigarettes already rolled. Jake would slip right through the gauntlet, unlock his door, and be on his way.

The tobacco would not go to waste. When he ran out of cigarettes, Jake would smoke it in an old corn cob pipe. He had a few boxes stuffed in a cupboard. It also came in handy for the bums wandering up into his yard asking for a smoke. When he handed them the roll your own, rather than a "tailor made", they almost never came back. The cigarette was just a ploy, used by the bums, to instigate a conversation. Jake was not stupid and sometimes used it as sport.

A conversation by an applicant bum, always centers around Jesus. Right out of the gate, they desire to determine, if a "pigeon" is right with the Lord. Jake never discussed religion. This forces the bum to resort to the next ploy, discussion of the Military industrial complex. Jake never discussed politics especially not with a bum. The bum usually would beat around the bush, searching topics of suitable conversation, trying to improve on the contribution of one cigarette to his welfare.

Sometimes Jake may contribute an old pair of shoes or a used shirt to an especially needy character. If he was in the mood, he may even allow the bum to unload a grievance, suffered at the hands of the social elite. The bum may stumble into a few words of condemnation, regarding the opposite sex, as another ploy to draw on Jake's sympathy. Jake did not discuss sex.

Once the bum was done with the rolling papers and tobacco they were on their way. On rare occasions, they may find Jake did have a few hours of work, they might earn. The old school said; no work, no charity. The new school seems to think concocting a cockamamy story was enough work in itself. Fabrication of half-truths with no basis in exculpatory evidence, was good enough.

Jake put it to the acid test; if a man was -what he said he was, he ought to know how to do, what he said he did. If a man said he was a carpenter he ought to know how to pull nails out of boards. If a man said he was a tile setter, he ought to know how to mix mud. If a man said he was a plumber, he should have no problem unclogging a drain. Tinker, baker, candlestick maker, every opportunity was extended, to verify the bum was truthful. Jake even made allowances for a method, unique to a geographical location. He would listen as they told him; "where I come from...".

The tools might be different sometimes, but not that different!

Most of the time he would cut them loose, after a hour of struggle with an unfamiliar concept. Paint splatters and all. The ten dollars he spent, was more than well invested, from the comedic value alone. He would load them in his truck and deposit them where they belonged, the homeless shelter. Ten dollars is a three-night stay at a homeless shelter with meals. A couple hours of work may earn a lady bum, a Greyhound bus ticket, to where she belonged. It was better than watching her degenerate on the street.

Every once in a while, there was someone who could actually perform the work in question. On these rare occasions, he would load them up in his truck, then drop them at a suitable trade union or construction site. Sometimes he would lead them to a temporary labor pool. Bums come in all colors, shapes and heave from all sexual orientations of ethnicity.

Over the years Jake had discovered a core group of talented individuals he called "Lackey and the boys". The epitome of the characters from the book Cannery Row. There was an irresistible quality, of comradery and human foible, in each of these men. They were all destined to allow their personal demons, to control their lives. There is not a social worker anywhere, to prevent the outcome. They would try the patience of a saint with their stupidity. Every last one of them, was a genius at their craft.

Moselle was a short fat Irish, New Englander. He was an extraordinary machinist. He was also a booze hound, who said he only drank beer, the truth was much different. Moselle would suck the alcohol out of a stick of roll-on deodorant. Richard, a Texas transplant by way of New Jersey, was much the same.

Moselle was a happy drunk, violent when sober. Richard was the opposite. The paradox of keeping both of them happy, was only solved by keeping them apart. The happy drunk would share his beer with the happy sober man. As the supply of beer ran out the sober angry Moselle, would blame the drunk, angry Richard. So, one guy spent all his spare time looking for beer, the other looking to sober up.

Richard was a humble man when sober, and a Baptist evangelist when he was drinking. Moselle was a brooding ex- Catholic all the time. From a philosophical level alone, they gravitated toward one another. Keeping them apart was a chore.

There was Leon, a small black man who was a landscape designer and interior decorator. Prudent enough to only exhibit gender, based on environment. He always affected a masculine presence around Jake, with much appreciation. He was creative, energetic and efficient. Always in a good mood, with a pretense to clown around, Leon would have made a great secretary. Too bad, Daytona was already taking up the space.

The last Joker in the pack, was a lanky tree trimmer and roofer called Wizard. When he did come around, it was always just to visit and pick up any loose project for a few bucks. He had a number of self-taught talents and somewhere along the line had been taught all the proper etiquette. Time would tell any trust in Wizard was a waste of energy.

All of them were a waste of energy. The first thing everyone had in common was none of them carried any identification papers. The next thing was they were not able to cash a personal check, a travelers check, any kind of payment except cold hard cash.

The Spook house was going to go as planned. Jake would write off the loss this year, with investment understood to be rewarded with the, Second Annual Spook House.

He was going to use Lackey and the boys, Daytona, Candy and anyone else who would work cheap. The job of Daytona, was expanded to include recording the work time of the men. Jake made them all fill out INS and IRS paperwork. He just planned to take a loss on his personal income for the year and get back to work at his professional career. Poor stupid, all the good intentions, milk of human kindness, Jake.

Two hours work, four hours pay. That was the way it worked out. Four hours work, eight hours pay. Before Jake reached his limit of investment, he was not finished the project.

There was obviously a bookkeeping error. If he kept going like this, he would take from monies allotted for special effects.

Consumables as they are called must arrive on site the night of the performance. Dry Ice and other things do not stay on the shelf. He had some of the bloody Mary mix fake blood. He had some of the grenadine syrup fake blood. He had the colored lights and mirrors but everything was a consumable needing replacement in the span of three weeks.

The salary of the actors was also in question. Everyone involved with the production, said they would be willing to volunteer, as some character or other. He even had two Elvira's, but they would have to call themselves lady vampires, to avoid any copyright infringement.

The time was running tight with the jail thing and all. Skip the first week only run it for two weeks. He decided to skip the second week, and only run it for one week. One week would be enough to prove it could be done.

Daytona was the spitting image of Elvira. Marcus was a mummy. Manuel was an acceptable Dracula. Three witches sitting around a bubbling chaldron, one dummy Moselle and Richard. Leon for a voodoo priest or priestess, who knew? Wizard as well a wizard. This left Jake to run all the special effects, collect tickets and fill all other functions. They might just pull it off.

All the tickets were printed. All the flyers had been circulated. All the consumables were either on hand or on hold. All that was needed was happy cheerful children.

CHAPTER THIRTEEN

The night of the opening was a farce. No one showed, not even the actors. He was standing alone in a haunted house filled with special effects. Like a true trooper he cranked everything on to see how well it played. Smoke and Mirrors, colored lights, bubbling caldrons, walls dripping with fake blood, it was all perfect. He had proven to himself it could be done. That was not the object, the object was to service the community. Jake was standing in a pile of debt, with nothing to show for the experience.

He opened the house for about six kids on the night before Halloween, or as some call it beggars' night. He got two lone attendees on the actual holiday. Of course, this may have been a couple of curious teenage hookers.

This was not the first party Jake had thrown, where no one came. He was a bit philosophical at first. He just knew the time was not right for a venture like this. So, what, he should have spent the money on other things. He would just go back to work and earn more money, and never think twice about the past.

Bad timing may have been part of the problem. The September 11th bombing of the World Trade Center had everyone upset, and looking over their shoulder.

He could even explain the actors not participating. Elvira did not like Manuel because he was a wet back. Marcus and Manuel had problems communicating. Moselle and Richard had problems centered on drinking or not drinking. Wizard was a repressed raciest who needled Leon. Leon was also a bone of contention with the homophobic Richard.

The Leon, Moselle dynamic was another thing. Moselle wanted to befriend Leon, but was afraid his past would be exposed. Nobody knew at onetime Moselle was teenage runaway. He survived as a transvestite male hooker, before he became fat and grew a moustache.

Jake packed in the project. Cut his losses and determined to go back to work ASAP. He had spent several thousands of dollars foolishly, with nothing to show for it, but a home looking like a Spook house.

He did not realize the activities had come to the attention of the vigilance committee who were busy guessing what he was up to, inside the house. He was not a slum lord like most members of the committee. The committee thought Jake was either to be up to the serious work of surveillance, or running a methyl-amphetamine lab. Checking with the sheriff undercover agents in the area, it was determined they could neither confirm or deny, he was preforming surveillance. So, the vigilance committee knew nothing more than they did before.

The sheriff; red flagged the location. In the interest of public safety, the building was earmarked, as a possible laboratory for production of controlled substances. Meanwhile they check to background of the owner/ suspect. Jake got straight ""A" s" in college organic chemistry. A factor which would prompt the further scrutiny of the detectives involved. They now had probable cause to pry into his bank accounts, check his mail, sort through his trash and scrutinize his blood bank donations.

His blood bank donations showed no use of controlled substances. Jake was clean. This did not however rule him out as a suspect. He could still manufacture anything from GHB to crack cocaine, although exposure to cocaine should leave a residue in his blood plasma. Some interesting spikes, on samples of the blood sera, showed elevated levels of hormonogenic compounds, thought to be nutritional supplements.

The next time Jake went into the blood bank, he was asked to donate plasma only. Due to technical problems with the equipment, Jake would urinate rust for several days after donation. As a result of ruptured blood platelet, his already diminished health took a dive. Technician error was ruled out.

Jake dropped another ten pounds. He was now thirty-five pounds shy of a healthy individual. He was beginning to look very much like a skeleton. The casual observer may determine he was either a crack-head or a victim of HIV. Patrol officers get good at sizing up a potential detainee, based on their physical appearance.

Jake who was willing to submit a urine sample; anywhere, anytime, was never asked to do so. Popular opinion was enough evidence.

The new buzz word was "Homeland Security". The vigilance committee of slum lords jumped on board. Nothing is more pitiless, or demeaning, than a slum lord with a badge. The concept of constitutional human rights of a renter, was the first thing violated. The practice was as mediaeval as it was merciless. Overnight the homeless rate skyrocketed, as evictions sent probable hookers, pimps and pushers into the streets.

If an army of rabble, is the desired effect, the best way to assemble one is put them out into the street, in mass. Without a hovel, to hide their improprieties, they will naturally form ranks. Once in ranks, they choose leaders to guide the assembly. The leadership then set about the task; of identifying targets of opportunity and enclaves of those sympathetic to the cause.

Poor stupid Jake. A home right in the middle of a war zone. Vigilantes on one side, crack-head army on the other. Anything not nailed down up for grabs. He did not even suspect he was under surveillance by the Sherif. He only knew he felt the eyes of a multitude pressing on him from every direction.

The only thing to do, in a case like this, was to delineate the tactics set down by the Knights Templar. Draw a line in the sand and set forth a discipline "this far and no further". To this end he posted "no trespassing", signs on four sides of his property. Neither friend or foe was allowed to cross without his spoken permission. Anyone allowed to gain access was accorded sanctuary within the rules of the house. Violation of the rules, was immediate withdrawal of sanctuary.

The first applicant was Leon. His affiliations with the rabble jeopardized his safety. He was not willing to join an unruly mob planning clandestine activities. Not being one of "us", he was viewed as one of "them". Jake had enough problems without being drawn into the fracas. All he could do for Leon was loan him a bicycle to outrun his pursuers. Leon was instructed to; return the bicycle on the following day, after Jake had a chance to think.

Jake warned the man "If you don't return the bicycle, it makes you a ...do I have to say the word?".

Leon shook his head. He was well aware how Jake defined the use of the word. He even indorsed the use of the word as utilized by Jake. Jake had often promised not to call a dope dealer, "the word", if they would only quit dealing crack.

Leon took off on the bicycle, promising to return. A promise he would not keep. He got within the city limits and was arrested for an outstanding warrant. The officer would never have noticed Leon except for being on a bicycle. The drug dealers play cat and mouse on bicycles, so the officer had probable cause. The outstanding warrant was Leon's failure to appear. Jake would never locate the bicycle. Insurance claim item one.

Jake bought another bicycle a few days later, along with some Brahma bull chain from a feed store. He padlocked the new bicycle to his roof rack of his new car and went in to sleep. He was too tired to bring the bicycle in that night.

Insurance claim item two, the new bicycle. Brahma bull chain cannot be cut with normal bolt cutters so whoever was responsible was also resourceful.

During the summer of that year Jake had purchased a new car. All his business was conducted from a mobile office. The old vehicle was not worth much as a trade in, so he kept it in the yard as a spare. Two insurances, two tags, two phone bills, a mobile phone bill, a pager bill. All to support a rolling office.

The original mobile phone came up missing some time around his arrest. He informed the service and canceled the line. He switched carriers and under a buddy plan gave a phone to Daytona in her own name.

Because she had failed to provide her end of the workload, Jake was disappointed. When second notices of bills started to arrive in the mail, Jake was outraged. He had made these the responsibility of Daytona. With his already diminished bank account he was forced to pay the bills, late fees and current charges. Adding this to the missing wallet with a few other variables could only mean one thing.

"Why didn't you tell me you used to be a Titty Dancer?"

Jake snarled across the yard, fenced in, with a bell on a post. "I would never have hire you, you pathetic sow".

"Get out of here nutcase before I call the Law." was her reply. She was going to call the law repeatedly, on the man from across the street. Their brief partnership was at an end.

The Sherif was dispatched on a weekly basis to Jake's home, always from an Anonymous Source. An anonymous source which could only have reported the activities in progress, from the vantage point of a singular direction.

Reports to the police were made on everything from; possession of a firearm, which turned out to be a barbecue lighter, to; cruelty to an animal, a friends unchained pit bull, put back on the tether.

In each case the Sherif responded in record time, duty bound to ensure public safety. In each case it was concluded the Sherif had participated in a Chinese fire drill. A process of conjecture, to produce evidence, had the opposite effect.

The States Attorney sent a Writ of Dismissal on the charges related to his arrest. Jake had spent fourteen days in jail for no good reason. But at least that was over and done with.

He was out thousands of dollars, had made none of his projected goals, and his every moment was scrutinized. He rationalized his missing wallet, was a used to cash the travelers' checks. That would explain why he was paying bills twice. He just could not prove the theory. He would have to somehow get past the events of the last few months.

Just when things were getting back to normal, his old truck broke down on the side of the road," during a torrential rainstorm. He put a note in the window as to where he wanted it to be taken and left. Again, he was walking, this time in a rainstorm. The truck was gone the next day, when he went to get it running. He checked with the garage where he had directed it to be taken, and they had not seen the truck. For several hours he telephoned various impound lots and came up empty handed. The truck had vanished.

Wizard was the next one to come to Jake for sanctuary. He was being chased from flophouse to crack house. Everywhere he went, he no sooner tried to sleep, when he was forced back onto the street. A few hours' sleep would do him some good.

Wizard confided in Jake he was a freelance undercover operative working for the police. Jake took the information as valid because the man was sporting injuries that only come from self defense. But if he was, what he said he was, then the police had a safe house he could use. This did not concern Jake.

These bums just could not get it into their heads, the charity ended, when the job ended.

On the heels of Wizard, came Manuel Cartagena. He too looked a wreck. He was being pestered by other street bums who had even less than he did. Both of them looked as pitiful as any refugee from a war zone.

Neither of these men were strangers to the allure of street walkers. A condition not tolerated by Jake. Rule One, no hookers in the house. A rule easily circumvented by Wizard by introducing the lady as a undercover operative. Jake did not buy the lie. He had seen the woman before. Wizard was asked to leave. The woman kept coming back. Jake finally had to firmly convince her to leave, not knowing she would carry off another mobile phone in the process. She vanished without a trace.

Every night at 10 o'clock, the racket started. The defining din of an army of guerilla warriors. The strike and melt back into the shadow's tactics of a quasi-militia. Unorganized chaos of anarchy plagued the dark streets. Smiling faces of the daylight hours, now shrouded in dark clothing, sinking into shadows. Light the only defense. They could only operate in the shadows.

Jake blamed the vigilance committee. They were the ones who closed all the vacant houses, the homeless use in cold weather. The homeless were now out on the street, adding to the chaos. The vigilance committee evicted all the suspected pimps, hookers and dealers. This only added to the flow of homeless.

The vigilance committee were closing houses under the pretense of Homeland Security. What they really wanted to do was improve property values. The overall effect was like jabbing a stick into a hornet's nest.

CHAPTER FOURTEEN

When a book jumps off a shelf by itself there is a good reason. Perhaps a magician has concealed a strong thread, which will pull the book from the shelf when the unwary brushes it while walking. A book jumping from a shelf after hearing a loud retort is another thing. If the book jumps from a shelf, where a man normally sits or sleeps, the book should be examined.

Examination of the book in Jake's hand, showed the bookcase was in the correct location, as planned. The book had slowed the projectile to a stop, within its pages. Pity to sacrifice a book to slow a bullet.

The only one who would possibly understand was Marcus.

He was the only one who had the necessary training, to deal with the shadows intersecting a lamplight in the distance.

Time would tell Marcus was one of the few who never compromised. Everyone else had surrendered to temptation but not Marcus. He might be nuts, he might be in need of a chemical straight jacket, but he was not compromised. He was no angel. He was just an honest man.

A few days later when Marcus dropped by for a visit, Jake showed him the book. Marcus immediately went to the outside of the wood framed house. He examined the location of the bookcase on the exterior wall.

"Spooky?" "Now." "Wasn't it?" He smiled his smile.

"No, I thought it was a little sloppy." Jake swallowed hard,

"They had a perfect shot through the front window. All they needed was to step into a porch light for a moment. They could have used a rifle from that vacant house across the street. Some young gang member probably."

Marcus had another fourteen minutes left before he would add to the conversation. While they waited; Jake outlined a plan to take Manuel Cartagena to Tampa, where there was already a integrated Hispanic community. Jake planned to drop Manuel off at a men's shelter, after alerting the Brothers Don Bosco Mission of his talents. Surely, they would know what to make of his training and education. The Catholic order ran a boy's home, where Manuel might even serve as a medical attendant.

"Sounds like a plan.", "Maybe", "Can I come along?"

"If you wouldn't mind, I could really use you to watch over the place while I'm gone." Jake suggested.

Marcus shrugged, going over to observe the only space in the bookshelf. Peering inside, he took a small wooden dowel from the workshop and sent it through the hole to the exterior.

A tight-lipped grin stretched across his face.

"Might have been the cable guy.". "I'm gonna need beer."

"How do you know it wasn't a white supremacist?".

"I don't know! To tell you the truth, that makes more sense than any other theory." Jake reckoned, "The method fits with everything else going on. All they need is a dead white guy, to assemble a lynch mob. There is already enough public condemnation of the people down here."

"White hookers showing up dead, just doesn't draw em in. like it used to!" Jake swallowed again real hard. "The way I look at it, we have to defuse this situation before it explodes." Marcus nodded in agreement. This thing was picking up momentum all the time. Getting Manuel to Tampa was the right thing to do under the circumstances. One dead innocent Hispanic could send the whole thing skyrocketing out of control.

Marcus held his belly "Sure am a little hungry" "Maybe a little biscuits and gravy?" "Who's side are we on?"

"We're not side were strangle middle." offered Jake.

Marcus lost his grin, now he swallowed really hard. He flashed back to Viet Nam. He knew no fear then, but it had played in his mind enough times, to know fear in retrospection.

Still, this was a different time and place. The rules were different. That was the jungle. This was an urban landscape with jungle out on the outskirts of town. The opportunity to test his metal, one more time was irresistible. He started grinning again.

Jake did not ask him why he was grinning, because he would have to wait too long for an answer. The biscuits and gravy were not going to cook themselves as they finished eating a knock came on the door. Monica, just happened to be in the neighborhood. She thought she'd drop by unannounced. Jake went out onto the front porch closing the door behind him. Monica speculated he must have a woman inside. Jake did not think it was any of her business.

"Well anyway, my new boyfriend makes me give him blow jobs for grocery money." she started.

Jake was not the least bit interested. It was a ploy she used to pique interest, while maneuvering an end run. The right to remain silent was wasted on Monica. She would sail right past what a mentor needed to know to assist her. She'd then jibe right back on the same course, and explain why they should not.

Jake did not care what two consenting adults did to run a household. He took the minority opinion, her lover probably resorted to this tactic in order to keep her quiet, while he still felt like giving her the money.

"So anyway, I was wondering...".

Here it comes, her whole reason for dropping by. She was going to put the pinch on Jake for more money. It didn't take a mind reader to forecast where this conversation was going.
Jake made a break for the mailbox. Maybe there would be some outstanding bills he could use as an excuse to fend off her plea's.

The mail box was empty.

Muffled by the wind he reached into his pockets. Standing like a plowboy, he slid a bill off the money roll, and folded it.

Palming the folded bill, he swung his arms up to the posture of a Cigar Store Indian. The body language told the woman he was going to need convincing. Monica knew instinctively to change the subject, wear him down with idle conversation.

Jake was way ahead of her. He pretended to scratch his nose while sneaking a peek at the denomination of the folded money. He then slipped back to the folded arms demeanor. She improvised humor to trying to melt his poker face.

She playfully poked him in the ribs with a finger, calling "gloomy Gus".

When he tired of the charade, he produced the money seemingly out of nowhere, mystifying Monica. Take it or leave it, just go away. "Do you have any idea, how many blow jobs you owe me?" Jake asked.

Jake did not want anything from Monica. He just wanted her to stop preying on his sympathy. Six months free rent here, another six months there. Forty dollars here, one hundred dollars there. He could add it all up, if she wanted him to itemize. He especially did not want a blow job. He knew she would just go to the next sucker, and complain about Jake. Get on your broomstick and ride, Monica.

Now she needed to use the bathroom. Meaning she still wanted to know who was in the house with Jake. She needed to dig up just a little dirt, on all her pigeons. Best way to solicit a back scratch, was to give the other monkey an itch. Jake considered evolution a waste on Monica, the succubus monkey girl.

He started back inside. She got in her car, rolled down the window and called after him, "How did everything go with the sponsor to the Spook House?"

Jake did not turn around, he went inside and shut the door.

A minor mystery solved; it was Monica all along. She had gone to the charity with some wild fabrication, making Jake waste months of time. It was the little she-demon who was responsible.

The following day, Marcus was loaded down with beer and video tapes. A pot of homemade stew looking much like Gumbo, was on the boil. If he kept it warm it would last all day.

While Jake made the Tampa run, Marcus a computer - savant, was given a brand-new laptop computer to configure.

The laptop had sat in the box long enough. Jake was going to need the digital camera package, as well as the Internet capability. He also Instructed Marcus to see to it, the word processing would be directed to the disk drives only. He did not want to clutter the hard drive with a bunch of project specific data. Too much of his hard craned work, was landing in the hands of the unqualified.

The Internet was changing the entire universe. People did not have to be qualified to give the correct answer. Everyone was solving the problems from solutions in the back of the book. Jake was the kind of person who solved the problem, then checked to see how close he was, to the correct answer. It is a process of producing a failsafe.

If Jake got the right answer he was dealing with a reasonably strong principle. If he got the wrong answer, he was faulty in some concept of the application. If he still got the wrong answer, perhaps the book was inaccurate.

One glaring example was the trust everyone had in the distance of longitude lines at forty-five degrees north latitude.

The books all said the correct distance was roughly sixty-nine miles. At the equator the distance is roughly sixty-nine plus miles. At forty-five degrees north latitude the distance is only about forty-nine miles between Meridians. Jake would have never discovered the error, by solving to a supposed correct answer. This was when Jake started to withdraw from traditional university study.

The popular answer was not always the correct answer. The whole concept of ability to make an educated projection, was the assumption the information was correct. A geomagnetic assumption made at one location, required a different correct answer, for each new location. This was Jake's personal enigma.

He tried to iron out the collaborative information, before an event took place which landed on the news. He was tired of puffy overinflated egos, explaining away their personal failures, on language or inept actions of underlings. Let nature take its course, but do not search for a scapegoat. Gospel according to Jake.

Boilers don't blow on their 5wn. Space shuttles are not supposed to come apart in mid-air. A building once targeted, remains a target so long as it remains standing.

Just like any castle wall, an enemy has not yet breached, the very fact it still stands is a goal for the next generation. The whole process of civilization is for one generation to build what the next generation tears to pieces. Followed by the next generation to rebuild anew. The answers were present before the parents and grandparents.

The answer was present before time itself. The question is what was yet to be discovered. The polite answer was but one of the solutions to the equation. Overlook one of the variables, and the polite answer is the wrong answer. All the lemmings run headlong off a cliff, into the sea.

It was fun while it lasted, a lemming lament.

History is written by the winners. The opinion of the losers is burned as heresy. The objective report is recorded, by those who pick up the litter and wounded, from a battlefield. The objectivity is based on the first-hand witness of carnage.

Jake did not want a computer hooked up to the World Wide Web, where a "cookie" allowed access to his hard drive. The "cookie" able to root out Heresy, then burn it, to preserve the polite correct answer. Jake never rolled over for a cookie, when he was a child. He was a little too old to start mimicking Pavlov's dog even in cyberspace.

CHAPTER FIFTEEN

Jake took Manuel to Tampa. The trip was hours longer than it needed to be. Manuel was hesitant to leave Orlando even if he had to endure the desolation of a street life. He had a wife in Panama, Jake learned. He had not seen his children in three years. Jake told Manuel, "He could have walked to Panama in three years. What was he doing spending time with hookers in Orlando, when he had a wife in Panama?"

Jake never told Manuel, that some of those hookers only looked like women. He approached the subject of cross-dressing prostitutes once, but did not follow through. The revelation of being an accidental Maricon, might be more harm to the man than needed. Maybe the man already knew. He was a hard one to follow, because his train of logic did not always stay on track.

The Brothers Don Bosco were an old Spanish missionary order who believed in work, study and prayer. They had monks, layman brothers, and priests. They were an odd bag of Dominican, Franciscan, and other Catholic orders.

The whole purpose of the Brotherhood was to settle differences in the practices of worship; to explore a compromise of the rubicon of Dogma. The priest may be a Jesuit with a tradition dating back to 1540 [Loyola. The Dominicans had carried the faith to the new world, where the Conquistador subverted Christianity in favor of Plantations.

The Franciscan were brought through Canada to the new world, by the French.

The Franciscans had a good relationship with the northern Mesoamericans. The Dominicans had a uncertain relationship with the southern Mesoamericans. The Jesuit were expelled from France in the mid eighteenth century, leaving a void that could only be resolved by revolution.

A remarkable occurrence on the New Mexico plains, with a tribe of Mesoamericans called the Zuni, would for all times link the three religious orders. As the Conquistador sought to subjugate the Zuni, the Dominicans were visited by Jesuit Franciscans. The Jesuit Franciscans demanded moderation in the treatment of the Zuni. The Zuni, sided with the Jesuit Franciscans, and as one nation converted to Christianity. The Dominicans were either going to share in the credit, or explain to the Vatican, why they let themselves take orders from the Conquistadors.

As a result of the favorable outcome, the Vatican took a experimental stab at forcing the cooperation of the divergent apostate. The Vatican would allow the brothers to remind each other; to stay out of the affairs of man, and get back in the boat with Jesus.

Two hundred years later this process meant, every time someone had a complaint, they would be forced to cross-reference the entire Vatican Library before anyone was placed on a Pyre. With the Vatican library containing every language on Earth, this process could take a very long time.

The Brother's Don Bosco was a good example of this experiment. The mission of the settlement, was to take in pre-criminal adolescent boys, and teach them Quid pro Quo.

Reward based on contribution, Quid pro Quo. Not; you scratch my back and I'll scratch yours, Quid pro Quo. Lesson plans were conducted with a "vis-a-vis" attitude. A student could succeed; vis-a-vis the easy way, or vis-a-vis the hard way. Vis-a- vis the book, or vis-a-vis the hickory stick. Future felons repeatedly chose the stick. Future politicians and lawyers chose the books, to qualify interpretation of the fore-mentioned Quid pro Quo.

Jake ran Manuel past the Brothers Don Bosco as a courtesy to the man, and the monks. Courtesy to the monks because they were going to eventually have to deal with him anyway. Courtesy to the man, to establish when the day came, Manuel would know who he was dealing with.

Manuel was too pious to be a criminal. He was too human to avoid temptation in the form of hookers. Too recently immigrated to understand American Law. Too disenfranchised to be integrated into his rightful place in society. Too emaciated to allow for proper mental hygiene. All together it spelled the man was nuts. He would eventually land on the doorstep of the monks.

Manuel and Jake arrived at the Spanish mission after Vespers. The time for quiet contemplation and prayer. Jake apologized for the interruption and stated his need with firm guarded brevity. Out of the corner of his eye he caught a glimpse of a feeble old monk who recognized Jake. With a quick glance he remembered the monk. They had once deliberated a small matter over a snifter of Benedictine liqueur and two cigars. Twenty years had passed yet the recognition was there. The assembly of clerics deferred to the old man, who remained silent with an unmistakable inspired countenance. The moment of recognition was all Jake needed.

He again apologized then loaded Manuel in the truck. As calculated, Jake had been instructed to deliver the man to a shelter where he could expect three nights stay. By the time they arrived at the facility, the shelter said it would honor seven days accommodations. Jake did not mention it to him, but he knew the good monks, were already working on behalf of Manuel.

Manuel clung to Jake with an uncertainty of the arrangement. He wanted to go back to Orlando. He was anxious of the outcome of being in a new city. Jake finally pried Manuel loosed, assured him everything would be fine, and drove away.

Today Manuel is finishing out his residency in a Tampa hospital. Somehow, he located a sponsor in those seven days.

He gained a lot of weight, and brought his wife and children up from Panama. He still does not know, a damn thing, about American law. This should change by the time he is sworn in as a naturalized citizen. Jake never saw him again.

The ride home was a blessing and a curse. He was free of Manuel. The man had drained Jake of all energy. It was as if he was sucked dry by an emotional vampire. Manuel had required so much energy, there was not enough left to concentrate on the road. Still, Jake had no regret donating his time to help the man. He told himself, he would be back to work in no time, this was just a chore left over from the Spook House debacle.

He arrived back in Orlando late and out of cigarettes.

Pulling into the first strip mall he could find; he purchased a pack of smokes and as it would happen the bright yellow box of "Top". A surveillance van across the street snapped a photo of a "White" man in the "Hood" with drug paraphernalia. Why else would a white guy need roll your own tobacco. White guys don't roll their own. Surveillance suggested the tobacco was paraphernalia.

Worse yet, this white guy was communicating with a street level dealer on the way back to his vehicle. Too bad in Florida it is illegal to make a voice recording of conversations. The surveillance van had long range microphones; it just could not use them.

Inside the van the conversation was guarded, "OK no exchange was made! Let him go." "Snap a photo of his tag just in case." "Hey who farted?"

Jake drove two more blocks and was home. Marcus was as jumpy as a cat, when he woke to find a key in the door. Jake told him to go back to sleep.

"Aw hell no!", "Spooky shit going on around here man."

"I'll see you when I see you." And Marcus was gone.

"Soot yourself.

.." Jake closed and locked the door. A quick peek around showed everything was in its proper place. Even the clock radio was there, which was a little disturbing. Marcus must really be spooked.

Jake had just enough time to sit down on the toilet, when a knock came on the rear door. He zippered up, task incomplete. As he looked out the window next to the door, he could see two decently dressed black men. He was puzzled, it was one O'clock in the morning. The men identified themselves as Orlando plain clothed police officers. They showed no shield.

"You're in the wrong Jurisdiction. Get off my property!" Jake threatened. Right now, he had more important things to do, than play games with clowns who didn't know where they were.

He shut the door, then went back in the bathroom.

Another knock at the door. They could wait he was busy.

More knocking, "Gee Zeus can't a man get a moment of peace". More knocking. "At least let me evacuate a colon full of driving back and forth to Tampa."

*. More knocking.

A white woman was at the door, at one O'clock in the morning, plus the time it takes to shit. What could she possibly want in a questionable neighborhood, at one O'clock. She was short with huge knockers. Her knockers were so large she was almost as thick as she was tall. The rest of her torso was proportional to a small frame. She would even be regarded as attractive, under less annoying circumstances.

Jake was not into short women. Had they come into contact at a company party or other function, he could see himself spending some quality time alone with this stranger. She knocked again. Jake went around from the window to the door.

She wanted a cigarette. A cigarette at one O'clock plus, in a questionable neighborhood, from a stranger. He made her wait on the stoop, while he went to get a yellow box of Top.

"Here roll your own".

She was a very clean looking woman for a street urchin.

Clean hair, clean complexion, clean nails. She fumbled with the rolling papers. Jake ended up rolling the smoke for her.

"Here you go", he passed her the finished product.

Now he just wanted to see her smoke the thing. She lit the cigarette without inhaling. He looked at her closer. She was twenty-five or thirty years old. A non-smoker. She requested something to drink. Jake gave her a glass of ice tea. She barely touched it. He went inside and closed the door. Weave the glass on the step!" he told her.

It was a real puzzling event. She was either a topless dancer out for a stroll, or vice squad bait. The calculated odds of either probability, knocking on a strange door at one O'clock in the morning was slim to none. The calculated odds, of a woman being put up to it by a third party, were greatly improved. If she was part of a pimp's plan, the effect was a simple equation.

If she was a part of a vice sting operation, the problem boiled down to a basic equation. Factor in the chance of a random coincidence, following another random coincidence, of the earlier visitors. His money was on pimp activity. A vice sting was a simple case of entrapment, even if he made her an offer.

Pimps had been offering him a sample for years. They wanted to maintain a presence in the hood, wherever they could find a susceptible alliance. He never took the bait. The marauding pimps, could not believe he turned down the offer time after time. He even earned a nickname on the street "Hey Fagot."

Maybe Leon was just another attempt to compromise Jake.

Test his fetish, see what he was all about. If he did not cave to the pressure, he would be a real disruption to "hood biz nee ss".

Sooner or later, he would have to break, "Ta jess de way it ss".

All this played on his mind as he dropped off to sleep.

CHAPTER SIXTEEN

It felt like he had just dropped off to sleep. It was ten O'clock in the morning. More banging on the door. Monica's usual knock. Very insistent knocking, Jake barely had time to piss away his morning erection.

"What is so damn important?" he fumed doing the best he could to cover himself.

"Did I come at a bad time?" she smiled, glancing down.

Jake did not bend to the suggestion. He went to the coat rack and grabbed a shirt. He was going to get to the point and get her gone. He did not want an update of her life story. He was not planning a biography of the succubus.

She waved for Sharon to come in from the car. Monica had used Sharon as a collaborative witness in the past, probably the only way to keep the story straight. Oh great, this was going to be a long-sorted tale, blown way out of proportion. He might as well make coffee.

"Cut to the chase how much this time?".

Sharon answered, "One Hundred Dollars".

"Nope, I'm going to have to hear the story, Sorry!" Jake was sorry. Sorry he was going to have to sit through a load of chatter. By the end of the story, he was sorry he could not take a red-hot branding iron and stamp a huge "S" right in the middle of Monica's forehead. At least; warn the next sucker, he was about to step in an uncovered manhole.

It seems Monica's present boyfriend was extraordinarily critical of the Lapdog John. The couple had a big fight, over John always sniffing around. Now that Sharon was almost an adult John had occasionally taken to sniffing her as well.

Objection, irrelevant information. Motion to strike from the record. Accepted, by Jake the judge.

So, Monica in the middle of the fight with the boyfriend, took the opportunity to approach the owner-roommate of the three-bedroom house. She made the mistake, of explaining to the roommate, she could have Jelly-Belly escorted out by the Sherif. All she had to do, was file a peace bond with the court.

She needed the roommate to verify, the boyfriend had threatened her.

Neither she or the roommate noticed Jelly-Belly sitting quietly on the porch in the dark. She even painted a portrait, of her and the owner-roommate, living happily ever after... in his house.

The owner-roommate could not make such a claim, having never interfered in the relationship between Monica or her boyfriend. He was only renting rooms he did not take sides in lovers quarrels.

It was then, Jelly-Belly made his presence known. By the time the boyfriend finished screaming, the roommate had every reason to worry for the safety of Monica, and himself as well.

"And you need the money to file the paperwork before he does" interrupted Jake, Growing weary of the soap opera.

"Yes, I have to file on Jelly-Belly, before he files on me!" So, another c-note got flushed down the Monica toilet. Fact was Jelly-Belly got to the court first. Not only, Monica barred from the residence, but from any and all five-hundred-foot radius that the man may travel within. Each and every place he worked was now off- limits to the stupid succubus Monica.

Every place he worked was somewhere she worked. She had no way to earn a living and no home. Jelly-Belly put her out in the street homeless, except for John the lapdog.

Jake would listen to the details at a later date. Right now, the money he loaned her, was being used for some purpose other than that, for which it was borrowed. One red hot branding iron could put an end of this nonsense. Monica would have to explain the "S" on her forehead.

The only thing good to come out of the loss of the c-note was Monica was gone for now. It was a shame, she was training Sharon, in all the tricks of the trade. Jake was more upset with himself, for allowing Sharon to believe; "Men are Suckers", than he was about the money.

On the subject of money, it was time to tighten up the flood gates. First, he had to figure out where his extra truck was located. Next, he better start making a list of all the stolen property for an insurance claim. If the thieves would only stop stealing his property long enough for him to make a claim.

Everything left in the yard for a few moments, was missing when he turned around again.

Richard and Moselle showed up in the middle of the afternoon. Both of them wanted to work for room and board.

The streets were getting too dangerous. Jake's place was no homeless shelter. He never pictured himself a charity. There was not one reason to assist either one of these men. Both of them went away, only to return after nightfall, and sleep in the bushes. One man covered in vine next to the privacy fence. The other under overgrown shrubbery. Jake discovered the ruse, and let it go unchallenged for the one night.

Moselle was satisfied with one night under the stars.

Richard was a different story. He dragged in every night around nine and crawled back under the vines. He was gone before sun up each morning. Where was the harm?

SUSPECT PROFILE O.C SHERIF DEPT.

INTERNAL DOCUMENT. The following suspect came to the attention as a possible ring leader, of a nuisance group, in a location under the jurisdiction of this law enforcement agency. A citizen action vigilance committee consisting of property owners, has brought to the attention of this department, reasons to investigate this individual. In the interest to public safety, this investigation was undertaken under the guidelines established for the Office of Homeland Security.

SUSPECT: James A/K/A "Jake" Dorado

LOCATION: Corner of West and 24" Hole Hell Suburb Option Florida.

COMPLAINT: Nuisance traffic month of October to present. Present complaint: frequent nocturnal encounter with known narcotic street vendors/prostitutes. Location frequented by persons suspected to be low level street traffickers. OC Sherif lacks resources to draw away from other surveillance projects. Location has been repeated regular source of complaint by anonymous concerned citizen. Attempt to establish undercover asset placement on location unsuccessful. Suggest matter be directed to Psychological Profile department for additional review. END SUSPECT PROFILE.

No good deed, goes unpunished. Any time the cosmic balance is upset, a vacuum is formed. The challenger to a predetermined stable orbit of events, is entrapped in the collapse of system. Extinction of social structure, is no different than extinction in the natural environment. The animal in a 200 may represent an extinct species, however, many of the unique traits are already lost. A caged animal is very simply an oddity.

Jake was the process of being examined as if he was a mountain gorilla, or some other endangered species. An alligator may be a better symbol of his present situation.

Whenever an alligator is discovered by the encroachment of man into a ancestral habitation, no effort is extended to directly communicate with the reptile. The threat to the community of newly relocated children and pets, is accessed, by quasi-qualified representatives of the people. A big alligator, in a small pond, is relocated or destroyed in the interest of public safety. It is the animal itself to blame for not staying on a evolutionary course, acceptable to the demands of the community.

A domesticated pet is awarded every convenient connivance as would amuse their owner. Small cute animals evolve into pets, or somewhere past utility of fondness, food.

Large domestics are likely regarded as a source of food. Given the incentive, most undomesticated evolution, could be seen as avoidance of landing on a plate. In other words, the undomesticated view remains the same, whether part of social evolution or not.

Jake, in the course of a lifetime, had developed a equation to handle the social-dynamical imperative. It involved differential and integral calculus. As with any complicated mathematical theorem the shortest solution is to solve for ZERO. Zero is a point where nothing happens. At zero a variable is introduced to place a limitation on the equation.

Jake's theorem resolution, as the product of trial and error, could be simply stated as "Eat Me!"

"Bite me, suck me and screw me" were all derivative functions of the integrated equation. Each represented the true result of a set of parameters, placed into the equation, by outside intervention. All Jake had to do was collect all relevant data and solve for Zero, then determine what the other individual actually was suggesting.

"You've got to look at the Big picture Mr. Dorado."

Meaning; while Jake did all the work, the other guy was going to take all the credit.

"You better loose that attitude!"

Meaning; Jake was asked to do work outside the agreed limits, at the time he was hired into a project.

As easy as it was to break down language into simple equations, there was always some variable not present at the time. The Zero(X) factor. Nothing happens, then (X) collides with Zero.

Popular Opinion sits there festering, and (X) lands right in the middle of the pile.

In the suburb of Hole Hell, Jake was the (X) splashing in a puddle of Popular Opinion. The good people of Hole Hell did not need a Sherif. They needed the National Guard. They need decontamination chambers to wash off neglect. The also needed a vaccine injection of the United States Constitution.

Poor stupid demented Jake. He still believed he could make sense out of a social condition that existed for so many generations. The police force was only there to suggest there was a correct way to conduct one's affairs. They were the last chance, before prison, to squeeze conformity out of a chaos.

The people who used self-serving Rhetoric, as an excuse for their own behavior, was the Anomaly. The only difference between prisons and plantations was the quality of life. All anyone could expect from prison was three hot meals and a cot.

The same was true of a plantation.

CHAPTER SEVENTEEN

Fools rush in, were, Angel's fear to tread. Fools, Firemen and Emergency Medical Technicians, all rush in. The only distinction between a fool and a fireman is training. The only distinction between a fireman, and an EMT, is advanced training. The only distinction between an EMT and a doctor is, a doctor will not make house calls.

Big frigging deal, a doctor may save the life of a patient, after an EMT already stabilized the life-threatening condition.

On the other side of the equation; a EMT does not have to explain to a HMO, the value of a procedure. So, who is the fool now, the guy hauling the gristle to the emergency room, or the man behind the pomp and circumstance of wearing a white lab coat?

An EMT only has to package up a heartbeat. The Doctor takes all the credit, but surrenders all the liability. Every moment of a doctor's time is scrutinized, recorded and later opened for pontificating. Regardless of how unseaworthy the vessel, at the time the good doctor took the helm, he is the captain. He is responsible for the condition of the boarded vessel, and all the actions of his subordinate crew. His only instructions to bring the vessel safely into port.

At portage, by the grace of God he may find; all the shoring of damage on the turbulent sea, was done correctly. A boat unlike a patient, never questions the presence of a poop deck where a promenade deck belongs.

Landing a vessel safely at the marina passes ownership back to the salvage company. Landing a patient into the safety of a hospital bed. allows pirates to climb aboard to pick through the incident, at a offering of Forty Percent of damages collected.

Jake among a host of other training, stopped while he was ahead of the game. He was satisfied with EMT training, to comply with any future needs which may arise. Under the Good Samaritan Law he could never be prosecuted for an emergency procedure for which he had received training. If, in the event, he was the first person at the sight of an accident, he could render a high degree of assistance pro-bono, without hesitation. When the jurisdictional authority arrived at the scene, Jake could turn his back and walk away, no questions asked.

With the American Students no longer required to study Physics in high school, the number of accidents was out of proportion to an acceptable level. An incident in his youth prompted the EMT training. Jake, time and again walked away from a miscalculated vehicular maneuver, soiled from participation in rescue.

Fire control was a requirement of all boot camp attendants of the US and USNR. Jake had an honorable discharge. He had the training, and protection of the Good Samaritan law.

Having to use the training, more often as the city grew, made him Jaded. If he happened to be the first man to discover a fire, he may try to put it out. He may also be the first, to openly suggest, the right thing to do would be to let it burn.

When Jake found a smoldering couch on the property line between his house and the next, he hauled it out to the street.

He planted the smoldering couch night on top of a culvert pipe used as a cache of neighborhood dealers, for storage of product. He also was in no hurry to alter combustion. With the couch on top of the culvert, the dealers could not reach their drugs. The smoldering would prohibit removal of the couch.

Jake went inside and shut the door. He attended to his chores, then discovered he was out of film needed for an upcoming project. As he drove away, he took notice of the smoldering couch the couch was an old dead Oak. He took a careful survey of the fuel and heat then determined the conditions safe, for the moment.

The old dead Oak tree was another former hiding place for contraband. When Jake first acquired the property, the house next door was a bonafide "Crack House". Upon trimming dead branches from the tree Jake discovered a big plastic bag of "crack" hidden in a hole in the tree. The hole was invisible from ground level. His activity in the tree, was closely watched by the next-door residents. Jake was resourceful enough to act like he was unaware of the hidden contraband.

As he climbed down from the tree a stray cat scuttled across the yard. A plan took place in an instant. That evening after dark, Jake climbed from his roof to the old dead tree. He was completely unobserved by anyone. Into the hole in the tree, he poured a collection of tuna oils, meow mix, and other bits of stray cat food. A freshly trapped field mouse was also shoved into the hole with the understanding mice love to nibble through plastic. As the mouse nibbled, the contents would be exposed to the tuna oils.

At this time Jake always stayed at his apartment, never at the property. There was no way the "Crack House" could connect him with any missing merchandise.

Feral cats are skittish, they eat and run, eat and run. They expect to drop portions of a meal, as they run back to the safety of their den. They are quiet and sneaky scavengers. They will return again and again to an available free meal, every time quietly, every time sneaky. Any city boy "crack head" that does not know this about feral cats, would be hard pressed to explain missing product.

Paranoia among addicts, is like the fuse on a stick of dynamite. Being Americans, they also expect immediate resolution to a problem. Combine the two psychoses, every man in the room started pointing fingers at someone else.

Missing merchandise, meant someone in the room was dipping into the stash, without permission. Discovery of the culprit, of paramount importance, to the posse. Nobody was going anywhere until the guilty party was found. Nobody was coming in until the guilty party was found. Under these conditions a "Crack House" cannot function properly.

Jake guessed the whole process should take about a week.

The decline was much swifter. Residents and visitors were gone in about three days. An occasional user would pop up, from time to time, knocking on an unanswered door.

The tree was abandoned in favor of the more reliable culvert. A culvert now covered by a smoldering couch. Jake did not set the couch on fire; he just moved it away from a location where it might affect his property values.

He picked up an extra pack of film at the drugstore to chronicle the tree, the culvert and the couch. At the store he happened across Leon the bicycle thief. Leon explained he was sorry about the bicycle; he had been in jail. Before Jake went to the slammer, he would have turned a deaf ear to the explanation.

His attitude was tempered by his experience.

"Tell you what, until you replace the bike, you're still a...

what the word I'm searching for..." Stuttered Jake

"Fill in the blank!" answered the quick-witted Leon, with a full toothed grin.

"Close enough!" Jake compromised.

"Mind if I catch a ride?" Leon groveled.

As the car pulled up in front of his house, Jake noticed the couch was now fully evolved. Flames were shooting from the top and assorted trash was catching fire from the heat. Jake was snapping photos as the fire truck pulled up, with a squad car closely behind it on the scene. Everyone stood around while Jake continued to snap pictures. The Fire lieutenant had a momentary word with the Sherif, as the flames continued to rage.

The Sherif asked Jake to step over and have a word with him. "Did he know anything about the fire? Did he know who put the burning couch where it was now? What else could Jake tell him about the blaze?"

"The fire started in the couch, I put the couch in the culvert, the culvert is used by street dealers to hide contraband.". Plain and simple. Watch how quickly things change.

"So, you set the couch on fire?"

"I did not say I set the couch on fire!"

"But you put the couch in the culvert?"

"Yes."

"Why did you put the couch in the culvert?"

"Because street dealers, use the culvert to hide Crack."

"You put a burning sofa in a culvert?"

"Correct." Jake admitted, he had nothing to hide.

"To stop dealers, from using the culvert to hide crack?"

"Also correct."

The deputy walked over to the fireman for a private conversation. He came back with a follow up question. "Why did you not put out the fire."

Jake pointed at the fireman and shrugged, "that's his JOB!" At this point, Jake was told to stand in front of the squad car. Presently the fire was extinguished. The fire truck loaded up and left the scene. Jake stood there, parade rest on a defined point on the pavement, in front of the squad car. The deputy was sitting inside the car with the air conditioning running. He was chatting on first a cell phone, then the radio, and again the cell phone. He finally climbed back outside.

"You a firebug?"

"Nope!"

"You got anything else to say"

"Nope!" Here comes the handcuffs thought Jake.

"Yer a bit of a wise ass aren't you" smiled the Sheriff handing Jake back his driver's identification. Jake did not answer, he took it for a rhetorical question. The Sheriff pressed the point; "Huh, couldn't hear you?"

"Around here, it pays to have a sense of humor, officer." Jake admitted. The Sheriff retreated to his air-conditioned car.

Jake loaded up Leon, to carry him the rest of the promised distance. Leon could not contain his complete astonishment of the last hour's activity. He was trapped between bewilderment and laughter. He kept mentioning how "If that had been one of the brothers, he would be heading to jail right now!".

Jake tried to convince Leon it was all a matter of keeping your mouth shut, and only answering the questions asked. Leon kept stressing the importance of being "white". Jake realized it was time to educate Leon.

"If I give you the key to my car, do you think you can drive it" Jake proposed.

"Hell yeah, I'd drive the shit out of this car." Leon grinned.

"Ok, right there is a good example. I wanted a yes, or a no, not a reason why I should not loan you, my car. Let's try it again. If I give you the keys to my car, do YOU think, you can drive it?"

"Why don't you give me your keys and find out?" came

Leon's annoyed response.

"Guess we know where you scored on the SAT exam. Why do you always answer true and false questions, with an essay." Jake prodded. "If I give you the keys, can you drive?"

"Yes?" Leon fumed.

"We're making progress." grinned Jake. "If I give you a violin, can you play it?

"What kind of a fool question is that? A violin takes all kinds of practice and training." muttered Leon. "Do I get to drive the car or not?"

"Sorry, I only loan my car to violin players!" laughed Jake.

"You and every other White devil, always keeping the black man down...." Leon trailed off into a soliloquy of rhetoric.

They had reached their destination. Jake only laughed, as Leon slammed the car door on the way out. He may as well have piled hot coals, on Leon's head, the effect would be the same. In a few hours or a few days, Leon would figure out Jake's ruse, and the embers would go out.

Leon's eventual grasp, of the concept of true and false, made it possible for him to enjoy a brilliant career as a paralegal. He never did replace Jake's bicycle. That was a pity, because it was a nice bicycle of a rare manufacturer. The vacuous Black Hole of the neighborhood had claimed another prize.

Mr. Espanto made it a family atmosphere, and the owner liked it that way. It was almost the last club in town, a customer did not have to order a cocktail, in order to attract the attention of a waitress. The chef was quick, clean and courteous.

When Jake was not using I-4 gridlock as an office, he relied on the Club to collect his thoughts. Most of the time the rear of the automobile office was festooned with charts, maps and manuals. Everywhere Jake plied his trade, the client would want to know; "where does it say...". Every time Jake was ready with the answer. Picking through the information, in the middle of interstate traffic, was a nightmare. The first thing he did, when he pulled up to the Club, was rearrange the disarray.

While everyone in town was selling snow cones to Eskimos. Jake was occupied with qualifying Eskimos, and quantifying available snow cones.

It was a long labor-intensive effort. The macro and the micro economic, long-range projections, with a margin of acceptable error. Responsible land stewardship, to safely provide soil and water conservation, all hinged on the efforts of people like Jake. Jake was an independent, a freelance. He did not have to kowtow to political goals. He only had to provide the right information at the right time.

The theory of land development is very simple. Business generates jobs. Jobs generate cash flow. Cash flow generates housing opportunities. Modest investment, results in modest housing opportunities. Grandiose investment, results in equally grand housing opportunities -for those who qualify. Education makes all the difference in qualification.

To the uncomprehending outsider, it looks like a system ruled by an inner circle of the elect, the Illuminate. In the American system, there are regulations in place, to provide a safety net. The regulatory process is so no one is left behind.

The overall effect of Corporate Investment is like the action of a Neutron Bomb, Alpha, Beta, and Gamma radiation spreads out from the explosion. Alfa particles, are contained by obligations like permits and investment. Beta particles, are contained by expenditures and economic impact to the community. Gamma particles, are the results which measure profit or loss.

The radiation in this case is cash. Cold hard dollars are the radiation. To provide a core of Critical Mass, is the corporate mission statement. A dreary document; the mission statement is a thick testimonial littered with irrelevant allusions, stifled by reciprocal agreements. A team of lawyers is required to dredge through all the "...where if's" and ". there fore's."

The mission statement describes in detail; Function of services, Desired value of services, and Economic impact expected. A corporate mission statement is generated to stimulate investment. The shareholder of a corporate offering, is presented with an endorsement of the potential earnings, to demonstrate intended results. A shareholder is issued a certificate to be honored at a later time. Long story short, shareholders are the critical mass needed, for an explosion of money.

No critical mass, no explosion. No explosion no jobs. No jobs, no housing. No housing results in homeless feral humans.

Homeless feral humans result in anarchy, pestilence, reversal of evolution, and unanswered social expectations.

In the American system of government, the democracy is intended to elevate the status of mankind. It seems to work pretty well most of the time. Fortunately, the city, has to answer to the county. The county has to answer to the state. The state answers to the nation. The nation answers to the people.

Take for example the Theme Park. The mission is to provide recreational tourism. As an employer the theme park has an obligation to investors. It also must provide for human needs of its employees. Housing, schools, hospitals, and shopping malls are all Beta particles of the Money Bomb, paid out of employee salary. The Gamma particles are Environmental impact, roads, soil and water conservation issues.

The County government serves to regulate uncontrolled growth. The citizens are what could be described a chain reaction. Their labor provides the money, which results in fallout, known as taxes. The county government, uses the Mission Statement, to issue a permit, to allow the Corporate Entity to construct a Neutron bomb, which when it explodes rains down money, to service the citizens and the fallout is taxes. Pretty simple right?

From out of nowhere comes the need for communication and education. There are some pitfalls; judging from all the homeless refuges, all clamoring to relocate from systems of governance, where a money bomb was defused.

The money bomb never goes off, when a tyrant tales' investment, without paying dividends to shareholders. All the foreign aid on the planet, won't stop a tyrant from draining the money bomb. All dictators do with investment, is purchase drugs guns and time. That is not how it is supposed to work.

A democratic republic makes allowances for language and customs. The citizens are given the ability to redress grievance.

A money bomb may be postponed for lack of significant documentation. There is no expectation of correct political outcome. The elected officials are prohibited from surrendering to temptation, even though there will always be Political Corruption.

Jake came into the endless cycle, at the only place the money bomb allowed him, the documentation.

Without documentation Jake would be another feral human, living out of a dumpster. Jake plowed under mission statements until his eyes bled. He cross referenced enough governmental regulations, to drive a man insane. All this, and still time to work a blue-collar freelance career. Independent research often meant, vocal minority opinion.

One of the major problems was a boilerplate approach to mission statements. Computers only made it easier to "boilerplate" a document, hack it up, change names and locations. Rearrangement of a chapter of a book in the wrong order, still makes it a copyright infringement. Every once in a while, a mission statement listed "Same as" without saying "As what?" Dead giveaway the author was a plagiarist. A plagiarist is a heretic. Clever heretics step aside, allowing the deceived, introduction to the bonfires.

CHAPTER NINETEEN

Marcus came dragging in from an extended weekend at the county Jail. Somehow, he abused his military training, by shooting another armed man in the knee with a gun. He was kept on ice while the detectives ironed out the details.

He was released, when it was discovered, he was acting in self defense. There was still some question, concerning a battered woman hiding in the shadows, when Marcus needed to defend himself. He was free on his own recognizance. The detectives must believe the other guy had it coming.

Upon release he made a bee line to Jake's place. The two spent time discussing the situation and cussing about the probable escalation of local violence. Jake cautioned Marcus to never again face anyone down like a gunslinger.

"Call 911, like everyone else!" offered Jake.

"Let the cops do their job?"

"Exactly!" agreed Jake.

Jake noticed Marcus was more focused than normal. He was not talking into silent reflection. Black on black violence was nothing new. The other man was lucky he was still alive.

Small arms training, meant Marcus used only what was necessary to disarm his opponent. Jake might have done the same thing.

"Except, my gun would have been pointing at his forehead"

"And that would be White on black! Don't forget that!"

Jake was the one forced into silent reflection. The whole reason for the conversation was to keep a lid on a tenuous social condition. They could not let the present paranoia get out of control. This place had all the ingredients as any other location where riots broke out. Watts, Chicago, Miami, Philadelphia, had all started from exactly this variety powder-keg.

"Only thing you need to worry about is if Louis Faracan shows up!" Jake finally argued.".

"….until then it might be a good idea not to discuss this with too many people."

"Don't blow it out of proportion?" smiled Marcus.

"Exactly!"

Shortly the conversation ended. Jake put Marcus out the door with a full stomach. The significance of the topic played on both their minds. Each man could feel the press of eyes on them. Neither one knew if they were being scrutinized by friend or foe. When someone casts an "Evil Eye", it pays to know the motivation.

Jake was accustomed to catching a evil glance from the slum-lords. His referring to them as "slum-lords" might have something to do with this progression. The poker-faced police had no reason to cast the "Evil Eye", they had the court system, as a fallback position. This left only the street people, who anyone with any brains, would maintain eye contact. When they lie, they look away. When they think a hand out is coming, they act sincere. When the handout is denied, they cast an Evil Eye.

Another cell phone was missing. This was the third one.

Jake reported the loss to the cellular service. He put it on the insurance list, then went out and bought another. This was getting expensive, one hundred bucks a pop. He needed the phone for work but this was getting ridiculous. Some hooker out there was getting a few hours of free cellular service. Who knows the compiled list of underworld activity being registered to Jake's phone. All he could do was notify the service and move on.

The device cost plenty, the interrupted service cost more.

Every time he got a new device it required him to notify all clients of a new number. He was starting to look flaky. Clients calling a disconnected number, throw away the Rolodex card.

This was going to cost him affluence in the months to come.

The whole freelance business is based on being available on the spur of the moment. Imagine the harm caused, by a man calling for a technical assistant being put in contact with a - hooker.

The actual diabolical nature of the phone thieves was much worse. The same posse crew sneaking in the bushes in the dark was responsible. Each time they got a hold on Jake's new phone they would scroll through the stored numbers. They would then call the number and offer a wide variety of services to whoever answered. A great deal of damage to Jake's credibility, was done in a very short period of time. A reputable business is not interested in a "Blow Job".

Suspecting the technology was responsible, Jake went out and bought new service contracts, and new phones. Every time obligating himself for the previous early cancellation fees. One hundred dollars for a phone, two hundred dollars to cancel a service contract. All of which was on a "bill you later" #Nicy.

Just when he thought things were getting back to normal, he received a notice of cancellation from his auto insurance company. They were dropping him; because of the abandoned vehicle. The insurance company had been notified by the police department. The same police department which had told Jake, they did not know where the vehicle was located.

In the State of Florida, no insurance means no license. The police notified, the insurance company, who notified the police. All done in cyberspace with any combination of data entry error. The insurance company notified the state of Florida, Jake was about to be dropped as a client. Jake opened a letter to the effect his license would be suspended if his insurance lapsed. He still did not have any idea, where the missing truck was located.

He had insurance on two vehicles, both would be canceled if he did not comply with the execution of the law in the state of Florida. He could not comply, because nobody was telling him where his truck was located. From pillar to post he ran trying to comply.

To compound his anxiety, everywhere he went Jake was getting tickets under the advanced preparedness of Homeland Security. He went to Deland home of Stetson University; he got a ticket. He went to the campus of the University of Central Florida, got a ticket. Driving anywhere, get a ticket, all in the name of Homeland Security. Cops have a foolproof way of checking out suspicious individuals, they write a ticket.

A suspicious individual is any stranger in a small town, after 10 PM on a week night. Beat up pick-up, or brand-new truck it did not matter. There is no smaller town than a university campus. Places Jake had visited a thousand times, were now off limits. Ten-, twenty-, and twenty-five-year projects were ending because every time Jake went to make a minor observation, he was given a ticket. The hazard of private funded projects, they don't come with credentials. They did not need credentials, before some lunatics slammed a few Jet liners, into a few buildings in New York and Washington DC.

Jake signed the tickets "They're only doing their job!" he admitted stoically.

No money coming in, everything going out. This could not go on forever. Someone hacked into the Utility Bill section. An astronomical utility bill arrived. Pay it, or risk power and water stoppage. Two cars and two homes, nothing coming in. He'd get hired, only to arrive on site to learn, the project was canceled.

Even the mail service was experiencing interruptions in the "Hood", fortunately not at the apartment. He was opening second notices, without the benefit of a first notice. Every time he mailed something out, it came back as undeliverable.

He woke up one morning in the "Hood" to find the entire mail box missing. No big loss, with no decent mail service.

Anthrax hysteria sweeping the nation. "Lava los Manos" you pathetic civil servants, just deliver the stinking mail.

The only mail getting through belonged to Monica. She was gone a year, and never filled out a change of address. Jake kept in contact as her personal mailman. He'd also slid her a few bucks for so long now, it was a habit.

She moved once, then again, and then again. The only person not kicking her, while she was down, was Jake. He had to hand it to her, she was making progress. She was no longer a victim or abusive. She was not susceptible to play into the party-chic scene. Those days were gone. She was steering clear of putting herself in a position where she could be abused.

One afternoon a process server came by, looking for Monica, he wanting to get her signature on some document.

Jake told him to hit the bricks. Jake didn't even know the address where she lived. He could drive there, if he had to deliver her mail. By the looks of this guy, Jake did not have to make the trip.

This guy was up to something not covered in the general textbooks. The scam was simplistic. Pretend to be working on behalf of the named individual, then locate their whereabouts.

Jake was glad this house was a dead end for those in pursuit of Monica. Odds were, if someone wanted to find Monica, there would be a constant presence in Jake's rearview mirror.

Sure enough, an unremarkable sedan hovered in the far reaches of direct line of sight. Sedan meant private investigator. Cops would be up front, or invisible on radio frequencies not open to consumer citizens. Just in case Jake made a quick scan of channel traffic with a receiver-only device he had built No it was not the police. Digital information was beyond the capabilities of his receiver-only system.

The channel check was not a complete waste of time. Some of the discrete signals of radio broadcast stations were operating more broad-band than normal. Modulated signals were overlapping. A decent radio-Pirate could exploit the possibilities. The drown-out of someone else's signal could mean reducing listening audience. This was nothing new.

A decent radio-Pirate could tag the overlapping signals, and reach a select group with a private agenda.

Jake determined to spend some time monitoring signal overlap. Spanish broadcasters were the worst offenders. Blame it on the metric system. Cuban Spanish stations were the absolute worst offenders. If Jake was going to smuggle cocaine he would use that signal, and a coded advertisement for free-the-Margaretta. Por quiza Taco Bell? Jake hated that little dog in the beret.

National pride aside, there are a few restrictions to personal freedoms. One was stepping on a radio signal; another is sale and distribution of contraband. If a merchant wanted to peddle cocaine there was always the pharmaceutical manufacturers, producing professional grade Procaine and Lido-cocaine.

Extra inventory is no reason to direct market contraband like an Amway vitamin distributer. It is not a question of national origin; it is marketing practices.

The technical term for a private investigator following another vehicle is "dingle-berries". The origin, of the expression, is lost in obscurity. There are many means of shaking off a dingle-berry. Dawn and dusk are good times to lose a tail. There is rush hour traffic. There are gated communities. There is always the opportunity to drag them along while a person runs errands. Ignore them and focus on more important business.

Someone with nothing to hide, and a lot of pluck, can sport with a dingle-berry. Wait for a break in traffic, whip a U-turn, drive past them stuck in traffic, whip another U-turn and pull up behind them. They will likely try to act innocent. This is all part of the game. Follow them anyway, make sure you have the right sedan.

If following them is a waste of valuable time, take a magnetic business card and throw it on the hood of the sedan.

They hate that. They'll act innocent as you dive by loudly shouting "Call me" while holding thumb and pinky finger up to your ear. Again, make sure you have the right sedan.

It should be mentioned dingle-berries are usually licensed to carry a concealed weapon. They might not be in the mood for humor. Playful antics are all in the presentation. They should never be given the impression; their safety is in question. Avoid throwing a magnetic business card onto the hood of a vehicle, already sporting a bullet hole. This guy is not going to be a happy camper.

Count the dingle-berries in the sedan. One is a low budget operation, some husband checking on his wife. Two is a deeper pile of do-do. Two persons, means anything from repossession to an attempt to locate a missing person. Repossession can be ruled out if the bank note is current. Missing person is really deep stuff.

People go missing for lots of reasons. Every hooker on the street is missing from someone. Hookers run away from pimps.

Husbands and wives go missing from alimony payments.

Topless dancers go missing from high-rollers who were expecting more than a thank you. Drunks with a bar tab, disappear.

The slimy implications of tandem dingle-berries, means some deep pockets, are looking for something specific.

Scummiest of all, was the search for missing children. This was something only a well-paid, professional detective should tackle. The condition of the located child, may be more than a parent should face alone. If the child was found, much professional counseling may be required.

Jake knew it was not a missing child case. He avoided any contact with children as a rule. No hookers, no drugs, no children, that was the rule. It was not that Jake didn't like kids.

Kids were always getting hurt. He just determined; he was not going to put himself in a position to kiss a bo-bo. Kiss one bo-bo and you get labeled a pedophile.

Out of work, almost broke, and time on his hands was too much for Jake. He had a favorite trick for the dingle-berries.

He got on a bus. Walking right by the dingle-berries sedan on the way, he waited at the bus stop. The bus stopped at every stop. The sedan stopped at every stop. Jake sat in the rear, watching the sedan pull over a block behind the bus, real time it stopped.

Jake rode the complete circle and got off where he started.

He entertained the notion of trading jackets with another passenger but decided that was too simple. He had a better idea. That afternoon he repeated the bus trip. This time he brought a pair of binoculars. Again, he sat in the rear. The dingle-berries could see him watching them, watch him, through their own binoculars.

This time he got off the bus. He went into a second-hand store on the route. They waited in the parking lot. Jake picked up some gigantic bra and panty sets. Another item of interest was Jane Fonda's workout video. A few blank tapes and he was ready to check out. He removed the labels from the blank Lapes.

He went home put his purchases into the trash. The following day was garbage day. Like any good homeowner he put the can at the curb the night before. At the bottom of the garbage were the bra and panties and the tapes. Trash is fair game to a dingle-berry. They would be forced to grab the can, go through the contents and return it before morning.

They would sit through hours of blank tapes, Jane Fonda's tape, and try and figure out the female garments. Jake slept like a baby. A happy mischievous baby.

For whatever it was worth, the sedan quit following him after the day on the bus. He must have convinced them he was not hiding anything. He was running out of dirty tricks to pull on them. His next move would have been, to walk right up and ask them what they were doing. They probably knew this was coming.

It was time to do a simple photographic job in Hernando County. Jake hired Richard to ride along. If he was stopped for another traffic ticket Jake wanted a wittiness. Richard was still hiding in the bushes every night so Jake approached him at the park bench where he spent the day. Without mentioning the bushes, Jake put the offer out there, and the man accepted.

As payment Richard agreed to share a steak dinner and a pack of smokes. They arrived at a restaurant just as the sun was going down. Being hours ahead of schedule, they decided to eat first, then get down to business. Jake had an Iced tea.

Richard had a beer, a beer, and another beer. His steak sat there until he was good and ready. Jake put the meal on plastic, American Express.

The rain was fierce, clouds threatened the angle of the photograph. The location was correct and the distance from the power station was established. All Jake had to do was wait for the moon to rise over the smokestacks and snap the picture.

He had the 35 MM film in the camera on a tripod waiting under a plastic bag. To ensure the shot, he used a Polaroid camera to test the angle. Even with telephoto lenses the picture was going to be questionable. The full moon looked like a speck of light in the Polaroids. The 35 MM would be better, but the film required processing to be sure. Focus was set at the top of the towers then a touch wider. With f-stop set, he ramped the shutter speed to longest exposure, dropping back with each frame to follow.

At the bottom of the run, he repeated the process with the focus at infinity. The whole roll was gone in a matter of moment. He reloaded the camera with a higher speed film, just in case. Again, the film was out of the camera and labeled in a heartbeat. All total he used four rolls before the angle was w/Tons•

They were loading the equipment into the back of the truck when the Hernando Sherif pulled in behind them. Richard took the pivotal role of spokesman. A mean drunk spokesman, what a novel idea. Jake managed to shut him up, in time, to convince the Sherif, Richard was the only one drinking.

"Just taking some pictures, officer."

"Of the power station?" Sheriff spoke a tad frantic.

"Of the moon, sir" Jake wisely did not mention his sudden realization how bad this might look. He was glad he was parked, that way no ticket could be issued. License and registration were a given matter of routine.

Who knows, how the conversation started on the trip back.

Richard offered up a little episode from his past. Seems in his youth he spent some time in Louisiana where he kept the Nigglers in line with a bunch of other good old boys. Jake mentioned a town known as Slydel just outside New Orleans.
Richard knew the place he had once kicked the shit out of white boy in Slydel. The white boy loaned a tool to a Niggler to fix his car.

"That's funny I once lost a fight with three white guys in Slydel." Jake mentioned tongue in cheek.

"How come?" Richard asked.

"There was too many of them!"

"No, what was the fight about?"

"I loaned a tool to a niggler!" Jake said softly.

The rest of the trip was spent with Richard explaining how he was a changed man. Jesus had showed him a different path.

Jake listened to the words without judgment. How much of it was true, or just an excuse, is conjecture. Jake knew, that Richard knew, it was a long dark stretch of road home, through a lot of swamps.

CHAPTER TWENTY

The trouble with money is; it is utilitarian. Making money is no big deal. It is never how much money is earned, it is what it is used for, that counts. The more earned, the more spent.

The more it is loaned, the less it is worth. Prices will always rise, as the flow of money keeps chumming along, trying to keep pace with spending habits. A one hundred-thousand-dollar house today, will be worth two hundred thousand dollars, at the end of a thirty-year mortgage. A new automobile is worth nothing at the end of the loan. That's the way money works.

Drunks fritter away a home in a lifetime, one shot at a time.

Crack heads go through a new car every month. These are examples of drains on the economy, because they really don't get any work done. Recreational drug use, takes utilitarian money and transfers real value, to the third world suppliers.

The third world suppliers then send refugees to live in the United States and other developed nations.

Jake took the same money and put it to use like a tool. Just like working with a shovel, "you dig yourself into debt, and dig yourself right back out". A couple of repetitions of moving a shovel full of money, makes the manager consider ways to save energy. A maneuver here, the right account there, consider the risk, save energy. Management is what is needed with money.

Jake had a savings account in one bank. He had a checking account in another bank. The bank with his checking account was his mortgage account bank. He was looking to open an account to use as a business account, to separate home finances from work finances. His American Express was a business-related credit account, but he was not satisfied.

The woman at the bank was a mock out. Tall oriental statuesque, she was a definite nine point eight-five. She tried to be helpful within the limitations of the banking commission.

Jake wanted to get her alone, it had nothing to do with banking.

Jake had a fond memory of two sisters who happened to be Amer-Asians. Who-me and Damn-me were both childhood sweethearts of Jake. Nothing more than a passing fascination.

Their real names were impossible to pronounce in English.

They were children of a Tokyo occupation family living in the United States. Who-me and Damn-me was just a nickname for the two of them as an English equivalent. Jake thought it was funny to hear them refer to each other as who-me, then when they got confused exclaim damn-me, in exasperation. They chattered away in Japanese pausing to announce Who-me, oh Damn-me. No one else, ever made the connection except Jake.

These children captured everything beautiful of both Japanese and American. Although he lost track of them as he grew older, he could remember how their mixed heritage was an improvement in the design of mankind. Anyone who argued against the mixing of races, only had to meet these children to be convinced it was a normal progression.

Even though he had never dated an Amer-Asian woman, he was now open to the suggestion. He was willing to test the waters with the woman at the bank. All he needed was a little nudge. She gave him a couple of signals that seemed to indicate she was open to his advances. Jake had trouble reading her. Was she just a professional doing an extra good job? Or was she really interested?

It really did not matter who made the first move, they were both adults. Jake thought of himself as a possible eight. He was not flush with cash, subtract two from ten. She was a nine point eight-five. Poise, grace, beauty, good with numbers, the only reason she did not rate higher, was Jake's refusal to hand out a perfect score. If he found her mind worked like a squirrel cage, he could always subtract points.

The banker was unable to help him without a tax number.

He could not get a tax number without an account. Chasing his own tail, was never a strong suit for Jake. He opened a second savings account. The idea was to combine his thirty or forty employers each year, into one account for tax purposes.

Jake only met one perfect ten in his life. He was in his twenties, and she was in her late teens. She had blonde hair and blue eyes. He went on believing she was a ten, for the next several years. This was during a time in his life when girlfriends were a dime a dozen. She was not really even qualified to compete, for his affections, by virtue of age restrictions. This did not prevent Jake from awarding her the high score for the competition. In the next couple of years, the other contestants lost interest. Jake cheerfully agreed, and removed himself from eligibility status.

They were two very happy Caucasians until the day Lancelot played to her Guenevere. Jake was forced to resume spectator status, as one of his best friends ruined the relationship. Two things came out of the turmoil, he was never confident of romance, and never again in need of a best friend.

As a former lover, he now awarded her a solid eight, where the vacancy required at least a nine. Upon the exit interview, the point in question was resolved, when a door slammed shut between them. She called once or twice to review her final score. Jake refused to re-tabulate, he could pick-up an eight anywhere.

By the time he reached thirty, he was only soliciting applications from solid nines. By the time he reached thirty-five, a nine point five was required. In comparison Monica was a five. She could dress up like a nine, but she had so much baggage, she was never going to be anything more than a five.

This Asian banker was a nine point eight-five. Nice thing about Asians they could count. With the highest population on the planet, it was important to know how to count.

Mexico City was highly populated, but no one seemed to be able to mentally calculate a square root. As a result, Mexico was feudal, when it was supposed to be democratic. It said it was a democratic republic for purposes of foreign aid, but it was feudal.

The Asians on the other hand, grow up doing mental gymnastics. Square it, cube it, smash it into sub atomic particles and rebuild it, all elementary to an Asian. Not just the scientists, the guy out digging a ditch. Stupid little pictographs were shorthand notation for words, paragraphs, even books.

The only way to assure a fair share, was to do the math.

How many grains of rice in a bowl? Go ask an Asian.

Americans think it a strange question.

"Enough to fill it up?" he says, then gives you a dirty look like you're an ass-hole.

Third century Japan was, twenty first century Latin America. Suburb to China, Japan was the cusp of shrinking planet. China was already in it's second millennium when Japan was colonized. That makes the second millennium America, forth millennium Chinese. The only reason the United States stays in first place, is open minded freedoms of Democracy.

Jake saw this Asian American woman as an opportunity to contribute a beneficial donation to all the selective inbreeding.

Push human evolution up the ladder one more notch. He didn't even know the woman, and he was working on improving the human genome. If he didn't find someone soon, he was never going to pass along his unique set of chromosomes. Of course, a child was the last of his worries. It isn't just a set of chromosomes that determine the fate of a child. A child also needs father and mother working together, to mold an individual into a contribution to the human race. He was going to need a lot of encouragement from this woman, to make him contribute his seed to her garden.

The Amer-Asian woman might just be another succubus.

Seemed to be quite a contagious condition. A brain virus.

Ignore the evidence and make everything a battle of the will.

Will he or won't he. Second guess, the outcome of something that has not yet happened. Waste time, trying to force everything, into a neat little pie chart. "If it doesn't fit on the chart, it can't happen!"

Jake was wise to the ripples on the waters back in the 1980's. Shirt manufactures noticed they were selling mostly tailored dress shirts. They ignored the factor women were buying men's dress shirts, because they were less expensive. All the bra burners were entering administrative positions. They needed to look as professional as the men, to compete with the men.

Soon a man could not find a shirt, cut to fit a man's proportions. The entire industry retooled to a tailored fifth Men started to look frumpy.

Jake simply changed careers, and started wearing three buttons pull over golf shirts with a collar. Why try and compete with a co-worker, who solved her problems, by removing a tailored suit coat to show the boss her mammary glands. No contest, who would get the next promotion.

Worse yet, she was only going to take the 'good old gal' to network her ultimate strategy. Will he, or won't he? A battle of the wills. Forget the Constitution, "Soon as we cram all the square pegs, into round pie charts he'll have to!" Jake was a square peg. "Cram it baby!"

"Who does he think he is, he's a bum!"

"I'm the bum who referenced the document your sweet little ass is sitting on, you bitch."

He could not even pull up to a University Library any longer. A few more tickets and he'd lose his license. Trouble was he had all the information he needed.

The United States was becoming a safe place for twisted logic. Everyone was clamoring to be considered a minority.

Even the term; minority, had been corrupted. Women wanted to be a minority. Everyone was using social advancement, to get ahead, by calling themselves a minority.

Those who wrote the Constitution had the expectations of a home, consisting of a husband and wife who would care for their children. They even made arrangements for amendments to the document because they expected social change. They expected men and women would always form a family unit.

They never expected the explosion of single parent households.

A single parent household was only acceptable if the good wife was a widow. Widows and orphans were an acceptable social expense. Wars had always produced widows. Somewhere welfare became popularized by kicking the man out of the house.

CHAPTER TWENTY - ONE

Cross referencing the Library of Congress, from the outside, was getting tedious. He had been in the library twice.

The first time to check information in the restricted reading room. The second time to correlate specific details.

The second trip was a real hoot. Jake was working on a small inconspicuous corner of a reference table. Some pompous jerk came up, and brushed Jake's work out of the way. Jake reached into his belongings, and fished out a huge fixed blade, diving knife, and placed it on the table. It was a work tool with his right hand, he placed the knife on the table, at arm's length. With his left hand he reached for the handle of the knife. He made sure the huge knife was firmly in the scabbard.

He then finished his work. The pompous jerk made no further encroachment on Jake's territory. Jake finished and withdrew.

The pompous Jerk remained sitting. The plumbous Jerk thought the Library of Congress, could only be cross referenced from inside the Library of Congress. Jake knew, every book on the shelf was a collaborative effort. The pompous Jerk would remain seated until the library was quite empty. The pompous Jerk, did not have a change of trousers, in his expensive brief case.

The Library of Congress started a screening procedure for back packs in 1988; the 101* Congressional delegation.

Something about a diving knife on a reference table. Jake did all his reference work from the outside of the Library of Congress after that. He could pick up the same information at any University, without having some overinflated ego to deal with.

A lot of information was not yet on the Internet. Some of what was on the Internet, was an oversimplification of very important work. Jake cringed at some of what he found.

Second generation information, was reduced to third generation drivel. On the Internet there was not always credit given to where the information originated. Someone like Jake, could not even find where speculation was separated; fact or fiction. The strange thing with the Internet it leaves no room for minority opinion.

Only so many square pegs will fit in a round hole. One too many pegs and the hole gets lopsided. Tolerance is a question of finding the correct number of square pegs, to allow a round hole to still be useful. Tighten a wheel too much it will not roll.

Loosen the wheel too much and it falls off, useless. Tolerance within unified goals, is a question of proper management.

Sometimes tolerance depends on the minority, to explain unseen problems.

In the "hood?

Jake voluntarily made note of a practice of mismanagement. He noticed, every time a meeting was planned, his invitation came one day -late. Clever little tactic. Push through a proposal by stifling opposition. All the covert opinions needed to push through a proposal, received their mail in a timely fashion.

Tolerance, as the wheel falls off. A slum-lord pushes formation of a vigilance committee. No minority opinion, to question why the cause of the problem is the solution. Slum, means the slum-lord did not screen applications. Vigilance h committee, means slum-lords think, they can fix a problem, created by their own neglect in the first place.

Tolerance as the wheel stays on the wreck. A minority opinion points out; the slum-lords are only going to start pointing fingers at each other. No one intentionally set out to be a slum-lord. It just happened. Unfit tenants, simply move from one rental to the next, using the slum-lords like a musical chair. The minority opinion; Communication between slumlords will be more effective than a vigilance committee.

Jake had a fool proof system to allow himself to know when he was in the minority. All he had to do was hear a simple phrase; "Who does he think he is?".

"I'm the guy who sold you a ten-gauge shotgun, with the FORESIGHT to sell you fourteen-gauge shells. Saw what you were up to, and took precautions."

"I'm the guy who pulled you out of a wreck just before the car exploded, thank you very much.".

"I'm the guy who pulled your whale physique out of the under tow, nine times out of ten. I let you bob around that one time, hoping you'd learn a lesson."

Or as Jake usually did, not say anything and walk away grinning. People had to be given the opportunity to put two and two together. Hopefully, they would tabulate four. People like Jake only needed to shine a little light once in a while. Drop a subtle hint. Maybe leave a book open with a point highlighted.

Leave a note in the margin, "you go Yahweh, I'll go mine".

He was of the minority opinion Americans had their work cut out for them. He only used the "Hood" as a measuring stick for how much work was slipping through the cracks. The Constitution was taking a beating. He looked at the slum as a project. Everything would be fine, just as long as everyone is invited, and they all get there safely. Calculate the risk, kick the ball to the good guys.

Right now. Jake was in no mood to kibitz with the clowns.

Most of what he had to offer, was going right over their heads in any case. There was a sonar ping, an echo, every time he opened himself to communication.

He would mention something to someone in confidence, it would circulate word of mouth, then return. Judging by the corruption of the original message, he could home in on the culprit clown. Stick an extra square peg in a round hole, and the whole assembly makes a lot of Racket. The clown thinks the noise is funny. That's what clowns do!

The only thing for Jake to do, was leave a lot of square pegs laying around, and keep his ear open for the cacophony.

Look for a laughing clown. Look for those laughing, those crying, and those running around like a chicken with their heads cut off.

The deafening din, of a few stray pegs in the wrong hole, is a sure sign of trouble on the event horizon. When every hole shows wear from the effects of stray pegs, it is time for action.

Anyone walking around calmly, in the calamity, is sure to have a intuitive understanding. Sometimes, but not always, the serenity was a result of carefully cultivated study of problems and procedures. Sometimes, complacency was a sign of conspiracy. Sometimes, contentment, was the result of being deaf to the noise. There was always the chance the peaceful composure, was because the individual chose to ignore, something beyond their control. This was something Jake needed to learn how to do, he could not go on taking everything personal.

Jake had ways to weed out the can of worms. He would separate the intuitive from the conspirator, the deaf from the disenfranchised. Echolocation, radar, sonar anything you wanted to call it. Ping, ping, ping, and wait for the echo return.

Ping-thud-ping, object to starboard. Ping-ping-thud, object to port. Thud-ping-ping, object dead ahead. Ping-pong, bogey sighted. Navigating the stream was no place for amateurs. The only reason to do a sounding, was to measure the expected cruise. est for turbulence, don't risk the whole crew on an unconfirmed echo. Send out a scout, then if the information is still unreliable, go out yourself and examine the likely carnage.

If a big storm is on the event horizon, put the women and children in lifeboats. Get the crew back to work. Let the conga-line of malcontents, wash over-board (they make good ballast).

One more marching band in this stadium, called America, looked like a violation of the fire code. The whole orchestra was breaking up into groups, each playing a different tune. It was a realization, deserving deep contemplation.

Divide and destroy. No other explanation made sense. All the minorities on the planet were working from the same game plan. Classic bar room brawl strategy. The only thing to do in a bar fight is to keep an eye on the cash register. See who makes a move. Only let the barmaid, stuff her bra so full, in the melee.

Find out who it is causing the ruckus, and wait in the parking lot.

This was more abhorrent than a child discovering the joy, of a playing card in the spokes of a bicycle. Someone was tuning the spokes, by listening to the squeal made by pork.

Someone was investing heavy in pork bellies. Someone else, was fattening the pork, with some pretty exotic feed. Audit the equation, it was more nefarious than comical.

Jake did what he always did. He ignored the extra pegs and started examining the wear and tear on the hole. By forensic inspection, a foreign object leads to the discovery of whoever had both access to the hole, and possession of offending substance. The conclusions being drawn were beyond any probability.

You can't blame it on a design flaw when you're talking to the guy who designed the thing in the first place. He did a thousand tests before he put it on the market. Nobody sold Yard Darts to parents who were unwilling to supervise their own children. It was not cost effective. Even a fool would not flood the market with superfluous garbage, without obtaining from the customer; a guarantee, it would be operated within specific guidelines.

Jake would read the small print. Major law firms always include a "Hold Harmless Clause". Smacking an auto, into a pole, while talking on a cell phone was already covered. Flip a Sport Utility Vehicle, by driving it like a sports car, and you have some explaining to do to the insurance institute. You cannot always blame it on the tires.

Physics, plain and simple. A plus B is equal to C. The hole is worn beyond the limits of normal use. The foreign object was found in the hole. Calculate the questionable. Get a second opinion if the evidence is quizzical. Trust no one.

Lead poisonings as a cause of death, does not rule out the possibility the lead came from a sudden exposure to a bullet.

Even medical examiners may wax - poetic. Heaven forbids, they should record Bala in the report as shorthand for ballistic, when it could be confused with Spanish.

Physics, plain and simple. A plus B is equal to C.

CHAPTER TWENTY - TWO

Monica was back in all her confused glory. Jelly-Belly was making her life miserable. He was not satisfied leaving her homeless and destitute. He wanted her head on a pike. Why this should have any effect on Jake, was beyond merit.

She only needed a little money to keep her going, long enough, to survive in a world of predatory possibilities. Even lap dog John was pressing her for a little -Gratis. He was such a slug the Quid pro Quo he requested, was anything but comfortable even for a succubus. She started to launch a vivid description, when Jake covered his ears with his hands.

"Here takes the money, never come back for another dime! I don't have it anymore!" Jake snorted in disgust. What was another c-note in mountain of bills?

The succubus was so concerned with her own needs, she had no time to worry about Jake. He was a man; she didn't need to move anything heavy. As far as she was concerned, he was a harem eunuch. She and her daughter could dispense with his services. He was dismissed, now that she had the money.

A foul mood, took control of Jake. Jelly-Belly had his fun.

Jake was paying the cost of the fiddler. He checked his watch; it was almost noon. Jake knew exactly where to find Jelly-Belly; the Club. Without hesitation Jake jumped into his car.

He roared into the parking lot. He stormed into the Club and found Jelly-Belly exactly where he expected. The man was half involved in a pitcher of cold beer.

"You better find your way to your truck before this Key goes to work!" Jake explained holding up the largest key on the ring. Jake was going to stick it, in Jelly-Belly's ear, and crank over the motor.

Mr. Espanto, acting as bouncer, jumped into the space between the men. He warned Jake to "take it outside". Jake would have to climb over Mr. Espanto, to reach Jelly-Belly's ignition. Calm entered the picture, momentarily.

"Yeah, let's take it outside!" growled Jake

"Dorado, I believe you are currently acting as an agent for someone who I have a restraining order against. Kindly stay five hundred yards away from me." The corpulent Jelly-Belly announced, with the contempt reserved for lower life forms.

"I'm not acting on the bequest of anyone but myself, you piece of crap. I am asking you for a moment of your time, man to man." rage exuded from Jake's very marrow.

Mr. Espanto showed Jake to the door. "Sorry to do this buddy, but you're way out of control."

Jake went away, out of respect for Mr. Espanto. He did not want to, but he was not going to risk losing a trusted friend over self-serving bravado. He went down the shops under the covered walkway and bought a pack of smokes. He was trying to quit smoking, but the situation called for some backsliding.

On the way-out Jake walked right by Jelly-Belly's truck parked in a handicapped space, no placard in the window. As Jake drove away, a man in a wheelchair worked on Jelly-Belly's truck like a beaver on a sapling. The wheelchair man was tired of people parking in handicapped parking. The nature of his militant handicap activities, sent him around to all the parking lots, issuing his own pro-active brand of justice.

Later Jelly-Belly went to his vehicle, and saw the damage, caused by the militant handicapped. He immediately called the police. The slightly inebriated man blamed Jake. He, in his intoxicated state, reasoned Monica had violated the restraining order. He wanted everyone in jail, in connection with the heinous activity. He had been violated and wanted everyone in connection with the crime, punished to the fullest extent of the law. That is what a fill pitcher of beer does to a slime ball.

The sheriff mentioned parking in a handicap zone. Jelly-belly showed him a placard from under the seat. The sheriff did not mention the frequency of attacks on improperly parked cars. When the sheriff suggested there might be some other explanation, Jelly- Belly offered evidence Jake was responsible. Pressed for a rational answer the drunk offered, "I saw him do it."

Jake was at home when a sheriff detective pulled into his yard. The sheriff was looking for Monica. Jake leveled with the man and told him she no longer lived at this location. How people kept coming here to look for her, was starting to get tiresome.

"So, you don't know where she is now?"

"No sir." You're welcome to look in the house if you want to." Jake was not surprised the law was looking for Monica, she had run afoul of the law in the past. He did think any outstanding warrants were already satisfied. He even drove Monica to the slammer one weekend himself. The Jail was in some other obscure County two hours away, four hours, with the return trip.

"G' Zeus, am I ever going to get rid of that woman?" Jake asked the cop.

The Sheriff, went away and came right back. "Can you give me any way to contact her?"

"Check with her Ex-husband, his daughter should know where she is!"

The cop left, and came back again. This was getting ridiculous. Jake was losing his patience. Something was all wrong about this situation. He was not harboring a fugitive. He was not interfering with an officer in the completion of official duties. What was the connection?

"She works for; Just Cameras, on Sheep Dip Road." The Cop came back one more time. "There is no Just Cameras on Sheep Dip." The deputy had Jake exactly where he wanted him. He was fishing handcuffs off his belt.

"There is inside Wall-mart." Jake mentioned, noticing with some trepidation the officer reaching for handcuffs.

This time, the cop never came back. It was all he ever knew about the interest of a police force, and the fugitive Monica.

Jake was unaware, the police went to Monica's workplace and slapped her in cuffs. She was humiliated in front of her boss, and his patrons. Jake never knew anything of her being arrested for violation of a restraining order. She sat in jail for half a day while Sharon contacted her father, Monica's ex-husband. Well one of her ex-husbands.

CHAPTER TWENTY - THREE

When Jake bought his new car, he paid extra for protection in the case it was stolen. If the Car was stolen it would be paid off by the lender. What Jake did not know, was this type of insurance is like buying a lotto ticket. One day it is in effect the next day, no good. A lot of the insurance Jake was carrying, was being conducted like a state lottery.

He had been able to locate his old truck. The impound lot had let it sit long enough to seize it for non-payment. Just before it went to auction, Jake paid eight hundred dollars for its return. Legal kidnaping, except it's a car not a kid. Even at that, hiding a car from an owner to run up a impound fee, still looked like theft. What could he do? He paid the impound fee, kept his insurance company happy, and kept his Florida driving privileges. It was some big privilege conspiracy. Driving was a privilege to motor to a crummy job and work until you die Jake considered walking.

Homeowners insurance was another scam. No insurance no mortgage. By the time the insurance lotto pays off, the homeowner already had replaced what was missing, with whatever he could afford. As more stuff disappeared, he put it on the list.

When his computer came up missing, he was running low on funds to replace things, without going uncomfortably low in any one account. He turned in the list to All-gated Insurance with a immediate five hundred dollar deduction. While he had them on the phone, he mentioned the roof damage which was still not fixed. An adjuster came out, saw the house all fixed up for Halloween and was told to "sue the workman" or he was out of luck The first claim payment finally arrived. After making five years of payments on insurance, it was worth about ten cents on the dollar. He had enough to replace the computer or wait and use the money for other bills.

By this time, he had gone on numerous jobs where the client failed to show. He even worked a couple jobs where he was not paid. Worse yet the homeless trio of Wizard, Moselle and Richard were dropping by all hours of the day and night.

Wizard borrowed a workbox of tools and returned the next day without them. Instead of tools the Wizard sported a grapefruit on his forehead where he claimed he was mugged. Moselle, when hired to do some light painting, snuck off to watch Jerry Springer every time it came on the television. Richard, when hired to do a little tile work ran out of energy in the middle of one place, and started on the other side of the house when resuscitated.

Jake had to keep the bums separated. He really did not want any of them hanging around, but the activities after dark were still in progress. People he had never seen before, were still knocking on his door with insane requests, like needing to use the toilet. With the bums around, at least Jake could get some peace and quiet. But give one bum a cigarette, they all want cigarettes. Jake started to make them roll their own.

The time came where lack of sleep and malnourishment started taking a toll on Jake. He could only handle being in contact with one homeless pathetic bum at a time. Wizard was the first to be offended by Jake withdrawing from playing nursemaid. He was appalled Jake was closing the Mission in the face of the needy. None of them would get it into their heads, Jake was not a charity.

Moselle and Richard both fell into an ass-kissing contest to validate who was to be next. Richard had the bushy vines; Moselle had the nuthouse. Neither wanted to limit their choices. They both thought Jake just needed sunshine blown up his pant leg. The trouble with Jake, was if he wanted a warm feeling, he could always go out and lay on the beach. He did not need an entourage, especially Moselle and Richard.

Through the rumor mill, came the news, a very old Yacht at the beach was up for grabs. Jake checked it out, sure enough this was an honest opportunity to change the losing streak. He checked three different times, with three different people, to his satisfaction it was an honest salvage operation. This was too good to be true. He knew exactly what to do with the wreck. It was beyond putting back to sea but it would make a fantastic cabin on a property he owned about thirty miles away from where it now sat.

In the city of Cocoa was a freight handler, who could accomplish the transfer. The cost was reasonable for moving thirty miles inland, with the forty-foot caravel style yacht. All Jake needed was to secure insurance for the trip, and liability at the present marina.

Martine underwriters don't give a damn if they sell a two-day policy. In fact, any policy they collect from a honest man is just fine with them. What they are concerned with is the vessel leaving point "A" and arriving at point "B". They don't stand for a sloppy ships manifest. They can tell without looking when a whale sized cargo, is claimed in a minnow sized boat.

They'll stop at nothing to verify the boat on the bottom is the same boat underwritten. Screw them one time, and that will be the last time. Jake knew and respected this contingency.

The leg work was done, all he needed was a little help.

Moselle was a damn fine machinist. He was also a happy drunk who would fit in fine around the marina. The whole job consisted of making everything sound for the journey. One load of equipment and Jake would see the underwriter in the mooring There was only one problem, when Jake showed up with Moselle, the homeland security was waiting. Homeland Security pulled them out of the car while, the cops searched the vehicle for just about anything. Jake hit the speed dial for the new owners of the marina. They asked to speak to the homeland security officer. The officer refused to talk on Jake's cell phone. As the vehicle was searched the old owners of the marina pulled up. Seeing Jake and Moselle being frisked was enough. When Moselle could not furnish any identification of any kind, things got worse.

A couple hours later they were driving back to Orlando with fresh no trespassing warrants. Go back to the Marina, ever, go to jail. Who, in times of a national emergency, walks around with no identification?

Jake wanted to drop Moselle off the Bridge to Cocoa Beach. Maybe a little example of thirty-two feet per second, would help Moselle get in touch with his educational potential.

If nothing else, Jake could time how many seconds it took to hit the water. He would then know; how tall the bridge was.

They returned to Orlando where in payment for work, never actually done, Moselle was placed with a homeless shelter. The sponsors of the shelter were given enough money, to keep the bum off the street for at least a week. Jake gave Moselle enough spending money to square the deal. He mentioned; maybe the man should not come around for a while.

Jake looked into the mirror; the face was a zombie. Skin shrunken down around bone. Eyes receding into sockets. The sclera of his eyes was white without jaundice. The pupils were dull. He considered hanging a towel over the reflection. The ritual of shaving was his only concern. Even growing a beard was preferable to staring in the mirror. The narcissistic adventure was an excuse to see how the rest of the world saw the person in the reflection. He looked like a survivor of the Bataan Death March.

Robust health reduces to an exposed rib-cage. Bones rattling at articulation of joints. Jake was taking on an uncomfortable appearance. He considered wearing a collared shirt with a bow tie. This made him look like the Jolly Roger, skull and crossbones. A Windsor knot was a better choice.

Jake was on his way to meet with the Asian banker. He changed again into something with a business appearance. Jake would learn all his accounts were now closed. The banker made the decision in the interest of the bank. Jake was appalled a banking relationship, cultivated over months, was now at an end.

The bank was of the opinion, Jake was using his accounts to launder drug money. At issue was an event which transpired in the parking lot. Marcus and Jake on a late return from a chore had been observed arguing. Jake took a clip, used to keep field paperwork from blowing away. He used the clip to trap all relevant banking documents and placed it in the night depository. He drove away, still in heated debate with Marcus.

Jake returned this morning to finish the transaction.

It was stated, the clip had set off an alarm at the bank. Jake knew there was no more metal in the clip than in a roll of quarters. He knew there was more to the story, than what he was told. A woman he considered a nine point eight-five, was now a six.

Although it was not directly mentioned, the allegations of laundering drug money were a serious charge. He immediately set out to locate Marcus. Perhaps he was involved with some unseemly extracurricular activities Jake should know about.

When unable to locate Marcus, he returned home.

The reflection in the mirror was of a man exhausted.

Someone being used, as a flotation device, by persons drowning in their own excesses. It was almost as if he could see the arms reaching up, from under the surface of a cesspool, to drag him under. Everyone hoping to preserve their own life, regardless of others in the murky waters. These were uncharted dangerous and perilous depths. The contamination was unexplored.

The first responsibility of a rescuer is to not be dragged down. Struggle away from a combative victim. Rescue yourself first, then rescue the others. Monica, Wizard, Richard and Moselle were eternally washed away by the tide, after being safely deposited on the shore. Ned and Daytona sat in the calm seas, directing worthy vessels onto the shoals, so they could pick through the cargo littering the beach. Marcus was a special case.

The only gratification for all the work, was Sharon. The now adult daughter to Monica, had been dragged out of the turbulence. It was still too soon for a reliable assessment of injuries received while floundering in the waves. She had brushed against the pollution of the intercity. She was contaminated by the corruption of the environment. It would be years before a clear picture of her experience developed. She had a pulse; this was a good sign.

As he watched the skeletal mirage in the mirror, he was reminded of the Samurai. Originally the Samurai was chieftain, warrior, spiritual advisor, judge, jury and medical examiner, even a fireman when needed. Expected to adhere to the highest standard, they lived to service the needs of the people. The symbol of authority was a big knife. As time went by, the biggest knife carried the argument. A standardized knife eventually surfaced. The focus shifted to the sharpest blade.

The Samurai at least had the luxury of social expectations.

Whenever there was a trifling influence within his hamlet the Samurai would react. He would dispense justice at the edge of his sword. His actions were predicated by concern for the other citizens. The Samurai would never allow streets to be havens of drug traffic. Headless corpses would replace street dealers.

Jake was no Samurai; he did not even have the guarantee of right to privacy. His every action was grounds for speculation. American law was prohibiting Jake from using the best possible equipment for the job at hand. He was a hundred years late, as technology in an urban environment is concerned.

Removing vermin at the edge of a blade was outdated. Yet, the intercity was ripe for removal of disease with surgical precision.

Drugs were the disease. Exposure started the vector. The carrier once infected, is capable contracting a secondary infection; addiction. They are still not yet responsible for transmission. The tertiary stages are where propagation of the illness takes place. The host organism transfers delivery to the newly afflicted.

The whole misunderstanding revolves around, when is a food really a drug? This has been a misunderstanding from the beginning of mankind. The whole Kosher tradition is an effort to answer this question. Purple flower in a mill was a sign of ergot in the wheat. A little ergot will not harm a human. A little more, and the human hallucinates. A little more, and arms and legs turn necrotic making the sufferer appear to have advanced leprosy. But it is not leprosy, it is ergot poisoning. The ancients made the choice to inspect the flour, so they would not be required to check the diseased patient. Thousands of years later man attempts to challenge the wisdom of the ancients. They regard the label unclean as a quaint custom, allowing language to confuse perception. LSD is a chemical derivative of natural ergot mold. The chemical is, and should be, regarded as unclean, even with so many using it for recreational purposes.

So many foods follow suit it is alarming. Crystallized sugar is still regarded as food. Crystallized coca is considered a drug.

No one ever traded sex for a Poppy seed muffin; but a lot of sex is exchanged for heroin. Money for sex, for drugs, must be the vector. But it is the narcotics, which are unclean.

Jake had a simple logic, anything eaten every day was food. If something was smoked or injected it was a drug. If someone took a prescription, and it did not cure the problem, it was food. Prescriptions were just as likely to be abused as any other narcotic. There were enough happy pills around, it did not make sense to score crack on a corner.

No one can pay a mortgage with sex. No one can pay a mortgage with drugs. Somehow sex must be exchanged for money. To entice those willing to make the exchange, there are drugs.

CHAPTER TWENTY - FOUR

Marcus stood by the mailbox, dressed in hospital scrubs.

He teetered above a pair of crutches with a bandaged knee. His right elbow was encased in a fresh orthopedic bandage net.

Hobbling between the crutches and his good right leg, he made the way to the front door. Every few paces he paused for breath. He crushed pink papers in his hand.

Jake watched from the front porch. Marcus presented the papers to Jake like a man checking in for duty. He was like a battle worn solider returning to front line duty. Jake carefully read the paperwork. It showed Marcus was released against doctor's orders. He was treated for injuries suffered while being thrown from a moving vehicle.

A few days earlier, Jake would have been resolved to chase down the posse who threw Marcus from the car. Right now, he was carefully anticipating the value of keeping the battle going.

If his property was so important, there must be a reason. He had to retrace the period of time before the abduction. Plan a plausible scenario leading up to the reason, why someone would throw another man from an automobile.

Events leading up to the accident were sorted. When he first learned his banking accounts were to be closed, Jake found Marcus. He posed the question, was Marcus involved underworld activities. Marcus denied any participation. Jake believed him but thought the matter deserved one of his acid tests.

There are means to determine how much Gold, is in the present in truth. twenty-four carat Truth, is rare. Truth is too restrictive, and the gold is malleable in its perfection. It only becomes useful when it is mixed with baser materials. A pure gold chain falls apart as soon as it is heated. Mixed with an inferior metal like silver, the chain is made stronger. Mixed with copper the gold becomes harsh, leaving a green tinge on the skin. As the utility of the gold is increased, the purity of its true composition is decreased. At some point the truth must be tested, as if it were gold. When it becomes too polluted, metal loses a gold standard.

Do you swear to tell the truth, and nothing but the truth?

That Judge, sitting on the bench knows, twenty-four carat truth, is as rare as pilot pork. They, like every other mortal, search for elusive perfection. They will not buy into a twelve-carat story, at a twenty-four-carat price. The very fact, the matter is under examination, is because some imperfection was discovered.

Jake was no fool the line must be drawn somewhere. How green must an arm be allowed to be tinted before it is determined a bracelet contains no Gold. When is the golden calf too pure to be touched? He did not have the laboratory to test his assumptions. He did not have the technicians, and eloquent experts, to ferret out a haystack looking for pinprick.

He did have a tried-and-true method. Twenty-four hours alone with someone, was usually plenty of time to rule out specific forms of substance dependence. To the observant even caffeine dependence is detected in a short period of time. Hand a man a decaffeinated coffee, see if he gets a mind-bending headache.

Nicotine, Alcohol, almost anything shows up as a habitual dependency Much satisfaction is provided by Nicotine in the blood stream. Removal of the satisfaction, may result in some exotic behavior. Smokers, in non-smoking buildings, spend a lot of time away from their desks.

Jake continued to smoke, only because he did not want to be provided with any excuse to be surrounded by whining. He knew some prescriptions, taken under the strictest of Physicians recommendations, was nothing more than laboratory purified nicotine. Odorless, tasteless tablets of rare compounds derived from tobacco. Mood enchantment, sold as miraculous to whining purists too self-involved to light up.

The first great miracle of mankind was fire. Smoking was only a way of remaining in touch with this singular event.

When everything is normal, the person striking a match is a pariah. When the lights go out, and everyone in the room panics, the same fellow with his pack of matches is a hero.

Suddenly everyone can tolerate the odor of a burning match stick, just in case the lights never come back on. If it was not for the man with the matches, the entire delegation would be at the mercy of the anyone with the practical knowledge needed to rub two sticks together. They often forget the reason the matches were in the room was to light a cigarette, in privacy.

Marcus with his fabulous human foible, agreed to escort Jake to a job at the beach. It required them to stay overnight.

For twenty-four hours Marcus would be in sight of Jake.

As they made preparations for the trip a woman from the neighborhood solicited Jake's assistance. She said she was willing to sacrifice an expensive and rare amplifier to secure grocery monies. The money she asked for, was not a fraction of the value of the rare equipment. Jake was not satisfied with taking her word for ownership or sobriety. He loaded her and the equipment into the truck along with Marcus.

The Acid test Jake planed, would work as well for two, as it did for one. In a few short hours, liars were going to change their tune. Nobody is perfect, it was only the degree of imperfection Jake was hoping to assay.

Marcus as expected, worked dutifully throughout the day into the evening hours. The woman became more disoriented as time progressed. She required a beer long before Marcus.

She also chain smoked, to the point a fog followed her. Her nervousness compounded itself as the clock ticked. As the sun went down, she took no notice of the spectacular sunset coloration.

In Cocoa Beach lived Nicky, an old friend of Jake's acquaintanceship. She was a survivor of the Timothy Leery era, where he promoted enlightenment, in the form of a sugar cube fortified with LSD. She survived just barely. Her mind was a squirrel cage of disjointed spiritual awareness.

She was a delightful person who Jake admired, even it he could only be exposed to her lunacy for short intervals. Unlike Monica who was a spiritual vacuum and an outspoken atheist, Nicky was a washed in the blood of Jesus, but spent many hours alone with Buddha. Her life mission was to examine all the prophetic advice of Hebrews, Islam, Christianity, Rome and China. When she felt confident, she had explored all these, she set out to examine the Aztec, Mayan, Inca and Zuni. She was of the opinion for all these cultures to show reverence to a Creator, was proof of the existence of God. God was manifest in a quest for perfection.

They had often treated each other to expensive meals at local restaurants whenever he was in town. Her unique perspective of the relationship of man to God was insular bubbles of study. She bounced from Peru to the Holy land, launched into Tibet, soared past Kiev, swung through Europe, banked off Spain, then brought the logic to rest exactly where she started.

Jake made every effort to show his interest, commenting on the topic, if for no other reason than to prove he was listening.

She would launch another balloon starting in Africa, hovering over Greece, slamming into Turkey, bounce off The British Isles, deflating somewhere in the North Sea. No effort was made to provide a time frame for any event. It all took place in the absence of time, space and gravity.

Everyone thought Nicky was Nuts. Jake didn't. He tried to superimpose real time frames, and actual geography, onto a moving object. It was mental gymnastics; most people should not attempt. He would come away from their meetings, exhausted from the stream of information.

Telephoning in advance, she invited his visit without question. He explained his plan, before trespassing on her home. Jake explained, the evening might turn tortuous. Nicky understood instantly the nature of his proposal. She owed him the favor. He had once helped her, in exactly the same way.

It was his turn to pick up the tab, as a legitimate business expense. She picked the restaurant, unfortunately she picked a restaurant where they did not accept American Excess. At the end of the night, Nicky paid for the meal, making Jake a freeloader. He thought she was now two up, on the loosely arranged dinner schedule. She thought Jake was a Bum. The thing about Nicky was the way she always seemed to have a special insight, without pronouncing judgment.

The time at the restaurant was spent between Nicky and the woman. Marcus was more than helpful keeping the meal moving with decorum and social energy. He danced with Nicky, then danced with the other woman, while Jake and Nicky caught up on old times. At no time were any of the party out of Jake's sight.

The late fall weather was cool but comfortable. A warm breeze swept from the south. Stars shown brightly in the seashore sky overhead. The stars raced behind a stationary waning Moon looking much larger above the Atlantic Ocean.

Cruise ships pulled into the harbor, in full view of the veranda.

A band played in the wide space between restrooms.

Alternating between Rock, Country and Zydeco music the band played: Jimmy Buffet, followed by Marley reggae, Beausoleil Cajun rifts made for an easy transition. The freshest seafood found the table. Everything served was heaped up, in help yourself portions. Drinks came sparingly, to allow the customer a comfortable level of intoxication without inebriation. Jake drank Iced Tea.

If Marcus was experiencing any discomfort, it was not showing. He was having a good time. He sipped on a beer then danced with Nicky. He took another swallow then danced with the other woman. The beverage would go warm before he finished.

The woman was revived each time she danced. She sank back into a catatonic state every time she sat back down. Jake kept force feeding her fried fish from the platter. The greasy food serving to cushion the withdrawal symptoms of which ever drug she was craving. She was no different than a diver going through decompression. The bubbles in her bloodstream were just atypical. Her nerves were screaming for a load of its normal atmospheres. She had become accustomed to surviving at sea level in an atmospheric pressure reserved for altitudes above twenty thousand feet. Plain and simple, she was way out of her depth. Jake did not judge her; he was satisfied with the fact she…Lied.

She was an attractive woman. Tall with pleasing features.

Auburn hair cascaded down her back. She always seemed well groomed never sloppy. The one visible imperfection being a tooth missing in front. This could happen to anyone involved in a car wreck. She seldom smiled, being a touch vain of her appearance.

There was every reason to believe her, when she said she was not part of any drug activity. In a few short hours Jake had unraveled the deception. She was a liar. By the same token Marcus had proven he was a good man.

Jake would learn exactly how beautiful the woman was a few hours later. She suddenly spiked a temperature where she needed to be disrobed and placed into a cold shower. Jake noticed no evidence she had ever injected anything, into an almost faultless body. She did not even have a tatoo. Whatever she used was either smoked, snorted, or swallowed.

He stood there dripping wet in a cold shower supporting the weight of the now collapsed victim. Marcus helped him wrap her in a sheet and place her into bed.

While Marcus sat attending the woman, Jake went out to clear his head. He drove to the beach in the predawn twilight to walk on the sand. He listened to the tidal surge.

The lopsided motion of the stars showed Cygnus starting to fade into the eastern sky. It would be morning soon. Big fat Boötes was still overhead. The stars were there. The earth was there. Jake was there. He surveyed north, east, south and west.

He needed no clock, no compass.

He was an infinite smiling speck in a gigantic galaxy. This galaxy was one of many. Somewhere out there, through solar winds, and magnetic flux, was another intelligent being looking back at Jake. It could be no other way. Billions of stars, with hundreds of billions of planets, meant somewhere out there was life. He stripped down at the shore, ran into the sort, then dove below the waters. The darkness, made the surf fluoresce iridescent, with a glowing luminescence. A microorganism in the waters, reacted with the sweat from his body, to glow an eerie yellowish green. He had seen it before many times, mermaid lightning bugs. Some scientist called it Luci fluoresces; it was now available in glow sticks at rock concerts. Mermaids don't patent nature. Jake climbed out of the water, to the familiar seashore.

He could leave this spot, going in any direction and never be lost for even a moment. Using only his collected understanding of the environment surrounding him, he could provide for his every need. He needed no book, no instrument, no interaction with other beings of any kind. He knew what he could stick in his mouth, wear on his skin, more importantly he knew what to avoid.

The only thing he required, for everything he was offered, was a good knife and a decent pair of shoes. The stars said it would be turning colder soon. Time to gird his loins, cover his nakedness for the sake of comfort.

There was not one reason for him to participate in the face of civilized man. The only value in participation was to avoid being hunted like bigfoot. Even the freedom to pursue happiness had eroded to the point, where delineation of happiness, was dictated by civil procedure. The right to privacy, gone! On the chance a hermit might construct a bomb, the homeowner Associations of America would find some way into any inner sanctum. Even if they needed to build a Internet they were going inside, to look around.

Jake had spent many years turning down offers, from those who suggested his life would be improved, by their intervention. Always some string was attached. Take a free lunch, get stuck with the bill. He was in the habit of rejecting offers from woman making a provocative suggestion. He learned to tell them; "to put their cloths on, and hit the bricks." The stars were there. Luna still orbited around Tellus. The solar plane was cutting across the eastern horizon. Everything was where it was supposed to be. A sea turtle scrambled back to the ocean froth, after making her contribution to the future.

A sand piper scurried the edges of the surf line looking for a guaranteed morsel of nourishment. It was all the same as it had been, for forty years of careful observation.

Jake left the beach, to motor around collecting the morning meal. Fresh fruit, coffee, juice, crescent rolls and doughnut were assembled on the back porch table. He even provided the local morning newspaper. No one was awake.

He returned to the beach. This was a big mistake.

Homeowners along the shoreline were protective of a strip of sand belonging to the National seashore in trust to every citizen. They did not come right out with a request he should leave. They just made sure he felt unwelcome. He was clearly an outsider.

How dare they! Jake had been part of this beach, before anyone thought to build a home. It would have been impossible for him to navigate the winding suburban roads unless he knew where he was going.

How dare these myopic gang of associated thugs, suggest they had control outside well defined property lines. Even that strip of tar, winding in front of the luxurious homes was the property of the citizens of Brevard County, Florida.

It was like the man building a wind mill, claiming he was owner of the wind.
A few moments of serenity shattered by the actions of man.

Serenity required by Jake to be restored. He was malnourished and sleep deprived. These things he could deal with, in due time. What he needed now more than anything was wash off the stench of the cesspool. To walk away clean and renewed.

How dare they deprive him of that simple need.

When he arrived at Nicky's the food was eaten, the paper was crumpled, and everyone was gone. He could not explain where everyone had disappeared. He made a few concentric circles of the area to make sure no one was left behind. He drove back to Orlando knowing; Marcus told the truth, and the woman was a liar. He also knew, Nicky was supposed to be to work by 9 AM.

Marcus was waiting for him when he returned. Nicky made the trip before she went to work. Looking no worse for the journey Marcus told him the woman ran off as soon as they arrived back in town. Nicky was upset, with Jake. The woman liar was upset with Jake. Marcus was a little hungry, mentioned with a grin.

To put the time frame in proper order, this was after Jake was told his accounts were closed, and just before Marcus was thrown out of a moving car. The twenty-four-hour observation was an utter failure, because Jake was deprived the morning status check on the woman liar. She was past the critical stage of decompression. If she did not promptly return to the substance abuse, she could shake it off.

Nicky did Jake no favors, by dropping the woman back in the pot, half cooked.

CHAPTER TWENTY - FIVE

Marcus came in on that pair of brand-new crutches. He plopped into an overstuffed chair. He was back to triplet sentences and long silence. First, he was fed, then he was provided with a poultice of herbs to vanquish his pain.

Some of the herbs grew wild in the yard. Fresh, they would be more powerful than required. Jake boiled the herbs in oil to form a soothing lotion. Topical it was better than any systemic prescription. Marcus applied the lotion to bruises and contusions. In a short time, he was free from pain. Application of the oil to his forehead was calming and restorative.

"What is in this stuff? Jake you a witch doctor! Got any I can take with me when I leave?" grinned Marcus.

Jake was way ahead of Marcus. He handed him a greasy bottle with floating residue. Marcus started to throw away the bottle of pain killers he was given at discharge from the hospital. Jake stopped him. Better to have them, and not need them; than need them, and not have them.

"I don't need them, I got you. You the witch doctor!

Where'd you learn this stuff?"

"Please don't call me Doctor. All I need is to go to jail, for practicing medicine without a license, you nut." Jake cautioned.

He settled into a long dissertation of the curative properties of the herbs he used. The literature was out there, all for the common man to cross reference. Most people used to rely on home remedies first, before going to the doctor. Every culture contributed something. Half the time a herb used by a Persian was known by a different name by an Italian. The contribution made by the Chinese was echoed by the Hindu. Swiss natural preparations influenced all of Europe. Mexicans had rediscovered a whole body of knowledge lost to Mesoamericans, when the Spanish entered the new world. The Spanish had made no less contribution to the process, by the careful examination of what they found. Most of the robust health of the peoples of the planet, was from a dietary intake of common herbs.

Every time Jake had contradictory information within a convergent body of knowledge, he had only to consult a withered old representative from the culture being explored. He may have to learn a little Spanish, a little French, and bank the learning off the Navaho tradition. A little Russian, combined with Turks Hebrew was very insightful. Creole with Huron influence was another treasure trove. Greek and Phoenician traders influenced Ireland, the British Isles, and the Scandinavian trade routes. Chinese used a single pictograph to illustrate an herbal prescription. Traditions and myths all shorthand for peaceful co-existence.

There was more to the story, but Jake did not have the time to fry neurons, in order to explain it in entirety. The only reason he had been able to deeply immerse himself in the subject was the guaranteed freedoms of his America. All cultures were afforded an opportunity to join together.

The present racial quibbling was a regular Tower of Babel, undermining the very foundations of America itself, Common sense was no longer enough to get by. Common popular opinion was forming discrete and insular Minorities. Even this was an understatement because the "Insular Minorities" were anything but "Discrete"

Before Marcus had a chance to leave, Wizard and Moselle show up looking to plead a case, for their Civil Rights being violated. Both of them were back out on the street, forced out of a hovel, by the slum-owner's diligence committee. Jake reminded them, he was not a Lawyer. He also reminded them he was not running a Charity Mission. This place was neither a bar nor a brothel. They had until sunset to figure out what they wanted to do for shelter. Moselle took it at face value and secured another night at the mission where Jake had introduced him. Wizard played the waiting game.

Marcus excused himself, then asked Jake for a ride, to give his benefactor an excuse to leave and lock the door. Wizard wanted to stay and wait for Jake. Jake told Wizard, No.

Wizard suddenly stormed out with all the indignity of a patron denied entry across the velvet rope. Marcus cautioned Jake he was going to need a bouncer. Jake commented he was well aware of his present requirements; he just couldn't shoot anybody.

After dropping Marcus off, Jake took his time returning to the house. Wizard just needed time to cool off. This was going to be the coldest night of the year to date. It was well above freezing however, it was going to be far below comfortable, for the street bums. The homeless would be up all night, walking, to stay warm. They would wait to sleep the following afternoon. on park benches all over town.

Wizard showed up after dark. He said he wanted to borrow a lamp for reading. Jake saw through the deception. If Wizard could find a place to plug the lamp, he could squat over it all night long to warm himself. Wizard got his lamp and was asked to leave. After wizard went away, Jake built a fine blaze in the fireplace. He had intentionally waited until after the anticipated visit from Wizard. Even if it meant seeing his own breath in the living room, it was preferable to offering Wizard any reason to stick around. Bums are pragmatic, they never want to share misery, unless they can profit from the deal. Jake was not going to share a cord of stored firewood, warming a homeless bum.

All that wailing and gnashing of teeth was part of the path.

Pain endured is a cosmic warning to cease and desist the excruciating experience. Jake was only doing Wizard a favor by making him face the path he had chosen. He had already been warned to seek shelter. If he was too preoccupied with some activity to take sound advice, Jake wondered what that activity could include. He had another acid test planned for Wizard.

A few more days of a special diet would make Jake smell the way he needed to smell, in order to be accepted into the presence of a Seminole shaman. Wizard was never going to get inside the thicket. Jake would have a musk without pollution.

Wizard would cast a bum's perfume. Not only would Wizard be lost on the trail, but his smell would show which contaminants he used. The swirling jungle was going to keep him busy for hours, or as long as was convenient. Jake would have his private moment with the shaman leaving Wizard twisting in the breeze, as long as was amusing.

The acid test was hardly necessary. They were on the road thirty minutes when Wizard was exhibiting signs of distress.

The trouble was, Jake stood the chance of missing his moment with the shaman if he turned back now. They were driving to Lake Okeechobee for a simple true false answer from a source most qualified. To neglect the appointment was to show disrespect.

Jake no longer needed to fill the jungle path with Wizards odor. He could smell it himself inside the car. He even worried the odor might taint his own cleanliness. He would be forced to rinse in waters containing tannic acid when they arrived.

The appointment was met. Never was one word spoken. A gift of Tobacco with an herb mixture was passed to the wise old man. He smiled, the answer was a resounding true, the herbs were combined in the proper order. As Jake rushed away, the wise old man swept his hand in encouragement to hurry.

Pausing to acknowledge instructions their eyes met. The old man pinched his nose, and repeated the instructions.

Everyone can pronounce Okeechobee. Where the Floridians are separated from the Yankees is when someone tries to pronounce Caloosahatchee, or Econolocahatchee.

Jake found Wizard was a liar, a Yankee with an accent, and he did not know how to bait his own hook. Also, he would not recognize a Ghost Orchid, if he was slapped with one, walking in the woods. He found himself no longer calling the man Wizard. He called him WIZ, because he really pissed off Jake.

"Exactly how many years were you on Ritlan" Jake asked

Wiz out of the blue, in the middle of a jungle path looking for Ghost Orchids. It was a rhetorical question.

"Started when I was Ten continued until I dropped out of school" came the surprising confession.

Jake was only making a wise ass remark, he was not really expecting an answer. Suddenly it all came cleaf. Wiz was abusing narcotics looking for a Ritan Buzz. When he dropped out of school his supply of Ritlan dried up. This guy was an inductee into the drug culture by way of a Tight Ass Teacher who slapped him into chemical handcuffs.

The teacher was too stupid to see he was acting out, because, the rest of the class was retarding his intellectual development. Instead of demanding the class excel at his level, he was drugged into submission and forced to operate at teacher clone level. The teacher probably was unable to operate above the level of the recommended textbook. The teacher's inability to answer his persistent questions, out of context, meant he required medication. Medicated, he eventually fell behind the level of his peers, and left school. But the boy was already a habitual drug user, Ritlan.

Jake was not in the practice of making excuses for other people, but in this case, he could make an exception. He had seen so much of it over the years. There was no avoiding the conclusion. Some pension seeking puke, in over depth, refusing to wade into the deep end. Convincing others, the right thing to do, is to throw not a floatation device; but a Ritlan brick.

The last brick Jake swam with, belonged to a professor who used students to collect a Doctoral Thesis. The Professor did not deserve credit for a work collected, on a pass-fail schedule. The greedy academic credited colleagues and bibliographies, never the students. The Doctoral thesis, valued status quo, more than accuracy. Jake stayed in the deep end, catching bricks, treading water. On the day it was time for Jake to stand and deliver, he turned in the report, keeping all references to himself. He crawled out of the pool, took all his bricks and built a bookshelf.

He also never looked back. Nobody needed a more efficient explosive ordinance package. Before someone learns to make something explode, they should be forced to learn how to build the damn thing. Gospel according to Jake.

The discovery of Wizards condition, tempered Jake's opinion. He was more inclined toward an optimistic overview.

The fishing and hunting Ghost Orchids, was doing Wizard better than Wiz himself knew. Somewhere deep inside his reptilian brain, stimulation was taking place, to wash away the narcotic trance. If Jake kept him out here a month, Wiz may even fully recover.

The question remained; while Jake was out here doing the work others were paid to do; Where were they? He did not even have to go inside the building to know the answer.

Some uninspired, untalented slug, was sitting in front of a computer screen scheming. Rather than doing what they were employed to do, they were cruising the Internet looking for hot stock tips, or dirt on the competition. Their tailored corporate uniform immaculate, after hours in an air-conditioned office, when the job required sweaty field work. The desk was on autopilot, while the social worker's clients were dutifully handled by uniformed officers. Perfumed, pampered and plucked: they were more impressed with the title, than the work.

Jake arrived at this conclusion, when he telephoned with mundane questions to be transferred ad infinitum, until he was speaking to the director of the project. He certainly was not complaining, but the questions he posed, were so trivial any competent subordinate could have answered them. If there was no one between him, and the project director, there was a lot of dead wood. He even felt embarrassed, to pester a project director, who obviously had more important things to do.

Maybe his inquiries were more topical than he himself knew.

Wizard was more than another example of someone who slipped through the cracks, he was an embodiment of the failure of the system. He was forced to face the world with a substandard education. He was constantly living at survival level, while the rest of society tried to ignore him.

Wizard was another petty thief. Jake caught him sucking gasoline out of the truck, with a garden hose one night. He was forgiven the indiscretion at the time, with promise to never do it again. The man was clearly living by the code: Survival of the Fittest. He was the Feral Hominoid cleverly avoiding cages.

Unlike Jake, the man relished his role as predator for all it involved. He only assumed a polished exterior of civility, when it served his purpose.

Wiz was the kind of man who claimed he knew ballistics.

Left alone with a cannon, he was the type to fail to compensate for recoil, and be unable to explain why the muzzle was now in the mud. He was the style of infantry, who climbs on horseback, then proceeds to shoot his own mount in the back of the head. Caught in the act, Wizard would explain his gun was too short. He might even offer; the action was to provide the troop with horse flesh.

Jake suspected as much. His suspicions were confirmed when Wizard jumped behind the wheel of Jake's new car, drove off, and never came back.

CHAPTER TWENTY - SIX

The fuel tank of the new vehicle was empty from the trip to Okeechobee. Jake figured it would only be a day before his car was returned. He filed a police report and notified the insurance company. The Auto insurance carrier, informed Jake; a parked car in his own yard, was the domain of his Homeowners Policy. He added the automobile onto the new list, of stolen personal effects.

The payment from the old list of stolen personal effects, had not even cleared the bank. As soon as it did, the Asian banker was going to close all the accounts.

The old truck was still in the driveway. It was in serviceable running order. Like any hunk of American steel, it was built to last forever, with proper maintenance. Jake and Jesus were the only ones who knew the tortures put to this truck. It still purred and begged for more. Please sir may I have another. All it needed at the moment was a new air filter.

He drove his old truck, down to his old bank. His old bank was the lender on his new car loan. When he bought the New Truck, he could have paid cash. He let the money sit in the bank, drew a loan with the new car as collateral on the loan.

The truck if stolen was paid in full, under fine print stipulated by the slick salesman. It was Jake's intently to advise the bank the vehicle was stolen. The vault slammed shut on his cash reserves.

The only thing going for poor stupid pitifully-honest Jake, was his American Excess account. After all, isn't that what credit was for? In case of Emergency, break glass. Pay it off at the beginning of each month, to avoid penalties so painful in comparison the Spanish Inquisition looked like a party.

All his bank accounts were vacated. All his insurance was based on having a winning combination to the lottery. His vehicles were alternating impoundment. His only trustworthy associate was tossed out of a moving vehicle. His other associates were all contributing to assist his plight. He was under casual police surveillance, with complete vigilante scrutiny.

Jake was a puppet all right, a marionette. A marionette, is the same thing as a Pieta, except when it gets smacked with a stick no candy falls out. Dangling by its strings, the only source of pleasure derived from striking a marionette, is in the smacking. A marionette has the disadvantage over a punching bag, because the punching bag swings back.

Jake was becoming accustomed to being used as punching bag. His assessment of his present situation; as a marionette he was hung too high. He only had to free his arms, and lower his attitude. If he could sweep closer to the ground, he could at least avoid being a target to quite as many sticks. A pendulum in motion, at the proper altitude, is just as effective as a helicopter. Everyone ducks for cover.

Monica went to court on the charge of: Violating a Court Injunction; Use of a surrogate, to Violate a Restraining Order.

She pled; not guilty. In a jury of her peers, she was found; not guilty.

Jelly-Belly, immediately pressed the Court to arrest Jake. If he had acted alone in the commission of the crime, he should be prosecuted to the fullest extent of the law, Vis- a-Vis, Posthaste, Muy Important, and any other excuse that sounded legal. The drunkard signed all the necessary paperwork, to put the wheels of justice into motion. Jelly-Belly then traversed to the nearest location where he could partake of his noontime dietary requirements, a pitcher of cold beer.

Had he gone to Jake directly, he would have learned something important. The wheels of Justice, like any other wheel, is only as effective as the portion of the wheel, in contact with the pavement. It does not really matter how large a wheel is, it has to contact cold hard reality, at some point in its rotation. If it is a gear, as it revolves, it must interlock with another gear. The wheels of Justice roll deliberately slow. A very pure lubricant is required to preserve the gears against damage. Even with the purist of lubricants, flat spots are worn into the gears.

Jelly Belly had been cushioning his gears, with the wrong lubricant. His gears were missing a few teeth. Jelly belly was describing road kill, by calling it a speed bump.

To the man being sucked into the slow-moving gears it is as if he was thrown into a wood chipper. He never sees the rotation of the cogs until suddenly being swept away. Jake never saw it coming. He was preoccupied with a host of other chores trying desperately to bail and shipwright a swamped vessel. Even Monica failed to warn him of the approaching storm.

For the moment all bills were paid, all expenses budgeted.

Money was going to come in eventually, one project or another. He had a few thousand dollars tucked away, for the American Excess payment when it eventually came due. The seas were showing calm on the horizon. One more board-side by a pirate could still send him to the bottom.

The boarding party of the pirates was in the form of Moselle. On the very coldest night of the year Moselle came crying to Jake. His tale was filled with tearful emotional distress and victimization of a cold cruel world, set on his ultimate destruction. Monica all over again. Put Moselle in a skirt and you had Monica.

Jake took the wretch to the proper authorities to get an identification card. Then he took him to a restaurant where Moselle was given a position as a dish washer. Then Jake took the little piece of crap, to the store to get him clothing for his job. Next was the question of transportation. Moselle was handed a bus schedule for the route from point A to point B.

This still left a question of where the bum would be housed.

Ten dollars a day seemed about right to charge the little scum bag. No meals, no cigarettes, no beer, no hookers, no drugs! Get up and go to work, no Jerry Springer Show. Three days maximum. The applicant had no money. He was handed a can of paint and a brush. Shape up or ship out, Pigritta.

Everything went fine the first night. The following morning Jake woke before dawn. He was attending to his normal business with coffee and a newspaper. As the yard warmed, he ventured out, to see if any plant specimens were damaged in the frost. Everything was fine, covered with sheets he could now remove.

He wandered around the yard wondering what to do with the Spook House decorations. He began crumpling some of the props, to leave for the trash man. The neighborhood was just not ready for a function of this kind. This 'hood would never be ready for anything except collecting welfare.

An unmarked police car, with a plain clothed officer, parked in the yard next door. At a glance Jake could tell the man was obviously a police officer, even before the shield in his belt was visible. Jake made no effort to escape, being unaware of any violation to public safety or outstanding tickets. He attended to his own business as the man approached.

"You know anyone named Monica?" the cheerful man asked. He approached from Jake's extended peripheral vision.

"Sure do, how's she doing haven't heard from her in a long time. She's not in trouble again, is she?" Jake answered as he folded a piece of plywood in half for the garbage man.

"No, she's just fine." spoke the man now dangerously close behind Jake. "You are the one in trouble."

Jake could have taken the advantage. He could have swept behind himself with a bent right leg. left foot pivot. Had he not just woken from a content slumber, he would have done so. He was well rested, and on his own property, this had to be a mistake.

The man straight armed Jake in the center of his spine and instructed "Put your hands behind your back, now!"

Jake didn't need to hear his rights read to him, but it would have been nice to hear them just the same. He was handcuffed and taken inside the house to be properly dressed for the trip down town. He asked why he was placed into custody.

"Failure to make a court appearance." was the only reply.

How could Jake be expected to show up in court if his mail never came in a timely manner. He had tickets out the yin-yang a stack of no-trespassing warrants and other assorted misery to choose from. Any one of which, may require a court appearance if he had received a summons to appear.

As he was leaving, Moselle came out of his room to find out what was happening. Jake said he didn't know. He gave Moselle the keys to the house and told him to keep it locked.

"Sell whatever was needed to post bond", were Moselle's instructions. Jake would call him from the jail with further instructions.

With everything Jake had done for Moselle, in the last few days, it was not a large request. Jake took nothing except his wallet. He even forgot his new Cellular phone. He was still confident this was a big mistake.

Jake knew the drill by now. When he was booked into the main section of the jail, he turned into a boot camp robot. He said nothing, to no one. When he was punched it the face, by another prisoner, he let it slide. When someone reached across his plate to take his food, nothing happened. He took a pair of barber clippers and cut his own hair too short, for anyone to grab with their fingers. To curb his craving for tobacco, he kept a tooth brush handy. If someone approached in a threatening manner he removed the toothbrush, holding it by the bristles.

He slept when he was supposed to, ate when he was supposed to, and every chance he could he would shower.

His bond was a thousand dollars, his bail was one hundred.

He kept calling the house to find out where Moselle was with the bail money. The one time he actually spoke to the bum, he was told the money: "was on the way". The following day Jake was still in jail. He reached his telephone answering machine, leaving a message for Moselle to "lock up and get out". The next message was; "He would find some other person to post bail."

Jake searched in his memory for every telephone number he could remember. He called the Union Hall, the Club, every friend and every business associate. Anyone he did contact, owed him at least one hundred dollars, meaning they were avoiding him. to avoid paying off the loan.

He was in the custody of the jail four days, when he finally called the one number, he dreaded the most. The one numbed his memory could never erase, His Mom.

Jake's mom was the quintessential smother mother. She was the kind of mother who would follow her boys into combat to jump on a hand grenade. Asking for her help, was like putting the Canadian Mounted Police on a case. No stone was going to be unturned in the pursuit of justice. If her boy was guilty of a infraction of any article of the rules; he would be better off inside the jail, than outside listening to her criticism.

She'd force feed with one hand, while smacking her boys with the other.

Every document in every file would be copied in triplicate and exposed to the severest form of verification by the highest authority. The President and the Pope, along with the emperor of Japan, and the Sheiks of Arabia were hard to find, when Jake's mom was on a case.

The only persons who did not block her calls, were the Pentagon and the Queen Mother. The Pentagon because it sounded like a national emergency. The Queen Mother who still maintained a curiosity of the workings of the rambunctious colonialists. Even the Israelis would, ducked and cover, when they saw Jake's Mom turned a corner. To say she was controlling, is like saying Attila the Hun was a boy scout.

He hung up before the call was received. He has to sit in jail a lot longer, before he made that call. Every time she got involved, he found himself strapped to a laboratory table being probed, x-rayed and analyzed. Psycho tropic drugs, everything imaginable to get to the bottom of the story.

Jake's mom was the kind of person who makes Martha Stewart look like a slacker. Everything must be in exactly the correct position where it was placed. The place setting was so tight a meal could be ruined, with the simple act of breathing too deeply. No argument was ever finished, the conclusion was only postponed pending additional information.

Still, she was his mother, deserving love and respect, with all acceptable distance to avoid an Anaconda like hug.

Somewhere along the line a temporary truce was instituted where Jake was allowed to determine when his efforts where good enough. He was allowed to choose perfection, in the outcome of a project, so long as he did not leave the immediate area.

Jake thought rotting in jail, was probably the best thing to do, considering the alternative. Too late, she checked caller ID.

As expected, Jake was transferred to undergo Psychiatric evaluation. The one Insurance Policy not operating on a lotto system was his health insurance. Holding up an insurance policy in front of a psychiatrist is like Cart Blanc to a real estate investor.

Everyone has something wrong with their mental hygiene.

This makes everyone an individual. Only clones, who are raise in a vacuum of similar environmental factors, are the same every time. A psychiatrist suspects anyone who is not a clone of the psychiatrist, has a critical need to conform, to being a clone. And to this effort is a plethora of psycho tropic medications.

The learned medical professional, can continue his evaluations indefinitely so long as the insurance policy is in proper working order. Jake's insurance just paid off a Porsche.

Jake refused to take his medications. His clinical evaluation was; he was resisting therapy. Never mind the fact he was malnourished and sleep deprived, he needed medication. He was not going anywhere unless he took his medication, or his insurance ran out, whichever came first. Take the medication and he was free to leave within twenty-four hours. Jake knew his Health Insurance was paid two years in advance. He still refused to take the medication.

He didn't even like the high from a glass of beer. He had no intention of smoking a joint. He did not need a happy-pill. It was a matter of principle.

He still did not have any idea why he was in jail. Failure to Appear, was all he knew. Good old mom and dad had the answer. He was being arraigned on a case of; Violation of a Restraining Order. They had all kinds of good news, his stolen car was impounded and currently going to the Drug Seizure auction. His mortgage was up for foreclosure, unless paid by the fifteenth of the month. Moselle had stolen his other truck, unloaded everything of value in the house, then brought the truck back and parked it with a flat tire. His bills were now all overdue. He also had a notice from the homeowner's association, if he did not mow his yard soon, he would be served with a Code Violation.

Jake still refused to take the medication. A needle nosed nurse documented his every abusive remark. She recorded every slang, colloquial, off-color expression in his vocabulary.

She was of the assumption this was a dangerous man. As they stood nose to needle nose, Jake suggested she service her sexual tension, herself.

All the alarms went off, a goose-stepping gang in white uniform, square danced around Jake. The "doe-se-doe" took Jake to his room, where a large hypodermic found his buttock.

They "doe-se-dos d" back out of the room, locking the door.

The room started spinning. When he awoke his legs did not work. He could shuffle, but not walk. Nice thing: the hangover was mild.

He languished a few more days in observation. The whole time he felt like a fish bowl was placed over his head. His game of basketball really suffered; he did not have the energy for a simple layup shot. Still, he was never going to get to the bottom of his legal entanglements inside a loony bin. He had two choices, tell the doctor what the doctor wanted to hear, or say nothing. Being Jake, he kept his mouth shut, and let the doctor do all the talking.

Muhammad Ali used to float like a butterfly and sting like a bee. Bruce Lee: said to bend like a reed. He also said: to fight water, you must become water. That was good enough for Jake. He was not going to swim the tide, against the current. If the doctor said Jake was nuts, Jake would become nuts.

He arrived at his home to piles of beer cans, unopened condoms and not much else. Anything not missing was only left behind because it was broken. The refrigerator and microwave were still there. Jake fixed the flat on his truck, locked the door and went to his apartment. He made a new list of all the missing and destroyed property to turn in to All-Gated insurance company; c/o spin the wheel maybe the lottery will pick your number.

With list in hand, he contacted the Sheriff to report the crime. They met him at the house and took the complaint. The law dogs were jovial and offered comment and criticism. It was their opinion; Jake should have known this was going to happen. "Where did he think he was Beverly Hills?" They could have told him this would happen in this neighborhood.

"Point taken. Tell me again, exactly whose job is it, to make sure this does not happen?" Jake scoffed, "Pardon me while I do, what it is I have to do, to comply with regulations."

CHAPTER TWENTY - SEVEN

Jake got a lawyer, a good one. He first had to prove his case to this lawyer before the man took it on referral. Criminal attorneys are like major league batters. They are scored by number of times at the plate. Runs, walks and errors. Most important are the errors. Batting a thousand while going to the plate only twice is no true measure of a batter. The lawyer Jake picked, was so good, he did not want to risk his standings on a spit ball. Jake made his pitch, and the Lawyer saw he could knock it out of the park.

The District Attorney tried to plea bargain Jake to a lesser charge. Jake would not be patronized by the offer. He went before the docket three times. Each time refusing to kowtow to the demands of the prosecutor. Even his own lawyer was amused by the gritty determination of someone, likely looking at more jail time. Jake already felt like he was serving time with no money, and no place to go. None of his client list, wanted to hire a jailbird. The only thing he could do was beat the charges.

Jelly-Belly eyeballed Jake on the day of the trial. Jake could see Jelly-Belly was already craving his liquid lunch. He hoped the case dragged on into the night just to make Jelly Belly suffer.

The jurors were seated. The opening remarks were made.

The prosecution showed its evidence, photographs of a vehicle scratched everywhere. The witness was called, he pointed at Jake.

Jake's lawyer got up and smacked it right out of the park.

By Jelly-Bellies own testimony it was proven he never saw Jake do anything. Jake had carefully photographed ever camera angle from ever seat in the Club, the walkway, and even outdoors. The pictures proved Jelly-Belly could not possibly, have seen, Jake from the location stated. There were pillars, plants and other automobiles in line of sight. The only way Jelly-Belly could have observed Jake, commit the deed, was to follow him out onto the pavement. Monica was never mentioned.

Jake had successfully defended himself in a court of Law with ten dollars of film and some color enlargements. God bless America the system still works. He was acquitted of all charges.

Jake only saw Monica one more time. Her years of torturing men were well behind her. All her self-abuse was worn into her face more deeply than any branding iron could have done. Her body showed the girth of a former coke whore, who without cocaine swells up like a balloon. Skinny arms and legs sticking out of a potato shaped torso, is not too attractive.

He wanted to feel sorry for her, even with all the damage she had done to his life. Upon introspection, Jake concluded he had done it to himself. He allowed himself to be taken for a ride by a succubus. She like so many other women of her era, was only aware of their power over men, without ever considering the consequences of their actions. His only resolve was that it would never happen again.

Somewhere out in the universe, is a location where the natural order of things, makes it impossible for one creature to control another. The Incubus and the Succubus, are only allowed a fleeting moment to find one another, and like a chemical reaction they consume each other.

EPILOGUE

On the island of Pathos, lives a man in a cave. He has chosen to devote himself to soil and water conservation on a personal level. Outside the cave a Windmill grinds wild seeds into flour for his bread. The windmill also serves to drive a turbine producing electricity. He has pens for chickens, rabbits, goats and a dairy cow. He is content to share a solitary existence, with his domesticated stock.

Within the influence of his attempts of land stewardship, he makes careful mental notes. When he takes time to commit an idea to paper, it often looks like a musical sonata of clever pictographs. He uses the notation as a memory device.

He limited his domain to five acres, most of which remains in a natural condition. His water is collected from rainfall then distilled against possible contamination. Strange fruiting vines brings seasonal fruits. He takes only what he needs from the land, sharing the rest with the wild creatures.

Inside the cave is an odd collection of useful objects Each serves its own purpose. Most run-on electricity, when some other fuel will not serve the function better. He stays aware of new developments by normal communication standards.

Choosing to shun the superficial, where a new face was selling an old product, he monitors satellite transmissions.

Sometimes he ventures into public, selling his handiwork to obtain money, to stay ahead of technology. His unassuming posture raises little attention from the people he contacts. The hubbub of large crowded areas, are tolerated for mere moments before he experiences sensory overload. His mind calculates results in nanoseconds. A momentary observation, causes him to cascade through cause and effect with every resultant, by glance.

Those who have been to his cave, all mention the need for a housekeeper. Few have ventured inside the cave for the clutter.

It is generally assumed the man has a lifetime supply of low caliber ammunition used for Animal Husbandry. Stuffed between books are jars with strange seeds, or leaves. The furniture is primitive, mostly bent with a curious odor of natural varnish. Tobacco lingers in the ambient air quality, along with a musty mold.

The mildew insures, an unwelcome guest will not remain long enough, to disrupt his papers. Many experiences an allergic reaction leading to their quick departure. Someday the townsfolk will come with their torches to cleanse the cave.

They will bum his notations and he will no longer exist.
On that day, the man will simply tuck a knife in his boot, and set out for a new refuge. He will pick through the crumbling after effects of an abandoned habitation, free from the herd of Lemmings and start anew. He knows he can continue without instrumentation and technology, as long as his mind is attuned to solving a single equation: A plus B is equal to C: true or false.

Bueno Rio

BY FREDERICK DALPAY

CHAPTER ONE
Blam! Blam! Blam!

Buddha, the rifle sounded. Bullets ripped through the dense undergrowth of the jungle Mesa. Down the steep embankment lay the relative safety of the river. Bullets do not care what they strike in their path. Right now, they ripped through overgrowth.

In a clearing, a drug lord's helicopter was exchanging currency for cocaine. Duffel bags of cash were unloaded, making room for the contraband. Night was falling fast. It was all part of the plan.

The plan, just grab two duffel bags, and run like hell. Twenty-five yards away was a sixty-foot embankment. It was only twenty-five yards.

Jake took the paper bag of black powder in his left hand. He lit the fuse with his right. Blowing on the fuse, he made sure it would not go out. Transferring the bag to his right hand, he made a lazy overhand motion. The bundle was lobbed between the Helicopter and the bags of money.

A huge plume of smoke rose up. Another chorus of Buddha, Buddha, Buddha, came crashing from across the mesa.

Jake made the run. He grabbed two bags, dragging them to the sandy cliffs. He dropped one, then rode the other down the slope to the river. A sixty-foot drop would kill a man. A sixty-foot slide at a sloping angle, with a sandy bed of friction could be survived, probably.

Ernie made his way around the shadow of the cliff, just as the crimson traces of nightfall fell on the mesa. He was circling around the dense jungle in water sometimes up to his knees. Clutched in front of him, like a suitcase, was an American made semi-automatic rifle. At moments the water threatened to be too deep. He would hoist the firearm to safety each time. The last thing going to get wet was that rifle.

Yelling and screaming from above, let Ernie know he was headed in the right direction. He should be reaching the boat any time now. A huge paw reached out of the gloom, clamping itself over his mouth. He knew he was, where he needed to be.

Jake released his grip a little at a time, no need to be reckless. Ernie shifted the M-16 to the side and butted Jake in the abdomen. Same reason...no need to be reckless.

"You were supposed to leave the rifle on the mesa"!

"We're going to need it!" Ernie responded, "Besides, I left them one of their own, an AK, with a spider web of trick line."

They were whispering, but they were also waiting and listening. The helicopter never took off. This was not what they expected. It was past twilight now. A few flashlight beams flickered about, but nothing close to their location.

"So, where's the boat?" Ernie commented over the sound of water tinkling in the shallows.

"You're sitting on it!" offered Jake.

"It's just a tree trunk..." stammered Ernie

Jake rolled over the log to expose a dugout canoe, containing two duffel bags. Inside the boat was a long pole, with two oddly shaped oars. The end of the oars, were like the spade on a deck of playing cards. They silently pushed it into the knee-deep water.

"You couldn't steal a real boat?" snarled Ernie, "This looks like some sacred Indian relic!"

"You gonna talk, or you gonna row?" smiled Jake, still wondering why the helicopter never took off.

The stars came out. The rarefied light illuminated the sides of the river. The sheen off the surface of the water reflected faintly in all directions. Beneath the surface was still inky darkness. The broken reflection the only clue of submerged objects to be avoided. The quick moving river itself, would not give up the location of the two men.

They covered fifteen miles, each hour, in the winding river. Miles away from detection in the morning. The helicopter pilot would have a large radius to search. The tropical jungle was only dotted with a view of the river. Jake knew, from the air, the river looked like a broken pearl necklace. To make matters worse there was no location to land an aircraft with limited fuel and no navigator. The best pilot could not search this river. With scattered tributaries feeding the Rio Meta, all flowing to the Rio Orinoco, any attempt to follow the river by air was futile. Jake knew this.

"You want some Gator Jerky?" offered Jake, "Gator, crocodile, caman something like that..."

"Where did you get it?"

"Made it myself, Cut the tail into fillets and smoked it in one of those Mexican tortilla ovens over at the mission."

"Where did you get the Gator tail?", Ernie knew to ask.

"I was standing by the river when this lizard came out of the river. It took a snap at me. I jumped straight up in the air then landed right on its jaws. I used my belt to hold the jaws, shut then carved off half its tail with my knife. I figured if he was gonna eat me, I was gonna eat him."

"Why only half a tail?" Ernie wondered.

"I think he learned his lesson. A gator only needs half a tail, the damn thing grows back. The sweet meat is on the tip of the tail anyway. So, you want some?", Jake again offered.

"No." countered Ernie.

"Suit yourself, you'll change your mind in a couple of days."

It was the time of the year where twelve hours of dark was followed by twelve hours of light. The Equinox. Twelve hours of drifting and paddling made the radius from dangerous detection huge. Not as large as one would calculate using a straight line, the river was winding. None the less, if a purser chose the correct branch of the river, there was a lot of real estate to cover. Somewhere between one quarter, and one half, million square miles of inhospitable jungle.

Somewhere else this would be the coolest portion of the day. In the tropical rainforest this was the wettest part of the day. Dampness clung to everything. It was even too wet to strike a match. The men were tired and wet. A small cook flame would be comforting. Even with a butane lighter, it was near impossible to find dry grass and sticks to fuel a flame. Just about the time they decided it was not worth the effort, Ernie dedicated some rotting vegetation to the flames. The fire smoldered for a moment then burst into an explosive blaze.

"Methane!" Jake announced with wide eyed examination. "We might want to put this out, before the whole place goes up!"

"What am I supposed to do with the fish I just caught?"

"Eat it raw like sushi..." suggested Jake.

Across the river a Capibara picked its way through the water to the opposite bank. The two men watched intently, knowing the creature would likely be attacked by a toothy river lizard. Jake bet Ernie, it would not make it past mid-stream. Double or nothing if it reached the shore.

The Capibara reached the bank swiftly climbing slippery mud. Out of nowhere an arrow struck the rodent. It stood for a moment puzzled then a delayed reaction the arrow knocked it down. Jumping back to its feet the animal acted dumfounded. Desiring to run and escape, it sank onto its knees then rolled over to quiver silently. Ernie looked at Jake in astonishment "But... he did make the other bank!"

A small brown man with hair colored red from Henna berries came out of the jungle thicket. He approached the Capibara tied the hind legs together then picked it up. Without a word, he forded the river ignored the men, then attempted to take the canoe. Ernie ran down to stop him as the native pulled the boat into the water. Jake stood watching as the native pulled a tug in one direction, countered as Ernie yanked in the other. The Henna covered native dropped the Capibara into the boat and in no time brought out an arrow from his quiver, leveling it at Ernie. The string of the miniature bow was being drawn back, in a methodical warning to his adversary.

Jake now stepped forward with the two leaf shaped paddles. He handed one to Ernie. The other he held tip up like a shovel. The Indian relaxed, slightly. The bow was ever so slightly allowed to slacken. Jake turned to Ernie, acting indifferent to the small man. "You do not want to be hit with one of those arrows. They are covered with tree frog mucus... some stuff called cure-are-re." Jake explained patiently, "Let's just have a normal conversation for a few moments."

"What do you want to talk about?"

"It doesn't matter...just act calm!" says Jake "This guy only wants to get down river with his dinner. In a few minutes he'll get the message we mean him no harm."

"OK, so why is the Capibara still breathing?" Ernie noted crossing his arms in front of him. The native relaxed his pull on the bow.

convulsions between nerve impulses." Jake spoke slowly ignoring the Indian. His eyes trained on Ernie. His ears concentrating on the sound of the bow string as it made a leather stretching sound.

"How was I supposed to know?" Ernie's voice broke into a desperate rasp. The small brown man now drawing back on the bow. Jake did not turn, he motioned with his hand to lower the arrow. The small beady black eyes under, page boy henna hair, showed recognition. Slowly he lowered his weapon.

"Now we rush him?" whispered Ernie out of the side of his mouth.

"No... now we shake hands, and offer our new friend a lift."

"Hey I thought these guys used blow guns?" Ernie smirked.

CHAPTER TWO

Flores, sitting at a small wooden desk, cupped his forehead in his hands. He was a large man, who could track his family's military career, to the conquistadors. He had a military presence, with a multi-generational sense of entitlement. He had never himself aspired to any lofty military rank. To be honest, this would have put too great a demand on his time. It would also have presented a problem for his private industry. Times like right now required his full attention.

Everything at the airstrip should have gone smoothly. No one should have interfered with the shipment. He cupped his hands to his face, not in bewilderment, but in furry. A knock at the open door brought the pensive man back to the present.

"The American pilot is ready for his interview." a young private in a poorly fitting uniform announced.

"Have him come in." Flores motioned from an overstuffed chair.

Two equally poorly dressed sentries escorted the American pilot. Everyone working for Flores whispered how, the CIA spent so much on cocaine, and provided such shabby uniforms. The entrance into the office was cordial and not threatening. Flores stood from behind the desk offering his hand to the stranger. "I understand you had some trouble with the last shipment."

The pilot walked in, a sturdy confident smallish man. He exhibited a cavalier swagger, typical of Americans. They shook hands. The pilot sat down, without waiting to be asked. Flores resumed his former position. The American glanced around for a moment then actually said "What no coffee?"

"Bring Mister Ryan some Coffee!" Flores gestured to his underlings. The gruff Columbian turned to the American, "While we wait, why don't you tell me about the mix up at the delivery sight?" Ryan studied his fingernails, palms up, fingers curling toward him. "The way I see it, one of your people went independent."

The small room began to warm, as the mid-morning sun climbed in the sky overhead. Flores could feel beads of sweat forming on his brow. He wondered how the pilot could sit comfortably, in a flight jacket. He suspected Ryan was a coke user, but it was too soon in the interview to labor the point. Flores never suspected his consumption of beer and tequila made himself sweat profusely. Ryan was out of his altitude which was usually sea level. In the lofty peaks of Columbia, the thin air was chilly. Flores was also sitting in the direct path of the sunlight a technique he used to intimidate those he held in servitude.

"And if all my men are accounted for....-?" Flores pretended to be seeking assistance from Ryan, "...there must be some other explanation."

"I am strictly a courier..." Ryan interjected, not the least bit taken in by the charade, "I never get involved with the cargo!"

"Ah, here is our coffee." Flores mentioned still playing the generous host. Ryan watched as the robust man stood and pulled the chain on a ceiling fan. Returning to his desk, Flores pulled open a drawer placing a bottle of clear liquid on the desk. He deftly poured a measured amount into his own cup, offering to do the same for the pilot. Ryan motioned with his fingers he would accept a tiny measure.

He was in no position to decline the offer. He did however wait for Flores to take a sip before tasting his own cup. When he did taste a full measure of the liquid, it was like being hit by   a hammer. "This libation must be an acquired taste!" Ryan mentioned, as he immediately stripped off his flight jacket.

Flores grinned mischievously, repressing a laugh that caused a bead of sweat to drip from his nose onto the desk. "It is a local recipe, made from the Agave Cactus and denatured snake venom. Very good for the heart! It will definitely give you a big...."

This left Ryan in a bit of a bind. He was in no position to offend his host. He also did not want to take any chances that would interfere with his ability to pilot an aircraft. He surveyed the bottle on the desk. It was half empty, and Flores looked healthy enough. Ryan took another sip of the tainted coffee, and hoped for the best. The concoction stimulated his already overbearing cavalier attitude.

"Senor Flores, you said all your men have been accounted for, yet it has only been hours since the situation." The pilot offered.

Flores held up his hand ending the dialogue in mid thought. "I choose my men very carefully. They come to me when they are eight or nine years old. All over South America these children are murdered, their small bodies thrown into shallow graves. I do not do this, I feed them and put clothes on them..."

"I get the point, throw in some small arms training you have a private army!" Ryan interrupted, hoping to speed the obvious conclusion.

"Not exactly..." corrected Flores without further explanation.

"What's this got to do with me?" Ryan wanted to know.

"I must do everything in my power to protect the people..." Flores growled, "I am presently conducting an investigation with the critical interest of my people."

Ryan noticed for the first time a small micro-cassette sitting on a side table. The presence of such a device could only mean this interview was on the up and up. Flores was indeed acting on behalf of the common good of his people. Ryan was sophisticated enough to understand this also meant to the exclusion of all others. He decided to play along.

"Senor Flores, I'd like to help you out with your little problem, I really would. I am just as confused; about what took place out there, as you are!"

"You seemed to find the landing zone, without any problem, Mister Ryan" Flores began his interrogation. He was disappointed his concoction had not loosened the pilot's tongue.

"I can find a freckle on a flea with the ground positioning satellite technology. Someone on the ground with a mobile radio and I'll drop the Sunday paper on your front porch."

"And how often are you called on to deliver papers..." smiled the robust Columbian exposing a gold tooth.

The recorder was still running. Ryan knew he could push the conversation in any direction. "Look if you want to go to a ski lodge in Aspen, I'll get you there. You need rescue equipment in the Mojave Desert I'll get it there. And if you need medical supplies in Brazil, say no more!"

"And... Who do you work for, Mr. Ryan?"

Without a moment hesitation, "Mainly I work for myself! I don't fix em, I don't fuel em, I just drive the bus."

An urgent knocking at the open door behind the pilot demanded immediate attention. Flores stood then walked into the hall, closing the door behind him. He returned shortly, escorted by an attractive woman. The light breaking through the window fell on her peasant dress, giving Ryan a view of her extraordinary body.

As she moved to a chair beside Flores, the pilot could see she was not as young as he had originally expected. She was tall, majestic, and even without the sunlight exposing her attributes, she had a presence lending itself toward distraction. Oh, what a body.

"May I present Senorita Mendoza?" Flores attempted to act business like, with obvious interest in attractions of Ms. Mendoza. She held in her hands a basket similar to ones used for marketplace tortillas. "Senorita Mendoza will administer the lie detector test." Flores advised. Ryan was already on his feet, offering a polite handshake to the maiden. It was the sort of handshake which gentlemen offer, taking only her fingertips holding her hand as if prepared to kiss it. As it sunk in, she was part of the interrogation team, he faltered. He could have sworn something inside the basket moved.

"You must follow my instructions very carefully. Senorita Mendoza speaks no English." Flores instructed with a patronizing tone. "She is very good at what she does. This will not take long."

Ryan now found the beautiful woman helping him to disrobe. First his shirt, next his boots, then his trousers. She removed restraints from the basket for his arms and legs. Using his own belt to strap him securely into the seat of the chair. A bandana blindfold was placed over his eyes. Next, she tugged at his boxer shorts.

"Hey, wait a minute..." Ryan resisted "I'm not into any weird stuff". His outburst may have been what prompted addition of a gag, to the Latin American version of a lie detector test.

"Relax Senor Ryan this will not take long." Flores instructed from behind the desk. He was preoccupied with a folder and ignoring the preparations. The woman Mendoza worked silently. The last of the manipulations involved tugging on his scrotum with a piercing sensation.

When the blindfold was removed the pilot noticed two things, the tape recorder was turned off, and a live rattlesnake's fangs were punctured through his nut sack. The rattlesnake fangs were buried into the seat cushion. He tried to scream but the gag would not allow this to take place. Sweat poured from his forehead, blurring his vision. Through the haze he explored the woman's face, then the face of Flores.

"Ah good everything is in order I see." Flores said placing the folder back into is top drawer. "Now we can resume our little discussion."

Ryan struggled with the gag; it eventually fell away. "You Son of a bitch, there is a rattlesnake sticking in my balls."

"Not your balls that would kill you. He will release no venom until he is milked. Senorita Mendoza will only milk the snake if you lie."

"Oh great, she doesn't even speak English."

"No, but she can tell subtle changes in your reaction to my questions." Flores pulled a single yellowing paper from the credenza behind his desk. Ryan saw it contained ten maybe fifteen lines. "This is going to be harder on me than it is on you..." lied Flores, "I have to translate from Spanish."

This prompted the ever-cavalier Ryan, to offer to trade places!

"Have you...?" "No!"

"Did you...?" "No!"

"Would you...?" "Yes!"

"Do you intend to..." "Yes!"

"Will you ever again..."

The pilot paused "I never did anything like that." He glanced down to consider the lie dowitcher attached to his manhood.

"Yes or no, please senor." "No!"

"Do you have any knowledge of the individuals who participated in the robbery of a shipment...?"

"No, I do not!" Ryan stared at the snake, checking for any unsatisfactory results. The veins in his neck stood out. His face was beet red. Sweat streamed down his body while his mouth was dry as sawdust.

"One final question, have you ever worked for the CIA."

"What is it with you Latin Americans...? Everything is CIA this and CIA that... No I Have never worked for the CIA!"

Senorita Mendoza with an expert flip of the wrist brough the snake away from the chair. "Bueno!" was the single word of encouragement she uttered for the pilot's benefit.

The restraints were removed. Mendoza helped him restored his clothing. Ryan walked over to a pitcher of water and drank deeply until there was none left.

CHAPTER THREE

"Naked, we have naked!" Ernie shouted as he ran back to see what was keeping Jake. Moments before the little brown man with the henna hair was pounding on the side of the canoe with a click-clack chatter. Jake correctly interpreted this to mean "Pull over here."

Ernie had followed the man with the Capibara into a village encampment. Jake brought up the rear with two duffel bags and a rifle.

"Leave that stuff, it'll be alright..." Ernie chattered "There must be fifty naked women down that trail."

Jake leveled a one-eyed stare at the man, "You mean leave the whole reason we are down here, so you can have your own peep show!"

"Well, no," Ernie trying to decide, "You take a bag, I'll take a bag here hand me the rifle."

"NO rifle, for the same reason we are not dressed in BDU's, I don't want to give anyone an idea we are guerillas."

Ernie took the gun, wrapped it in banana leaves, then buried it above the high-water mark on the river bank. As soon as he was finished, he launched into a description of what Jake would see for himself shortly.

"Naked, not a hair on their bodies. There must be fifty of them!"

"Where are the men?" Jake soberly interjected.

"I don't know but were not going to find out sitting around this canoe!" Ernie was clearly in a frenzy.

A short distance up the trail was the encampment. True to his word, the camp was filled with nubile womanhood of all ages and sized. The morphology suggested they were from more than one common ancestor. To Jake the variation of eye color was also interesting. Ernie in his wandering explorations would not be able to describe eye color. Green eyes were common, with variations approaching yellow brown. The older smaller women were probably more representative of the genotype of the encampment. They showed a darker complexion with light brown eye coloration. Even these matrons were in good health with supple skin and proud bodies. Like the singular male they preferred to adorn their hair with henna. It was difficult to determine the texture of their hair, however the younger pre-adolescents had thick mains of uncolored dark straight hair. Jake had seen such hair on the Polynesians.

"Where are the men?" Jake again wondered aloud, "we should keep our distance until they arrive."

Jake was so absorbed in his observations, he would have missed a minor miracle, except for ironically Ernie. "Hey Jake there something you don't see every day."

The two men moved toward a pen where the capybara was being revived by the canoe thief. The man stabbed it with a sharp needle dipped in a clear yellow liquid. Moments later the huge rodent was up on its feet the Indian checked its eyes and blew into its ears.

Jake waited for the man to exit the caged pen. With his best practiced smile, he attempted to persuade the brown man to trade him a small measure of the clear yellow liquid. He made animated gestures, using his hand firmly on the serum, reinforcing the language of barter. It was finally concluded each side would contribute to the deal.

"Ernie let me see your pocket knife."

"Why don't you use your pocket knife?"

"Because mine costs seventy bucks and yours is a four-dollar Swiss army counterfeit."

Ernie previewed the knife for the small brown man. Opening each of the blades, fingering the toothpick, corkscrew and tweezers; he handed it as a trade. The Indian took the knife cautiously. A few more moments of concentration, and he reached into his medicine bag removing a vial. When handing it to Jake he gestured this was the sleeping potion. The brown man placed his hands as a pillow to his face, making a snoring sound. He slowly reached into the pouch removing the second vial, holding it firmly.

The native dropped to his knees, smoothing out the earth to draw and instruct. The pictograph he drew was a curved line. Indicating the sun in the sky, he drew a sunrise to the east. At the center of the curve, he made a crude sun circle with rays surrounding it in a pattern. At the end of the line to the west he placed a set of parallel squiggly lines to indicated sunset. Slapping the vial, he washed his hand across the drawing, from sun up to noon. He made a smiling face as he did this three times. On the fourth pass, his face changed as he crossed over the noon line, into the later hours of his pictograph.

Past noon he made a grimace with his mouth, cumulating with his tongue sticking out as his hand reached sunset. To emphasize the point on the next pass he flailed his arms. On the final pass he let out a sinus sound to warn the customers. Moments of discussion followed, where Jake and Ernie tried to decide if they interpreted the instructions correctly.

Jake placed both vials on the ground, pointing to the sleeping potion. He placed the second vial at the noon mark. The native grinned and shook his head. The results were not conclusive. A small tribe will use its own mannerisms within the community. When the brown man shook his head, he seemed to be saying no in the western fashion, but to his tribe this could mean yes.

Jake looked away from the drawing to make sure he understood what was being told. As he glanced in Ernie's direction, he noticed the man making lurid gestures, in the direction of a group of nearby women. Without thinking he used a backhand motion to ring Ernie's chimes. The women thought this was funny, but the small brown man roared with a staccato laugh, slapping his feet on the ground where he sat. Even Ernie smiled after a moment.

"Pay attention this could be important!" Jake insisted.

"Sunrise to noon approximately six hours..." Ernie pointed to the drawing "Noon to half way to nightfall approximately three hours, nine hours total. Is that what you got?"

"Yep..." Jake was amused.

Ernie squatted down like a Turk to show the little brown man he understood. Pointing to the first vial he pretended to sleep. Pointing at the second vial he pretended to wake up. To the men assembled, the message was, the antidote must be administered within six hours.

"Give him your watch." Jake instructed.

"Why not your watch?" countered Ernie.

"Because mine is a Rolex, and you wear a Timex!"

The little brown man looked at the bracelet without interest. Instead, he reached out and stroked the duffel bag.

"No Deal!" stammered Jake.

"Jake, he doesn't want what's in the bag, he only wants the bag." offered Ernie.

"Well, what do we do with the stuff in the bag -then. We can't even show them what's in the bag in case someone comes snooping around. And... I just know they will." It occurred to Jake they had never actually inspected the contents of the bags. There may be contraband to throw away. Then again, there may be some way to pack everything more carefully to fit into one duffel bag. "Let's find us some privacy!"

Better than could be expected, upon dumping the first bag. their eyes grew large. The top third of the sack was large American currency banded into one hundred bills to a stack The center of the pack contained a basketball sized cache in a coffee bean bag. The bottom of the bag was loose twenties, tens and five-dollar bills.

"So, what do you suppose is in the coffee bean sack?"

"Cigarettes, whiskey and porno magazines." offered psychic Ernie.

"How did you figure that?" scoffed Jake.

"Tell you what, I'll bet you this stack of hundreds and explain it to you after we open it up." wagered Ernie.

"Ten thousand dollars says you're wrong."

"There may also be playing cards, dice and stolen jewelry." added Ernie, hoping to improve the odds of being correct.

Before exploring the contents of the coffee bean sacks the men emptied the second duffel bag. It was set up in similar fashion. Jake transferred all the stacked cash into one duffel bag. He shoved loose bills into the top until it would hold no more.

The little brown man, who had been quietly watching, smiled widely as he was handed the empty duffel. In exchange he handed the second vial to Jake. No longer interested in the activity he threw the duffel over his shoulder to show his trophy to the rest of the tribe.

"The name of the game is distraction..." Ernie explained as he began to unwrap the first coffee bean sack. Little shooter bottles of liquor were intermingled with plastic bags containing watches, and other jewelry. A couple packs of playing cards fell out along with a odd set of dice. It was a strange pile of booty.

"You lose, no porno!"

"Not so fast... "Ernie begged, pulling a pack of playing cards out of the pile. He held them up for Jake to take a closer look. The face of each card was a pornographic vignette. Jake took a peek at the cards then threw them back on the pile. The second coffee bean bag contained similar objects, with a few flesh monger magazines.

"All part of the El morder, the "Bite"." offered Ernie, "Three maybe four men go into a room to count the shipment money. The leader distracts the others to skim from the top of the count. A shot of whisky, interruptions to look at the pages of the magazine, all part of a carefully constructed attempt to insure no one knows the true value of the shipment."

Ernie went on the explain the subterfuge. The confidence game was based on distraction. The watches and rings only made it more difficult to keep the total straight. Each man pilfered his fair share from the pile some keenly fond of libation allowing generous disposal of the trash. When in the end everyone, is satisfied with the total, they pack up the loot. The leader, who also serves as banker, then distributes shares to the others.

"And the shares are smaller because of the manipulation!" Jake mentioned growing bored.

Ernie stood up exposing an irregular eagle nest of booty under the area where he had been sitting. He made an apologetic smile. Jake now stood, showing he had been even more successful spiriting away items from the pile. Jake's take, included everything except the porno magazines, which he had occasionally used as a screen to palm cash and jewelry.

"You were just going to let me prattle on..." smiled Ernie.

"Well, it seemed like you were enjoying yourself. "Jake mentioned as he began stuffing his nest into one of the coffee bean sacks. "I'll let you take charge of the porno, just in case we need to hypnotize someone down the river."

Clouds had formed a thick blanket over the immediate area. An almost perceivable mist had been falling for t longest time. Equatorial heat was causing it to evaporate a ground level only to add to the increasingly thick atmosphere Sunlight was diminished to the point where one could almost witness vegetation give off a fine water vapor of its own.

Retracing their steps, the two men emerged from the jungle at the village. A large common building stood at the center Stout timbers were capped with a thatched palm fiber roof. The workmanship was so sturdy a storage and sleeping area for children was apparent in the rafters. Hammocks lined the interior, sometimes two high, allowing parents to acclimate older children to sleeping at ground level. The hammocks were hung high enough from the ground, to presumably keep out stray animals. None of the hammocks were in use at the moment as the people were busy preparing food and other tasks.

An older woman smoothed the dirt floor with a broom made of palm leaves. She moved slowly and melodically, as if in prayer. It was as if she were invoking a talisman of good fortune to the tribe. Her frame was sturdy, age was only apparent in her face, breasts and gnarled hands. Even her hair was dark and healthy.

Where Ernie saw only naked women, Jake saw the stone aged industry of survival. Women collected into a sorority, going about the mundane chores of everyday life. As the rain began to fall some of the women withdrew to the shelter of the common great house. They did not enter the interior, but clustered around the perimeter. It was apparent they did not want to disturb the swept floor.

In a few moments the only ones getting wet were Jake and Ernie. Jake insisted they wait for an invitation. Like mocking birds on a wire, the women nudged each other. Finally, one of the women went out to bring the men under the shelter. She was taller than most, more ample and bountiful. To Jake's pleasure she had radiant green eyes. To Ernie's pleasure she was naked and now wet. Wet, meant cold, and he studied the effect.

She stretched out her arm with her palm down, making a flicking motion with her hand. She conducted them to an unused corner of the pavilion. Now out of the rain, Ernie made a gallant effort, by removing his shirt to assist the woman dry herself. She allowed this for a moment until it was obvious the man was only amusing himself. She placed the palm of her hand on his forehead and pushed. Ernie landed on his ass in the dirt. She went to rejoin her friends.

"Can't take you anywhere!" scoffed Jake.

Hey, at least I act, like I got a set." He snarled, "What are you some missionary?"

"Do you even know where you are? You want to come in here upset the status quo of the village, get your rocks off. Then what?"

"Tip my hat. Hand out some jewelry and head down stream." offered Ernie.

"Name that river out there?" Jake pointed down the trail.

"Hell, I don't know. What is these twenty questions?" Ernie snapped "Just some little creek running into the Amazon eventually..."

"Where do shrunken heads come from?"

Ernie started to laugh, and then swallowed really hard before spitting out "Let me mull that over for a bit, I'll get back to you. By the way the rains starting to let up, don't you think we should get moving."

"Yeah, I do." Jake answered in a soft southern drawl.

The green eyes were a real puzzler. Surely Jake and Ernie were not the only northern Europeans to have come in contact with this tribe. Probably some remote male ancestor had contact with one or more of the women. Maybe a Spanish moor from the conquistador era had introduced the coloration. Some mulattos from the Caribbean had green eyes. It was a hansom characteristic. These were hansom women. Well formed. Even the older woman sweeping the pavilion was sturdy and healthy.

Jake seized on the idea of thanking her for the hospitality. He wished to engender good will; in case he ever came this way again. Picking through the coffee bean sack, he selected a gaudy bauble of a necklace. Leaving the rest behind, he then walked the perimeter of the hut. She was just finishing the sweeping when he approached. He expected a toothless grin as he placed it around her shoulders. She smiled a faultless smile, white against tan fawn skin.

She held her self-more erect to gaze down at the necklace. Jake had to admit for her age she was a beauty. What he was after, was a glance at her eyes. When she finished admiring the gift, she raised her face to look at him. He noticed two emerald pools, the very color he had expected.

Jake turned to catch up with Ernie; who was about to hand out some jewelry himself. He was testing the waters of charging a kiss for a bauble. Ernie turns to Jake and says "I never took you for a Granny Grope, but hey whatever gets you going, is fine with me!".

Jake did not say a word he just hefted up the duffle bag, leaving his hand free to retrieve the second coffee bean sack. He turned in the direction of the canoe making giant strides to leave. "Boats leaving!" he finally announced over his shoulder.

Ernie who loved to hear himself talk fell in behind Jake muttering, "We've got booze and cigarettes, we have jewelry. There are fifty naked women...you know that's one hundred breasts... What else do we need?"

Jake was still wondering about the men. Where were the men of the tribe? Folk lore spoke of a tribe of women living independently in the South American jungles but that was only folklore. Primitive habitation required the efforts of well-defined social structure. Even the relatively advanced pre- Columbian cultures were limited to twelve family groups within a defined area of cultivation. Crunching numbers, Jake reasoned there had to be a sizeable hunting party out there somewhere. The single canoe thief was probably one of the ones who preferred to stay with the women. A jungle mama's boy. Where were the other men?

CHAPTER FOUR

The fat man was sitting behind his desk. Glued to his ear was a telephone. "Flores, don't give me any more crap about poor communications. I am the guy who arranged for the telephone system in that shit-hole pueblo of yours!"

"Sei Senor Mercer ..." Flores sweated and grit his teeth, "I was just trying to stay on top of the situation."

"Not by screwing with my people, you were not! "Growled Mercer, "You better hope his sperm count is right as rain... or yours won't be!"

"Oh, so you know about the lie detector..."

"Yeah pinta. I want you to know, I do not use dirty people. I thought I told you that before. My pilot thought he was delivering medical supplies, until someone wished him up!"

Flores now adopted a more business-like voice, "How do we put this incident behind us?"

"Put my pilot in his aircraft with my shipment! I want padlocks on the bags, with tags reading medical supplies. He is to deliver it to the exact same location as originally planned. Oh, but that is instructions I will be discussing with the pilot personally...!"

"Senor Mercer what am I to do about the payment? ... I have expenses." whined the fat Latino Captain.

"Get yourself a better ground crew! My obligation is only pickup and delivery. The cash was delivered and your people dropped the ball. I am dealing with a logistical nightmare, pal."

Mercer had only a few discreet clients, who bought in bulk. His people claimed, they were all purchasing, for personal consumption. They insisted on quality Peruvian flake. Over the years, he had weeded out the clients who were too flamboyant for his business. It was of course true that some of his clients did contribute to the street level trade. This was not his problem. He was not concerned about crack heads and hookers. Mercer ran a squeaky-clean operation. What the client did with the product was none of his affair.

Disruptions of the product delivery at this point, could send his clientele to the Columbians. He knew his screened and select customers. If they went directly to the Columbians they would never come back. At first the product would seem pure. Later it would be stepped on with magnesium citrate or any number of white chemicals. His customers would turn into Cocaine sheik fashion models, as a result of inhaling baby laxative. In a short time, the quantity would suffer. Explained away as production problems.

The Columbians offered not only an inferior product but a shorter measure. There was also the consequence of the broker moving right into the residence with the customer. They would impose themselves into the daily activity of the household. It starts off innocent enough, where the dealer stops by on a Bible salesmen schedule. He may offer the lady of the house a morning picks me up over coffee. A little toot for the co-ed daughter at the home coming game. Before long the household has a live in, undocumented domestic servant, keeping track of the life of the family.

Mercer somehow convinced himself, he was providing more than the product. He was providing a service to his clients. He was preventing his customers from being held prisoners, of their well-groomed estates. He even pictured himself as a medical professional, delivering a rare and exotic panacea for the well healed professional.

At the other end of the spectrum were the Jamaican and Haitian trade. Strictly street end product, whores, pimps and violence. They would grab teenage runaways off the streets turning them quickly into slaves. They only needed an oven and a cook pot, to whip up a batch of Crack. Jamaicans knew any white crystals with trash coke would render crack on cookie sheet. Five dollars for a five-minute escape.

The whole inner-city decline was a result of their influence Those receiving welfare from the government, were very often participating in distribution. The women would receive just enough crack to service a customer then they needed more. To Mercer it was a cesspool, which he was not a participant.

This went through Mercer's mind as he brought his annoyance into check. "All-right Flores..." He shifted into a cordial tone, "I'd be willing to pay ten percent, above wholesale, for the next five shipments."

"I will have to meet with my associates. This could take some time." Flores was stalling and Mercer knew it. The man had no partners.

"OK you tell them this: You have merchandise with no buyer and you owe me, two-point five large from the last time we did business!" Mercer remained calm. He allowed the gravity of the situation sink into Flores's consciousness.

"Senor Mercer, I hear the Helicopter leaving even as we speak" Flores lied, "Your merchandise is on its way".

"Very good. Now remember those five wells we drilled last year?"

Mercer was suddenly all business again. "I need you to provide the engineering reports, and billing, for three of them all over again."

CHAPTER FIVE

The two men were in the process of loading the canoe. Their guide showed up dragging his new duffle bag. He had painted symbols on it which looked like paw prints. Inside was some living creature, but because he gave it a soft kick, they ignored it as unimportant.

Ernie was the one who reached into the gear pulling out three whiskey bottles. He handed one to Jake, one to the native, and swallowed one. Jake was about to mention, "You don't give whiskey to Indians."

It was too late. The little friend followed the example of his companion. First beads of sweat formed on his forehead, he started gasping for air, next snot shot out of his nostrils. The man stuck out his tongue hacking and coughing sucking air back into his lungs. Finally, he smiled a coy embarrassed smile. Ernie laughed and patted him on the back.

"I think he likes it!" offered Ernie.

Suddenly Jake seized on the idea of using the little empty bottles to store his Tree Frog serum. He transferred the serum, then the antidote to the tiny square Bushmills Irish Whiskey shooters. The volume of the serum was not substantial; viewed in the new container. The color of the two liquids was similar with the antidote having a pronounced green tint. Jake scratched an "A" into the label of the bottle.

When he was finished making the transfer, he offered the stoneware containers to the little guide. The man placed these into his medicine bag, then extended this hand to receive the two bottles. He motioned with a down turned finger for the men to wait for his return. He was not gone long, only the time it takes to reach the village and return. The bottles were to full.

Jake fished around in the coffee bean bag looking for article of trade for the man. He came upon a key ring with eagle with arrows, which seemed to have military distinction and handed it to the guide. it seemed fitting for an archer, and was solid gold. It impressed him very much but was quickly placed into the medicine bag.

"I hate to break up this flea market but we should be moving out. The plan was for us to be sleeping this whole time so we could travel by night." Jake offered.

"Oh, so now we have a plan?" Ernie jested.

"Three hundred miles of river is all you need to know at the moment." Jake replied.

The rifle was retrieved from its hiding place. The three men shoved the canoe to the water's edge. Standing at the shoreline they remembered now the duffle bag belonging to their guide. He raised his hand to his mouth and giggled like a schoolboy. Reaching into his medicine bag he retrieved a small bone object which proved to be a flute. He then unsnapped the top of the bag. As he played softly on the flute two small hands appeared. While he continues to play the rest of the body emerged. It was all in the fashion of Boa snake dance.

Both Jake and Ernie ware hypnotized in that crystallized moment associated with a deer in the headlights. The body was perfection, not a mark on it, not even a vaccination scar. She had long dark hair to her waist, with an up turned nose, and generous lips. Her eyes were not only green they were seductive. When at length the dance ended, she picked up the duffel bag, and shoved it down over the flute player's head. A soft kick landed on the man's butt, showing what she thought about the whole idea.

Ernie to the rescue, produced in short order another salvo of tiny Bushmills whisky bottles. He offered one to the dancer with the advisory, "This will make your nipples stick out sweetheart." Said Ernie.

And it did. Her nipples stuck out so far, they looked like New Years Eve whistles. Ernie stared, and the little Indian stared. They got so close they were almost cross eyed to keep the nipples in focus. She put the heel of her hand on forehead of each man and pushed. For the second time in the same day Ernie landed on his butt in the dirt. The little Indian sat right beside Ernie. She stormed off dragging the duffel behind her.

"I'll help you find some party girls, Ernie..." Jake shook his head, "All you got to do is get in the damn canoe!"

"Well, I might as well, I damn sure cannot put up with the rejection around here." Ernie spoke as he dusted off his trousers.

Pushing away from the shore bank they revisited part of the river. By returning the way they came they were able to pick up the main flow as it traveled east. Ernie was soon to discover how reasonable a craft the dugout canoe was in reality. Instead of a simple portage where the craft would be hand carried, the men let the boat careen over rapids from the safety of the shore. The canoe was nothing more than a log, so it was not damaged by the rough treatment. Jake controlled loss of the canoe with a stout rope. He deftly moved from rock to tree to vantage point allowing the rope to take momentum away from the rapids.

The Indian had followed them for a few miles, finally turning back in the direction of the village. Jake pointed as he mentioned "There goes the last honest man you're going to find on this river."

"We're honest aren't we Jake?" inquired Ernie.

"Nope, we are too civilized to be honest!"

CHAPTER SIX

Fourteen days of travel on one of the Earths largest rivers found them in Venezuela bordering on Brazil. Only the first few nights did they travel by darkness. The chance of losing the cargo was too real to tempt fate on the winding river. Traveling by day made it possible to forage food from the jungle. Ernie would not try any of the gator jerky Jake had made. With the only other provision a bag of dry dog food, Ernie was on his own for food. Jake, on the other hand, had no problem munching dry dog food. It was a trick he had used on many explorations. It was the easiest way to pack in high protein of low weight and no spoilage. As a last resort, he could insure a week of travel, in a twenty-five-pound bag. A simple filter provided just enough fresh drinking water to keep them going.

Ernie with his rifle had other ideas. The trouble with Ernie was he just never seemed to make a clean head shot. For all his bragging of marksmanship, he kept making gut shots. Jake thought he might be using this as an excuse to leave the boat. The gut shot meant, they would have to stop and cook the meat, before it spoiled. Luckily for the game, Ernie was short on ammunition. He had to wait for an absolute successful shot, before squeezing off a round. So, the weeks of travel saw Ernie waving around a loaded gun he was timid to fire.

"Who does your housekeeping?" Ernie announced walking into the bamboo and timber shack. His eyes swept the large airy structure. "What's with all the baskets?"

"You ever try and find furniture in the jungle?" Jake answered.

Emie flopped down on a bunk against one wall. Looking down he recognized a large tail protruding from beneath the cot. He pulled his legs up out of harm's way, screaming "Call the exterminator!"

Jake laughed while explaining "That is the exterminator, she is the best little rat catcher I ever saw. Just try not to let your fingers dangle when you're sleeping."

The end of the trip was uneventful. They traveled almost three hundred fifty miles effortlessly. Being in unfamiliar surroundings made it impossible to relax, so now at the bungalow they fell into a deep restful slumber. Jake determined if anyone was looking for them, it would be in a hotel, resort or an airport. Still the river was the heartbeat of the Jungle. He did not want to overlook the possibility of being discovered.

Everyone knew about the crazy Gringo living in a small pueblo outside of town. They knew he disappeared for weeks on end into the bush. They also knew he had nothing of value up at the pueblo. He did have a few modern appliances, but the town was too small to use any of the equipment if it were stolen. To steal the electrical appliances required theft of the generator. It was a very small town.

Even the telephone to the shack only worked some of the time. Jake had to string his own line out to the pueblo. Because he used trees and not poles the telephone wire frequently needed repair. Even in perfect working order he had to energize the line from his end to make a call. And that was not always worth the trouble. The single operator in town did not speak English, so Jake had to read off the number in Spanish. Frequently the number dialed was incorrect. To add to the confusion the operator worked from eight AM, to Eleven AM, she then took lunch. At roughly two PM, she returned to her station post, until five PM.

Most of the important communications were transmissions over Citizen Band radio. It is true that no one can have a secret in a small town. Between broadcasting business over the radio and an operator who was going to repeat what she heard, even if she could not speak the language, this was a very small town. The old pirate motto applied; two can keep a secret, if one of them is dead!

There were all kinds of quaint back woods customs. After being put in jail, the prisoner would eventually be released if they had nothing to hide. Meaning any number of accusations, allowed the corrupt police force to pick through personal property until they were satisfied the prisoner was not guilty. Popular with the townsfolk was a brand of Christianity intermingled with pagan rituals of the Santa Rita.

When a town is part of the pagan system of belief, there will occasionally be reason to burn a witch at the stake. Just quaint customs. The village priest may be consulted for absolution of the accused, but not always. Even the parish Priest had to sidestep local customs. The Ten Commandments, with generous exceptions were local practices. Many attributes to the Major Deity, gave practitioners every excuse to do just what they wanted to do in the first place. There was only one God but just as it was before the conquistador, the One God had many faces.

When the early Spanish used the bon fires to establish Christianity, it was viewed as sacrificial to the Inca, Aztec and Maya. The Mesoamericans saw no difference between their own bloody rituals, and the ones performed by the Spanish. It was no stretch to join the Inca Sun god, to the Spanish tradition.

Worse yet were the actual practitioners of the dark arts. Some people cannot wait for God to provide for their needs, they subcontract with Satan. Again, it is a question of getting what they want. Of course, mayhem and even murder is no obstacle to the dark arts.

The Old Testament describes animal sacrifice so long as it was offered to the one true God. Santa Rita an earth-based religion transplanted from Africa. Influenced by the Spanish tradition, Santa Ria also uses animal sacrifice. The mystical Kabbalah plays into the practice of Santa Rita. As an earth-based religion it has both; an aspect of enlightenment, and a dark aspect. The effort toward enlightenment is universal to all mankind. The sinister aspect usually is to establish domain for an individual practitioner.

Apart from the "evil" eye, there is not much to the dark arts. Most of it is harassment until the target is overwhelmed by paranoia. Small totem figures are left in obvious places to be found later. Offensive dead creatures slip into merchandise brought home from shopping. Sometimes the decorations of the home are purposely moved to make the victim question his own sanity. The ultimate goal is to reduce the quarry to a nervous, sleepless and obvious madman. After being escorted to jail or an asylum those who participated in the magic, divide up his personal belongings. Many abandoned shanty cabins stand as testament to this practical method. Unoccupied homesteads just waiting return of owners.

For two generations the populace had been victimized by the constant presence of freedom fighters. Somewhere in the distant past the freedom they were fighting for had become hazy. They alternated from allegiances to the Kremlin and the United States. The guerrilla throngs swayed to the side of the highest bidder, then eventually went autonomous with the cash from drug traffic. The truth of the end of the cold war, was the Kremlin could no longer afford to ante up, what the troops demanded.

Drug profits were higher than the charade of establishing a Socialist Republic. The United States, hoping to install a Democratic Republic, continued to lend its ear to the lip service of the freedom fighters. Never admitting defeat was a mistake for Latin America. Sham democracies continued to apply to the United States for assistance, this time against Drug lords who were formerly sponsored by the Kremlin.

It was by no stretch of the imagination, one could evaluate. the United States was now sponsoring both sides in Latin America. Narcotics on the one hand, narcotic interdiction on the other hand. Billions of dollars in the center of a bureaucratic dance. Constitutional governments of Latin America wisely looking the other way. Hoards of Latinos descending on the United States with the disposable income from the narcotic trade.

Jake had enough. He was looking for peaceful surroundings, free of the turmoil. He liked being a nonparticipant, right up until the opportunity to score big fell into his lap. A few days in advance of the plan, he was not the least bit interested in the Mesa above the river. His enlightenment came only form the activities. He just happened to be in the right jungle, at the right time. Even Ernie was a coincidence. They had become acquainted in a cantina, over some warm beer. He and Ernie were just passing through, when they hatched the plan. By one of those strange twists of fate it worked.

Five or six hundred miles of travel, it was hard to tell in a winding river, put them deep in the Amazonas territory of Venezuela. This should be way out of the search pattern of anyone coming after the money. In all the years Jake had his homestead there were very few outsiders who would venture to would get lost looking for Esmeralda, a not-too-distant town. This was the part of the plan Jake was most comfortable with, he was going to lay low. He was El Loco Gringo on a river! It was a title he could live with.

Still the river was the heartbeat of the jungle. He could not overlook the possibility of being discovered. Having the money was not the problem. Having the money in his possession was a different thing. Discovery by one of the bandits could be disastrous. A bandit would not think twice, leaving the two men as crow bait in the wink of an eye.

The State police could not be trusted any more than the bandits. Who could blame them? They get a pension in pesos after a lifetime of paying for their own uniforms and bullets. Still the police official for this area was an alright sort of guy. He was not so young as to be overly impressed with himself. Nor was he too old to take care of business. He was a man to be respected. This was a good thing considering the scum he had to deal with. Drug addicts, rapists, and cut throats; fire a shotgun into a crowd and anyone with a pellet in them was likely guilty of something.

Women who were not of a sporting nature, needed to be home by dark to be safe. This unfortunately included livestock and pets.

To be fair, in the closest town were many hard-working good industrious people. As hard as they worked, it did not make up for the influence of the criminals. Of course, these criminals just happen to be uncles, cousins, sons, daughters and spouses. One tends to overlook the peccadilloes of family members. In the world where nothing is more important than family. Many crimes go unpunished if not un-forgotten.

The balance is maintained by someone trying not to ruin the reputation of the family. Still many newborn infants are abandoned on the doors of a church, because either the father or mother has bad blood.

Out here in the bush, the practice of foundlings is almost nonexistent. The families are too tightly joined. Sometimes a woman leaves for a larger town amidst whispers. She returns in the course of years entering into a monastic lifestyle, if she returns at all. The foundlings are cared for by the world churches, if they survive.

Way down here in the middle of nowhere was nothing like the border of Mexico and the United States. No one expected to find a domestic position with the high pay of America, and the low tax structure of Mexico. No one here, was ever murdered because of envy, over a job as a maid or gardener. The criminal mind unable to rationalize the reason they did not get the job, was poor personal hygiene or bad temperament. Incommodious mannerisms, with a spirit of entitlement, leave law enforcement on both sides of the border scratching their head. Por Que?

Why murder a maid?

Out here in the bush there was no reason to second guess a decision. Jake learned early not to hire anyone. He had to abandon one compound to escape from the employees. He hired one man for some light work. The man very nearly moved into the camp within a week. This in itself was bad enough, without the ever-increasing number of applicants. At an alarming exponential rate, he was exploited for a few dinero. Those who did speak English were firm in demanding to be hired; "because they were just as good as the man with the job".

Like any good manager, he packed up everything he gave two shits about, hired everyone present, and marched them three days distance into the jungle. Most of them were done in, after the first day. This increased the burden to the rest on the second day. Some abandoned the project that night or early the next morning. It was cosmopolitan view of the nature of man. Jake who was looking for solitude, knew he had found it, when the last of the crew threatened to turn back. Interesting enough his last employee was the first man he had hired.

By boat the new camp was no more distant from town than the old camp. Only by woodland trail the distance was greater. Occasions where an applicant wandered out of a cantina, looking for a quick source of cash were greatly reduced. Being upstream from town, made it unlikely a drunk would challenge the river. He did sometimes receive guests, for no other reason than the townsfolk keeping track of a recluse. Part of the problem in Latin America was education was not commonly available. The Catholic Church was the source of most of the schools. Here a disparity existed between well-funded private schools and those available to orphans.

Fifty years of insurrection by antigovernment forces had seen a growing population of non-educated peasants. The revolutionary forces used the church as a representative pawn to the established governments. The revolutionary rhetoric placed attending Mass; as plot by the land holders to enslave the people. The original communist influenced rejection of the Deity, was now a watered-down manifesto. Freedom fighters do only what they were trained to do; attempt to overthrow the government.

At the same time the rich land owners are contributing to the schools and the churches. They know the better the education the richer the land becomes. The animals are healthier. The crops are more productive. Education is the key to productivity. But they are also faced with; too great a population, on a land devoted to crop production.

The revolutionary knows full well they will fail unless proving there is injustice in the system. Under the Marxist influence; the proof was how unfair it was for some to have so much, and others so little. The Marxist form of rebellion ended, with the fall of the Soviet Block. The revolutionaries were forced to sign on as hired guns, or go extinct.

The narcotic traffic had room for a private army. So very quickly rag tag idealistic freedom fighters, became well-manicured, opulently funded -storm troopers. Their existence changed from taking away property from the rich land owners, to protecting the Coca and Marijuana fields. They went from a offensive guerilla army, to a defensive army of occupation.

Still to be successful, the insurrection force needed to challenge the authority of the Catholic Church. Not only the Catholic, but any church compelled to assist the impoverished population. What the church schools attempted to provide with a book, insurrection forces did with a gun.

To a supermarket shopper a sanitary wrapped chicken is no moment of veneration. Even for the farmer who dispatches his evening meal with an ax, there is only a momentary remorse in what is commonly good animal husbandry.

The same chicken in earth bound religious practice may hold a much greater significance. The dappled sloshes of blood taking on a profound meaning.

In part, the practice of Santa Rita and voodoo served to give the rebels an identity. Bodies found on the Matamoros border with the United States showed signs of being sacrificed in the Aztec tradition. In this arcane religious practice, a victim empowers the priest. Just another example why you shouldn't skip school.

CHAPTER SEVEN

"Oh Shit!" muttered Jake looking out the window, "What are they doing here?" He swung the table out of the way. Peeling back the grass mat on the floor he revealed a trap door sunken into the floor.

The pit looked bottomless. A wooden pallet was suspended by chains within the space. On the pallet were small arms and ammunition but Jake did not have time for these. He dumped the duffle bag and two coffee bean bags on top of the stack and closed the trap door. Replacing the rug, he checked to make sure the floor above the trap door made the same dull thud as the rest of the wood. In one motion he replaced the table then swung open the front door.

A tall plain looking woman stood there with her hand raised to knock. Her hair she wore in a bun held in place with a chopstick. Tortoise shell glasses drew attention away from her slight over bite. Her skin was creamy with bright clear eyes. This was why Jake loved her and had told her so on more than one occasion.

Over her shoulder to the left was a gaunt man, English maybe, no one knew for certain. The man could have been from New England. Slacks, walking shoes not boots, plantation owner's shirt, a white Panama straw hat with a only a modest sweat stain at the crown. Jake did not know what the fellow did for a living. He seemed to be on permanent vacation from wherever he was from.

Sarah smiled at Jake and he swept her into his arms in a big bear hug. He could feel her shrink slightly. She did not recoil, only shrank.

"How long were you out there this time?" She wanted to know.

"You have a two-week beard, and three weeks overdue for a bath."

He knew it was true so he disengaged from the embrace showing Sarah into the front room. The front door swung shut under its own weight, as he knew it would. Sarah's escort was forced to push back to enter. Jake spoke to the man over his shoulder "What happened Ceryle, the cantina run out of Gin?"

"Be nice..." Sarah interrupted "Ceryle offered to come up here with me. You don't expect me to cavort all over the jungle by myself, do you?" She flashed him a smile she knew he could not refuse.

"I noticed from my motor launch your canoe had returned, so I fetched Sarah." Ceryle said begging for gratitude.

Ernie recumbent on the cot sat up sheepishly. When introduced to the visitors he rose to shake hands. Jake mentioned Ceryle Smyth, then turning to the woman he stated succinctly; "This is Doctor Sarah Cross my eventual soul mate, if she would just stop rejecting my advances."

"I never rejected your advances dear boy. I just am not ready to play Jane to your Tarzan." Sarah corrected.

"How long have the two of you been wrestling with this relationship?" Ernie ventured.

"About three years." both answered at once.

Ernie reached down and picked up a magazine "According to the article I was just reading; if the two of you were not shaking the bushes in the first three months you never will."

Sarah took the book to glance at the story. She smiled as she turned to the cover. "Well Ernie I'm sure that a publication as prestigious as Group Grope Quarterly must have done exhaustive research to gather information for this article..." She then thumbed the pages mentioning a number of conditions from the swinger submitted photo section, "Chlamydia, gonorrhea, herpes, syphilis and HIV, all avoided by abstinence..." Handing the magazine back to Ernie, she left it open to a particular explicit page mentioning only "...I hope someone knows the emergency first aid for choking."

Ernie took the magazine back rolling it into a tight tube. He stared at Sarah with a combination of awe and admiration. This was the first time he had met an attractive woman who cooled his carnal nature. He had expected her to recoil in horror from the photos. He was only making small talk in the first place; he had not counted on the woman's academic nature. Finally, the severity of his mistake took hold and he headed for a door. "Think I'll burn this book and take a bath in the river."

Jake followed as far as a portable generator. It turned over on the first crank. As he came back inside, he paused to turn on a fan. A large black teapot was placed into the microwave oven as he asked "Coffee or tea?" His guests did not voice a preference. He pulled the pot out and poured a large quantity of coffee grounds into the water. "Coffee it is..."

"So Ceryle what's the news in the real world?" asked Jake, just making small talk while he searched around for some clean cups.

"Same as usual... Except some pistolero's showed up yesterday asking a lot of questions. They got the locals all stirred up."

Jake used a strainer to pour the muddy liquid into the cups. The coffee would be as strong as it was hot. "Did they go to the police?"

Ceryle noticed for once he got the clean cup. "No, they did not, that was the strange part. They just seemed to confine their search to the cantinas and restaurants."

Jake finished pouring the coffee, sliding a cup to Sarah keeping the stained cup for himself. "Out with it Ceryle don't keep me in suspense, what did they want?"

It seemed like they were looking for anyone spending a lot of money in town. That is all I could make of it. But it did stir up interest by the more unsavory element in town."

"You mean like Miguel and his cutthroats..." introduced Jake.

"Exactly," Ceryle shrugged, "It must be a lot of money because they spent the rest of the night carousing Cantina to Cantina looking for strangers. They got so loud and obnoxious the police had to escort them home. Miguel made a scene over Civil Rights probably thought he was still in Miami."

Sarah interrupted, "Why didn't they throw them in the slammer?"

"I suppose the police did not want to listen to them rant and rave all night long!" Ceryle submitted.

Sarah took a sip of the coffee quickly jerking her lips from the cup. "My God this coffee is as strong as espresso". Not wanting to be a bad guest she continued to sip at the mud in her cup. She would just have to deal with the way it made her want to grind her teeth. Ceryle meanwhile, thought it should have been served in those tiny demitasse cups.

Jake just smiled, "Good huh?"

No one spoke.

"So, what you are telling me is do not do any lavish spending in town, and my coffee stinks!"

"Don't forget you need a shave and a bath..." smiled Sarah playfully. Jake did not say a word. He rose from the table went out back and upended a galvanized tub used for watering horses. He filled the tub from an electrical pump connected to a shallow well. When the bath was full, he shut down the electric pump. In about an hour the water, sitting in the sunlight, would be warm enough to bathe.

Returning from this chore, he plugged in a barber's sheers, chopping his beard close enough to shave. With a tube of Palmolive, he lathered his jaw. He made short work of the beard with an old Schick retractable razor. It was the only blades he could buy in town.

Turning back to the bathtub he took a hooker bath, dunking his head and upper body then toweling away the wetness. From a foot locker he donned a fresh shirt. To complete the ritual HE, slashed some Persian rose water onto his face, then lifting the bottle to his lips swirled the liquid in his mouth. Returning to the table he asked "More coffee anyone?"

In unison the twain guests replied "Please".

Ernie who had been gone the whole time was back. He wore boxer shorts that could be confused with a bathing suit, it was unlikely he would be embarrassed if they were not. Ernie explained his boxers by remarking how he had also washed his clothes. He looked no cleaner than when he went down to the river. Jake in contrast looked immaculate.

"Why didn't anyone warn me about Parana in the river?" he asked. Ceryle was the first to speak, explaining "there are no Parana this far north in the Orinoco."

"Whatever it was, it almost made me half the man I used to be. Maybe the doctor should have a look at this. Ernie offered as he began to show the wound to the crowd.

"I'm not that kind of doctor!" shouted Sarah as she covered her eyes. Jake handed the injured man a bottle of Iodine and asked him to please go out back to use the medication.

Jake had an evil grin on his face as he displayed his outstretched palm, fingers widely spread. He closed his fingers one at a time. Five, four there, two... "Yow, Ow -Ow -Ow!" resonated from the back yard.

When he came back to the table the color had drained from his face. "What kind of a doctor is she?" he whispered.

"A biochemist a Ph.D." she confided.

Ernie wandered away cursing and muttering to himself. Every once in a while, came the sound "yeo-ow".

CHAPTER EIGHT

Sarah's eyes lit up almost without need for explanation, as Jake placed two miniature whiskey bottles on the table. Her automatic reaction was to pull out a small pad and pen. She noted the day date and time then set in examining the contents. She again reached into her purse for disposable syringes and sample vials. She listened to Jake explain how he had come into possession of the find. Her keen mind growing more excited from the story. She took a sample of each bottle, jotting down the particulars of each on the small pad.

"Where did you say you found these...?" Sarah stood poised with pen to record every detail.

"This is not for public knowledge. I do not want the primitives molested by a bunch of research hooligans. It was up on the Rio Casiquiare." Jake almost whispered the name of the river.

"So, you found something special then..." Ceryle said hoping to be included in the circle.

"No offence... Mr. Smyth, but this is private business between the doctor and myself." Jake corrected.

"Perhaps I'll check on Ernie." offered Ceryle diplomatically.

"Then you did find something remarkable?" asked Sarah after the man left the room.

You have no Idea..." Jake mentioned the neurotoxin and the antidote in passing. He thought she would be interested in the matriarchal group of primitives, governed by a post- menopausal elder. He mentioned the common genetic trait suggesting low contact with the outside world.

Smiling Sarah interrupted, "How many naked women were in the colony?"

"Fifty, and I was basing the genome on eye color." Jake's schoolboy grin told Sarah they were indeed naked. "We made contact with a single observable male, but I have no doubt there were more hidden in the jungle."

"Fifty is a pretty large number to go undetected." Sarah frowned, "in aboriginal circumstances twelve family groups form an encampment that is forty-eight individuals."

"Not when you see how they live! They are true nature children."

Sarah picked up the blue colored bottle, turned it upside down to check for sedimentation. She rocked it side to side to see if there was any separation of the liquid. Fifty cubic centimeters of this liquid was a valuable asset, but nothing special. The neurotoxin had been identified in the 1950's and heavily studied during the Cold War. Rumor of that period indicated the bullet intended for Fidel Castro was coated with the substance inside a hollow point. Although the plot against Castro may have been only a rumor, some micro-projectiles were used in European espionage.

"So, what's in the other bottle?" she turned her attention to the greenish tinted sample.

"That dear lady is a mythical elixir, which if I were to reveal the very nature of its power would make you swoon. You would experience such rapture as to demand I satisfy your every desire. We would frolic in a paradise so sublime, neither of us could stand to be parted for even a moment." Jake could pour it on when he wanted something.

"OK, P.T. Barnum..." She playfully grabbed Jake by the throat with both hands and started shaking him. "What is in the bottle?"

-"Antidote!"

"Meaning Antidote to the neurotoxin?" She gasped. Her eyes were great beacons with dilated pupils. "Oh, this is big. Do you know the ramifications of this discovery... what it could mean?"

"Yes Maam, and the best part it works on mammals."

"You've seen it work on mammals, what kind of mammal?"

"Capibara."

"Good, good, good higher order rodent similar in weight and structure to a pig. Pigs are often used for human trials...." Now it was her turn to wax poetic, you were right I am stating to swoon, all the cognitive channels in my mind are racing at once."

Then a remarkable thing happened. Sarah grabbed Jake and kissed him, not as colleagues or coworkers but as a lover. Their limbs entwined around each other into a protracted embrace. This was no mistake it was destined to happen. Jake felt it, and at long last, Sarah felt it too.

"Ahem, ahem." Suddenly a wet blanket walked into the room in the form of Ceryle Smyth. Sarah was abruptly aware of her surroundings.

"Another five minutes and you would have walked in on a real show." Sarah commented only half joking.

She had long questioned whether the antidote was present in the jungle. To have a sample in her hand was like holding the Holy Grail. Returning to work on the samples she transferred 25 cc of each to vacuum blood collection tubes. That should be plenty for the tests she would perform. Gas Chromatography, spectrograph analysis, gel electrophoresis, a ton of information was at her disposal. She toyed with the idea of sending a small sample to Atlanta. With Jake's help she could perform tests in the wild. Primate research, using the ever-present jungle monkeys.

"I don't know when I have ever been so excited about the research...Do you have any idea what this could mean." She prattled.

"Oh, you mean like vindication for all the years invested in jungle research?" Jake mentioned casually.

Sarah never shared her dissatisfaction with the present grant she worked under. She also did not mention the project was coming to an end.

Her present grant: Effects of Fauna and Flora on drinking water quality in the Highlands of South America. It was damn boring stuff. Take a sample, analyze the sample. The results were to be expected; animals foul the water with feces, rotting plants cause algae blooms turning the waters turbid. Drinking water needed to be filtered, end of story. You did not need a Pd.D. to qualify the resultant data.

Somewhere on her desk was a letter informing her the grant monies for next year were non-existent. If she wanted to continue basic research in South America, she would need to submit a new application with a new mission statement.

Now out of the blue, good old Jake drops a bombshell right in her lap. This was Bio-Chemistry, more than she could ever hope for. The Neuro-transmitters were well known within the confines of western medicine. This new substance would be a decisive gain to the body of knowledge. This was legitimate research grant material.

"Jake what did you think when you first saw this in use?"

"I thought it was pretty neat!"

"Pretty neat?" She laughed grabbing him around the neck, kissing him all over his face.

The wet blanket again chimed in "Sarah we should be going I do not want the risk the motor on the boat in the dark."

"He's right we should be going. Is there anything else you' like to tell me before we go." Sarah was fishing for tender notions.

Jake completely missed his chance when he launched into a description of the tools used by the native. The aborigine had used a bone flake arrow head, very small but very sharp. It had an indent like a sewing needle at the barb. To administer the greenish fluid the man had removed the arrowhead placing it in a wooden handle. Jake was being obscure about the nature of the antidote in front of Ceryle. He was hoping Sarah would take the hint so they would have a private matter to discuss. He did not feel threatened by Ceryle, just crowded.

He walked them down to the river. Shaking hands with Ceryle, sneaking a last kiss from Sarah, Jake mentioned he would come to town in a couple of days. They got into a clean little Cris-Craft with inboard motor and the engine roared to life. Ceryle's Panama hat went flying into the back of the boat.

CHAPTER NINE

Jake was sitting in the galvanize tub thinking loud enough for Ernie to hear him, "How in the hell, are we going to get this money out of Venezuela to some place with currency value?"

Ernie was right there in ear shot but did not say anything He was going through the pantry. Everything was in a can, even cooked ready to eat chicken legs. There was canned ham, sardines, canned clams. A glass jar calling itself caviar but looking very much like fish bait caught his attention. Saltine crackers, shortbread cookies, mincemeat, fruit cocktail cherries, and a half case of pork and beans were all crammed onto the shelves. Then there were peas, limas, tomatoes, carrots and beets lined up like little solders. Inside a large cookie box was a three months' supply of tortilla shells. Refried beans, canned oysters, jerky of a dubious nature, dried sausages all neatly canned and protected from the jungle environs.

Ernie selected the ready to eat chicken legs and cranked off the lid. With the opened can in his paw he proceeded to tell Jake, "We've got to go shopping there is nothing to eat around here!"

"What is up with the Saran Wrap, you must have a case of the stuff?" Ernie wondered between bites of chicken.

"All part of the plan!" Jake threw his arms behind his head comfortably soaking in the afternoon sun.

The plan, you just keep making this up as you go along. I don't think you have a plan."

Humble by the accuracy of the statement, Jake immediately told Ernie the plan. "If you must know tonight, we take all the money and wrap it in saran wrap. Then tomorrow we disguise the bundles to look like brick...."

"You are making this stuff up as you go. Why bricks?"

"Because bricks are so common no one will question seeing a pile of bricks. Do you question this patio I made with homemade brick?"

"Seems like a lot of work. I say we go down the river hire a bunch of models, fly them into Miami International, wearing a saran wrap body stocking of money."

Jake dunked his head to smooth out his hairline. "That would be the last time you saw the models or the money."

It took a while to get the count right. Fifty bills to a stack. Five stacks to a brick. That was the easy part. The greater portion of the haul was already in stacks. The predominate species was the one-hundred-dollar bill. There was also the fifties and twenties with a odd assortment of ten's five's and one's. Jake pushed all the loose change into a pile.

They secured some empty coffee cans from the kitchen then pretended to tuck away the loose currency the way a housewife would squirrel grocery money. The money was arranged face up in the same direction. One layer at the bottom of the can with a wad of paper on top.

First can under the sink. Second can in the back of the pantry. Third can on the bedroom linen shelf. One can on the entry way closet.

The one can a wife uses to take the kids, and run home to mother, was an unsolved mystery, Ernie would have to do the best he could.

"So, if someone does break in, they will find a can of money and leave?" Ernie ventured.

"Something like that. If you hadn't burned the girly magazine, I would tell you top off the cans with clippings." "I didn't burn it." admitted Ernie.

"Well go get it and chop it up. Nothing will confuse and confound a sneak thief like pornography. They forget what they came for, a different part of the brain takes over and they become disoriented."

"That's the way it affects me, why doesn't it affect you the way?" Jake got a big smile on his face, "College, it happened while I was in college."

Back in Jake's collage days they used to have porno night where they sat around with the sound turned off, making dialogue for the actors. One of the frat boys would treat it as a documentary nature show. He would make up terms like Mammary-us Gigantic-us and Penis Elongate-us to give it credible dialogue. One of the other students would do a war movie sound track;" Pilot pull out -pull out, or you'll be stuck with the bitch financially for eighteen years." Still another made sports commentary out of the spectacle, "... illegal use of hands, First and down!"

But there was this one pre-med student who ruined it for everyone.

When it was his turn, he spent all his time explaining; how a certain mole should be examined, or the ramifications of exotic positions. He prattled on about the diagnostic technique of pap smears and yeast infections. He used complicated jargon to clinically describe the various positions. After a short while the crowd was really grossed out. It wasn't much fun after that and eventually Porn night was abandoned all together. Everyone began to think of it a childish.

"Glad I never went to collage!" offered Ernie.

During this time Jake had assembled eighty bundles of cash. After toying with the stacks, he determined a total of $27,500 was the proper ratio. Two stacks of hundreds, one stack of fifties, one stack of twenties, and a odd assortment of bills to make up the five hundred.

"Why $27,500?" chimed Ernie

"If we do put them into bricks, I want the same amount in each brick!" Jake stood back to examine the deceptively small table of bundles, "Who knows, maybe we'll come up with a better plan."

"Yeah, like something that floats when it's in a canoe!" Ernie grimaced, "That brick idea is lame."

"Alright you come up with something three feet, by six feet, by six inches that you hide in plain sight without worrying about it wandering off." Exploded Jake, "Just wrap the stacks so I can get some sleep."

Ernie was quiet for a short while. Finally, he remarked, "When I do monotonous things like this, I just got to talk..."

"Go ahead and talk." Jake mentioned as he continued wrapping stacks of cash. "Tell me how you ended up in South America."

CHAPTER TEN

Specialist Ernest Copeland was placed in country at 142 N-89' 17 W. It was a minor disturbance in the hemisphere Military advisors from Cuba were still working the o revolution, despite the lack of support of the Kremlin and the fall of Soviet Union.

He and two spotters, spread out from the drop zone after dark. Night would lift in another eleven hours, there was plenty of time to get into position. Ernie was there to make a six-thousand-yard shot. The target time was 10 am so atmospheric distortions would be at a minimum.

Papa and baby bear clucked away on the two-way radio sets. Mama bear was on a receive only frequency. He could not even radio to tell them to shut up. The target zone was acquired without much problem. He unpacked his equipment and began assembly. The Jute blanket he packed in made the perfect Gilli suit. He transferred the natural foliage to the Jute blanket in the same order it was removed from the terrain. Within a short time, he was invisible. Nothing to do now but sleep if he could, but not too soundly.

More clucking in the morning. Ernie did not like clucking. radio telemetry homes in on clucking. Transmissions tell the other guy you are there, and also where you are. He knew he was safe with his receive only headset but the gear also had its limitations. A limitation that would come back to haunt him.

The code to fire was Red-Red or in case of static Green- green. All the crew members had a mug shot of the target. Papa bear had a radio link to an off shore ward room analyzing the progress. They had the final say if the target got dusted or not.

It was not until Ernie lined up on the target, that he realized he had seen him before. It was either Somalia or Angola but it was the same guy. One of those places where the law was anarchy. What gave him away was the jowls and scruffy beard, set off by a blue stone earing twinkling in the sunlight. The rakish tilt of a dirty brown Caesar Chavez beret, told Ernie this was the same guy.

Over the radio came the signal Red-Green and again Red- green. Papa bear was saying take the shot. Baby bear from his point of vantage was rejecting the order. Man on mission, Ernie, lined up on that blue earing. The next transmission would be the take down order. The call was Red.... He took a deep breath, slowly exhaling. The second call was Green.

MOM now made a decision to take a shot. Not a kill shot, just a turkey shoots personal satisfaction shot. He squeezed the trigger. Seventeen hundred yards away the targets left earlobe disappeared. With all the noise suppression, and the extreme distance, the intended target was still having trouble processing what may have happened to his ear. He just stood there put a hand to his ear, as he would a bee sting. MOM chambered another shell; he was now waiting for the take down message. The target was still in the kill zone, examining his bloody finger tips, unaware he was in harm's way. The take down order never came, instead he heard the order: "Proceed to the extraction point." Ernie dissolved into the brush, only to reappear at the landing zone some five kilometers distant. The other members of the team were already on board the helicopter. It didn't even land, it dropped a cable with a hook which snapped into a hook on the pack harness. The chopper lifted ten feet and headed west plenty fast, leaving Ernie to momentarily deal with some eleven- and twelve-foot trees.

Off the record Papa bear thought the earlobe thing was pure genius. It was even better than killing the guy, because when he did figure out what happened he would be sheepish about exposing himself to fire. Baby bear had a different take on the subject. It was insubordination and failure to follow a direct order. The Army agreed with Baby Bitch. Before Ernie knew what happened, he was up to his neck in psychological profiles and red tape. So much so, that when he was offered an Honorable Discharge, he took it. King of the world to court jester in one signature.

Bumming around the civilian world did not suit someone like Ernie. He took his last two thousand dollars, booked flight to anywhere and checked into a Venezuelan hotel. After spending a week drinking and groping cantina whores, he went up to his room put a pistol to his temple and squeezed the trigger.

"Jake, do you have any idea what it takes to be a sniper?"

"Yeah, I spent some time in the service." Jake half listened to the story. His hands were still busy wrapping the bundles of cash.

"Do you want me to tell you about training and drills?"

"No, I'd rather not I'm kind of tired..."

"I can knock the stone out of a guy's ear from a mile away, but I can't hit my own melon from point blank. Not to mention all the crap you witness looking down a scope. Brutality to women and children, rape at gunpoint, or just plain prostitution when the only thing a woman has is her own body." He was getting overly intent in the telling of his story, ".... And I can change it all with the squeeze of a trigger.... No one would give me the clear signal!"

"Emie it's OK. I've been there myself, sometime I'll tell you, my story. The point is the gun did not fire."

"Oh boy what a hangover I had the next day. The maid came in to change the bedding and started screaming like a banshee. Before I knew it, I was out of town heading south."

"And I found you on the banks of the Orinoco, End of story. "Jake concluded. "Let's get some shut eye!"

They counted the packages of money twice, with two different totals. Seventy-nine or eighty bundles plus the spare change from the coffee cans. A deceptively small pile for the actual value. It would fit into a foot locker with room to spare. As they packed the loot into the floor pocket they counted once more, with a total of eighty-one.

"That's a lot of phoney bricks!" Ernie suggested.

"Maybe we won't do the brick thing... forty or fifty, but eighty?"

"Yeah, I told you it was a Lame Idea!"

"SHUT UP!"

CHAPTER ELEVEN

Sarah gave Ceryle a peck on the cheek with a friendly hug He toddled off to a westernized cantina as was his habit. He would nurse a couple of Gin and Tonics, while pumping the locals for regional news and information. He would listen intently for hours to crop reports, land deals and personal gossip. Never offering his opinion, Ceryle would simply listen keeping mental notes until becoming board. Anything of importance was recorded in his personal diary before he retired for the evening.

Continuing excitement allowed Sarah to begin at once on her research project. She entered her modest bungalow traveling through her messy living quarters to a spotless room she called her lab. In marked contrast to her living quarters, which could be politely called comfortable, the lab was perfectly arranged for someone five foot eight inches tall, weighing one hundred thirty pounds. No experiment was closer than eight inches from any other procedure. It was by no mistake the lab was kept in order. She had long ago decided she was nothing more than a robot to the chore of checking water quality. She unlocked the door of the hazardous materials cabinet, withdrew a descant jar and replaced the lock. Checking the lid of each sample she placed each in a plastic specimen container. She then lovingly dropped the prize into the descant jar. These extra steps were essential to prevent cross-contamination of future tests.

She could not jeopardize the tests with sloppy results. Now came the tedious task of determining how to record the sample. Years of training told her segregation of the details, information: She chose two composition booklets, one for each would make it easier to cross reference the results. Should she choose to work with an assistant later she needed to use clear scientific notation and verbiage. At the same time the findings should be closely guarded against just anyone having the opportunity to filch the results. On the one hand was the collaboration of a colleague, on the other, a document as complex as the Rosetta Stone.

Keep it simple. Day, date, and time of observation. The observer should initialize findings. Inside the cover of each book was a legend of shorthand notation. And as always, she placed a note card on the cover with a paper clip. The note card read: LOCK IT UP STUPID! This was a carryover from her undergraduate studies. Everyone wanted a peek at the work of other students. The note card did two things; the first was obvious, the second, if the note card was missing, she knew someone was pilfering her stuff. She regarded someone looking at her notes, as a violation of her privacy. Why should she share her thoughts with Cliff Notes students?

She looked around the lab and suddenly felt unprepared for the task at hand. She could perform some of the analysis here but the equipment was going to be inadequate to the task. Titration was necessary to determine solvents for the sample. She could do an electrophoresis, where a sample is run through a gel to separate components. The components then tested by Gas chromatography. Some of the tests like infra-red and ultraviolet photography would destroy the samples, by denaturing the protein. Dr. Sarah Cross Ph.D. suddenly felt weary.

Her treasured twenty-five milliliters of antidote were not enough to perform all the tests. Even then, the conclusions made at a backwater lab, with its limited resources may be inconclusive. The tests may be better preformed at a state-of-the-art facility.

She rejected that idea. Sweating it out in the jungle was her way of rejecting the politics of laboratory research. She had learned years ago not to trust anyone, even the director of a project.

Dr. Judy Jones was chairman of the department, when Sarah was doing post graduate studies. She educated Sarah the hard way. The chairman had a habit of sneaking into the labs at night with a skeleton key. She said she did it; "to keep on top of things". What she really did, was redirect projects at critical moments. The technicians usually overlooked significant datum, until after the doctor wrote a report. The egocentric doctor proved her superior intellect by side tracking two- and three-year projects belonging to her colleagues. She would go so far as to add her name to an abstract during the review process. She might even simply substitute her name as author, to a work submitted on floppy disk. The trick was to publish in her own name while the true author was making exhaustive changes to the document, under the Chairmans direction.

Sarah Cross on the other hand would never take credit for a work not her own. She looked back at the time she kowtowed to the chairman and cringed. Sarah thought the woman must have been on the witness protection program, with a name like Jones. That and the fact the woman was such a criminal.

There was another means of gathering datum. She could invest the small amount of serum in primate field work. This would give her a better understanding of the nature of the material. Do the field work first, then squander the remainder of the serum in laboratory tests. Working late into the night she was able to complete the protocol. She labeled the samples and prepared tranquilizer darts with neurotoxin serum. Administration of the antidote would be conducted in the laboratory.

Locking the lab and preparing for bed, she thought of Jake. That funny man, always saying how much he loved her, knowing the least encouragement would send him packing.

She was probably the only woman in the tropics who wore a flannel nightgown. Brushing her hair she thought of Jake. The sex would be good for both of them. Trouble was neither of them could even consider an encounter not based on a relationship. It was almost as if both of them preferred to keep things the way they were, never moving on to the next level.

Sara needed more of a reason to become involved with Jake than he was the only attractive male in a thousand miles. Jake seemed to have a different suppression, something dark and quiet made him wait patiently. She went to bed aching for Jake's touch, his overpowering hug.

At that very moment, upstream, Jake was rolling over trying to get comfortable. The bed was a raft tossed by the tumultuous currents of a stream. He was bouncing up and down at the whim of the raft. He was thinking of the lady doctor. Not able to find a position where his muscles would relax, he sat up in bed.

What he needed most was a woman's touch. He wanted to enjoy the fragrance of her hair, as he folded her in his arms. He put the blame on himself. He was no big catch for a Ph.D. He was only able to share a deep long-standing love without benefit of reward. Then he thought about the money. Maybe he did have a chance after all. As soon as he figured out what to do with the money. There was no sense of urgency over the money except for his desire for Sarah.

Money was only part of the equation. Women like Sarah needed mental stimulation. He had ten years in the backwaters of the Rio Negro the Rio Orinoco and even the headwaters of the Amazon itself. Until now nothing significant by scientific standards had come out of his dabbling in fauna and flora unique to Venezuela and northern Brazil. Now he had something to trade, while he warmed up to the prospect of telling her about the money. He had the serum to dangle like a scientific bauble.

In the next room, Ernie was having a Special Forces nightmare. One hour to get to the landing zone, one hour to get back to the pickup point, one hour on the ground. Total three hours. But he doesn't have three hours he only has two hours. If he gets out at the drop zone, he will never get back what happened to the other hour? He is shaking uncontrollably, sweating even in an intense chill. Then he is visited by a fawn-colored woman with iridescent green eyes. She calms his fears. He settles down into a restful slumber.

CHAPTER TWELVE

An early riser from childhood, Ceryle was knocking on the door to Sarah's bungalow. It was only the crack of dawn. She came to the door in her flannel nightgown. Long ago they had fallen into the habit of Ceryle being received at strange hours. Ms. Cross never wore makeup, there was no reason to leave him standing at the front door. Pointing, in the direction of the coffee, tea if he preferred, she then scuttled off to perform her morning rituals.

Here in the jungle, there were too many tiny creatures looking for a home where ever hair grows. She kept her legs shaved all the way up to her waist, even though she always wore long pants. Only vanity prevented her from shaving her head, as she so often wished she could. The hair up in a bun, held in place by a chopstick, was a much of a compromise as she was able to make to the humid jungle.

Ceryle was puttering around the kitchen. The sounds echoing through the louver door of the bathroom. Somehow it was comforting to have someone else in the bungalow. Other times during shaving she would hear a stay noise which made her jump and nick herself. The nick made dangerous by the possibility of infection. At the end of her customary habit was a generous lather of Dr. Bronner's Magic Soap. The peppermint acted as an astringent, cleansing the skin making it feel fresh. The jungle climate never allowed anyone to feel really dry. Even the act of toweling after a shower was a futile act. Immediately the heavy atmosphere would have the effect of making exposed skin feel clammy. The soap which she special. ordered from Escondido, California made life bearable. Otherwise, she would spend all day, every day, in the shower.

"Would you care for a cup of coffee?" Ceryle called through the louvered door.

"Keep it hot, I am almost finished."

"It's alright my dear don't you know all Englishmen are homosexuals!" He lied.

"Ceryle that is a pathetic attempt to catch a peek. For every Englishman who claims to be a Fay, there is a child to prove he is not."

"I suppose with the proper encouragement I could curb my perversions!" said the man leaning against the doorway.

Sarah had left the shower running giving him the impression she was still nude. "I am not the one to reform you or redeem you." she stepped into the hall way fully clothed. He hair waded up in a chopstick bun. "Besides if you want to see me in my birthday, suit you only have to look in the photo album on the desk."

While hanging the towel and replacing the toothbrush there was a distinct quiet. The absence of a reply caused Sarah to sneak up on Ceryle, who now stood at the corner of the desk. The page was indeed open to the page of Sarah on a bear skin rug. She tapped him on the shoulder and he jumped. He recovered quickly his mind sharp as ever," My God woman you have just confirmed I am not only a sodomite but a pedophile as well."

"How old were you when this photo was taken?"

"Three months." smiled Sarah taking the album.

"Would you have any photos of similar composition not quite so vintage?" Ceryle explored "For all my faults, I am a student of the Arts."

"Sure, you are buddy...I am sure you are." returning the album to the desk, placing a paperweight squarely on top.

She reached for the wad of laboratory keys and led Ceryle to the locked room. He was no stranger to the inner sanctum.

His schooling prevented his hands from wandering, a trait much appreciated by Sarah. Among his other skills; were the ability to find north on a compass. He could also find down on a map of a river, and up in a differential survey.

"How are you with a dart gun?" she asked.

"Absolute pro!" Ceryle picked up the rifle, checked the safety, and sighted down the barrel. "I can knock the whisker off a warthog."

"Yeah, but can you hit a monkey?"

Jake said he would be by in a couple of days. In Jake terms, this could mean anything up to a week. He was not a man fond of civilization. Somehow, he always seemed to be preoccupied with small things, out in the bush. His enclave was a well-kept and spacious dwelling where everything seemed hand made. Once, he mentioned he could build better furnishings, than he could purchase. The compound from the thatched roof to the wicker table were all proof of his cunning.

Sarah decided not to wait for Jake. Choosing instead to head up-country into the woodland area close to the village. Monkeys were plentiful, to the point of being a nuisance.

Ceryle took his time selecting an adolescent male who was not yet part of the social hierarchy of the troop. Such an animal would not place the rest of the colony in condition of stress. The adolescent males sometimes disappeared on their own or joined other troops where there were available females.

Standing below the unwary monkey, Sarah extended a large terrycloth beach towel. She would catch the monkey in the towel to prevent injury. Because they sometimes carried the herpes virus, the towel was as much for Sarah's protection as the monkeys.

The shot was true, landing in the fleshy part of the monkey's thigh near the buttocks. The target animal seemed to sit down on the branch, then flip over clinging by one hand, before finally letting go. It landed safely in the middle of the woman's outstretched arms.

She ignored a commotion behind her, as she gently gathered the monkey into the towel. Turning to view the altercation she noticed Ceryle laying on the ground. A local brute named Miguel was standing over the man. It was only nine o'clock in the morning but she could tell he was drunk. He suddenly stormed at her slurring "Coma se Disa!"

"What an ugly bambino..." Miguel shoved his rough hand inside Sarah's blouse, "Maybe he doesn't get enough to eat." He stood there leering, stinking of tobacco, tequila and sweat. His hand exploring her breast, while his other hand cupping her bottom.

Sarah was startled. She did not know how to react, because she knew Miguel was a dangerous man. Ceryle had recovered in the meantime. He approached the man in a fury. Unfortunately, Ceryle was a gentle man and Miguel was an animal. Ceryle tried to turn the ape to face himself. Miguel took a big meaty paw slammed him in the chest and sent him sprawling. The distraction did end Miguel's assault on Sarah, who was still cradling the monkey.

Tequila is not like other alcoholic highs. People do strange things. Miguel grabbed the monkey like a rag doll. "Look what you've done to my pet..." he screamed. He then turned ending the encounter. The man walked away down the path to town, with the limp monkey dangling from his fingertips. They did not have to follow him he was going to the cantina behind the bodega.

"Let him go." instructed Sarah, as she caught Ceryle wind up the rifle to split Miguel's skull. She stopped him just in time. Ceryle was in a murderous rage, something completely foreign to the man. He was ever cautious and polite, not one to sponsor violence except as a last resort, theoretically.

Instead of following Miguel to the cantina, they went to the bungalow. Sarah thought it would be better to explain what had happened to the constable now than later. As fate would have it, waiting for them on the stoop was Jake and Ernie.

"Sarah why didn't you wait for me?" Jake mentioned not angry just disappointed.

"I didn't know when you would show up..." She admitted lamely, I was so excited to get started on the project I just couldn't wait. Besides lover boy, I don't hear from you for months at a time..."

"Hold it right there...you just started sounding like a woman, not a research scientist." Jake smiled.

Ernie rolled his eyes and coughed loudly. He went to the front door and opened it. "We only have about three hours to save the monkey can you two works out a translation later."

"Translation?" questioned Sarah.

"Sure, Man says this-woman thinks that, Woman says this- man thinks that. Someday I'm going to write a dictionary so the sexes can communicate. Ernie led the others down the street to the cantina.

"Give me an example?" Sarah queried.

Ernie chuckled, "Only one, I've got thousands. How about when a woman asks how she looks. She doesn't want to hear fine; she wants to hear gorgeous. Which makes no difference at all because she is going to change clothes with or without her partners approval."

Sarah stopped dead in her tracks. "Why should a woman need a man's approval?"

"Exactly my point, women only pretend to seek our advice. In reality, they are using the interrogatory, as a means of promoting their own agenda." Ernie stood facing Sarah while Jake knew to stand aside.

"So, it is all one big conspiracy?" she ventured.

"Not until you include sex as the big bribe!" Dead panned Ernie,

"Women use it for everything from getting a promotion, to paying rent."

Ernie now found himself in a headlock. Sarah raping her knuckles on the top of his head. "Some women; not all women. Besides, if men were not so easy to distract, women would not be able to charm then out of everything." explained Sarah.

"Could you repeat that," Ernie begged, "Your breasts are blocking my ears."

By now the cadre found themselves outside the cantina. Jake had Sarah and Ceryle waited outside, so the monkey thief would not be alerted. Miguel sat at a table in the rear with his back to the wall. In the center of the table was a glass half full, a bottle, a candle and a monkey. In between swallows from the glass the man rambled semi-coherently about Gringos, revolution and the monkey. "Look what they have done to my pet!"

The scarce other patrons placated the man. Partly to share from the bottle. Light shown through the cracks in the walls of the old building. An old paddle fan churned up an odd mixture of odors. Stale alcohol, tobacco, sweat, urine and vomit all lingered in the churning air. The room had never been finished, interior walls were non-existent. The two men had to wait for their eyes to adjust to the gloom.

Miguel made the first move. He shoved the table away, pulling a large bore handgun from his waistband. Jake and Ernie split up. Jake behind a column of insufficient girth to provide adequate protection. Ernie still working on his death wish, moved out into the open. He maneuvered around clear of the table between himself and the drunk. When Miguel coked back the hammer, Ernie saw his opening.

Every eye in the cantina raised as Ernie started slapping his feet on the wood floor. He was tapping dancing; through it all he kept a menacing grin on his face. Everyone looked on with a secure knowledge the man was crazy. Plant the seed watch it grow. He slowed the staccato beat of heal and toe. Waiting, waiting...slower, slower.

Miguel fired the weapon into the wooden floor, "Dance!"

Which is what Ernie had planned all along. He cleared the eight feet of space between himself and Miguel. Jamming a knee into the mid-section, he grabbed the gun with one hand and folded his arm back with the other. The gun was now pointing at Miguel's head. Ernie with a final stroke of genius coked back the hammer. If the man tried to move, he would blow off his own head with the old single action revolver. Everyone in the room, including Jake, were not sure what they had just witnessed.

"Sir may I have my monkey back?" Ernie asked politely, as if he were in a pet store.

Miguel nodded his head, his face drenched in sweat. He was much more sober now. "Help yourself to the pistola Senor", he smiled a gold toothed smirk. Ernie backed away slowly closing the hammer, almost wishing for an excuse to pistol-whip the man.

It was only in the last few moments he had come to the realization the Miguel was a Cuban. He opened the chamber of the old Smith and Wesson .38 caliber gun and dumped out the bullets. Into the palm of his hand fell Chinese -9 mm shells. Where would a guy like Miguel get Chinese shells? And, how would he know they fit into a .38 caliber revolver. He had to be Cuban.

After the fall of the Soviet bloc, a lot of people like Miguel went freelance. Freelance revolutionaries meant guns, drugs and money, not always in that order. And, he was missing his left earlobe.

"So, what... he can't be the same guy!" Jake suggested.

"Maybe not..." Ernie agreed.

"Besides, everyone dumps their armory in this jungle, with all these dictator types. It's been going on since Pancho Villa!"

"Here's your monkey lady..."Jake snarled, still angry she went out with Ceryle instead of waiting for him. The idea of being cuckold did not sit well with him, regardless how innocent. "You better run along now; you only have a couple hours to administer the antidote."

He continued to walk not even looking back. Ernie stood for a moment with a puzzled look on his face. Then he followed Jake, heading back to the canoe at the water's edge. As they pushed away from the bank the water slid effortlessly under the boat. The surface waters were warm and held no strong current. This time of the year strong current was in the deeper waters. Rowing the canoe was no great chore for the two men.

"You don't have to say anything if you don't want to," said Ernie.

"Shut up, I'm thinking" came the gruff reply.

CHAPTER THIRTEEN

Overnight the tropical jungle releases water vapor as a byproduct of the dark cycle of photosynthesis. Microscopic dew droplets form on all surfaces of the jungle canopy. The severe angle of the morning sun heats the water vapor into a moisture laden cloud formation. As the angle of the sunlight changes more gaseous water vapor is lifted higher into the atmosphere. By early afternoon lower elevations experience a micro climate. The sky is full of the water vapor, quickly collecting into droplets and falling as clean rain.

Jake and Ernie had just landed the canoe when the rain began. It would not last long maybe an hour at the most. They rushed to pull the boat clear of the river before it filled with water. Unhurried and already soaking wet they ambled into the compound.

Ernie was letting Jake brood. They had not said two words from the time they left the village. Jake for his part was only ignoring his company. He was used to living alone. From childhood he had always spent time by himself, making observations. Then when he had collected enough information, he would seek the council of qualified experts. Many times, he agreed with the experts, but occasionally he would find small errors in the judgment of the authorities. Sometimes the experts justified expected results without valid proof. And this was his present problem he was trying to weigh all the evidence.

At the compound he put everything out of his mind. He decided to focus on the problem at hand. What was he going to do with eighty packages of contraband money? He was not even concerned with the small fortune inside the coffee tins. The bulk of the money was his only concern.

Compounded to the problem was the fact; they were only safe as long as the money remained a secret. The moment it leaked out they had anything of value they were as good as dead.

Good people who will drop everything to help a stranger, turn into bandits when money is involved. And, that is good people. Miguel and his cutthroats, just barely qualified as people. If word ever did leak out, almost any of the other inhabitants of the village might find the money too much of a temptation.

Jake suddenly realized why he was so angry. The little altercation with Miguel at the cantina was sure to have a consequence. The backlash was unable to be calculated. It was a question of honor. Miguel was not the kind of man who would leave it alone. He was probably at this very moment plotting his revenge.

The most he could hope for was Miguel was not part of a network.

The cartel in this area was not very well established. If the man was a Cuban, he might be part of an advanced guard looking to stir up trouble. Jake rejected the idea. No one would use Miguel as a front man, he was too neanderthal. His present occupation was cantina drunk.

Options, there had to be options. Traveling against the Orinoco back into the heartland of Venezuela, was not feasible. The Rio Negro into the Amazon was too dangerous. Going up over the mountains to the north would put them in Surinam or Guyana, both desperately poor but friendly. Jake began to realize, he did not have the money, the money had him!

Now he wanted to talk with Ernie. They were in this together. The money was a trap both of them shared. Whatever took place was going to affect the outcome of a poorly constructed plan. What was more disappointing, he had always included Sarah in the plan, but now it looked like she was a liability not an asset.

"God damn it, Jake what do rich people do with the money they have?" Ernie offered, "After a fancy home, and a fancy car, and fancy furnishings, what do they do with the money?"

"How the hell am I supposed to know?" grinned Jake.

"They use it to make more money, plain and simple." "Real estate development, commodities, brokerage of farm produce, textiles, heavy machinery."

"If it is all the same to you that sounds like a lot of work. We already have the money. What do we do with it now?" Jake scoffed.

"Import, export!"

"There is nothing in this jungle to export, except contraband. That is why everyone is leaving for the United States. And, if we import there is no money down here to purchase anything!" Jake corrected. "The only thing they produce down here is arts and crafts that only sell to tourists!"

"Well then we have a big problem, no wonder you're walking around with a bug up your butt."

"It's the governments fault you know...they do not spend enough on education. These third world countries, will always be third world, until they educate their people."

In short order it was determined Ernie had no more insight on how to move the money then Jake. The one thing they both agreed on was the brick thing was lame. Now that Miguel was part of the scenario, they did not have the time to allow the trail to cool. They could not afford to wait six months to a year. It was always part of the plan to wait to allow the trail to cool, but things change in the world of high finance.

The one thing that never changes is the need to grease the wheels. Trouble was, as soon as they started spreading money around, the secret was out. Still Jake wanted to somehow include Sarah, which meant full disclosure to Ceryle, which Jake did not think was a good idea.

On the contrary Ceryle had been in the jungle for years and no one knew what he did for a living. Everyone took him for a pensioner from England. He had that good natured quality of a retired bureaucrat. If as some believed he was still working for the British foreign service, he might be a valuable tool.

Even though he was unaware, the money was beginning to change him. Jake would never have brought Ceryle into the plan, but now that he needed assistance, he was willing consider the possibility. For that matter he had befriended Ernie who was now a side kick, because of the money. The only reason he allowed his privacy to be invaded was the money. The money had a life of its own and Jake was just it's pawn.

A few weeks ago, he led a simple life with its moments of pleasure. He only stole the money from the Cartel to prove it could be done. He was philosophical; no money, no antidote. He was more concerned with the antidote because of the link to Sarah, than the money. But the money was already forming a wedge to the relationship and he could not tell her why.

Sarah in the meantime was having her own problems. Someone should have told her the antidote effect took place immediately. She had carefully examined the monkey for fear of the rough handling. If it had a broken arm, it was one thing, a broken neck another. If it did have a broken neck, she would perform euthanasia. It would be the humane thing to do. As it was the animal looked fine. She readied a cage with the door open. Three insulin sized hypodermic syringes stood ready. She cleansed the injection site with alcohol, with the first syringe the monkey sprung alive. So quickly did the transformation take place, she only had time to grab it by the chest and abdomen, with its arms and legs flailing. With a gloved hand she attempted to put it in the cage. The monkey screeched a deafening cacophony, doing everything in its power to sink its teeth into anything it could reach. Sarah stood there with the monkey at arm's length.

Ceryle could think of nothing to help the poor woman. It was not going to fit into the cage unless the arms and legs cooperated. Sarah might just well have had a hornet nest stuck to the end of her arm. Worst yet was the more the monkey struggled, the harder it was, not to crush its tiny body. Finally, Ceryle peeled off his shoe and sox. He placed the sox over the head of the monkey and the struggle soon ended. Even with the sock in place, twenty tiny fingers and toes locked onto the door of the cage.

Clearly the monkey had the advantage. It was still able to make ear piercing screams to addle its opponents. The chore boiled down to trying to juggle two spiders, a muzzled set of teeth, and a rag doll. Sarah got the feet in the cage, when the arms twisted and turned. She got arms in the cage, when the little buzz-saw body changed places, feet up arms down. And again, all fingers and toes locked onto the opening of the cage.

Ceryle ran out to the kitchen, and grabbed an oven mitt. He knew Sarah had the patience of a saint, but he did not. He worked his way onto the lower portion of the buzz-saw body, shoved, leaving the oven mitt in the cage. He shut the door on the monkey's fingers. The small primate pulled the sox up like a drunken sailors watch cap.

A momentary reconnaissance of the confines of the cage, then another screech, with an assault of the door's lock. She had just enough time to pull the chopstick out of her hair, and jab it into the door lock, before the monkey picked the latch. Sarah started wondering if she gave the monkey too much of the antidote. Two of the three insulin syringes still lay on the prep table. Mere micrograms of serum in each of them. This was powerful medicine.

She surveyed the damage to her lab coat and gloves. Nothing to worry about, as she counted her fingers. The excitement was more than she bargained for. They were almost afraid to approach the cage.

Ceryle pulled his flask from his coat and took a sniff. Sarah wrenched it out of his hand. A long drought was ended in a courtesan style swallow. This left Ceryle perplexed. Sarah had drained a day's supply of his tonic. No worry, he would just have to schedule an earlier tea time.

CHAPTER FOURTEEN

"You're not really thinking of making Ceryle part of the deal?" Ernie exploded, dead set against the idea.

"Well, he has a Land Rover, that's a plus..."

"Yeah, so where is your truck? Why don't you have one?"

In stoic fashion Jake laid out the reasoning, "If you have a vehicle, you need a road. If you have a road, you have visitors. I don't want any visitors!" He went on to mention how he was content as a back wood's hermit. The less he saw people the more he liked it.

"Then why don't you just give me that duffel bag of money you've got stashed in the floor boards, and let me worry about it?"

Jake smiled, "That hardly seems fair, letting you take all that risk on yourself."

"Tell Ceryle, and you've got to tell Sarah!"

"Somehow I don't think she's going to be too upset about us stealing cocaine money. She's been down here long enough to see the damage it has done to the local people." mentioned Jake off hand.

Ceryle was a man of the world, no doubt he would have a readymade plan, for the liquidation of a large sum of money. They could cut him in for ten percent. That was a reasonable amount for a broker. Ten percent, plus expenses. That plan stayed on the table all of a nanosecond. If they told him at all he would no doubt want ten percent just to keep his mouth shut. So, there they were back to square one.

"Caracas! We go up over the mountains, down into Caracas. We buy a boat then motor our way to the Caman Islands. We open two off shore accounts, one for me one for you!" Ernie was serious.

"We're going to be stopped along the way." cautioned Jake.

"Nobody's going to question a load of bricks." grinned Ernie.

So, the brick idea was not as stupid as it sounded. That evening they built forms to make bricks. It was going to take a few days to produce eighty money bricks. A realistic brick is four by eight inches, two and a quarter inch thick. Jake had done his homework on that one. The packages of money fit neatly into the center of the bricks. The trouble with real bricks is, they are fired in a kiln. They could not risk incinerating the money by firing the bricks, so the concrete mixture they used, would have to cure naturally. This meant twenty-eight days drying time. Plenty of time to cosy up to the unsuspecting Ceryle and commandeer his Land Rover. The new plan was to use the money in the coffee tins to rent, beg or borrow the vehicle.

There were tens of thousands in loose currency, more than enough for a decent bribe. This way Ceryle didn't have to know anything so Sarah did not have to know anything. They were only delivering a load of handmade brick, to Caracas.

This is where the plan had its faults. A brick even eighty bricks are a dime a dozen. By themselves they carry little value. It is only in the hands of a mason they become anything important. The mason is a skilled professional, setting a plumb line, holding the horizontal line level. What the men had to do was improve on the nature of the brick in some way. Jake whittled a figure of a mermaid out of wood. As they made the bricks, he embossed each with the stamp. Now they had handmade, designer bricks. Works of art, needing delivery to Caracas.

This only increased the subterfuge. If they were going to pawn off these bricks as art, they were going to need a lot of samples. Jake figured they would get stopped at least four times on the way to Caracas. So now they were up to one hundred mermaid bricks. Some to give away as samples at road block check points.

The fortunate occurrence was the paper inside a dried brick, was almost the same weight as a solid brick. The unfortunate occurrence, the money bricks and the decoy bricks were almost confused coming off the assembly line. Ernie quickly provided the phoney brick mermaids with nipples, and tragedy was avoided. The phoney bricks, were now more collectable, than the money bricks. They would have to wait twenty-eight days to see how well the ruse would work.

Fool Ceryle, and it was all downhill. Before they even started on the project, they met the man in town as they picked up supplies. It was then; they planted the notion of travel, to the north. Ceryle saw them carry away Portland cement and water based, rust colored dye. They never mentioned bricks. Instead, they allowed him to wonder about the cargo in the canoe. They did mention Caracas, letting the subject drop abruptly. In due time, the man may even believe it was his idea to make the trip.

Any trip to town would include a visit to Sarah. The monkey trials were turning her world upside down. Monkeys eat with their right hand and fling excrement with their left. At least, this was the pattern of this monkey. Here immaculate laboratory was punctuated with monkey droppings. She had tried hanging plastic over the bars. The monkey quickly turned the plastic into a chew toy. She tried handing plastic curtains away from the cage. This made the monkey try to aim for the gaps in the plastic.

As a rule, she never allowed the windows to the lab to be opened. With the stench of monkey dung, she changed the rules. She had just decided to release the damn thing back into the wild, when she heard a commotion coming from the lab. Normally the monkey only let out a screech when there was someone to hear him. He was screaming his head off. Small cage, large snake. Enormous snake!

One of the local pythons had followed the monkey odor, right through the open window. It was now curled around the cage with its head trying to swallow the corner of the cage. Sarah was going to need help, lots of it. The thing had to be at least ten feet long. As luck would have it, there was good old Jake. Jake, Ernie, Ceryle and Sarah took a moment to pause. "I say we let him have the monkey..." Ernie offered.

The monkey did not like the sounds of that. It let out a round of desperate screeches, even offering to stop throwing feces. The snake in the meantime was stuck on the bars of the cage, with teeth pointed in the direction of its stomach. The cage was showing no damage from the activity of the constrictor.

Jake took command of the situation. He ordered a tarp and a fire extinguisher. Sarah had both in the lab. The three men rolled the cage off the counter onto the tarp, as Sarah pelted the snake with cold carbon dioxide. The monkey just kept screeching. As a team they dragged the bundle out into the street. Jake reached over opened the cage, the monkey escaped. They stood back as the snake uncoiled, eventually working it's jaw loose from the corner of the cage. This was not an animal used to hasty escapes. Indolent would be a better term. Sarah kept pummeling short bursts at the creature as it slowly slithered away.

Good old Jake, always around when Sarah needed a hero. She hugged him and everything was better for the moment. Ernie mentioned something to Ceryle about a belt and boots, they then followed the reptile. The reptile for its part, soon concluded these men were more than curiosity seekers. It began moving in a more deliberate manner, searching for jungle environs.

"Sorry about the monkey."

"I was getting a tad tired of him anyway..." Sarah related.

They stepped back inside the bungalow to view the shambles of a once immaculate lab. With stoic determination Sarah shut the door, escorting Jake out to the living room, where they could rest in each other's arms for a moment. Just as they were getting comfortable the others arrived and the mood was spoiled. Ceryle presently excused himself, mentioning unattended business. Ernie sat there, a lump on the arm of the sofa, not considering himself any distraction.

"You couldn't take a hint?" Jake snarled an hour later, as they walked down to the riverside.

"Hey buddy I was doing you a favor..." Ernie explained, "Now is not the time to make the big move. We've got work to do!"

"Let's, see? Spend time with you, or spend time with Sarah. I think I'd rather spend time with Sarah."

"I'm telling you there is going to be plenty of time to spend with her after we get back from the Caman Islands!" enjoined Ernie.

"You dolt, life is a collection of moments in time! You have to live each moment as it happens!" corrected Jake.

"Oh yeah, what happens if we get back from the Caman Islands and she is not here! You ever think of that. You ever think how miserable you'll be, without someone, you have had a consummate relationship with?" Ernie the philosopher stated.

"It is better to have loved and lost...."

Ernie interrupted him, "That's a load of crap... You never even remember the ones that got away, you only remember the ones you got in the sack. And then, you only think of them -when you wish you were not in bed alone! Think about it. Do you remember a single date from college where you didn't get lucky?"

Jake just smiled. Ernie for all his lack of couth was right on target. Not that it had any bearing on the present romance. Jake was sure he would remember Sarah, with or without coitus. Their relationship did depend largely on geography. Not many attractive singles to choose from out here in the jungle. Yet they both had in common their disdain for the civilized world. It was something to ponder.

CHAPTER FIFTEEN

In between the back breaking work of making bricks, moving bricks and hiding bricks, there was plenty of time for playing cards. Jake was not fond of the practice when they started but soon warmed up to the challenge. He with his coffee tin of gambling loot, Ernie with another. They started out replacing the money at the end of the game. Later they kept what they won. Fate sided with Jake one day, Ernie the next.

Ernie sat there chomping on a unlit cigar. He was down about a coffee can. This meant he was going to have to fold or bluff. Bluffing was doing no good. "I can see you did not waste your youth on any of the usual dalliances.", he checked to see if Jake was awake.

"Dalliances, where the hell did you get that word?" Jake laid down three of a kind.

Ernie picked up the pot with three Jacks. His little ruse worked, keeping Jake from drawing fresh cards, which could have made him the winner. The play became fast and furious. Ernie went on a winning streak to replace virtually all his lost money. The tide of battle turned as Jake won nearly all of it back.

Hours drifted by, until it was time again to crank out a load of brick. The form would hold five bricks at a time. That was not much mortar to mix. The wet brick shrank as it set up, allowing the form to be removed. They could get three loads done, on a single pass, before it was too messy. After standing overnight the brick could be carefully moved. It was still soft but the sand and dirt it collected made it look authentic.

As the pile of brick started to accumulate the men began to have second thoughts about the whole idea. Anybody else would have just left it in the duffel bag, booked an airline ticket to the states and declared the money at customs. Someone else might already be sitting pool side on one of the islands. Jake and Ernie were simply too pedestrian to go that route. They knew there were feelers out, from the owners of the money. The people involved with the cartel certainly would be interested anyone with two million dollars and change to spend. Anyone flashing a lot of cash would raise the suspicions. Then again, the cartel was not above stealing money that didn't belong to them.

Not Jake and Ernie. They were still trying to get over the shock of having the money in the first place. Making a load of brick was just a charade; an attempt to actually earn the loot, through hard work. The brick thing, to let the trail turn cold, was not the worst they could do.

It had been about a week from the incident at the cantina. Just about time for the local police to get involved. The men had finished for the day, put away the tools and were waiting for the bricks to dry sufficiently to be hidden under the floorboards. Six hours was about right. A motor launch tied up to the dock. A dutiful civil servant stepped out of the boat, trudging up the slippery path.

"Don Shoot!" the man smiled, holding his arms up. He was a funny little man with an oversized khaki uniform, which had never been ironed, and might just fit if it were starched. On his head was loose fitting, broad brimmed officers' duty cap. It too, was comfortable, from removal of all the internal hardware keeping it tidy. About his waist, in gunslinger fashion was a large bore antique, in a holster covering the handle. The relic was something Pancho Villa may have used in Mexico.

From the look on his face, he was only doing his job. At the moment his job was to take a statement from the gringos. It was the face of a student told to stay after class. He was not happy to have to come all the way out here, but it was his job.

One could tell her kind of liked the gringo Jake, not enough to visit him, he just liked him. But then most of the towns people were used to Jake and many admired his hermit lifestyle. For the most part, he was not so much well liked, as tolerated. But the Guardia-urbano liked Jake. Jake was the kind of man who checked with the authorities before he did something to his property which might affect the town downstream.

The Policia's real business was with the stranger; Ernesto. It was Ernesto who tore up the bar, with a little help from Miguel. The Guardia-urbano, told Ernesto what happened, more than asked him any questions. Reading from a carefully prepared account, the man penciled in the margins any additional information. Ernie was never a big talker around officials. He mainly said yes; and no, to the questions. In no time the law officer liked Ernesto too.

Just the same, because the Guardia-urbano had traveled so far, he allowed his eyes to wander about the property. There was no reason to waste the trip. He was invited inside for coffee, spiked with un poco Mezcal, if he was so inclined. It was too early for the tequila, but he took the coffee just the same. Jake knew to make the coffee strong. Even with the heat of the day. It would not show on the man's sweat stained uniform. Perhaps, he refused the Mescal, to prevent the unpleasant odor.

It was not a game of cat and mouse. At least it did not start that way. From the kitchen they wandered into the yard beyond. As most of the villagers did, Jake grew a number of peppers, cilantro and bean pods. Where others included marijuana, Jake did not. Not that the constable would have had any comment one way or the other. Tomatoes and green peppers were looking good, as was sunflowers and corn. Even a small stand of sugar cane bordered the garden. Animals was the one thing Jake lacked. The villagers all had scrawny chickens keeping bugs out of the garden. They penned goats and pigs. Jake was so far away from town he refused to own livestock which would only feed predators. As for the bugs he was content to import insecticide. He even made a tobacco juice bug spray to keep away some of the ants and aphids.

Returning to the sunlit patio, the men came across the brick making operation. The law man even went so far as to begin to pick one up, then hesitated when he noticed it was still soft. He did not consider fabrication of bricks at all strange. He went on to explain; his father was a brick mason for a number of years, before returning to town with his wife and children. In the eyes of the community, he was a wealthy man. Now his son was a respected law officer.

Ernie nervously rolled the extra wet cement in his hands. Without consideration, almost like a compulsion he produced small spheres. He made one, then moved on to the next, as they chatted. A row of the small globes began to line up on the brick bench. The constable watched him with a growing desire to also share the feel of the wet cement. He picks up a tiny portion forming a little snake. As he flicked his finger back and forth the snake curved and danced. Fond memories of childhood.

Ernie ran around to get the Policia a sample of the brick work, one with nipples. "Here ya go, this one's a bit more cured than those others."

"But senor, why put a figure on the brick when it will not be seen?

"These are designer bricks!" replied Ernie without a glance." They're for around a pool in a mansion!"

As all similar meetings go, the news from town needed to be told.

The local missionary was dead. He had died of natural causes, most likely boredom. Jesus Christ was a well-regarded local hero, and as such needed little reinforcement from the outside world.

The missionary was able to bring improved water treatment to the town, something it needed. The one thing he was never able to accomplish, was to establish advanced commercial ventures. He tried everything under the sun to put in place mercantile business. As close as he could come, was to have the ten cantinas in town purchase hooch from the same vendor. This was far below his original expectations.

The whole problem came from the failure to adequately explain the concept of wholesale and retail. He had envisioned setting up a dry goods establishment to stimulate commerce. Initially he brought in an assortment of farming implements, with textiles, and sundries. The wholesalers were supposed to supply the retailers, something that never happened.

Even the stratagems of industry were lost on these children of nature. They could not be expected to put something away for a rainy day, when it rained every day. So far as they could see the jungle was always going to provide for their every need. Owning any farm implement, regardless of how cheaply acquired, only meant having to use the damn thing. They would labor at small chores ad infinitum. Any chore in need of a tool, was simply too large to tolerate.

The cantinas were quick to see the advantage of locating high grade hooch, at the lowest possible price. Quickly the practice of buying in bulk caught on with the Cantina's. The missionary, against his better judgment, became the supplier of spirits for all the cantina's. The justification was; eventually other mercantile ventures would prove valid.

Try hard as he could, he was never able to sell the idea of retail verses wholesale. The populace, other than the cantina owners, never did understand how; ten of some items, was cheaper than one. He explained the shipping was the key. They could collectively defray the cost of shipment. The important stratagem was for the community to act collectively. This was the hallmark of government, severely lacking in the jungle, from a missionary perspective. He hoped to bring democracy to the stone age.

Being such a small community, they would buy one shovel, then loan it out, when it was not in use. They did not need another shovel until the first one broke. Even then they could fix the thing.

Stimulating the economy was a hard thing to do, when the items remained on the shelves collecting dust for years. In the end, the missionary was content with the sale of spirits to the cantinas. Even sales of the Good Book, paled in comparison to liquor sales. For one thing, to sell a book, the customer has to be able to read.

The missionary originally considered teaching himself Spanish, as he taught the population English. This far away from civilization Spanish was more of a dialect than a language. It was easier to teach English as a language written and spoken. Not that there was anything wrong with Spanish. Except the spoken tongue of the jungle was not more than sugar coated variety of Spanish. If even one in ten words, was in any way connected to Spanish, it was a freaky miracle.

Right about the time, he discovered he was a liquor barn, he made the discovery; these people did not know anything more about Spanish than he did. So now he had a case of Spanish bibles on his shelf, he could never sell. The very next day English class began. He wrote a hasty letter back to the United States: send English bibles, with lots of pictures.

He toiled for twenty years in the humid dank jungle. Even after he was to retire, he stayed on. In part, to cover for the peccadillo of being a part time liquor salesman. Most of the original merchandise remained on the shelves. None of it making any difference, now that he was dead.

The whole trouble with a town like Bueno Rio was the progression from jungle village to the modern world. The people were hunter gatherers only a generation ago. Grandfathers still felt more comfortable in a loincloth than pants. Their children learned both the jungle and civilized traditions. The grandchildren were the ones who encountered aspects of the world beyond the jungle.

Then there were the negative aspects which filtered into the collective consciousness. Most of the new arrivals were criminals from the civilized world. People like Miguel, who's social development, limited itself to drinking in a cantina. Two day's north were mines of precious gemstones, where these men labored a month for a year's salary. Periodically they would leave town, only to bring a debauched lifestyle on the return, at the expense of the permanent citizens.

The older tradition, one of Elders collectively considering the needs of the people, was changing. The town now had a mayor, not a chieftain. It had a police force of several armed officers, instead of a collection of armed braves. The odd assortment of modern buildings and homes were a curious result of outside investment, or charitable donations, from people who never had been to Buena Rio.

A shallow pocket of oil fueled a small electrical generator plant. Phones were available to those who could afford them. Mainly the modern conveniences followed the migration of people from the outside world.

Plantation owners and cattle barons were still at the top of the food chain, with the villagers unable to make democratic progress. As it had been for five hundred years the peasant was chattel, to the land holders. The people of Buena Rio were not even peasants. They had never been part of the servitude, of a feudal system of government. They were attempting to establish democratic reform, without first exploring myriad political landscapes. Flint and stone one day, satellite communication the next. Something was bound to be lost in the translation.

They were being expected; to bypass ten thousand years of trial and error, to arrive at a moment in time, where the rest of the planet lived. The co-mingling of Aztec tradition and Christian morality, cumulating in regional democracy was a disappointment. Somewhere along the line humanity forms ranks, some -for and some -against democratic policy.

After fifty years of political activists working in the region, there were armies without leadership. At this moment in time; the armies were on either the side of one argument, for or against the drug traffic. Communism and Democracy were not even in the fracas.

The fall of the soviet bloc caused the rebels to reinvent themselves as drug couriers. The assembled armed camps could not be expected to put down their weapons and go home. A multi-generational mixture of armed thugs arose.

Critical to supporting this army, was the developed countries and their demand for recreational substances. Taken to the extreme, every crack whore on the planet, was an advanced scout, for the armies of the cartel. Every customer, of a crack whore, contributed to the enemy of constitutional government. Anarchy was the only political agenda, for a people who sought to enlist as many as possible, to a narcotic slavery.

This tiny village, in the jungles of South America, was an outpost on the war against narcotics. It was only a matter of time, before it would fall victim to the dictates of the outside world. At present social science was at an infancy. Harbingers of doom, such as Miguel were already in place to support anarchy. The tiny political government of the township would not be able to prevent him, if he tried. One of these days, he would wake to an intoxication of power, and make his move. If not Miguel, someone exactly like him. The only thing standing in his way were a few altruistic individuals like Jake, Sarah, and the dead missionary.

CHAPTER SIXTEEN

Flores was busy in his bakery. He needed to make up for the shipment which was lost. One more delivery and he would not have to cut the cocaine any longer. He was glad of this. The time he spent blending magnesium niter into the coca, was time away from more important things. His wife thought he may have a new girlfriend. He did. The time he spent mixing at the bakery, was making it too noticeable. He never allowed business to conflict with pleasure, or he could bring the girlfriend to the bakery while he waited for the product.

Years before he had made a similar mistake. When the woman tasted the powder, she was an instant devotee. At the time he was much enamored with her. Enough so he married the woman, who to this day tried to visit the bakery unannounced.

If it were not for his wife, he may have not stayed in the business. He had always been afraid of losing her to her addiction. She never progressed beyond a maintenance level user. It was just something she needed to stay normal.

What Flores hated most was trying to package the powder after it was mixed. To make it look as if he had not tampered with the shipment, was as much of a chore as anything else. He had to compress the coca into blocks, then wrap it in cellophane. Next was outer layer of butcher paper followed by a counterfeit label. Everything had to look genuine. The trouble with the man was his own dependence on coca made him a perfectionist. He spent far too much time on critique, not enough time on work. Sooner or later the job was done.

His time with his girlfriend was limited but not enough for his wife.

In the short time he had known the girlfriend, his wife had developed another gruesome habit. Whenever he came home, she demanded sex from him. Proof he was not unfaithful. No matter how well the girlfriend had squeezed his lemons, the wife demanded satisfaction. She was not content with a quick friendly hello. She started at the first page of the Karma Sutra, and worked her way through.

The only way he was going to prove, he had no girlfriend, was to provide his husbandly duties. This only reinforced his need for a woman, who's caress, was not so much work. The long-term consequence of such a relationship was for the girlfriend to become disenchanted with the bedroom activities. So, Flores found himself in a damned if I do, existence.

One more load of doctored coke and he was home free. Mercer would stop pestering him about the quality of the product. Flores had been lying these last few shipments. Telling senior Mercer, the supplier was to blame for the quality. He had almost made up the lost revenue.

Way down stream some of his scouts had encountered a native village of women. They told of a pair of white men who traveled that way on an earlier -new moon. A gaudy trinket was left with the tribal elder who would not relinquish ownership. They were sure it must have been part of the shipment, but without proof they did not want to steal it back. Flores was past worrying about baubles. He wanted the money. As close as he could count, there was only a thousand dollars of gold, in a shipment of almost three million.

Word came back from the jungle there was a fork in the river at the location of the village. They could go south or north. The crew were waiting on Flores to decide what he wanted to do.

It was having his own private army which he enjoyed the most. The wife and occasional girlfriend meant nothing to him in the context of having an army. He was a born dictator. A small-time drug smuggling tyrant. It did not matter to him, there were a hundred other men in his position, between here and the money. One hundred drug smuggling dictators. He sent word to the front; continue downstream.

Fielding a contingency of troops, to carry out your orders, was more difficult to do; than Flores imagined. He would have to send supplies, ammunition, and payroll. The scant amount of ammunition was a joke. Food is everywhere to a trooper born in the jungle. Most important was payroll. It was a matter of good will, on the part of Flores, the men get paid. Sending the money, even when they had no place to spend it, was just good military management. The troop would just keep going if they were not paid. Somewhere out there, they would find something, to attract their attention. Soldiers need a reminder of what they left behind.

As a tactician, Flores was a mimic. He talked with other men in his situation throughout South America, to find what they did to evoke loyalty. He found they all used the system of elitist conscription. No matter how few men made up a cadre, some were to be Elite. The hundred odd men of Flores' private army had ten elite storm troopers. It was a number he could tolerate. Half of them were sent into the field with the search party. This would make for envy by the other troops. They would all be trying to distinguish themselves in the meantime.

As a punishment he also sent the men who were in charge of the missing shipment. It was an opportunity for them to earn redemption. If they recovered anything. Flores would retain them in his service. He was being kind beyond reason, as a minor potentate.

Some of his contemporaries had told him to murder the men. Stage an accident where they died, as heroes to the cause. Martyrs were important to bring sympathy from the people.
Flores resisted the suggestion. He was still down playing the existence of a small troop of armed men as a police force. Sure, they were uniformed, and they did military training, but they were to protect and defend people in his town. At most his men were a Militia, not a private army. Flores was only an employer to those worthies of his patronage.

He was just a benefactor, not a war lord. As a sign of his generosity, he included fresh uniforms for the men in the field. It was a onetime gesture, to prove how well he supported them. He also included a cache of trinkets and baubles to be traded to the native tribe as a bribe. He hoped the next time he heard from the men; they would have found his money. He did not want them gone too long.

The jungle had a hypnotic effect on people. It is constantly changing, growing, expanding. Wandering through the lush landscape a machined and tooled firearm is a complete deviation. Most of the jungle has no definition, gravity is only a suggestion. Water, plants and animals are all blended into a biotic soup. The presence of a firearm in stark contrast gives the impression of an orderly universe, somewhere beyond the horizon. The weapon defines space in a scalar coordination of time and dimension. The same may have been true, of the Conquistador and his blade. A man alone in the jungle, has only himself, and that which he has on hand to define reality.

CHAPTER SEVENTEEN

Cleaning up after the monkey was a chore; Sarah did not want to repeat. She took her precious serum, placed it into a mail pouch, then returned it to the refrigerator. Even if it meant sharing the discovery with some laboratory back in the States, it was worth it. Many times, the field work, stood alone, in critical research papers. After all it was about the paper, not about the research. Being pelted with monkey feces was not noteworthy. Still there was much to learn about the relationship of the two compounds. If it worked on monkeys, it would work on humans. Imagine sedating a patient before surgery. The world of emergency surgery would be turned upside down. No longer would an accident victim bleed to death on the way to the hospital. A gunshot wound, or an automotive accident could be immobilized at the scene. The more she tried to talk her way out of continuing with the project, the more reasons she found to continue. Monkey Shit or no monkey shit.

She had seen the effects on the damn monkey. No respirations, no blood pressure, pupils dilated and un- responsive, all from a microgram of serum. In a hospital the monkey would have been pronounced dead. Another microgram of antidote, dead brought back to life. But what did the monkey experience. Was the monkey aware of the surroundings. Was it asleep in a fitful slumber. These were questioning a monkey could not answer. She wracked her brain for experimentation to prove the monkey was not dead but only sleeping. The possibility of human trials was a subject she avoided. Back in the United States it would take forever to clear the project for human trials.

Zombis, the living dead. She was aware people in Haiti were sometimes pronounced dead, only to be found alive later. Available in the literature was one interview with a Zombi. He was aware of the entire ordeal. He could remember being taken to the morgue, being placed in a coffin, the dirt covering him up. Then he lost track of time, until the grave was dug up and he was released. Even with this evidence, no clinical trials of the Zombi drug were ever preformed on humans.

Another thing troubling to Sarah was the lack of control over scientific documentation. Way back in the 1950s, research was conducted on Ergot fungus. A powerful hypnotic drug came out of the research. LSD escaped from the research laboratory and into American counter culture. Over the years, other less dynamic recreational pharmaceuticals came on the market from time to time. Medication was over prescribed to a public looking for permission from the doctor to use recreational drugs. Mixing prescriptions with alcohol, allowed for a high which could only be described as date rape, even to the point of same sex partners.

Sarah considered the effect of sending an abstract document to her project coordinator. She knew she had better do it soon. Funding for her present project was being pulled. If she wanted to remain in the Jungle, she needed something spectacular.

This neurotoxin, antidote was just the ticket. She sat down at the computer hoping the words would flow. After several tries the abstract began to come together. On one hand, she wanted to sound detached. On the other, she could not contain her enthusiasm. She down played the action of the toxin, to focus on the antidote. She knew toxins were a dime a dozen. A stimulant able to raise a corpse was another matter. She glossed over parts, concealed what she thought was obvious, and closed the document. She sent along a list of equipment she would need. Pediatric blood pressure cuffs and paper towels along with an odd assortment of muzzles and soft restraints. Knowing the bureaucratic system, she requested many things she did not need, so she would get the things she did need. At the bottom of the list, she included a Land Rover as she always had. If she did not include it now, they would only get suspicious.

Ceryle Smyth had a Land Rover. For as much as he used it the thing could have been up on blocks. She had once asked to borrow it with a negative result. A couple of other older cars in town couldn't even muster a traffic jam. The one lifeline to the outside world was a Tuesday, Friday bus. It carried mail and passengers who did not mind traveling with chickens. The chickens were supposed to be caged. Often, they were not. Occasionally a pig was shipped, which is an ordeal for any passenger. Pigs get motion sickness, they don't throw up, but they are very messy. One can smell the pig in the slip stream of air behind the bus as it moves.

Sometimes it would be nice to have a car just to get out of town. She pictured going on a picnic. The bus service was no help. Unless you went on Tuesday and came back Friday. On those days it came through town twice. The early morning run was always on time. The return trip was never scheduled. Any mail or packages needed to be on the early trip to avoid waiting hours for the bus to come back.

She had once ridden the big loop of the morning run. It stopped like a school bus at indiscreet cross roads. It bumped and banged along a sandy path jostling every bolt and bone. Instead of an adventure it was more like a roller coaster, except you get a seat belt at the amusement park. The only other time she rode the bus was coming to Bueno Rio.

It had seemed so quaint coming upon a town with market stalls. Bright colorful tent roofs leaned to block out the sun. Live chickens for sale along with fresh garden produce. Spices of every variety for sale or trade. Handmade trinkets, mostly silver was available. It was a medieval bazar atmosphere, quite distinct from the modern American expectation.

When she arrived, Sarah was replacing another field research Scientist. The bungalow was built two years before her arrival. It was nothing special in the modern world, but years ahead of the community. The former occupant must have had enough credentials to merit decent living conditions. Strangely the architecture seemed to impersonate that of the only modern hotel which was built at the same time. A mining conglomerate had footed the bill for the small tasteful hotel. It seemed the local fresh water supply was adequate for the investment.

Bueno Rio was located in a wide part of the river, making it good port to use as a marshaling area for heavy equipment. Some fifty miles north were working diamond mines. South American diamonds were inferior and smaller than African diamonds. They were known as industrial diamonds used in polishing and fabrication. Every once in a while, a decent sized stone came out of the mines but the color and clarity was usually wrong for the precious gem market. The engineers needed a remote location from mining activities to plan for the future, they chose the small village. This should have been a economic windfall to the area, but there was never enough engineers in the hotel to make a difference. Water, electric, and telephone service were greatly improved but this never impacted the villagers. They were still wondering what to do with a general store. Life went on, as usual, around the modern conveniences.

When commercial development failed to materialize, her predecessor pulled out, opening a slot for a soil and water mangers position. Sarah saw it as a once in a life time opportunity. Her funding came from the university system, was all she was privileged to know. She suspected the university stipend was charged back to the mining operation. The previous person in her position was a note book freak. They had set locations all over the region where water samples were taken. At each location was a notebook recording observation, day, date and time. Samples were carried back to the lab for analysis. More notebooks. It may have made perfect sense to her predecessor, but it was Greek to Sarah.

As with any scientific investigation, she had to catch up to the rest of the class. The notebooks in the field were the problem. The longer they sat the more incoherent the information became. She started collecting the notebooks then bringing them back to the lab. Soon a pattern emerged, giving her a new respect for her colleague.

He had dutifully recorded the information from the field books onto the samples. Back at base camp he transferred the information to the laboratory notebooks in greater detail. Sometimes charts and graphs are needed to explain details. The crafty old former resident of the post somehow did without such nonsense. He knew he could produce such as were needed on demand from the margins of the laboratory notebook. After sorting through his archaic system she had one of those moments of pause where it all made perfect sense. Total annual rainfall, ground percolation, it was all there. Primary, secondary, and tertiary contamination of ground water along with the natural causes, was all there. Natural antibiotic effect of beneficial microorganisms was there. As was the pathogenic reaction of bacteria, mold and fungus. It was all there!

Scattered about on thirty locations was a treasure of information just waiting to be harvested. She quickly abandoned shorts and halter tops. The information as presented showed the job required a fair amount of protection. Long sleeve shirts and long trousers with boots, were the required uniform. This was also when she adopted the use of a chopstick to hold her hair in place. There was so much to do she never tired of the routine. It was as if she belonged here.

Then there was Jake. Big brooding hulk of a man. Not too big, not too brooding. Quiet and unassuming. If he only tried harder, he might be in for a surprise. She did not take herself to be a spiritual person but she knew she was here for a purpose, and part of the purpose might just be Jake. But Jake was not helping matters by being so distant.

She asked him once "Did you ever serve in Viet Nam."

"I was never there!" he replied with a haunty tone, that she took for him somehow telling a half truth.

Either he did not want to talk about it, or he was never there. She overlooked the possibility he was somewhere in the region. As women do sometimes; she waited a few months and asked him again. The same haunty tone reached her ears. It was almost as if he had been programed to repeat the phrase if he was ever asked. This was the first time she had ever hugged him, because she knew he had something to shelter. This may have been why she liked him so much.

He was the exact opposite of the rest of society. She had never met a hippie, who did not attend Woodstock. If every American hippie of the era in had been at Woodstock, there would have been a human pimple three hundred feet deep in upstate New York. At the same time on the other side of the globe, men were experiencing a separate reality.

If every person claiming to be a Cherokee Indian really was one, The United States would be one big reservation. No one is ever a Choctaw or a Zuni even an Apache, everyone is a Cherokee. It is remarkable.

Just from an academic framework Jake was a refreshing challenge.

People who told the truth, the whole truth, and nothing but the truth, were hard to find. Most people string so many nouns and verbs together so quickly, they can't help but get some of the information wrong. Even if they're not lying, they still cannot be counted on for the truth.

Jake was different. He paused before answering most questions. Not like some dolt, he weighed the information. He knew most people are not ready for the correct answer, they wanted to hear, what they wanted to hear! Many times, his answers would require a disclaimer; " To the best of my knowledge...", "In my humble opinion...", or the old standby; "Where the hell did you get an idea like that?" It was just this practical wisdom that made him so attractive to a woman like Sarah.

The academic mind is constantly aware of proofs. A mathematical formula must balance before it can be proved or disproved. Jake had a way of balancing the equation in his mind before he spoke. If there was one thing, she could appreciate it was precision. Even when as a woman both hemispheres of her brain found conflict in an equation, she could rely on a friend like Jake. He would tip the scales in favor of the right answer.

She was not a needy person. She did not require a man under foot. Long ago she had determined; if she ever did find a man, it would not be to complete her as a person. She would only accept a partnership. The whole concept was something she could blame on her grandmother. The kindly old matron told her: "A man and a woman are like a team of horses. Don't ever team a plow horse with a race horse. The team will only pull in circles." The elderly woman had grown up in a simpler time. She was not a product of the age where the population had surrendered to the demand of individual automotive transportation. A return to the womb. The universal devotion to shelter inside rolling steel.

Sarah was just as much a hermit as Jake, in her rejection of the mechanized sterile condition of modern environments. There was still so much of the natural world in need of exploration.

To sit behind a wheel, while music served as a catalyst for advertisements, was such a waste. The common experience of man reduced to rush hour traffic. What was worst was the commuters all got to where they were going without ever sharing the experience. If there was any sharing going on it was all negative; Road rage, horns honking, fender benders, and vehicular homicide.

Here in the jungle, life was much more real. One could actually see a vine grow. The trained eye was able to attune itself to the release of water vapor by plants as the clouds blocked the skies. The plants shifting to the dark cycle of photosynthesis in the changing conditions. Hydrogen rising aloft as a mist, carrying pure water droplets. Then the Hydrogen proton richly charged atmosphere; explodes. Gravity is restored to the escaping gas as it combines with oxygen, then it returns to the water cycle.

Only one of the events a motorist is likely to ignore with the flick of a windshield wiper. All the physics in all the libraries ignored, in a banal attempt to reduce the landscape to one singular dimension of travel. Jake would be the first to demand physics as a prerequisite to obtaining a driver's license. No matter how hard the automotive engineers tried to improve safety: Two objects cannot occupy the same space at the same time. Simple elementary Physics. Mass and gravity, object and inertia, all explained with a little math. But then were the lawmakers really aware of physical requirements? If a Toyota traveling 60 MPH slams on its brakes in front of a Mack truck traveling 60 MPH: Who has the right of way? Break it down to the X, Y, Z components, throw in the element of time, it doesn't take Einstein to calculate the Toyota had it coming. The Mack truck driver can watch, as the EMT pry the other driver from his plush little mechanical womb. Poor grasp of elementary Physics.

It was this mutual disdain for the direction of the sophisticated world, which lead both Jake and Sarah to live in the third world. It was an opportunity to investigate, where civilization was going wrong. The trouble was the third world was advancing so rapidly it was not a true representation. Technology has been abused from the time the first hominoid turned a rock into a sharp rock.

As kindred spirits, it was only natural they should be attracted, one to the other. As victims of a time, where every pleasure was instantaneous, they were overly cautious of making a profound mistake. Jake could be a bit of a plough horse on occasions. Sarah was sometimes overly anxious. The only way they remained friends, was by making excuses to themselves, about the other's conduct.

CHAPTER EIGHTEEN

Miguel had waited long enough. No one would remember the pistol wiping at the cantina. He was like a lot of men with limited mentality. He had been humiliated in a public place, vexed! Many of his waking hours were spent trying to imagine a fitting vindication for the gringo. He only needed something to show it was him, without leaving evidence to convict himself. When it was over it should look like the gringo man had been punished by fate. He was not above superstitious hocus pocus. The mystical fabric of the rainforest was more than enough fodder for his fertile imagination. He wanted to put a hex on the gringo. He wanted to perform a ritual where Ernie was consumed by his worst fears in a jungle of uncertain fortune.

Christianity had never erased the shaman influence of the people. Many accepted Jesus Christ as a lord and savior, adding to a host of other jungle deities. The shaman taught there was a God, because of the order in nature. Many found the man Jesus just another manifestation of the gods they already held in esteem. Accepting Jesus was the quickest way to treat the priest complementary, while not discriminating against any of the other gods. Their observations of piety, could always include a man nailed to a tree. This was no different than a blood sacrifice offered to a tree. Inside his holy house they would worship Jesus. Outside his house, they worshiped all the gods of nature. How could Jesus feel defiled?

The casting of spells for fortune was common. No more common than wishing on a star. It was always known some had the gift over others. Every village had its chieftain and a shaman. The shaman had an assistant. The assistant had an apprentice. The apprentice had a student, who had a beginner, who had a neophyte, who had a helper. No matter who begat whom, somewhere along the line, someone would conjure up an unfortunate spiritual apparition. And, if they could do it once, they could do it again. It was this dark side of the magic, everyone guarded against.

Every once in a while, there would come a time to evoke the dark side, to deal with a pressing problem. It was the dark side Miguel wanted to use against his enemy. He wanted to be in two places at the same time, so when he was asked where he was, he could comfortably deny whichever he chose. He could swear on a stack of bibles without offending Jesus.

In civil law when someone presents a cup of poison to another individual, they have assaulted that individual. If the person drinks the concoction, the charge is attempted murder. In the climate of jungle shamanism some mysterious force was supposed to be present to prevent the injury. That way the tribe is not responsible for murder. The individual is at fault, or the poison would not cause death. Every member of the tribe may have participated in presenting the poison, yet no member forced the accused to drink. One may sprinkle herbs into a meal, another into a water cask, and another onto the bed linen. Each assault, a test to the censured.

It may take weeks or even months of fitful slumber before the accused begins to incriminate himself. He may have broken out in boils or experienced fevers, maybe vomiting, all evil omens. He has one choice either experience a cleansing ritual, or perish a lingering demise.

This was the hokum Miguel hoped to use against the gringo. In order to accomplish his work, he needed to gain access to the ranch house. The trouble lay in the location of the compound. It was almost an island, when it rained it was an island. Traveling by boat, was the best way to get there, however he could not do this undetected. He attempted to cross the mud flats on the west side but sank up to his hips. The north side was firmer, but as he crossed, he detected the men returning from town so he decided to wait for another chance.

As consumed and determined as he was toward revenge, he was just as concerned he not be caught. It was not cowardice it was self-preservation. He wanted to be known as a man to be feared, not a petty criminal. It was the mystique he savored. The macho machismo. He did not want to be remembered as a bushwhacker. The town needed to know he met the gringo face to face on the field of valor. Such was the crippling effect of the tequila on his mind.

One of the men got out, heading up the steep hillside to the compound. The other man pushed off from the bank of the river. From this distance Miguel could not tell the difference. He was sure the gringo Jake was the man who stayed behind. He had no business with Jake, it was the gringo Ernie, he hoped would drown in the waters. Miguel ran ahead to a point where the bank narrowed. If he could get there in time, he might just be able to cause the canoe to have an unfortunate accident.

Some children from the village had stolen a rope, making a swing at a swimming hole. The same swimming hole where the river narrowed. Miguel found the rope. He tied a log to the end. When the canoe came by, he would set the log free. He swung it once to practice. The trap was set.

He anticipated the arrival of the unsuspecting victim. Once more he tested the rope swing in the gathering darkness. On a pendulum, gravity is greatest at the point where the object stops, and moves in the opposite direction. Poor Miguel was unaware of this natural ratio of mass and acceleration. The limb of the tree has to be able to handle the strain of the load. When the log reached its limit, the branch of the tree broke. Gravity being what it is, the limb fell directly onto Miguel. As this took place, the log floating in the water drew the rope taunt in the current. The craggy old limb of the tree, grabbed onto Miguel's clothing, dragged him off the bank into the water. All he could do was hang on for dear life as the swirling river brought both floating ends together. This left a fair amount of rope free to catch every snag. Each new snag caused the log and limb to violently crash into each other. Poor Miguel, could not decide, if he was being drowned or pulverized.

Jake was in a good mood. He had spent a little time that afternoon with Sarah and would spend some more this evening. Ernie would have been a third wheel. Jake took him back to the camp to keep him out of trouble. He didn't even waste time going inside; he just dumped him at the dock. Sarah was preparing dinner, an overdue gesture. Neither of them was children so this could mean she was finally coming around. Maybe it was how he handled himself, now that he knew he was a millionaire. Nah, that couldn't be it. He was never going to feel like a millionaire until the money was in the bank. Funny how, while he went through life nickel and dime, he never had use for a bank. Now all he had on his mind was getting rid of the currency. Somehow it was like radioactive waste, it needed to be handled cautiously. Maybe that was why it ended up inside bricks. He had subconsciously juxtaposed handling the money, like it was contaminated. The more he thought about it, the more he was sure he was correct. It was dirty money. It was drug money. The only way to wash it clean was to run it through a bank.

He had the same aversion to gold. Gold the noble metal was polluted. The Nazi death camps had stolen the fillings out of the teeth of the inmates. Brick after brick of the metal was produced from the suffering of the people. Franklin D. Roosevelt must have suspected as much when he took the United States off the Gold Standard. Sure, lots of Jews died, but so did many others, whose only crime was ingenious dental work. To Jake the whole supply of gold was polluted, unless it came right out of the ground. But he had no bias against gem stones.

The money supply was just another example of his delusional side. He merited the confiscation of drug monies, as keeping it off the streets. If it was off the street teenage prostitutes had nothing to work for. It was a big triangle, Money, Drugs, and Sex. Just like they teach in fire safety, to control the fire, you have to control; Fuel, Oxygen, and Heat. So, money was only fuel for the fire. Sex and drugs are going to happen, that is the whole understanding behind participatory addiction. The multi-billion-dollar pharmaceutical industry would have to close its doors, if every habit-forming compound was removed from its shelves. Lots of times a wife will not find her husband attractive until after her evening dosage. A man is happy as long as his wife is happy. All too often the women are only happy with the help of prescription medication. Many women would dump their husband tomorrow if it were not for his excellent health insurance. So, in the short version; sex for drugs, is just going to happen. The triangle money, sex, drugs; can only be broken by removing money. Sex and drugs have an intrinsic confidential value. Money is a sliding scale, supply and demand. No money, no supply. No supply, no demand. As if the demand for sex is ever going to stop. Some do it for the money. Some do it for the drugs. But if they do it for the drugs it is white slavery.

All of which; told Jake, he had rational reasons to hold onto the money. It was his fair and square. He would do it again the first chance he got. He just wished he got more of it the last time. It wasn't the money it was the principal. He'd like nothing better than to burn all the money and start over. But then he was a one woman, man. What did he know?

Up to the port side of the canoe was a tangled mess blocking the river. It looked like a log and a tree branch. If he hit it just right with the canoe, he could drift right over it. Funny he had not noticed it on the way to the cabin. As he came closer, he noticed the rope and a snarled jumble of old clothes. It was just the rope swing the children had hung. He had often wondered how long it would stay up there. He braced for the collision jumping cleanly over it, sending the confusion straight to the bottom.

He kept going unaware of Miguel, who in the darkness was helplessly spewing out the last of his tequila. The sudden impact broke the branch holding him prisoner. The tail wake from the canoe sent the gnarled heap into shallow water. Moments later Miguel collapsed on the bank, thanking his poor excuse for a god, he was still alive.

He cursed the man in the canoe, and the canoe, and the river, and the branch, and the rope. He never once regarded the mishap to be his own stupidity. He prayed to the wrong god, at the wrong time, he told himself. A less insulant creature would have looked back at the scenario and discovered he had -prayed to no one. He had acted before thinking through the consequence of his actions. Placed in the same position a thousand times, he would forever make the same mistake. And every time he would fault the same Deity. The money for the candle he was going to burn in his god's honor, would go to tequila. The god that saved his life would surely understand, that after his ordeal he would need a tequila before an offering was made. He staggered away promising to burn a candle to the river god, just as soon as he had a tequila, maybe two.

CHAPTER NINETEEN

Twice a week a Curtis Seaplane landed on the wide part of the waterway. The hotel catering to mining engineers was supplied with all the perishable niceties of the outside world. Among other items were the foreign newspapers at a reasonable price. Ceryle Smyth was a frequent guest whenever the plane was due. It was always a treat to share a cup of tea with one of the pilots. They often were forced to lay over to the morning, but still could not drink at the bar.

An Englishman and his tea are only civilized with proper preparation. The leaves must steep in a pot. One scoop of sugar and a dapple of cream. One of the luxuries delivered biweekly, was small portions of dairy creamer. These were only available immediately following the flight and at no other time. Ceryle was annoyed enough to want to discover, why the creamers were not available throughout the week. Surely the damn things come in a case. He pugnaciously requested a bowl of the tiny creamers be brought to the table.

No stranger to the inner workings of a kitchen he turned an adept eye, to the location of storage. Begging pardon to retire to the restroom he slipped into the kitchen and found two cases of the tiny creamers. That was more than enough to carry over between flights. Returning to the table he was confounded to find the waitress had removed the small bowl. It stood on a bus cart, empty of the tiny creamers.

Again, he requested a small bowl of the tiny creamers. The procurement of which took the same steps as before, pulling from the storage supply. It was still puzzling, now even more so. What happened to the hand full from the first batch? Now he did have to go to the restroom. When he returned, no creamers. He had, about enough. Something was not right. This time he ordered the creamers and the waitress brought them from the cooler. He made some pretense to rush off with the acknowledgment he would shortly return. He went outside on the veranda and watched through the glass. The waitress tipped up the bowl into the pocket of her apron. Mystery solved, almost.

The woman was a thief this much was true. Why she would steal these insignificant objects was something else. He returned with a copy of the paper pretending not to notice the missing creamers. He would wait for the proper moment in time. He watched her a sullen bovine woman. She had that hurt look, that "I do this because I have to do it" look. It was the kind of a look which was calculated to evoke pity. It was the kind of look a bum use, when handed a sandwich instead of a dollar.

Ceryle waited until she went on break. He called the manager over giving him a quick overview. They rushed together into the employee locker room where they found the woman pouring the creamers into empty baby bottles. Ceryle was horrified, how could he be so heartless? How could he be so cruel? What business was it of his anyway?

"Quitar -Vaminos" the manager spoke to the waitress. As bad as Ceryle felt this guy was heartless.

"My good man, surely you would not deprive a child nourishment."

The manager laughed, putting a hand on Ceryle's shoulder to escort him back to the dining room. "If she is guilty of anything it is being caught! The baby bottle trick is pure sympathy. She has no children. They all do it you should see what they do to the individual portions of butter. She'll come back in a week and I'll hire her to dust rooms. Hopefully no possessions will be noticed missing."

"But... the baby bottles?" Ceryle was confused.

"Evidence...if I have her arrested the bottle is evidence! By the time the case gets to court she'll conger up a baby!"

Ceryle went back to his paper, sitting at the same table. Somehow the tea was not attracting his attention. In through the door walked Jake and Sarah. Always the gentleman he invited them over. They noticed him one moment too late. They had to accept the invitation. He poured out the sorted details of the creamer caper, seeking absolution.

"What's the big deal, you get caught you get fired!" scoffed Jake.

"I was just annoyed; I was not trying to cause trouble."

Sarah was able to help Ceryle out, her intuition was tuned to this ambiguous argument. "You, as a patron of the hotel, should have every right to feel cheated when the domestic help steal right off your plate."

This made him feel better. That was all he was asking. He had done the right thing. If he was more of a sleuth, he might have uncovered a conspiracy of the workers. They ate twice, even three times a day, at the hotel. At home their cutlery was all stamped with the hotel crest. Even the sheets on the bed came from the hotel. They all had garden furniture from the pool deck near the cabana. As an overwhelming gesture to the herd mentality, whenever one of them pilfered an object, they all followed suit. Slowly the hotel was being carried away bit by bit. Like a procession of ants in a documentary film, the property of the hotel was spirited away.

Seeing three people at the table the manager sat down. He knew Sarah and Jake were looking for an excuse to dine alone. He resumed the conversation with Ceryle, directing his attention to the bar with the offer of a gin and tonic. The couple knew he would eventually return, so they quickly ordered from the menu. This would at least give them a little time alone. They talked and laughed, even cuddled a tiny bit.

The restaurant had a coat and tie requirement. Long ago Jake had put a coat and tie in the coatroom for just this purpose. For once he did not look like a back water swamp thing. The sophistication of Jake in a tie was refreshing to Sarah. Both of them acted with a sense of urgency. Sarah may be leaving soon, if the grant was not renewed. Jake would be going on an extended absence from the compound. It was as if the life they were living, was going to end, and they both knew it. They had been such friends; it seemed ashamed to not explore its full potential.

That evening they spent hours, where every human contact had a meaning. First a short shower, with a long bath. No hurry, just simple talk. They found they both loved fresh powdered snow in the Fir trees on a mountain crest. They loved finding starfish on the beach but, hated those who collected the living creatures. Numerous other topics came and went as the water turned cold.

Even then there was no rush. They wrapped themselves in bath sheets, sitting close to one another on the sofa. Neither of them touched the wine in front of them. They were so complete in the moment; the wine would have ruined the sublime. When Sarah fell asleep in his arms he was not disenchanted. If not tonight, some other night.

She was only proving how much she trusted him, by being able to relax enough to fall asleep. Her rhythmic breathing soon caused him to enter a deep slumber.

Hours later she woke and dragged him into the bed, where they both were more comfortable. With the morning light they woke, each nibbling and tickling without the slightest sexual overtone. They were kissing, deep wanton kisses with full body embracing, only without the need to culminate with coitus. It was as if; by mutual understanding, it was still too soon for them to cross over into the absurd requirements of a sexual relationship. Jake was not the least bit disappointed, and more importantly neither was Sarah.

For one thing they could skip the conversation about, "was it good for you?" Even having the conversation, meant the participants should have waited. Anyone who can't tell if they and their partner are satisfied was doing something wrong. It was the difference between fornicating and enjoying the human experience. God would never have given man complementary body parts, if he did not expect people to use them. But he also gave man a free will, allowing the possibility for mistakes to be made. What Jake and Sarah had just experienced, was a test drive, without the guilt of postponing ownership. They had breakfast.

Miguel was coming to in the dank hacienda where he hung his uniforms. He was never able to fulfill his promise to light a candle. Too many shots of tequila were required to dry out from the river spirit. His immediate need was met with a demijohn from the corner of his room. Inside the bottle was a nasty homemade brew. It contained seeds, leaves rancid fruit, and berries. It was as close to moonshine as his jungle supplier was ever going to come. He had two demijohns, just in case one of them went dry. Stronger than wine, weaker than liquor, it was the perfect morning tonic. The supplier warned it was sacramental use only. To Miguel anything that knocked loose the crust, from his bleary eyes, was a damn Milagro. Being rescued from a watery grave was just proof the gods were stupido. His lifetime preoccupation with Nihilism, rewarded with the comfort of emptiness from alcohol.

He rose slowly in a guarded gait. His whiskered jowls wet from drooling. He took another swig from the jug. He felt better now. His morning ritual; a dunk of his head into a pail of fresh water. Now that the water was tainted, he rung out his faded shirt. The trousers could wait.

It was his habit to refresh the bucket of water in the mornings. His day would be spent as a friendly face, begging sympathy, at any number of bake ovens. To his part of the bargain, he would occasionally provide a dressed fowl from the jungle. No one ever questioned his generosity was just the result of plucking feathers from the looser of a cockfight.

When he filled his stomach, or wore out his welcome, he went looking for trouble. Part of his lively hood was derived from inspecting all the chicken coops, in the absence of the owners. He would separate out the hatchlings sorting them by sex. The rooster chicks he would slip into his pocket, then deliver to the sporting cages out of town. His contribution was tolerated, even when the fight promoter, had to raise the chick from a hatchling. In this way, Miguel claimed to be a champion raiser of fighting Cock's. No matter which bird won, he claimed it was his.

By late afternoon, his day was done. He would grace one of the cantina's with his presence, and hustle drinks from the other patrons. It would always start the same. He sized up his benefactor. This man enjoyed war stories, another bedroom dramatics. Some went for the nostalgic, where he could vent his anger over the encroachment of the outside world. The latter was pure fabrication, for he himself was one of the outsiders who had simply drifted into town. Truth was not a requirement in storytelling. His tale would reach a highpoint whenever the glass was empty. Excusing himself to visit the toilet, he would always return shortly after the benefactor put new drinks on the table.

Tonight, he had a new tale to tell. His narrow escape from drowning, and the gringo who disregarded his perilous struggle. Each time he told the story he relished new details into his predicament. He had been worried for the children, so he took down their swing. He did not let the rope get away because it would be a nuisance to navigation. The gringo deliberately ran him down, seeing he was struggling for his life. It was a three-tequila story, he would tell five times.

He was feeling pretty good as he stumbled home to fall face first onto his cot. His heavy breath forming drool in his beard. His remembrance of the events changed by -retelling.

CHAPTER TWENTY

First thing in the morning, Ceryle was not the least bit hesitant to drop by Sarah's bungalow. After all, she was one of the only cultured persons left in town, now that the minister was dead. The hotel management personnel did not count, they were handsomely paid to pretend to be genteel. The Engineers were all ciphering, integrals and differentials. Besides she should be the first to know the hubbub concerning Jake.

"I'm sure he would have mentioned it to me, if he had done such a thing!" She argued "Not that drowning Miguel would be such a crime."

"Shoot him, drown him, just drive a stake through his heart so we know he is dead." Ceryle agreed.

"Not too fond of Miguel are we?"

"That putz once conned a round of drinks out of me with a war story. He was crying in his beer, when he mentioned using an AK47."

"Meaning, what?" Sarah shrugged.

"Meaning he was on the wrong side! I'm not inclined to buy drinks for someone who was the enemy." Ceryle stated firmly.

"And here I thought you were a pacifist!"

"Conscientious Objector, my dear girl. Conscientious enough to serve as a medical attendant." proudly he announced.

"Get shot at without shooting back!"

"Quite so!"

"But you'd shoot Miguel?" she smiled.

"In a New York Minute. From the proper duck blind." he stiffened his neck inside his shirt collar.

"Why?"

"The man is from the Lunatic Fringe; he wants nothing more than to cause chaos and anarchy. "Ceryle bit his lower lip, "As long as he lives' he is going to, try to, kick start the revolution here in South America."

"El Presidente del Bueno Rio."

"Don't you scoff at him. All he needs is a squad of a few men to get the thing started!" Ceryle ventured, never knowing how prophetic his words would be.

That very afternoon a small troop came in from the river. They had been out quite a while. Perhaps a month. Finding themselves in a small town they made bivouac, then toured the area to spend their wages. Their olive drab trousers made them easy marks for the crafty Miguel.

He immediately ushered them into a Cock fight pit not too far out of town. He waved the favored bird around, then kissed it on the beak, for luck. The fine-looking bird was sure to win, over its scrawny competition. Everyone bet on the handsome strutting rooster, without questioning if their winnings were secured. What no one noticed, as Miguel kissed the bird, he forced tequila down its throat. This was the only wager Miguel had with the strangers, where he could not afford to lose. The drunk bird, who richly rewarded him, was knocked out in the first round.

Had the betting gone the other way, he was going to expose the drunken bird, as means to postpone payment. A few rounds later he had money enough to comfortably quit cheating. He still persisted kissing the roosters who now sometimes won. He could send the para mutual bet either way, to suit his purpose. All he had to do was substitute a concoction of tobacco and coca leaf herb, instead of tequila.

After a while he pardoned himself and sat quietly on the side lined with a pocket full of winnings. The others continued to game until they were bored. He used his time, sitting off to the side, to learn about the men. When they were not calling each other pubic hair, or some other insult, they used names. Even in his alcoholic haze, he learned who they were. More important, he put together pecking order for the small group. He came away knowing who was in charge. This was going to save him a lot of drinks, when the time came to impress someone.

He was still curious about the mission they were on. No one really mentioned anything of substance he could manipulate for his own benefit. They just seemed to be an anonymous guerilla band from somewhere to the west. Watching the group he could pick out; one lieutenant, one sergeant, one petty officer. These men were keeping track of the frivolity. Half a dozen grunts kept to themselves.

Miguel would try to befriend the officers. If this did not work, he had already focused on one of the grunts as a weak link, to the information he wanted. One of the regular troops suffered harangue by the rest of the group. His name was either pubic hair or Pedro, from listening to the others. He looked bright, probably smarter than the rest, and this is why they picked on him.

At length the Cock fight wound down. His misfortune was the timing of the event. Many of the town regulars did not add to the revelry, not knowing the impromptu event was taking place in the late afternoon. With the gathering darkness the troop found it reasonable to return to camp. They were after all in an unknown region, even with the hospitality they had been shown. After escorting them to camp Miguel begged to be excused. He now did an unusual thing for Miguel, he bathed, shaved and made himself presentable.

From the bottom of an old foot locker he assembled a uniform. Nothing more offensive than safari clothing it gave him a distinct military bearing. He still did not know exactly what he dealing with. It was better not to expose his Cuban boons, to a cadre who for all he knew, were hunting Cubans. He reminded himself he was expatriate, retired, whatever the squad wanted to hear. He would have to substitute local jargon o make his deception complete.

Jake saw them go by, just about noon. Three boat loads of backwoods Militia. He went right into the shed grabbed a shovel. Those coffee cans of money were going to be trouble. He left one can in the house, because everyone needs money. Not having any money on hand would be a worse mistake than having a little too much. The other four cans he took out near the compost pile and buried four feet deep.

This only left the brick. It was all sufficiently cured; he could do something with it around the yard. In a flurry of activity, he relocated the stack of firewood. First moving it to the side, next throwing down a herring bone pattern of brick, where he didn't really have to measure. He put a plastic sheet under and on top of the brick to keep it clean. His samples could not look used. Plastic under a wood pile was nothing uncommon even out here in the boony's.

Ernie returned from fishing on the river, just in time to see Jake complete the project. He just smiled as he walked past the man sweating profusely. Putting away his home-made cane pole he remained silent. He knew, to say one word, was only going to complicate matters. Besides Jake looked too winded to engage in conversation. Ernie put down his fish to clean them. Maybe if he handled the situation right, Jake would stop giving him that dirty look.

The fish were large enough to peel the skin off. He ran the filet knife down the back bone just so far. He reversed the knife and peeled the skin from the other end. In no time flat they had six fresh fish steaks. Out of the corner of Ernie's eye he could see Jake cooling off. He ran into the hut coming back with tin foil. Each fish steak got its own jacket, with onion, mango, coconut oil and spices. Here in the jungle, it was hard to keep dairy products. The coconut oil took the place of margarine. The mango would keep the fish from drying out over the fire.

He kept checking on Jake, who just stood back with his arms crossed over his chest. Ernie took a few choices logs off the wood pile, making a fire in an old drum, cut vertically, and laid on its side. To get the fire started he poured a stream of gasoline onto the wood. He knew he used too much. When he threw in the match, he didn't even duck out of the way. A fireball exploded from the top of the barrel with a loud crackling-voompa. Jake didn't say a word he just went inside to bring out a couple of plates. Ernie could see the man was smiling. What is the loss of a couple of eyebrows, when it amuses your friends.

The way to make the fish perfect, is to fully cook it in the foil, then dump it into a hot frying pan with cayenne pepper and Spanish paprika. Let all those juices boil away, and just before the fish sticks to the pan, pull it out. It works on any fish, anywhere. Even if you can't pronounce the name of the fish, you can cook it. Of course, some fish stink more than others, which is why you were cooking on a drum in the first place.

They had just about finished two pounds of fish each when Ceryle appeared. He had news from town and it was critical, or he would never have come this late in the day. Jake was quick to provide another plate.

"Yeah, I saw them come through around noon," announced Jake. "Seemed strange they just kept going, unless they knew where they were!"

"Oh, so I wasted my time coming out here?"

"Not hardly, you're getting fed a pound of fresh fish!" chuckled Ernie.

"What happened to your eyebrows?" asked Ceryle.

CHAPTER TWENTY-ONE

Ceryle as a man of the world did not like to brag about his associates scattered through South America. Some of whom were nothing to brag about. Kitty and Charlotte were a couple who Ceryle had once befriended. He had made their acquaintance soon after they quit San Diego. They left the United States for southern climes under a controversy from the Quartermaster Corps. It seemed they each had too many husbands, missing in action, at the same time. The brief interval before the discovery of their complicated marital status, gave them just enough time to bank roll enough money to skip town.

They teamed up to survey resort life at the expense of gullible bachelors. Not that they catered strictly to unmarried men. Their motto: Free, White and over mumble, mumble. They were among the most charming women Ceryle ever met, to his unfortunate mortification, following a scam. While he was duping them, they were duping him, and the result was so hilarious they kept in touch.

Funny how he never got around to inviting them to Bueno Rio.

They might just liven up the stuffy old engineering crowd. Still, he did not want to muddy his own pool. This was his home not his office. Extreme times call for extreme measures. Why let the ladies age gracefully pool side, at some resort, when he could use them down here. After all, it some guerilla action was imminent, he was only protecting himself.

What he needed, he explained to Jake and Ernie was a matching contribution, for the monies he would extend to Kitty and Charlotte. Without a moment's reflection, Jake dipped into the coffee can, presenting Ceryle with five thousand dollars Uncharacteristic of his usual demeanor the man's lower jaw dropped. What were Jake and Ernie doing with this kind of money out here in the bush? He had not even laid out the full plan, when he was being taken seriously.

No matter, the pedicure and perfumed lovelies could be on the next sea plane into Bueno Rio. If anyone could find out what was going on with a militia it was those two. Any military man who could cut the muster would fall out to carry baggage. A Channel #5 dipped hanky, would likely clear out the jungle. Ceryle wouldn't have it any other way.

Sarah was unaware of the preparations in progress. She likely would not approve. With the strangers in town, she did stay closer to home. When Jake stopped in, it was as if she never wanted him to leave. He did not mind, yet the he never took her for the clingy type of woman. It was a little disturbing. but understandable.

More disturbing than the rest was the way Miguel was catering to strangers. He was almost an aide-de-camp for the men. His favorite cantina served as an officer's club, while his next favorite was given over to the enlisted combatants. He would circulate between cantina's like a chaperone. The former lumbering hulk of a man was shaven, with an esprit de corps. Even Ceryle found him less loathsome. Something was brewing and the ball was in Miguel's court.

No one in the tiny village had the slightest idea why the men were here. For the most part they did not care. They had all been able to sell small items, food and the like, to the men. The villagers were not threatened even with the prospect of arms and ammunition. The one man whose business it was keep track of the peace was objective. The sheriff only wanted to be disturbed in case of an emergency. If anyone wanted him, he would be in his office.

So, one day drifted to the next, with very little changed. Peasants from the outlying areas brought in produce to the marketplace. At two in the afternoon the rains came, and by four the peasants all returned home. Those who lived in town went to lunch at eleven and came back a two. The mundane, taken to such an extreme, as to make a visitor scream at the ridiculously slow pace. The whole experience, made that much more excruciating, by the presence of strangers.

The Seaplane landed and everything changed. A motor launch sent to convey passengers took an unusual loop around the lagoon. Two occupants, one in large blue polka dots, the other in a highland plaid were being given the grand tour. Both had red hair which could have come from the same bottle. The polka dots wore a white wide brimmed hat, while the other chose a conservative garrison chapeau. Each carried an outlandish handbag, large enough to be mistaken for a hat box.

Their wardrobe was conveyed in quite large steamer trunks. Handles everywhere, the vaudevillian trunks had wheels on the back and the bottom. In no time the ladies were installed in a suite. By the time Ceryle arrived moments later, an explosion of colorful garments swirled in all directions. When they were sure the room would reflect, they had arrived, they greeted their Duma with kisses, not quite connecting to his cheek. The activity did not end here. Kitty was quick to suggest a prowl of the market place before dinner.

Quite detached from being an escort, Ceryle wondered at the antics of these dramatic artists. They marveled over the most mundane items, squealing with delight. Each time making the merchant feel proud of his offering as if it were indeed special in some way. Even though they hardly bought anything, all the vendors took notice of the rare sight. At length Charlotte found a chicken she wanted for a pet. Kitty demanded she not buy the creature. Not without a leash, she found at one of the closer stalls. Now a procession of chicken on leash, was followed by the ladies with Ceryle bringing up the rear as porter.

One of the cantina's observing the commotion was quick to set out a sidewalk tableau. Four chairs and a setting of water with bread sticks graced their arrival on the return from shopping the market. Knowing this was a ploy for their patronage, they sat down. The wine they ordered tasted like someone's poor attempt to create a malt beverage. The only grape in the glass was Kool Aid. The alcohol was not from fermentation, it was from distillation. The bouquet was too coarse to be anything other than Vodka, and a cheap one. Still the ladies not wishing to expose their knowledge of such things, politely sipped at the concoction. They knew the whole ruse was to turn to their advantage.

Other tables were assembled at the entrance to the cantina. A chicken on a leash was a quick tool to conversation. Even in this backwater, where chickens were common on a plate, one on a leash drew comment. Eventually a uniformed man sat down.

The girls just loved a man in uniform. From his fresh shaven and coiffured presentation, his appearance at the table was by no accident. Bread sticks, anyone? Soon he was followed by a subordinate who appeared to have been ordered to duty station. The momentary flirtation rendered; name, rank, serial number mother's maiden name, location of headquarters, men in the field, where they were and what they were doing!

Kitty and Charlotte at the same time remained as mysterious as fog on a marsh. The macho military men did not have a chance. As the ladies politely returned to private conversation, the soldiers were trying to entertain them with their whole life story. Even with Kitty's attempt to rearrange her highlander bodice, to cover her charms, the men were persistent. Charlotte closed the curtains on her leg show, with a quick snap of polka dots. They had gone from bawdy to chaste in moments. This only encouraged their "pigeons" to further bombastic antics.

The cu-de-ta, Kitty began fanning her face with manicured grace. The wine had gone straight to her head, wink. Charlotte pulled a perfumed tissue from her handbag, handing it to Kitty. The woman dabbed her nose as she made a petit sneeze. They then rose from the table leaving the tissue with the bill. Ceryle quickly arranged payment then hoisted his arm load of trinkets, to follow the girls. Looking over their shoulders for the welfare of Ceryle, the tissue was now a military conquest, as expected.

Arriving at the hotel Kitty turned to the concierge with the chicken. He reached out, without a clue, except he was being diligent. She handed him the leash with the instructions: "Have this Fricasee'd and brought to my room!"

"Maam, what about the leash?"

"I should think par boiled!" she smiled wickedly.

Ceryle didn't even have time to put down the packages, before Charlotte poured them each, two fingers of Bushmills's Irish whiskey. Kitty put Her's to her lips almost trembling. She slugged the first shot and wrestled the bottle away from Charlotte.

"Where in the freebooter universe do you have the nerve to invite us into such a screw-up? "Charlotte screamed softly. "What?" Ceryle demanded in self-defense.

"Those clowns are hunting for a missing load of cash from a drug deal!" She announced, refilling her glass and handing Kitty another.

"We don't do drug deals." squeaked Kitty as she swallowed.

"See here, I had no idea. I thought the military presence was another Cuba or Honduras, I never thought it was renegade drug dealers."

"Well think again pal! This is a new world. There is no nationalistic agenda. The only game in town is DRUGS."

"We don't do drug deals." squeaked Kitty as she swallowed.

"Surely you are not going to try to tell me GNP and Gross domestic production are leveraged on drug traffic." Ceryle reasoned.

"No not those who are already Corporate! But those who have rinky-dink third world policies are all guns and drugs!"

"We don't do drug deals." squeaked Kitty as she swallowed.

"What the hell is the matter with Kitty?"

"A couple of years ago we were playing a long con on a executive in San Juan, some Banco Popular official, he turned out to be a real case history in clandestine trafficking." Charlotte refilled her drink "That son of a bitch had his fingers in everything."

As the story unfolded the cloak and dagger was way beyond the scope of a couple of girls trying to set up a mark. Evidently, they did not fold tent and pull out soon enough. It took them months to lose the tail this scoundrel placed on them. In part the only reason they agreed to play the backwaters of Bueno Rio, was to test if they were still free of bogey men. Every time they thought they were reestablished another spooky skeleton fell out of the closet.

"We don't do drug deals." squeaked Kitty as she stared into space.

This guy was so well connected he had a man in the INS in Miami in his pocket. The INS agent could slide anyone of Spanish descent from the whole Caribbean basin, Puerto Rican papers. Especially young boys. The bank was buying up property all over the southeastern United States. Guns for drugs for money for property for Visas, all in a day's work.

"This guy was a regular piece of shit."

"And you were playing him?" queried Ceryle.

"We didn't know! He was just another business tycoon with a wife at home." Smiled Charlotte. If Helen launched a thousand ship, that smile could sink them.

Kitty's nerves were finally starting to calm down. "This time I was the bait in the wife trap. He was all primed and ready to be plucked, nobody leaves their wife!"

"Don't tell me he would?" chimed in Ceryle.

"Oh, hell no! I was his beach side mansion, motor boat driving, Gold card using, fiancé pending further instructions." Kitty explained.

"Where were you while this was going on?"

"In the guest house, of course!" Charlotte acted like it was a silly question. "The mansion was as big as this whole village..."

"Long story short, what queered the deal?" Ceryle grew tired of the sorted details.

"Beach front, motor boats, Drug smuggling, is that concise enough for you, you turtle!"

"You saw something you were not supposed to see?" he offered.

"Let's just say when you're shopping with a Gold card you want to take your time!" Kitty smiled, now somehow cheering up from her former catatonic state. "Money on one side of the table, big pile of dope on the other. Us with our shopping bags."

"The next thing we know, we're blindfolded, on a motor launch headed out to sea." Charlotte described.

"I thought I was dead. Didn't you think so?" "Yeah, I thought we were dead" And the conversation began to exclude Ceryle as the two started gravitating into a private reconstruction of events. He refilled his whiskey, sipping slowly listening to the yackity yack.

As he sat there, he knew he loved them both dearly, even if he never saw them again. From the bits and pieces of chatter he pieced together the rest of the story. They were taken to the equivalent of a Puerto Rican gulag, where they remained for about a month. A hurricane blew through after which their captors were missing. Forced to work as domestics for a few days, in order to earn bus fare, they headed straight for San Juan. Once in the capital city they went on a vindictive spending spree with the smuggled gold card. The high point of which, was to purchase twenty-five duplicate sets of non- refundable tickets, to all corners of the globe in the name of the banker's wife and daughter. They then sold twenty-four sets of tickets at buy one, get one free. Naturally the banker would have to look everywhere for the ladies. As a final twist in irony, they mailed the gold card back to him at the office. They were a class act, these two.

Over the years, they had put a little aside, in various bank accounts. Enough to lay low when the time came. It was the only way the two could stay out of trouble. With the sale of gold card merchandise, the vacation was prolonged. Eventually the banker was arrested for racketeering. When they read about it in the papers, they came out of hiding.

A knock at the door, delivered a well-cooked chicken. The presentation included a leash with interwoven wild orchids coiled around the serving dish. The whiskey had heightened their appetite. They tore into the bird like Henry the Eighth. Nibbling first delicately, the savor of the meat, they soon were shoving handfuls into their mouths like wolves. Ceryle was the only one, who found the necessity to use a plate or utensils. Not the least bit appalled by their table manners, he thought the spectacle fit perfect with their character. Being frivolous persons, this is exactly the flighty behavior he expected behind the scene. Soon the chicken was no more than a pile of bones.

"So why were you so shaken earlier?" Ceryle asked Kitty.

She hesitated to fix her makeup. "Drugs and guns, weren't you paying attention?" She snapped the compact closed, near his nose like a castanet. "In our line of work, we spend more time avoiding high roller dopers, than we do setting up a mark."

"They're everywhere..." Charlotte proceeded to explain, "Find a highroller with too much time on his hands, you've found a smuggler!"

"Or a DEA agent, don't forget the DEA Agent" Kitty added in lilting sisterly tones.

"That's right I almost forgot..." she intentionally turned to Kitty, not Ceryle. "Off season at the resorts, it's all dopers at one table, DEA at another, with hurricanes on the horizon." the two ladies laughed.

Kitty turned, "Ceryle it's getting really bad for business, we haven't been on a yacht in years."

"That's right, the high rollers are bringing their wife and kids. You can't set up a mark with wife and kiddies" Charlotte explained. "We used to do so much better, when it was only wealthy industrialists, catering to the third world."

"It's hard to believe, none of them were involved with arms shipments..." Ceryle tried to pry the truth from them.

"Oh heavens, there was a time we were practically on the DOD payroll...." started Kitty suddenly interrupted by Charlotte "We were bankrolled under entertainment, every Department of Defense meeting with South American Nations." Kitty "those men were such gentlemen, not that we didn't get groped" Charlotte "Yes, but we were never treated like common prostitutes!", "No we weren't".

"Ladies!" Ceryle butted into what was quickly becoming a private conversation of two nostalgic women.

"Those men were not gun runners. They were ordinance salesmen of the finest nature, Jets, radar and satellites." Charlotte announced.

"Don't forget communications, dear!"

It was a losing battle. It was clear they were just loaded enough to want to spill their guts. Also, clear; they were going to walk down memory lane every step of the way. Much of what they wanted to talk about was personal agendas. Ceryle wondered after the future of the charming broads. Not that there was any need to worry they seemed capable to take care of themselves. He stopped even listening to the details of the conversation. He rested back in his seat to the warbling of doves, twittering away in human form.

Kitty was pretty, but it was Charlotte he had always favored. She was the true redhead, a strawberry blonde. Her breasts a creamy white right down to her pearl pink nipples. In his day, her legs were like stilts climbing out of stiletto heels. Not that they were no longer attractive, he was just too familiar with the women to be willing prey. He was better off conducting business on their bequest, then trying to satisfy their appetite for mayhem. In due time he made his way to the door almost unnoticed, except for the envelope of money he deposited on the credenza.

They didn't stop chattering even as the door closed behind Ceryle. He smiled to himself, wondering where on the planet was a place these two could finally retire. It just was not possible. Their work was their life, and even a billionaire would have trouble keeping them amused. It wasn't the money it was the sport. It was the infinite devious details of perpetrating a connivance, that made their life worth living.

If they ever ended up in a rest home, they would be charming their way to extra pudding portions, just for the sport.

CHAPTER TWENTY-TWO

"Flooseys!" smiled Sarah looking Ceryle straight in the eye, hoping he would blink.

"Beg your pardon?" the man concealed his guilt behind an impeccable poker face.

"You fly em in for the troops or the engineers?" she chided.

"I'm sorry, what are we talking about?" the polished diplomat choosing to veil his complicity. He could neither confirm or deny.

"Two hot tamales fly into town and spend the afternoon with Ceryle Smyth, never gonna happen by accident, in this galaxy!".

"Oh, you mean my cousins!" that was stupid, he knew it was.

She was only fooling up to this point. Teasing him just a little tiny bit. She did not care if Ceryle found companions out here in the middle of nowhere. But! He had something to hide and all his attempts at deception were piquing her curiosity. A moment ago, she would have been happy with any old worn-out salutation. Now she was primed for answers.

Ceryle looked at her. She returned his gaze. Something unsettling was in her face. It was the look of a big of Doberman, the moment play time is over, and it really wanted the stick. Running was not an option. He was a man who had wondered how long he would last under interrogation. At this moment he had reason to doubt himself. Suddenly he found he had plenty of pluck left in him. "The redheads my cousin, and the other one is her sister."

Too late, baby wants her chew toy. He knew Sarah as well as anyone in town. She had an aggressive tomboy side, when she got going. Right now, he was in a headlock, with the added inconvenience of a wedgie. And, she was not laughing.

"I can see a nipple" he joked. Taking a page from Ernie.

"Well keep looking for the other one, there's two down there!" she remarked, increasing the strain on the wedgie.

"All right alright I'll talk!" he laughed "but I can see your nipple!"

"No, you can't, it's a mole."

She agreed to wait for his explanation until they got up river to Jake's Place. He explained he only wanted to tell the story one time to a select group of people. He would have to service the engine to the boat, a ploy to buy time, hoping the girls would find their own way to the pier.

Off in the secrecy of the jungle, Miguel knelt in front of an elaborate altar of his own fabrication. It was laid out in a circle, favoring the major points of the primitive compass. The five points were not the usual pentagram of Hollywood horror movies. His points of the compass were: Pole star, summer morning sunrise, winter morning sunrise, summer sunset, winter sunset. All observable from a point of convergence, referred to as a nadir by chart makers. He had chosen the location years ago when in a drunken delusion he found himself flat on his back looking directly at the moon. To his poorly cultivated spiritual awareness he was in communication with the lunar apparitions.

He cleared a circle large enough for him to lie outstretched from the brush of the location. Over the following years he made observations of the key points of his compass. Only rarely did the moon position itself directly over the circle. With his head pointing at the pole star, he charted the movement of the sun across the sky with his arms and legs. The exorcize left a circle, very much in the shape of a pentagram.

Just outside this circle, near his feet, he collected objects of dubious spiritual devotion. The original five stones and a bolder, were in the course of time, to be decorated with shells and bones. He valued skulls as additions to the altar. Holding them in place with wax dripping from candles. He worshiped the animalism of the departed spirit.

Eventually, they required blood sacrifice. Small lizards and snakes were impaled on strips of bamboo. In the event of an auspicious full moon, he offered armadillo's or chickens.

He was inventing the ritual as he went along, hoping to be favored by the gods. As time went by, an element of devotion surfaced, where each ministration was an act of wonder. The armadillo was a favored offering, because it remained in position, as the jungle hollowed out its lifeless form. The chicken was always devoured by the jungle, leaving feathers strewn about the clearing. The chicken spirits were active. The armadillo spirits contemplative.

In order to arouse cosmic activity, he must sacrifice a chicken. Then he would light the candle, from the inside of the circle. After working himself into a trance like state, he placed the candle on the altar. He had been using his hocus-pocus for so long he had lost his sense of rational thinking. The tequila made his mind soft and pliable. From the time, he first tried to contact the spirit world, tequila was an important function of the ceremony. The only time he had been to a catholic service, he remembered the observance included a cup shared with the Lord. As author of his own religion, he filled the cup with tequila.

Sharing the celebration with the gods of the jungle, sometimes took a lot of tequila. He placed himself inside the circle, devoutly kneeling. A jigger of spirits for the spirits. A jigger of spirits for Miguel. He would talk to the altar, sharing drink for drink. When the bottle showed signs of being emptied, he would cut off the altar's share. It had, had enough.

Then he would taunt the stack of rock and bone. Come and get the tequila. He would dance around inside the circle refusing to share. He would lift the candle to his lips, sending a fiery blast of the flaming liquid in the direction of the altar. This was his practice, his ceremony. He had conjured his own gods.

Tonight, Miguel was here to ask the gods a favor. Solders were looking for money. He needed to find the money before the solders did. This time he was devout; he left the whole bottle on the altar. He would only take a drink with the spirits permission. So, he took his first drink.

"Mirada, I have a surprise for you!" he pulled a fully cooked chicken from a bag, laying it on the pile of stones next to the bottle. Miguel mumbled some incantations in the direction of the chicken.

"? Que, you want me to have some pollo?" He reached out grabbing a leg quarter. Greasy fingers swinging the bone as a lecture tool.

"I have come to ask you to grant me a small request...Not for myself...For the people!" He should have known not to lie to gods.

Each time he took a portion of the offering, he lit a candle as a distraction. Soon the whole altar was washed in candle light. True to his nature he washed down the chicken with tequila. He did not use his goblet, hoping the gods would not notice him drinking their liquor, from the bottle. The heat from the candles raised the temperature of the liquid. He was so busy trying to communicate with the spirits, he never noticed vapor forming in the bottle. As he reached for a piece of chicken, the vapor caught fire with a whoosh.

Miguel stood in the center of his circle, swinging a flaming forearm in all directions. The altar was an inferno of melting candle wax, tequila and half eaten chicken. Overhead, in all directions birds took to wing, squawking as they went. The rush of heated wind, rising straight up, sent leaves drifting to the forest floor. The rustling leaves brought moisture from the canopy, dropping like rain, quenching the flames.

One would suppose the god's answer was no. Miguel felt; "if the gods could not hold their liquor, they really should not drink so much." Maybe he could find his answers in town.

CHAPTER TWENTY-THREE

Ceryle stalled as long as possible trying to act like he knew what he was doing. He had the cover off, delicately picking over the Volvo Penta engine parts. Oil was good. Air cleaner was brand new. He went as far as pulling a spark plug to inspect for carbon. Sarah sat by patiently with a nail file checking her manicure. She knew he was just trying to come up with an excuse to not run up the river to Jake's.

When he replaced the first spark plug Sarah turned to him and announced "You know how I like to check em? I like to see if they run!"

She reached down twisting the ignition key, the motor cranked right over. Ceryle could hardly argue with a craft so tight it sounded like a sewing machine. He replaced the cover, adjusted his straw hat, then cast the lines off from the dock. Sarah in a wicked mood, demanded to drive.

"My hat!" he called as she roared off.

"Really Ceryle I don't know why you wear that thing. It doesn't do a thing for you." suddenly she turned fashion consultant.

"Normally! When the damn thing comes off, I know I am going too fast!" he glared at her.

Jake was in the middle of a row of vegetables, weeding with a hoe. This was one of the things he loved in life, tending the soil. He cared for the garden and it provided a modest reward. Ernie had been out scouting for wild game on the back side of the property. He did not exactly sneak up on Jake. Jake was too absorbed in thought to notice anyone.

"Something big tried to cross those marsh flats -twice."

"How big?"

"Judging from a stick I used to poke at the mud, it was about my size" As they went to take a look it was quickly concluded it had to be a man. Any animal with a snout, would smell the water, before stepping into the mud. The dried prints on the other side were spaced bipedal. They had worked their way down the marsh to a sandier area but never crossed

The discovery was not too dramatic. Anyone from town may have been out wandering then got themselves stuck in the mud. The confounding notion was, they tried twice, to cross the marsh. Jake noticed from the sandy area; the river was in view. This may have been their whole objective, to line up with the river. Nothing to worry about, probably!

Jake went back to his cultivation, while Ernie sported with the need for defenses as a diversion. All he needed was some claymore mines, a little entrenching of a machine gun nest, a handful of grenades, side arm and rifle. He might need some night vision glasses. The situation may even call for ground to air support. He wondered where Jake kept the communications gear.

Jake smiled at the list. He did not ridicule Ernie, he just smiled. If he was serious, Jake would just patronize the man. Ernie was given a few hundred yards of trip line and a bunch of empty cans. That was as high tech as the compound could afford. Rather than being insulted Ernie dove into the project. At least it kept him busy for a few hours.

The tight little boat came screaming up the river. Even from a distance Jake could see Ceryle's white knuckles. Sarah didn't slow down on the approach. She maneuvered the craft to send off a strong bow wave, then pulled a three hundred sixty-degree turn. As the wave returned from the shore, she cut the engine. The bow wave slapped against the side freezing the boat in a moment of time. As the water leveled itself, the boat settled quietly at the dock. Ceryle was still looking for his hat.

Sarah saw Jake in the middle of the garden and wondered what connection such a simple man had with floosy's. Ceryle was just using Jake as a decoy, she thought. But it was a good excuse to visit. She left Ceryle to anchor the boat while she ran ahead to embrace her farmer.

He was glistening, sweating over the labor. His shirt was off. This was a turn-on to the normally sedate professor. Everything but the soiled hands which he tried to turn away to avoid contact. "What do you know about the flooseys?" she interrogated Jake, keeping an eye on Ceryle's progress down at the boat.

"What the hell are you talking about?"

This sounded a bit familiar to poor Sarah. She wanted to give Jake the benefit of the doubt. She was of the opinion; all men were part of a conspiracy when it came to extracurricular activities. Maybe it was her approach. Substitute a less offensive word for the term floosy's, pour some sugar on top. Too late here comes Ceryle.

"If you have any of the tranquilizer serum left, perhaps you could sedate Sarah. She been nothing but a pest all morning!"

Jake still had her in his arms. She was smiling like she knew she was safe. "So, what has she been up to this time."

"Perhaps we should take this inside." concealed Ceryle.

Sarah wasn't anymore thrilled with the story of militia. searching for a lost shipment of drug money, then she was with the earlier explanation regarding the floosies. Jake on the other hand was all ears. Ernie when he returned from booby trap duty was likewise inclined.

It was an ugly business, sorting the details. The glamor girls' portion of the equation, was easier to sell, now that Sarah saw these men were serious. There was a clear and present danger to the village if the militia took up permanent residence. Even the local constable was not prepared to deal with the cadre of armed insurgents. Ceryle made mention of the tiny Island of Grenada, talked about Panama, explained the fiasco of Honduras. For foreign gentry, he sure knew a lot of regional politics. Sarah became fearful of her small jungle paradise. This was her home, her Shangri-la. She had too much time in country, to allow common thugs to ruin it for her. She wanted to know what the men planned to do about it. Fly in as many floosies as necessary, just save the town.

"What floosies?" Ernie demanded.

CHAPTER TWENTY-FOUR

A shadow swept across the street, up a wall and into the hovel where Miguel collapsed on a cot from time to time. It was not his main residence, not that it was any better or worse. A steely blade poked the perimeter of the room. The earthen floor gave up a resounding thud. Moments later a trunk lay open, its contents strewn throughout the room. The shadow escaped through a window down the street into the night.

The shack like so many others belonged to no one. The only reason it existed was to provide temporary shelter to fruit pickers at the plantations of wealthy land owners. For most of the year a drunk need only stagger in and make himself at home. Via con Dios.

Anything left in the building, belonged to the next person who came along. In this case, a bunch of old uniforms and some military ribbons. Cockroaches had already eaten most of the papers, leaving pellets. A framed picture was chewed on all sides. The dog-eared photograph of an attractive woman was shielded in plastic. Even mothballs had no effect on the vermin. In the morning someone would find the mess and alert the constable. He would take an inventory making note of what was present then walk away, leaving it up for grabs. He may even keep the ribbons for himself. Some fruit salad for his dress uniform.

The only serious effect from finding the squatter shack in disarray, was looking for Miguel. The constable had been keeping him under eye for a long time. From the beginning of his stay at Bueno Rio, the man had tried to impress everyone with his military background. Finding uniforms could mean, he had finally crossed over the line to Loco.

The guardia made his way around the other shacks, some distant from the first. When he found his way closer to town his efforts were rewarded. Miguel lay sprawled on a straw cot. He almost did not recognize him at first because he was shaved and his hair was cut short. Miguel did not look as wild and fearsome as usual. Poking with a night stick he woke the man. The one thing a shave will not fix is the bleary-eyed gaze of a drunk. It was Miguel alright.

Long moments went by, while the hangover prevented Miguel from understanding the constable. He looked around his room, explaining it always looked this way. When he realized it was some other shack they were discussing, he denied having any thing to do with it. He changed his story again, when he found the visit was to locate the owner of a large trunk. Reward, for cooperation, was an easy sell.

Back at the original site Manuel was less blusterous. He had seen none of these things before. These were not his uniforms; he had never seen the beautiful woman in the photograph. As for the ribbons they were hardly something he would wear, they were US Special Forces. The constable let Miguel go on about his business.

This was a curious find in the village, so soon after the arrival of so many armed men. Miguel was as intrigued as anyone. It had him looking over his shoulder. He was still not sure what the armed men wanted in town. He knew they were not part of the revolution. Judging by the roach pellets, the locker had been buried years ago. There was hardly anything in inside such a large box. The revolution would have packed it full of a cache of weapons. A bulb clicked on in his tequila saturated brain. He waited for the guardia to leave. The uniforms and pictures were in custody, but the box was still in the hole. Miguel got down on all fours with his face in the box. A faint odor of rifle grease could be detected. There was another odor, the sickly-sweet ammonia of a plastic explosive. He pushed the litter away from the bottom of the box showing six indented impressions. He rose to his feet knowing it was no mistake. Someone was sending a message to Bueno Rio to be on its best behavior.

Eight men stood in line, as the other two inspected the troop. As it goes, they were inferior to another Cadre, but they passed muster just the same. The officers announced they would be leaving the following morning; everyone should get plenty of rest. Troop dismissed.

The only thing on anyone's mind was spending time with the beautiful Cabeza Rojo senoritas. It did not matter a tortilla shell the ladies were out of their league by a couple levels of credit. The men only wanted to gaze upon the sublime. They were tired of the thick ankles of the serving wenches of the cantina's. The redheads were as if heaven itself was sending a message, of what lay in the next life.

While the men had no problem spanking a cantina girl on her generous bottom, the brutes were on their best behavior around Kitty and Charlotte. They might not even tip a cantina girl, but for the Rojo they bought the most expensive drink in the house. Make it a double. They descended on the hotel lounge, despite the coat and tie requirement for the dining room. Even here they continued their apish behavior. It was only after Kitty and Charlotte entered the room anything like decorum was achieved. As with any occupation force, the officers percolated to the surface. They took their time naturally, allowing the subordinates to empty their wallets. At the point where the ladies had been properly lubricated, the officers took command. A familiar tactic to the ladies.

The highest-ranking member of the goon squad hardly outranked a cabana boy. Truth was a cabana boy probably had better prospects that these guys. The girls could have dusted him off, in the blink of an eyelash, but instead toyed with him. Just like a cat toy with a mouse. Kitty had fully recovered from the discovery of the quest to recover drug monies. Tonight, she was swirling a tiny parasol precociously. She played the dumb blonde better than anyone. One of her talents included heaving her cleavage around like a juggler. Keep your eye on the ball style. It was as distracting as entertaining. The operation was smooth and uncomplicated, looking perfectly natural, like a snake charmers' flute.

Charlotte had her own routine. She would squirm in her seat allowing her dress to rise up on her thighs. The unsuspecting males would be drawn in for a glimpse. Hocus- pocus, she would rise to visit the ladies' room with the dress bunched around her excellently structured legs. She would make one step, and the curtain came down on the performance. It was as if the dress had a mind of its own. The performance having an appearance of genuine grace. Even in crowded bars, her seat was always vacant for her return.

Ceryle walked in and stood to the side for a few moments admiring the program. It was his good fortune to know the behavior was a act. A recital and nothing more. Once upon a time, he had been the anxious gentleman holding the seat for Charlotte's return.

He was one of a handful of men, ever able to grace their salon. His mistake at that time was an inability to choose which love muffin was the sweetest. Moments later, did he discover, it was all a big bamboozle. His male pride restored by the confession he too, was a con artist. That moment was one of his fondest memories, and darkest nightmares. No confidence man wants to admit he'd been taken; hook, line and sinker. Worst, he had made his decision a microsecond too late. He chose Charlotte, it was always Charlotte.

Ceryle sent coffee to the ladies, with a message to meet him in the dining room. He was not going to risk challenging the thugs to a question of manhood. He knew Kitty and Charlotte could handle the situation.

The goon squad had no coats and ties. Soon they were not welcome at the bar, for without women to impress, they had no reason to feign decorum. When the girls had gone, they started demanding "Cervezas". The beer was delivered "too warm" and "too monkey piss". Soon the bartender refused to take their order. The whole troop got indignant. For a moment they threatened to tear up the place. An eight-foot-tall Samoan dishwasher   brought   clean   glasses   to   the   bar.   They   then   just went away.

"I thought you two were on the next Flight. "Started Ceryle.

"We would have been sweety, but the plane...." Kitty smiled. He could read her like a book. They were going to stay on a few days. No particular reason, just looking around. They could see the possibilities a town like Bueno Rio held.

"This could be the next Cabo St. Lucas or Veracruz." Charlotte offered. "All it needs is a facelift!"

"Don't we all?" interrupted Kitty.

"Then where will you buy vegetables? You can't just run around making tourist destinations out of anywhere you please." Ceryle advised.

"Ceryle, -I never took you for a tree hugger."

"Well think again! I like this place just the way it is, Primitive." He was working up a head of steam. "...donkey carts, live chickens, tables of fresh fruit..."

"Donkey shit chicken shit!"

"Muggers and rapists..." he chided.

"Hot and cold running water!" she mentioned weakly, sitting in the dining room of a modern hotel.

Ceryle was not done talking. He just knew he could never come up with an argument, sound enough, to satisfy the ladies. He used the breakfast order to switch conversation to the weather.

He hardly recognized Ernie when he sat down at the table. He was properly dressed with a decent manicured appearance, right down to his polished shoes. His tropical weight woolen suit held enough of a press to be presentable, without looking stuffy. Such a person would not require an invitation.

He traded salutations with Ceryle and swept right into introducing himself to the ladies. Kitty looked to be the loose end, so Ernie naturally drifted toward her. In moments they were thick as thieves. The breakfast bounced along merrily with common banter.

Luckily, the ladies excused themselves, to go powder their nose. Ceryle was waiting for the break. "What the hell are you doing?"

"Looked like you were over the limit, you needed to throw one back!" Ernie smiled, so full of himself he could just burst.

"Where did you get the clothes?"

"Where does anyone get a suit in Bueno Rio? I rented it from the mortician."

"Look, you got to get out of here. This isn't what you think. These are old friends of mine who are doing me a favor. Jake knows all about it." Ceryle pleaded.

"Yeah, well I'm doing you a favor by being here." cautioned Ernie, "As long as the ladies have escorts, the military presence can just go march up a flag pole."

True, but it didn't matter, because the girls were back in any case. Ceryle did not know what to make of it, but Charlotte winked at him, as she sat down. Any other time, he would have considered it a flirtation. With these ladies it could mean anything. Maybe they took Ernie as a mark. Ceryle had mentioned the hotel was full of engineers. The way Ernie was dressed it was likely the ladies would have made the mistake. But then it dawned on Ceryle; Ernie was not wearing a wedding band. Even a hint of a tan line would be acceptable. No wedding band no action. It was a puzzling development.

Charlotte and Kitty were not acting normal. They should be playing the bimbo act; if they were working Ernie. They were being clearheaded and cheerful without the usual extravagant adulated mannerism. Maybe they were just too hung over.

No, that could not be the case. Kitty always had trouble with clingy eyelashes when she was hung over. She would just keep adding mascara until she looked ridiculous. She wasn't having that trouble at the moment, so she could not be hung over. It was far too early in the day, for them to be drinking, too heavily.

Kitty now winked at Ceryle as she turned to Ernie "Oh, we'll be on vacation for a few more days..."

"Vacation..." said Charlotte softly, placing her hand on Ceryle's firmly. A gesture meant to calm his fears. It did anything but make him calm. He didn't know what they were up to, but something was going on. "Ceryle, you never told us you had a motor boat!"

CHAPTER TWENTY-FIVE

Sarah had a decision to make. She had sent samples of the serum to be studied at a laboratory in Atlanta. Her confirmation of arrival was short, nothing more than a cryptic notation. Bureaucratic gibberish was all it was. Soon behind the confirmation, came a letter to inform her the funding for the following year had been found. Separately it would not be unusual, for a basic research project, to find last minute funding. In combination with her serum samples, it was sinister. Someone back in the States was taking her research and running with the ball. They were going to keep her buried in the jungle, while they took all the credit.

On the other side of the scale was her sanctuary. The jungle had grown to be more than a job. This was her home. She was not even sure she could go back to the dirty overpopulated cities of mankind. Here there was a fresh cleanliness to everything. Every creature had a purpose. There was no urban decay. What had lost its purpose was reabsorbed back into the primordial soup of the jungle. Every creature, every bug, every stone reabsorbed; by a living life essence.

Her study of water was only a common denominator of the diversity. Every creature depended on water as a source of life. Her rudimentary tests, were nothing more than a qualification of the potential of the planet.

She sometimes stared into the gathering storm clouds in awe. Elementary Hydrogen would rush up to meet the Cumulus formations, furnishing the grounding connection for a lightning strike. Even the shape of the clouds gave her pleasure, knowing that the atmosphere was divided into layers. One layer was at seven thousand feet, twenty thousand feet, thirty thousand feet, her spirit soared.

A bird would catch her eye. She would see it diving from dizzying heights, to open its wings before crashing into the ground. The larger avian hovering on thermal updrafts, wings outstretched. Swooping down to snatch a meal from the forest floor. This was her jungle. How could she ever leave it behind.

It was a troubling decision. Some other clown was going to publish a paper; they had no right to publish. Doctor Jones would be sitting on their fat ass back in America while Sarah toiled away in the tropics. Doctor Jones would be well up the ladder to a Government Service Forty while Sarah hovered at a dismal GS fifteen. Doctor Jones would retire to the lap of luxury. Sarah did not consider retirement an option.

If there was any justice to the planet, Doctor Jones would die a lingering slow cruel death with plastic tubes and beeping machines. Not that Sarah wished anyone harm.

Not even the Doctor Smiths of this world. The potentate posing bastards. The type who earns a degree on the flimsiest of pretense, then walk around forcing everyone to call them doctor. She once knew a guy, who got a doctorate for turtle research, and ended up teaching pre-med course work. He always gave preferential treatment to the ladies of the class. She had once considered dropping a flaming Bunsen burner in his lap, as he ogled her in lab class. She reconsidered, only because professor flambeau would have hurt her academic standing.

She had to make a decision quickly. She knew she could hide out in the jungle indefinitely. It was only a matter of time before things had to change. Some day she was going to have to face the real world again. Conceivably now was as good a time as any. As she pondered the question, she began to ask herself, if she had any unfinished business.

Sarah did have one piece of unfinished business. She walked out of the bungalow, down to the river and borrowed a canoe. Up the river she paddled. She did not stop rowing until she arrived at the front door to Jake's cabin. She took him by the arm marched him into the bedroom and slammed the door shut.

Miguel worked his way around the swampy section of the low-lying area. He avoided the mud. Poking with a long pole he avoided his earlier mistakes. The man was determined to creep up on the gringo casa. He only wanted to sneak around, maybe find something to use to convince the town the gringos should leave.

Who was he kidding; he was there to steal anything not nailed down. It could not be anything unique. It needed to be something of value, yet common to Bueno Rio. It had to be something which would just naturally come into his possession. He would make up an elaborate story, after he found something to take away.

Waiting at each hiding place he made a slow approach. No one seemed to be around. Confidence grew as he advanced from bush, to barrel, to wheel barrow. If someone did discover him prowling, he was prepared to pretend to be lost and taking a short cut. The trick was to pop up out of the hiding place, acting like nothing was out of the ordinary. "Bienvinida", was always a good approach. Welcome the owner to his own residence. Put on a show, like it was all a friendly visit, from a good neighbor.

The back up plan was flimsy. Jake was never going to buy it. As he came closer to the house Miguel was more confident. His senses started to heighten. Ecstatic buoyancy was beginning to replace fear of being caught. Creeping around, felt like being inside a fish bowl. His sensitivity to noise increased. His heart was pounding, but his breathing was almost no existent. It was exhilarating, a drug like no other.

The tension only increased as he made his way inside the structure. Quietly, with determination, he picked through the effects of other people's lives. Looking, searching, poking into private recesses of the domicile, nothing seemed to catch his attention. What kind of people were these? It was as if they had nothing to hide. Everything was clustered in an attitude of utilitarian conformity.

He found something out of place, a coffee tin in the linen closet. As he examined the contents a new desire began to emerge. These filthy gringos had dirty pictures put away. He unfolded the top one, then the next. He could feel his crotch forming a ligature around his genitalis. Soon he would need three hands to continue examination of the contents of the can. He was losing the feeling of exhilaration, masked over by a swooning sensation. Finally, he dropped the can on the floor with a loud clanging sound. He held in his hand a few folded remnants of a cut up book of pornography.

Suddenly, something stirred in the next room. A voice asking another voice, "if they heard anything?"

Manuel's panic was like a trapped animal searching for a way out. An animal who would do anything to extricate itself even chew off a limb. He still had the pornography in his hands as he sprang from the rear door, trying to make it to the safety of the marsh. He ran like a rabbit. Scurry and hide. Scamper and run.

This was the flip side, of the high he was experiencing earlier. The absolute terror of having been discovered was a pitiful downer. His nervous system clicked over from the sublime to the chaotic in nanoseconds. To reinforce his confused status, the gringo was taking pot shots at him with a large bore rifle. All he could think to do was scamper and run. Scurry and hide.

Jake had taken one glance of the coffee tin on the floor. That glance was all it took. Behind the door to his room, he kept the rifle Ernie brought with him from up river. The slamming back door told him which direction to follow. He didn't even wait long enough to put on pants. He did not need anything but the rifle.

The shots landed dangerously close. Flecks of river pebbles flew in all directions. Scamper and run. Something gathered around one of his legs. Wire so ingeniously installed, it immediately was tangled, around his foot. Scurry and hide. Tin cans clattered as he ran. Oh, the horror of being hunted with a calamity of noise to give away his position. The whistle of a bullet rippled the air right beside his ear. Scamper and run.

Sarah was beside Jake now. She had the good sense to dress before leaving the bedroom. "You're not trying to hit him...are you?"

"Nope, trying to work him around into the deep muck!"

"Good let me have a shot at him" Sarah smiled evilly, "I don't like to be disturbed!"

Jake showed her the gun, present arms "Here ya go..."

Suddenly the bullets were a hailstorm with much greater accuracy. One of them almost nicked him. Scamper and run, clang- itty, clang, clang.

The further he ran; the more cans were trapped around his foot. Worst yet he had somehow stomped his way into knee deep mud. The cans were getting heavier by the moment. As he waded across the marsh the gunfire trickled down to an occasional blast tossing up mud.

He lay on the opposite bank heaving and writhing in agony. His lungs burned. The whole world was cut away from his vision. The line of cans was sunken in the mud holding him prisoner. If he had the energy, he would hold his arms up to surrender. Why struggle the inevitable would soon overtake him. He closed his eyes and passed out.

"So, you're just going to leave him there?" laughed Sarah.

"Yep" Jake turned and walked into the house suddenly aware he was without clothing.

"What if something eats him?"

"Well, I guess he should have thought of that before he broke in!"

They went about their business. Every now and then Sarah would peek out the door to see if Miguel was still there. Closing in on sunset she forced Jake to go check on the man. She knew if she didn't, she was never going to sleep that night.

As she paddled back to town, she was no closer to a decision than before. The unfortunate run in with Miguel showed her a side of Jake she never knew existed. Just when she was getting to know Jake better. He was still unfinished business.

After Jake sent her off in the canoe, he took a pair of lineman's plyers around to the other side of the marsh. He cut the wire holding the man prisoner. That was all he was willing to do. He knew it might be a mistake to let the incident go, but he was sure it would be a long time before he had any more trouble out of the man. He glanced down noticing the crumpled porno photos in the man's hand.

CHAPTER TWENTY-SIX

Charlotte and Ceryle were sitting alone at a table. They mature nature of the conversation was almost corporate. It was a merger of his acquisitions, with a leveraged purchase, of the properties held by the ladies. All of which; was a joint accounting, of twenty-five years' time invested.

"He's got the look!" Charlotte confided

"What look?"

"You know... the look" she rejoined. Seeing Ceryle was still foggy she turned his face to watch Ernie as he fawned over Kitty.

"He does look confident, doesn't he? returned Ceryle, now sharpening his vision. The man he saw was not a third world stumble bum. The fellow was calm, clever and cajoling. The look of a man without a care in the world, the least of which was money. Funny he had never noticed it before. Ernie was always, just Ernie.

"If I had to put a price tag on it...." she pauses waiting for Ceryle to catch up, "It would be a hefty amount."

"Hefty enough to make a goon squad take notice?"

"Why Ceryle you are a clever boy aren't you!"

Ceryle sat there for a few moments letting it sink in. He had never considered it before yet the provocative was plausible. Call it woman's intuition, call it an ingenious hunch, Charlotte was on to something.

"So, I suppose the two of you will play pluck the pigeon with the poor boy?" he ventured.

"I really can't say, um I'll have to let you know. Right now, Kitty seems to have the claws tucked in. She does that when she truly likes someone. If she starts prattling on about how wonderful he is, when were alone, I'll know for certain" Charlotte said with the air of a conspirator.

"So, it's true, you two are retired!"

"We are always retired, right up to the next caper!"

"Is that how I got you down here, on such short notice?"

"That and the opportunity to see a dear old friend, who is too much of a turtle to mix business with pleasure." She looked him square in the eye. Not the least glimmer of a smile on her face.

"Now Charlotte please, you know how I feel about you! You just never give me any clue as to when is a good time to..."

"Say it! To be ro-man-tic."

"To be romantic. I never know when to be romantic."

It was not a case of jungle style courtship. No one was swinging from the trees. Ceryle sliding his hand, to take Charlotte in tow, took an eternity. They did find their way to an observation window overlooking the river. Even here he had a problem working up the courage to put an arm around the woman. When he kissed her, it was a technique usually reserved for a sister.

Charlotte did not seem to mind. Over the years she had always treated him coldly. There was a good probability they were too close as friends, to ever be lovers. He was going through the act like a mechanical man. Looking into his eyes she found only desperation.

She decided to take pity on him, and kept direction his attention to sites through the large plate window. That he was willing to make the effort, was good enough for her. She did not need an immediate commitment; they had plenty of time.

Ernie on the other hand was blazing away. He was into Kitty like a ferret with a ball of string. In the short hours they had known each other he had mortgaged his future to a fanciful blueprint. White picket fence, dog in the yard, two car garage, anything he could think of, that she would want to hear. Never once did he make reference to ways and means of bringing this fantasy alive. He was having no problem planting petit kisses on her necks and ears. She did nothing to ward them off. He held one of her hands hostages while stroking her hair with the other. It was all so sweet as to make a diabetic lapse into a comma.

The evening rolled around, putting everyone in the diningroom. Ceryle with his hesitation. Ernie with his bravado. Charlotte as cool as a judge. Kitty just as confused as the seamstress of a Persian rug. It might as well have been a poker game. Everyone at the table had something to conceal. Most of the conversation was not small talk, it was minuscule. They may well have been talking about atomic particles. Every time someone started to bring up a subject, they realized they might- ought not.

The food arrived delicate and savory. Now there was something common to discuss. Of course there was wine. There were so many things on the table it was difficult to decide what to try next. With so much to try Charlotte was having a time deciding which dish to blame for her migraine headache. They all looked so good.

Just like prize fighters going to their respective corners, the party ended company. Ladies to their room, gentlemen out the door. Kitty was going to have a fair amount of explaining to do. Ceryle and Ernie tried to share a civil word. It was not they didn't like each other. It was like they were from two different dimensions. Finally, they just gave up trying and walked away in opposite directions.

Miguel was alive. He knew he was alive. He lay for a few moments wondering where he was. He remembered the events of the afternoon. He reached down after the injured leg and found a white gauze encircling the injury. Stumbling to his feet he found the chill of the night air comforting. He had woken in many strange places but this was different. This time he was sober. Usually, he did not offend himself with his personal hygiene. This time the stink of the mud, and the sweat, made sobriety bothersome. He limped off into the dense overgrowth, looking for fragrant foliage to towel off his body. His bowels came gurgling to life. He wiped himself with the same leaves.

This was just one more violation to hold against the gringos. His twisted logic always made him the victim. Two men had been shooting at him. He was the hero, standing up outnumbered, two to one. His mind set about the task of arranging the event, into a courageous assault, in the face of superior forces. He was not a sneak thief; he was a patriot. The same way a ghetto hoodlum makes a stand against the establishment, by ripping off an apartment. His severe mental disorder made everything he did righteous. At the moment he had an overwhelming desire to spend time at his sacred place. The gods would hear his problems. They would show him what to do, as he licked his wounds. He would never make it all the way home on a night like this anyway.

A shadow swept past the squalid shack Miguel used for his living quarters. Again, a steel probe examined the dirt flooring. The clinking of metal on metal was cause for examination. Silver plated dinnerware was buried in the hole. Nothing of value just transient trash belonging to anyone. The steel probe kept searching.

Again, there was the sound of metal on metal. This time the clink was muffled by a sturdy cloth. A gun wrapped in oiled cloth. No doubt who owned the AK-47. Inside the oilcloth the weapon was poorly maintained. It had the odor of a piece put away without being cleaned. The hole was wallowed out slightly deeper. Under the weapon was positioned a booby trap. The ordinance would only go off if someone went looking for the hidden weapon. Remove the gun from the hole, and hello St. Peter. Carefully the earthen floor was restored.

The shadow lingered just long enough to erase any footprints from the dirt floor. Just like a puff of smoke it vanished into the night mist. It was the perfect justice. Execution of the guilty. Whoever put the weapon in the hole was guilty by association. It did not matter if the punishment was delivered in days, weeks or months, the guilty would be executed.

"I'd a plugged that bastard...." Ernie was passionate.

"Look, you never want to kill anyone!" Jake pleaded.

"That guy is never going to stop being a pain in the ass, as long as he's walking the planet!"

"I know that!" grimaced Jake

"You missed the perfect opportunity..." Ernie's voice broke "We could be done with that guy forever."

"Thou shalt not kill..."

"Save it for the pulpit, no jury in this jungle would ever convict you for protecting your own property."

"You really don't get it, do you?" Jake looked him in the eye.

"Get what?"

"The spiritual connection of all things!"

"Jake you are gonna have to save the bible thumping for someone else. I'm an agnoticator."

"I'm not talking about the Bible! It's in all the books, the Torah the Koran, even Zen tradition. When you take the life of someone else, you project a portion of their spirit, onto yourself. Your spirit is tainted by the spiritual essence of the man you killed."

"Maybe you ought to talk to somebody else about this..." Ernie demanded, then for no reason he added; "OK tell me more!"

"I think it was the great plains Indians of the last century who had a handle on the subject. They thought the spirit of a warrior went on to serve the victorious."

"Kind of like a spirit guide?"

"Exactly, except they did not have a concept of evil. They had fortunate and unfortunate, but not evil."

"Well pal, I got news for you; there is plenty of evil in the world."

Jake watched him patiently "That's what I am trying to tell you." He fell silent, not sure if he should continue to preach. These were his own private thoughts on the subject. Years of reading trying to make sense out of jumbled documentation. He himself had participated in grand displays of National superiority. It was one of the reasons he chose to hide himself away from the world in the backwoods of a nameless jungle.

Ernie out of the blue provided, "Oh, I get it, by killing an evil person, you attract their Evil!"

"Something like that." Jake crossed his arms in front of his chest, "As a matter of fact, there are cults which believes as much."

"What if the guy is just another grunt, on the other end of a bullet?" Ernie the agnostic was warming right up to the subject.

"I don't know, I have never been able to work that out..."

"Well, if the guy is basically good, just on the wrong side, killing him is not a problem."

"Boils down to self-defense! How much are you gonna let the other guy take before you stand up to him." Jake pushed back in his chair. "That man didn't take anything, so I didn't have to kill him!"

There was much more to his philosophy. That damn war in Southeast Asia spilling over into Cambodia and Laos. The Communist party trying to persuade the American public to picket Congress for Peace. The whole thing was sloppy. Fifty years of a Cold War.

Fifty years of two colossal war machines keeping peace in their respective hemispheres. The minute Russia relaxed its grip an avalanche of internal conflicts erupted. It was like the baby sitter was caught napping. The soviet presence was withdrawn and the people used any excuse to go kill a neighbor. What moral depravity, ever condoned killing a fellow human being, was beyond the grasp of poor Jake.

What about now, what about the present. Nations had agreements favoring the two giants of power. Now there was only one World Wide Policeman. All the nations would do any ass kissing, they could think of, to cozy up to the United States. Some of the people seemed to enjoy their butts tongued by foreigners.

The Good Cop-Bad Cop role, of the soviet years was impossible to pull off. A Good Cop has to catch the criminal in action. All the emerging nations had only one standard to consider; Democracy.

What a cluster. Most of them had never attuned themselves to anything servicing natural resources. Go to the border of Guatemala, and see how the Mexican population has stripped their side clean of anything to fuel a cook fire.

It is no mistake the Mexicans want into a country where even firewood is plentiful. Even the overly ambitious, pompously, bureaucratic; North American Treaty Alliance could not keep up its promise. All it did was send workers north looking for training. They weren't going to get training in Mexico; consequently, they weren't going to get jobs.

America was being invaded and no one thought twice about it. Wild fires in the California Hills. A small coincidence, right in front of bulldozers and cranes. Homes being slapped up so fast, it was a wonder any of them made it past a wind storm.

Maybe this was why Jake was down in the jungle. Maybe he was ahead of the mass exodus sure to happen eventually. Maybe he was hiding from a civil war based on ethnic variation. He sure was not going to kill anyone based on the color of their skin. He did not even know if he had it in him, to form ranks against an opposing army, regardless of the cause. Just how far he was willing to surrender was another dilemma.

He could have gunned down Miguel, and probably should have, but he held back. If this was a subdivision somewhere, the man would be a simple prowler. So, in his own way, Jake brought with him civilization. A point requiring reinforcement by the actions of others.

The town of Bueno Rio was only a civilized as it allowed itself to be. It was also as lawless as it's people. This Miguel was only testing the limits of village tolerance. Jake was not the conscience for the town, its ethics, its morals. He did not have to have things, his own way. This was a luxury that comes with age, he thought. Once or twice over the years he was not given a choice. Stand and deliver, for old glory. Hold the line by whatever means, at whatever cost. That doesn't really give a guy too many options.

All one can hope for, is that man he just killed was not harboring an unclean spirit.

"That's what I was trying to explain; the transmigration of souls" Jake looked around he was sitting by himself.

CHAPTER TWENTY-SEVEN

Ernie thought they were done talking. He had taken a piece of hard wood with a bend in it, fashioning a putter. Using small balls of the brick material, he was playing putt-putt golf in the next room. Each ball had an erratic roll, different from the next This only made the game more challenging. If he smacked it too hard, the ball cleaved in two. Every once in a while, the ball actually landed inside a tin can turned on its side.

Jake was as amused as Ernie. The only thing to do was go out and search for a putter in the wood pile. He found something long enough, and hard enough, with a wooden knot at one end. One ingenious stroke of a hatchet put a putter face on the wooden knot. The front room was too small for competition. They moved into the yard. The single hole became two holes, followed by eight holes. Ernie insisted they put in a odd nine holes, to make it official.

"Golf, now there's a game. Ernie insisted, "You against a hole in the ground. You don't even need a partner."

"Shut up I'm trying to putt." grinned Jake.

Allegations of impropriety naturally surfaced. Allowances for the imperfection of the balls was administered. Each player was given a choice of ball in play. But Ernie was the master of distraction. Whenever Jake had a good position, Ernie would get him to smack it hard. Hard enough, to send half of it one way, half another.

It didn't even take an hour, for them to become serious of the outcome of each hole. Soon the tee off marker was a recessed brick. Each hole was a tin can sunk in the dirt. They even took to using scorecards.

Now, it was skill at the play of the ball, which mattered. Skill and in Ernie's case guile. He had more conversation whenever it was Jake's turn.

"What did you say about the transmigration of souls?"

Jake was as much of a natural born duffer as the next man. He would quietly make the shot and turn the tables, by answering the question on the other man's turn.

"You ever hear of Exorcism?" Jake muttered, knowing that would take a lot of concentration. He planned Ernie's next shot would be goofy.

He was wrong. The lineup was dead on the hole. Ernie was able to empty his head at will. "Beg your pardon, what were you saying?"

Jake knew two could play at that game. They went on for another hour. Each asking a question, just before the other man shot the ball. Never answering a question. Ernie was up. One ball to take the impromptu tournament. He drew back, inhaling on the up stroke. Pause at the top of the swing, exhale. The ball cleaved cleanly in two. Jake the winner by default.

Nothing if he was not a good looser, Ernie showed Jake some of his other hand made clubs. He had a driver, a pitching wedge, a five iron which was really a wooden club. He was working on a whole bag of clubs. Just something to pass the time, waiting on the day, they would leave for the Cayman Islands. They lined up a handful of stones down by the river. Each took turns pelting the rocks as far as they could.

Jake really got a hold of one, and it felt good. It didn't slice, it didn't hook, it didn't fade. It just took off. That rock sat in the sky forever, before dropping into the river. Both he and Ernie stood there in amazement. It was the kind of shot where a man is instantly addicted to the game. Were it a driving range, Jake would be going for another bucket of balls. Knowing it would never happen again, he handed the club to Ernie. Ernie declined the offer, choosing to work on his pitching wedge.

"You know this gives me an idea." said Jake.

"Are you thinking what I'm thinking?" Ernie pelted one sideways.

"That depends! How much do you think it costs to build a golf course?"

"Who do I look like Jack Nicholas?"

"I'm serious! Look we already have a hotel. Engineers need something to do besides drink in the bar."

"Hold on a minute..." Ernie clubbed one into the brush ten feet away. "After we set up a Caman Islands account..."

"Who says we have to open an account?"

"Anybody in their right mind! That's who!" Ernie teed one up, looking at it like it was a diamond. He was considering every aspect of the rock. Inhale on the back swing, let the club head fall, control the face of the club. Cer-plunk, the stone soared. "Golf course, Huh?"

"Eighteen holes, carts, the whole enchiladas."

CHAPTER TWENTY-EIGHT

Jake could see Ceryle pull up at the dock. He was not in his usual leisurely attitude. The way he worked the lines looked all business and professional. He even tossed his hat back in the boat as he came ashore. Ceryle always had a worried look on his face, today it was even more pronounced. Jake greeted him at the doorway with hot coffee.

He took the offered cup then announced "Twenty Percent!"

"What the devil are you talking about?" Jake demanded.

"Twenty percent after expenses, to keep a lid on the pot of gold."

"Ceryle, have you been drinking?"

"Don't play games with me. I know you and Ernie are the ones who have the money those armed thugs were looking for."

Jake did his best to act like he didn't hear, what he just heard. It was not like he could trust the man, if the cat was out of the bag. He started looking around for Ernie. He found him, grabbed him by the nape of the neck, and sat him down at the table. "Ceryle, tell him what you just told me!"

"It all came to me while I was watching Ernie with Kitty. I asked myself what could make him so confident in the company of such women. I mean, most men tremble in their presence. But not Ernie."

"Maybe he's just a commodious fellow. You ever think of that?"

Ceryle puckered up his school master face. It was a look of the wise flushing truth from errant students. "Yes, I did. But then I have to count on the intuition of two very sensitive ladies"

Jake and Ernie looked at each other. Neither of them felt the least bit of guilt regarding the stolen money. It was just a lotto jack pot. Actually, the odds were better than lotto. Stumbling over a drug shipment in South America was not even a thousand to one odd. They took the chance, and they were holding the payoff.

"Say, that Kitty is one fine woman, isn't she?" Ernie kibitzed. He was trying to steer the conversation.

"Yes, yes, but its Charlotte who is the keen observer..." Ceryle said, "She can tell exactly; how much a man has in his pockets when he walks into a room. For instance, the other night you had five hundred dollars when you joined us for dinner."

"Wrong! I had four hundred and eighty-eight." corrected Ernie.

"How much was the rental of the suit?"

"Twelve bucks...." He smiled broadly.

This was not going the way Ceryle planed. He was ready to make them an offer, yet he was shy, one confession. They had to admit they had the money. Jake and Ernie shut up tighter than a couple of clams. He decides to turn tactics. "Where do you have it hidden?"

He turned to Jake, then to Ernie. Both of them acted like they wanted to say something, neither one did. Ernie was using his best military face. It was the look of a man at parade rest. Jake too was giving the nine-mile stare. Looking off into the distance, completely isolated from the present surroundings, the two waited for a signal to be; at ease.

"Alright, perhaps I was wrong..." Ceryle turned tactics "But if the two of you don't look like a cat with a canary, I don't know who does!"

Ernie broke the silence."Ceryle, you ever play golf?"

It took a while for Jake to fashion a putter for Ceryle. Addition of a third competitor made for exciting play. The whole time Ceryle kept chipping away at the ball, he kept chipping away at the truth. He only had to smash a thin veneer before he knew the men would crumble. He made every excuse to leave them alone from time to time. He needed his hat out of the boat. Would anyone care for a Cuban cigar. He needed a sip of water. Each time he observed them in heated conversation, which ended abruptly, when he returned.

Upon tallying up the score, Ceryle was in the lead. His opponents were distracted. The players went down to the driving range at the river's edge. Hardwood cracking against stone was a world away from elegant. Yet they waited for the inevitable. Ceryle caught one just right, and he was transformed. It felt so good. The shot was at least two hundred yards right down the middle. Now the two men pounced on him.

"We want to build a Golf Course." Jake mentioned as he lined up on a stone. He swung away, a gentle lob with the pitching wedge. It was clear he had been practicing. The stone flipped out seventy-five yards and sank. It was all one fluid THIS motion, like a machine.

"A Golf what? You silly whankers." Ceryle teed up another stone. The rock went flying, skipping on the top of the water. It skipped about nine times before stopping. It was almost as satisfying as the earlier lob. "Go on tell me all about it." he conceded.

Ernie burst into a sales pitch normally reserved for new cars. He started drafting pie charts in the dirt. Nine holes to start, with a putt-putt course, and driving range. Eventually twenty-seven holes with a tennis court. The hotel already had a small pool.

"You really are daft the both of you...a golf course is a major project. Who do you think will play the course?"

"Ranchers, planters, and engineers!" Jake offered.

"We could be a real boost to the Bueno Rio economy." added Ernie, slapping down a stone, and swinging without even looking.

"Have either of you ever even played golf?"

"Well, no, but that's not the point. The game wouldn't even exist if people did not play it!" Ernie mumbled. He dabbed around in the dirt drawing a map of the town. Here was the hotel, there was the church, another stone for the market place. Then he drew separate fairways. It was clear he had given it some thought. The course was almost all clear of jungle growth. It was stripped of firewood faggots over the course of many generations. The people of town hardly bothered with the denuded area. They went further out into the forest floor, to collect fuel for their small clay ovens. The open areas were perfect fairways.

"I think what my partner is saying is that the potential for profit is well within the scope of investment." Jake clearly stated.

Ceryle saw an opening. The word partner was the sinker. It came off Jake's lips just a smidgen too professional to be a mistake. They had as good as admitted they had the capital for a large project. Now it was for him to devise a strategy, to link his own contribution. "Let's just say I deliver to you, the equipment you need, at a twenty percent markup from wholesale. C.O.D."

"Could you excuse us for a second?" Jake took Ernie the one side.

"What do you think?"

"Sure, beats the lame notion you had, of making bricks!"

"I don't know, sounds like we're asking for trouble. It's all a damn fool business. I say we forget about the golf course and just keep the money." Jake pleaded.

"Who gives a damn? He knows we have it. Let's get him on our side. Twenty percent is nothing!"

"What do you mean nothing? That's a fortune by itself." Jake's face turned red in emphasis of his point.

Ceryle could not help but notice Jake turn red. He was thinking to himself of lowering the charge to ten percent. No that would be a weak posture. He would increase his demand to thirty percent and then allow them to whittle the fee back down. At the same time, he was entertained at the whole idea of putting a golf course in Bueno Rio. What a hair brained idea. Even if every engineer bought a full set of clubs, it was only...! Wait a second...! That was a chunk of change. Greens fees. Golf balls. Not to say anything about membership in a club house.

Bueno Rio was due for a facelift. It was only a matter of time before it was developed. Latin America was always developing from the center out, squashing the landscape into an urban nightmare. This was an opportunity to set aside a park in the center of the town. It might even be a chance to influence a planned community.

His head started to swim thinking about the prospect. He was no urban planner, but he thought like a capitalist. One square mile was enough ground to build almost four thousand residential units, spread out in a subdivision with roads. They would need schools, churches and hospitals. A suburban community, centered around a municipal golf course. The idea almost seemed plausible. A little agriculture, a little tourism, Bueno Rio might be the next Branson, Missouri.

"Thirty percent? I thought you said twenty?" Jake snarled.

"I heard him say twenty." Ernie chimed in.

"Ok, ok, twenty percent over wholesale. Do we have a deal?"

CHAPTER TWENTY-NINE

The first thing off the seaplane was a couple of crates and four wheels. Nobody ever mentioned who would assemble the golf cart. All three of the men took a stab at the directions. It was a calamity. The instructions were in hieroglyphics. Nothing seemed to have the right sized bolt for the myriad holes. Somehow in the hours they worked on it everything finally fell into the correct position.

By unanimous decision the crew decided to give the cart to the Chief of police, as a gift. When the chief of police, is also the mayor, it makes for easy cooperation to shower him with favors. It is never too soon, to lubricate a friendly relationship with the guardia urbano. He had many errands to run every day. A golf cart would suit the task nicely.

An old Gravely tractor was left over from the construction at the hotel. The cost to ship it back was more than the thing was worth. Ernie struck a deal to purchase the tractor from the owner. It only had a drag bucket, but that did nicely to scrape a long narrow center of each link. He'd go out a hundred yards then spin a donut with the tractor. Another hundred yards and another donut. He kept it up for days at a time. It looked a confused mass of crop circles. Gradually it came together. So far, the cost was nothing special. They could bail out at any time and no one would blame them.

As the shipments came rolling in, the pilot started complaining he would have to get a bigger plane. They needed a mower for the Gravely tractor, which to be transported, had to come in pieces and parts. A load of grass seed came on the same trip. When they assembled the mower, they realized they had no way to spread the seed.

The obvious grabbed hold of them, they should hire people to help. There was no shortage of a labor force its Bueno Rio. If anything, there were too many unemployed. The agricultural interests of the region kept them waiting most of the year for the times they would be needed. Young people usually left to make a mark in the world. Some stayed at home caring for their parents. A job with wages was almost as foreign as moon rocks. It was a wonder the town even existed at all. Even the scant few jobs as maids and porters at the hotel were coveted.

Ceryle suggested they wait to do anything with a labor force. Word spreads quickly. People start collecting from the country side. Even a part time job would have people fighting for the position. Jake agreed, knowing; in the border towns of Mexico, maids were sometimes murdered to grab her spot as a domestic servant.

Ernie just kept running the tractor over the same forty acres, Some of it on one side of the road some on the other. Ceryle made the pitch to the mayor, for discovery of who to contact to buy the property. The man seemed to be confused. Just so happens the ownership of property in the area was seemingly a case of Squatters Rights. So long as no one came forward to complain, those forty acres belonged to the Golf Course.

"If we improve it, we own it!" Ceryle explained to the others.

"Does he know forty acres is only enough room to put in nine holes?" Ernie countered. "We eventually want to go twenty-seven holes that's...one hundred twenty acres." He counted on his fingers.

"He doesn't seem to care just as long as no one else claims the property." confided Ceryle.

"Where is the loophole?" Jake wondered aloud.

"Well, I did mention the possibility of a taxable donation to the city of Bueno Rio."

"What do you mean -City? If it wasn't for the hotel this wound not even be considered a town."

"Exactly, there is no city. When the two of you came up with this lunacy, I was skeptical, but now I am blown away with your insight."

"What the hell are you talking about, what Insight?" Ernie asked.

"Have you ever heard of a City Charter?"

"No!"

"Well, it is a puny little document confirming a geographical location is a city." Ceryle patiently explained.

"So, what does that mean?"

"Bueno Rio does not have a Charter, and they never will, until someone sits down and draws one up."

"Palooka-ville!" A bulb went on in Jake's mind.

"Beg your pardon?"

"We are living in Palooka-ville. We don't count because we don't have a piece of paper to prove we count. Palooka- ville, don't you get it?"

"Sure, whatever, as I was saying, all we need to do is..."

"Lay out our one hundred twenty acres for the golf course, then get the mayor to charter the city of Bueno Rio." Jake interrupted. "We end up with a town center!"

"Exactly!" Ceryle agreed.

"It would be like owning Central Park."

"No, it would be better than owning Central Park. We could form a corporation holding the Golf Course as a taxable revenue for the city of Bueno Rio. In other words, we become the government to the city."

"I don't know if I want to get involved in politics in Latin America sounds pretty risky." Interrupted Ernie.

"No don't you get it...The only thing wrong with Latin American politics is despot government. With a charter we can have a constitution. With a constitution we can have free democratic elections."

"Yeah, right up to the next cu de ta. These people just don't seem to handle freedom to well." was Jake's pessimistic opinion.

Ernie looked up from the bolt he was working with, and said, "Aw for Christ's sake who's gonna attack a golf course?"

Ceryle set about the task of composing a significantly long and boring City Charter. Hour upon hour was spent making the document as complicated as he could.

He was looking for volume, calculated by sheer weight. He was looking for five pounds of paper. In the text he tried to specifically contradict each "whereas" with a "therefore". He wanted to be able to later change any argument, to suit his purpose.

As a matter of formality there was the question of taxable contributions to ensure the success of the project. Knowing the golf course would be the major contributor, he was inclined to go as low as possible. He considered a one percent tax. It didn't seem right. Eventually the cantina's would be contributors, as would the hotel. Right now, they did not legally pay anything. Whenever the mayor needed anything, he simply passed the hat. They all kicked in something and he went away happy.

He thought about two percent, but figured it would cost that much, just to collect and administer the fund. The magic number was three percent, sales tax. He kept the document wording jumbled enough, to include other taxes later. No need to scare anyone with income tax, and property tax, and luxury tax, and motor vehicle registration tax. He included them all; he just buried them in fine print. If he needed to, he could always drag them out later, for a referendum bail out.

Even bringing up the concept of taxation was going to be a hard sell. These people did nothing unless there was some visible benefit. They were not going to support a tax on anything. Ceryle was going to have to present his plan as free money, from the golf course. That way no one could argue they stole the land.

He avoided tampering with the system of kick back to law enforcement. Here in Bueno Rio, just like in New York City, there was graft. Nobody had anything, so nothing ever got stolen. Just in case something did happen, a few police officials were on hand. They would do to sort things out. Just like in a New York delicatessen, the cantina's fed the Police to make sure nothing did happen. Unlike New York there was no money exchanging hands. No body had any money.

The few pesos in circulation, all came from odd jobs, handed out by planters and ranchers. Even the larger portion of the town budget came from this source. It was like a maintenance agreement. The land owners allowed the town to exist, in order to secure labor on their fiefdom.

In portions of South America this practice was nearly five hundred years old. It was only in the last one hundred years, where the population grew faster than the labor demand. There was always an overburden of crops, harvested for the world marketplace.

Places like Bueno Rio were lucky, compared to the shanty towns of the major cities. Latin America just seemed to avoid a middle class. But then Latin American political intrigue runs hot and cold. Whole portions of the population migrated, to more favorable living conditions, without benefit of basic education. That is easy to do, when everything someone owns, they can carry on their back

It was a multi-generational fiasco. Civil war went on for so many years, with each new wave of revolution, sweeping away the goals of the last revolution. The history of Latin America was littered with unanswered prayer. Somewhere along the line people forgot; the Lord helps those who help themselves. The overly pious population expected a angel to deliver their daily bread. When they got tired of waiting, they made a habit out of picking up guns. Too often a candidate for national reform was assassinated right in the middle of a speech. How rude!

Western political theory was constantly charged with providing a new improved version of the same old worn-out diplomacy. Everywhere a new adventure in urban planning was ripe. Give the people what they need to build a orderly social climate. Food, shelter, medical and spiritual care the freedom to choose a destiny, all part of the political quest.

A golf course. Why not a golf course as a focus of a community? A small grain of sand in an oyster, forms a pearl.

CHAPTER THIRTY

Sarah did not like the way the golf course was laid out. She had the education and credentials to back herself. Part of her undergraduate work was geology. If they kept scraping the hill side vertically the rains would wash away the whole hill. She surveyed the carnage. Her recommendation was to only move dirt horizontally. She dug out old magazines with photographs of terraced earthworks, to support her proposal. She was a clever politician, most women are.

She was not saying it could not be done. She was saying, it would be better to do it, a different way. As with most women, it did not phase her one bit, that she was not the one doing the work.

Ernie was the one doing the work. His take on the subject was she was just another bon-bon eating, - interference. Fortunately, the woman had Jake on her side. He was willing to listen to what she had to say. When he decided she was correct, all work stopped. He was not willing to risk a mudslide to prove her wrong. Ceryle put in his two cents worth and the project took off in a new direction.

The Maya and Inca had uniform earthworks running horizontal to the lay of the land. Here and there these earthworks were marveled over by a whole generation of scholars. Some called them timeless. Ceryle was the first to mention; it would make for a very attractive South American golf course. He was agreeing with Sarah, without disagreeing with Ernie. Finding himself to be in the minority, Ernie decided to obey the democratic process. It wasn't any big change. All he had at the moment was a bunch of donut shaped points of reference. In his mind's eye, they were connected vertically. He could just as easily connect the dots horizontally. Having made this mental adjustment, he saw the project unfold in a completely new direction.

"That's gonna be one boring golf course." he mentioned, to reaffirm control more than anything else.

"How so?" Sarah played the consulate diplomat.

"You just cannot have a staircase course. It's got to have tricky spots with dog legs and sand traps." He argued.

"Just do the best you can." She advised.

The whole town of Bueno Rio was beside itself with questions. How, this was going to help the local economy, was unanswered. The people saw it as just one more unnecessary influence on daily life. Even the prospects of jobs were met with disdain. The hotel had offered jobs, maids, porters and the like. They all worked a rotation at the hotel, in between being fired, for some misunderstanding. It was the way they were treated. They were forced to follow rules. Better to be drinking in a cantina, than being berated on infractions of the rules.

As one toured the market place the tension was present. A thin veneer of civility sheltered the vendors true feelings. Over the years Jake was never made to experience being an outsider. Now that he was, all those years cloistered on his own homestead meant nothing. They all treated him well during those days. Now that he was part of a change coming to the town, they looked at him in a different light.

As he passed between the stalls, he could hear whispers. He had never had this problem when he minded his own business. When he first arrived there had been whispers, but he never noticed it, when everything was new to him. He had a new appreciation of the plebeian power of rumor and innuendo. He did not want to stand out in a crowd. Especially not now. He wanted to do everything in his power to blend into the town.

Out of sight, is out of mind. He tried to avoid everyone as much as possible. They would have nothing to discuss, if he and Sarah acted normal. She was well liked only for the fact she was a strong woman. Somehow a woman especially a strong woman is always accepted. Towns just seem to enfold a woman into the community.

It may have been the towns people who approached Sarah with concerns about the Golf Course. The way things work, she may have been chosen spokesperson, without her knowledge. They put her in an unenviable position. This person would speak to that one, they would speak to another. Finally, someone would speak to Sarah. Sarah was then supposed to speak to the men.

Ernie's first impression had been; "I don't take orders from...."

"You better not end that sentence." Jake suggested.

"...newcomers. I was going to say newcomer." he lied.

As it was the small change was not going to affect the project in the least. They were still toying around with design. Nothing was going to happen overnight. Better to go slow, in the beginning, where mistakes were not going to cost much to fix. They were still working out of coffee tin money, and there was still plenty of that.

Strangely, the interference came at a time where the project needed some development. Better to make mistakes on paper than in the jungle. If they put in nine holes it was forty acres. Eighteen holes would take eighty acres. Ernie would have torn up the whole one hundred twenty acres for a twenty-seven-hole golf course. This was a bad idea. Business acumen required having a saleable product. Get the engineers onto the course, then wet their appetite by enlarging the facility.

Put in a putt-putt course. Mention how nice it would be to have a driving range. Put in a driving range. Mention how nice it would be to have a nine-hole course. Put in a nine-hole course. Mention expanding.

Ceryle liked the new plan. He needed the time to conjure up a five-pound document. The way things were running it was going to take some time. He was shuffling between the mayor and the hotel lounge like the ace of spades in black jack. Every single engineer he spoke to said they would play the links after they were built. The mayor was more than happy to see a sports complex in his tiny town. Perhaps Ceryle could include a small area for soccer. Ceryle was in no position to say no. He left the subject, pending examination of the committee.

The whole time he omitted mentioning the committee was a small one. For his purposes the spoke of an outside investment conglomerate. Better to speak in abstract terms than to let everyone know he was bluffing.

The grant was in place for Sarah to stay on for another year. She was finished trying to snare a portion of the neurotransmitter biochemical research. To hell with it! Eventually they would need to contact her, one way or the other. When they did, she would be able to gain some recognition for her contribution.

She could even ignore Jake, as the reason she chose to stay. Their relationship was now real and tangible. But she refused to believe it was his fault, she still wanted to escape the outside world. With the planning of the golf course, she had a new passion. Photography, was going to consume her free time as never before. She wanted to document the pristine jungle before the encroachment of man.

The town as it stood, was a quaint picturesque riverside. She wished she had seen it before the hotel. Most of the modern homes were of concrete block. The earlier houses were wood framed of a local lumber. Before this, the houses were mud brick, painted ornate colors on the exterior. These were the ones she marveled over. How anyone, could live so close to nature, piqued her curiosity.

The normal lay out of a mud brick house was simply four walls with a thatched roof. She had been inside one or two, examining the clever roof beams and interwoven palm leaf shingles. Above the main floor was a sleeping loft. At one end was a cooking oven built into the wall. The dirt floor was covered by intricately woven palm leaf mat.

Some of the more ornate mud brick dwellings were quite sophisticated. Of these, there was one with a courtyard, surround by three rooms and a barrier wall. From the outside it looked very simple. On the inside the home was quite complex. The three ground floor rooms provided enough support for four lofts. The central courtyard, complete with a passive cistern, hosted an area for weaving. This close to the equator heating was not a concern. The sleeping lofts were kept free of insects by the cook fires smoke. It was easy to see how someone living in the jungle could be self-sufficient in such a structure. It was a happy place. Sarah felt compelled to include these structures in her photographic journal. Already some of these were lost without a trace. The mud brick leveled to build more modern structures.

There was also the amorphous combination of tin roofs on the mud brick buildings. This was a bad design, for now when the wind blew the whole structure rattled. The mud brick was only walls. The roof was held in place by stanchions sunk in the ground. As the roof swayed, in the wind shear, the mud brick came loose. The older design of thatched palms was more resilient in a strong wind. So, the people living in harmony with nature were actually more advanced than those trying to improve the design. Vainglorious to prove tin roofs were better, the whole blueprint for a structure had to be redrafted

So, the next oldest structures on the town were wood framed. With tropical hardwoods in abundance there was still no shortage of building supplies. The river once provided a saw mill with power. Nails were the only thing not available locally. Nails and tin roofs. Then when everything started to warp, they needed paint. As long as someone was shipping paint they might as well send a sample of a cinder block

When enough cinder block samples arrive at a location there is always someone going to put them to use. That is known as progress. Back to the blueprints. Someone built a house. Then another house was built. The town of Bueno Rio never saw it coming. Next thing they knew, there was a hotel standing, down at the water front.

Sarah wished she had started taking photographs sooner. There was so much to chronicle. She had saved a tidy sum living humbly here in the jungle. That is why most people take the position. She became a regular at the dock, dropping film off, picking it up on the next flight. It was expensive, but the processing was better than doing it herself.

She became a regular snoop. Always on the hunt for a moment worthy of capture. It did not interfere with her work; it enhanced the job. She even used black and white to see if she could match the work of Ansel Adams. She would constantly be caught in a moment of awe, at the prospect of severe camera angle.

The talk of that stupid Golf Course was what tripped her fuse. Ernie bouncing around the open field, spinning donuts. The landscape she had come to know was changing. She was the Indian, with settlers on the horizon. She felt it her duty to record the change. Everything took on significance. a new special

She even tried to appreciate the afternoon cockfights held in a clearing close to town. The lens of her camera trained on the lunging vicious birds. Moments crystalized where the swirling motion of the proud roosters took on a surreal aspect. Beaks and claws, with proud strong wings, as the opponents struggled to be victorious. Blood dripping in small pools around the vanquished.

In sharp contrast were the shots she took of a woman grinding corn to prepare tortillas. The slow rhythmic rolling of a stone on a well-worn mortar. Dried corn was added at intervals, pulverized, then wetted to make a nourishing flour cake. The un-leaven tortilla shell dried on a small clay oven. Nothing escaped her frantic fascination.

She even snapped a whole roll of the girls leaving. Kitty and Charlotte were not small town enough, to share her sympathies. They were willing to return after the golf course was up and running. One photo caught a tender moment shared between Charlotte and Ceryle. It was a keeper. The other keeper was Ernie with Kitty. Both pictures were good enough for the cover of some dreadful romance novella.

Sarah had overcome her prejudice of the ladies. When she finally met them, it was almost like she was rescued from a deserted island. They had plenty to discuss; news of the outside world, hemlines, cosmetics. Not that she cared about those things when she was alone. It was just a compelling subject in the company of strangers. They even helped her through the process of remorse over a town in renewal. They told to quit worrying over small things, seize the day. Tomorrow would come, rain or shine. Worry only caused wrinkles.

Her photographs helped her deal with the moment. She gained an insight into how things could be changed for the better. If they were careful, if they were modest in demands of the environment, they could make it a better place. Some of her fears were well founded.

The Mayan jungle had once supported an advanced race.

Pyramids in the Yucatan, proved to her, even the best plans are sometimes wrong. The people took crop cultivation to such an extreme they over extended their living space. Of course, it did not happen overnight. It happened gradually, while they slept contentiously in a political system where everyone had a place. Just like Easter Island they denuded the environment. The crops failed and the culture collapsed.

From her understanding Babylon fell for the same reason. The Egyptian culture had a similar demise. These examples went back to prehistory all with cataclysmic endings. The Roman empire had its day. Even then, were the virtues of contour farming, held up as proof of the cleverness of man. The natural environment proving every attempt to be harnessed a fleeting moment. Some prospered as others declined. The body of man's knowledge weighing heavily on explaining; what went wrong. Somehow man survived, making excuses for the failure.

She often wondered of the complexities of modern culture. Exactly how complex where the social orders of the Mayan or Inca. The records of Aztec culture were known from a Spanish perspective. They had a unique method of dealing with overpopulation. They would round up surplus citizenry, foreign or domestic, and have a festival. When the Spanish arrived, there was only one way to view the native culture, barbarians with gold. Skull racks greeted the Spanish explorers. Wholesale slaughter of peasantry, vanquished warriors, and any other undesirables.

The Spanish, for their part, were fresh from the end of the Inquisition. They had no problem sending pagans to meet God. If it helped deliver gold to the Spanish Crown so much the better. So, the Mayan experiment was never really concluded. A political landscape superceded the fruition of a remarkable culture. Perhaps it was going to self-destruct of its own excess. This would never be known.

This town, Bueno Rio, was such a strange mixture of backgrounds. Everything was represented, from Mayan survivors to the modern engineers. That woman grinding stones might have the cultural memory of the time before the conquistador. The cockfights were carried over from the colonial period. The planters and ranchers were part of the plantation expansion of post-Columbian exploration. The law was certainly Spanish Indian, a suggestion, more than a policy. The law seemed to evaluate the consequence before taking any action. There was no shortage of lunatics in the jail, all there for good reasons.

They even had a middle class. The pensioners, former government employees who retired to this place. For the most part they were friendly to Sarah, but seemed to cherish their isolation. They were the ones who owned sturdy homes with all the amenities. They were the ones keeping the town moving toward the modern era. They were the ones who foot the bill for the electric plant, and the telephone network. It was their contribution allowing the hotel to locate in an unremarkable bend in the river. They were the moral backbone of the town.

If there was anything missing it was the elite. Sure, the planters and ranchers, but they never came to town. The engineers never left the hotel. There just did not seem to be an upper crust to the social order. The minister when he was alive, tried his best to service the spiritual needs of the community, but that is not an elite function. The mayor was as common as the next man. He was never even challenged in an election. He would probably be the chief of police until he was old and grey.

All that was going to change with the plan for the golf course. Sports mean competition. Competition means some would win and some would lose. A looser is not one of the elites. When there is an elite, there has to be a bubble headed bimbo, to act as town crier for success. Thank God it was only golf. Golf is a gentlemen's game. Golfers don't require too much in the way of a cheerleader squad. They have their bimbo's; however, these are discreet. Sort of like Kitty and Charlotte.

Sarah's quest for a photographic record sent her deeper into the lush tropical jungle. For the most part she stuck to the trails, never knowing if it was made by animals or man. The wide footpaths had to be human. There were other less traveled routes, sometimes covered with animal tracks.

On one of her explorations, she happened across an odd ring with a gruesome display of animal skulls. At first, she thought it may be a very old site of veneration. As she came closer the altar stone was covered with fresh wax. She kept snapping pictures. Her curiosity was growing. She avoided tampering with anything, not really sure of what she had found.

Five stones formed a circle, with the head stone opposite the altar. It gave her the creeps. She was suddenly aware it was a vulgar worship site, of one of the earth religions. Those five stones made a pentagram.

Sarah thought of herself as a spiritual person, just not anyone who would spend too much time at church. Her scientific background gave her more solid answers to her questions.

Many mysteries were held inside the holy books which on occasion, explained scientific principles, better than science. The question of Noah's Arc was more than an account of survival. Science, short of finding the Arc, supported the evidence of a flood at the conclusion of the last Ice Age. Noah through some enlightened perception was able to preserve mankind. He gave the credit to God. That was good enough for Sarah.

Behind her a twig snapped, a man pounced. She was down on her hands and knees. He kicked her, climbing onto her back forcing her prone. Her breath was gone as soon as she hit the ground. His hands were forcing her face into the dirt. She struggled against the dead weight of the attacker. There was nothing she could do. She was only making herself more tired by struggling. She tried to play dead.

It seemed to work; the attack became less violent. Whoever it was turned her over onto her back. Her eyes were full of debris however she could make out a faint outline of a figure. Her attacker seemed to falter.

This was not a rape, at least not a premeditated rape. He started for her clothing, ripping at it, wrestling with it. Still, it was not as if he knew what he was trying to accomplish.

Her breath returned. She took the camera on the end of the neck strap and turned it into a one-pound hammer. One pound of brutal force striking the intruder squarely in the cheekbone. He went tumbling off her onto the jungle floor. She was still too shaken to be able to see more than rough outlines. Her hair was matted in her face with leaves and twigs. She saw the shape move, amble to its knees. She swung again. It landed with a thud. Moments seemed to expand. She brushed the rat nest away from her eyes with her free hand.

She prepared the camera for another assault on the would-be rapist. He was gone. Vanished into the overgrowth. Nothing more than rustling leaves marked his path.

Many emotions surfaced all at once. Sarah was all alone. She began to cry but caught herself. Then she was glad, and happy. And now she was angry. She picked up a tree branch and started smashing the altar. She picked up the stones forming the circle, and hurled them in all directions. She kicked and stomped until she was exhausted. Then she picked up her camera and took pictures.

She was not finished by any stretch of the imagination. She marched into town, and jumped up into Ernie's tractor. Like a demon unleashed, she tore down the pristine jungle path. Overhead branches slapping at her the whole way. She didn't care. When she got to the site of the attack, she spun a donut. Rubble flew in all directions. She was still spinning when Ernie arrived.

It took him a few minutes to calm her down. She was so intent on what she was doing, she ignored him. Now that she knew she was with a friend she broke down and started blubbering. She didn't want to cry she just wanted to explain what happened. Everything happened so fast, her mind was a caldron. The only way to describe the events was to blubber. The attack had reached the little girl, inside the research scientist.

Ernie held her in his arms the way a man holds his sister. He let her get it all out. "I guess we'll be looking for someone with Kodak stamped across his forehead." he joked.

This seemed to cheer her up a bit. "Just look for a 35 mm dent."

CHAPTER THIRTY-ONE

Miguel had a sudden change of fashion. Normally he regarded hats as too bourgeois. Today he wore a large hat kicked to one side. It didn't make him any less gruesome than usual. In fact, anywhere else besides Bueno Rio, that hat would be another good reason to get into a bar fight. Everyone in Bueno Rio knew Miguel was quite simply crazy. They all knew some day they might have to put him down, like a rabid raccoon. But the trouble was crazy people sometimes have a special relationship with God. Nobody wanted to interfere with God's work. Maybe God was punishing him by making him crazy. Maybe God was showing him things no one else could see. Whatever the case he was crazy, and no one wanted to tempt fate.

He was especially quiet this evening. Sitting by himself slowly sipping at the tequila. He was lost in some ethereal landscape far away from this place. Even the bartender noticed the change. Normally the man would be slamming the empty bottle on the counter. Tonight, he sat almost trance like, at his favorite chair. Every time someone came in, he glanced around nervously. When he finally went home, he left a small tip for the bartender. The tip was so unusual it bore notice.

"Those Gringo's..." He muttered to himself as he drunkenly stumbled down the block. He blamed all his troubles on the Gringo's.

By now there should be no white people in Latin America. The revolution should have chased them all to Los Angeles, Dallas and Orlando. La cucaracha, nobody had time for La cucaracha. Where is the glory of conquest without a revolution. Sneaking into the suburbs like a cockroach was not glorious.

Why had he spent so many years in Somalia, Angola, Honduras. A lifetime devoted to the revolution never to be rewarded. His face was too well known outside this river. He could never be part of the guns to drugs business. He could only wait in the stiffening jungle for the next big purge of imperialist interests. He would hide out, waiting for the day a platoon of armed freedom fighters needed a leader. Time was on his side. Yet he had barely escaped the Panama incident.

A lifetime in the field, first as a soldier, later as an advisor. He looked at Panama as the pearl in the oyster. He could have settled down into a quiet retirement, helping to export the revolution. Even then the effort was financed by the drug trade. President Noriega ruined it for everyone. That jack ass, kept asking the United States for financial support to fight drug lords, when he was the biggest dealer in Panama.

Miguel knew it was over, when the army surrounded the Noriega compound. He stripped off his uniform, and headed south. Weeks he traveled to find the sanctuary of this small town. Only to find Gringos.

Miguel was not a stupid man. He had no formal education beyond what was needed to learn to be a solder of the revolution. Many subjects were a mystery to him. He very often invented a train of logic to support his actions. He got what he needed, by cunning and deception. This alone takes an obvious amount of intelligence.

He was just like any other hoodlum. If he was in the United States he would be locked up with the rest of the under- educated population. The high school dropouts, the fantasyweavers.

"Oh those Gringos" he cursed them. "They think they are so special." He lamented his own circumstances.

It never seemed to make any difference to him he was not equipped to deal with the parity of education. Jake was no slouch; he earned his degree. Ernie was more of a technical person. Sarah had double, even triple, the amount of education of an average person. Ceryle it was hard to say, he seemed always to study. Even the dead Minister had a significant level of understanding above the common man. None of them supported the people's revolution.

Unless there was a revolution there was no room for Miguel to advance. He needed it. He needed to tear down the established governance. He needed to wipe away the very order of society, to make the people accountable to no one. Of course, in his demented world view, he would be the leader. He would be Chairman Mao, or Fidel Castro. Just because there was no Soviet Union, did not mean there was no place for communism. If he could just pull together a small brigade, he could bring freedom to the freedom fighters.

He studied the popular news. He saw how the Islamic countries were involved in the cleansing of the infidels. He did not know anything about Islam but he could learn. A front page of the press saw Fidel Castro marching at the head of an Islamic Parade. Death to the infidels. A holy war, what could be more confusing than that. Kill everyone let God sort them out. Let Allah sort them out.

That was the problem with the United States. They valued freedom too much. The soft underbelly of the fat citizens was too much freedom. Let them fight on all the continents of the known world. La cucaracha, La cucaracha. Maybe there was time for the invasion. One man at a time.

Miguel grew weary. His head was throbbing. This always happened when he tried to think beyond his learning. He had never read the Bible or the Koran or the Talmud. As a matter of fact, he could not remember ever reading a book. He had trouble with newspapers, except the captions under a picture.

To get what he wanted out of life, there was only the revolution. Revolution for the sake of revolution. Tear down the very fabric of civilization, rebuild anew. Just like the Conquistadors did to the Aztec. No make it worse than the conquest of the new world. Kill all the men, rape all the women, throw all the children into concentration camps. Leave nothing but orphans and wailing women.

Then he would hand out a small portion of the spoils of war, to those deserving. Not so much they have anything of value, just enough that they do not notice their shameful existence.

He had waited long enough. In the morning Miguel would dig up his old assault rifle. He would start his private revolution, here on the banks of the Orinoco. He was only waiting for the return of the troops who were seeking the drug shipment money. He could enlist them to the cause of jungle justice. Tomorrow, they would return, and the slaughter could begin. They would be the first recruits to an illustrious army.

He slumped down onto the woven cot. The hat bothered him. He laid it to one side. The throbbing would not go away. As a last resort he placed a wet towel over his forehead. In the morning it would be dry and crusted with blood.

Bright and early the sunlight patches danced through the dappled overhead branches. It was a festival of light. One hundred shades of green and gold beamed down from the sun's path through the heavens. Birds darted tree to tree. Off in the distance a howler monkey sounded. Roosters crowed and went back to sleep.

Miguel came around to someone banging at the door to his hut. The banging was strong enough to loosen the mud brick of the place. He accidently picked up his hat and put it on. This was absurd, no one was supposed to disturb his rest.

Jake and Ernie stood there, arms folded, chatting to themselves.

"What if he won't go peacefully?" says Ernie quietly.

"He doesn't have a choice!" Jake answered.

The ferret of a man appeared behind the wobbly door. He was not willing to come outside. Anything they wanted to say they should say from the where they were. "I am not afraid of you...but you have me out numbered." was his explanation. "I have no witnesses!"

"Let me make it short and sweet, I'll give you a thousand dollars to leave right now and never come back." Jake offered.

Miguel came out of the house a bit further. "Why would a gringo make such an offer?"

"Call it anything you like, piece of mind, a bribe whatever makes you happy..." Ernie started to move forward.

"But Senor Jake, this is my home. Where would I go?" Miguel groveled trying his best to act innocent.

"Yesterday this was your home then you made a fatal mistake." Jake spoke really slow and deliberate, letting it sink in.

"I don't know what this es...what es this es..."

"Plain and simple, I can put you at the scene of an attempted Rape!" Ernie was losing his patience.

"Me, rapto never. I would not do such a thing." he backed into the doorway.

"Look I can go get the guardia urbano or you can come out here and talk to us. The only reason I didn't get the constable is you're not worth the trouble. They'd lock you away for a few months, and you'd come right back, like a damn rash."

"But Senor, I swear I do not know what you are talking about."

Ernie was tired of the runaround. Jake could tell he was about to kick in the door. He stood in front of him holding him back.

"Do me a favor..." Ernie growled "...Take off the hat!"

"Stop Ernie, that's not why we're here. We're here to offer him money to leave town." Jake wisely interrupted.

"Why should we give him a dime, he's guilty look at him!"

Jake took a look at a man trying to act invisible. He was cowering in the doorway. Miguel was doing his best to act defiant in spite of his situation. His indignation was that of a gamecock. He held his chest high, neck extended to give him height, chin pronounced. It was a wasted effort for the hat on his head. He still looks like a buffoon.

"What's it gonna be Miguel? One thousand dollars American, I'll even throw in my canoe. It'll get you all the way to the Atlantic Ocean."

"Jeu know senor something tells me, jeu can pay more than what jeu es offering." The very nature of the comment was offensive.

Jake was not sure what he was hearing. The only reason he made the original offer was to find some civil way to move past yesterday. He would like nothing better than to snap Miguel's neck like a straw. The body would be a problem. Not that the investigation would be very intense. This was why they were not contacting the policia in the first place. There was no actual rape, only attempted rape. It wasn't a sure thing the case would ever go to trial.

"Let me talk to him..." Ernie said softly. He stepped forward.

"Careful there Ernie, If you kick his ass he'll only come back later with a gun." Jake advised.

Ernie was smiling, shaking his head "See here Miguel, I know I haven't known you too long, but you've been a screw up for as long as I've known you. I could leave right now and come back in a hundred years and you would still be a screw up." He rubbed his palms together, opening them face, toward the man. "What do you say we end this discussion right now." Ernie's hand swooped out lightning quick snatching the hat.

Manuel was shocked by the speed of the attack. A large circular bruise matted with blood sat along his hairline. Ernie threw the hat back right into the man's arms. They stood eye to eye, neither one speaking. Moments passed long and silent. Manuel slammed the door, throwing a bolt to lock it against the intruder.

"You know he's going for a gun, don't you?" Jake predicted.

"Not if I get to him first..." Ernie started break in.

Jake grabbed him, walking him away from the building, "You don't want to go in there". Jake started running motioning for Ernie to follow.

They slowed as they came around the corner of the street. Jake went to the bar of a Cantina and ordered Dos Cervezas. He stood there looking at Ernie as a tremendous clap of thunder sounded outside.

An eye witness described the scene. The thatched roof went straight into the air, as the walls of the building folded out like a magician's prop. The roof then landed on top of the fallen walls. Someone was searching the rubble looking for Miguel.

They finished their beers and went out to help. It was a regular Chinese fire drill. Everyone running in different directions. All wanting to be part of the commotion. Five or six people elected themselves to be in charge, without anyone listening to them.

Right in the middle of the ruckus was Sarah. She had located Miguel, and was holding positive pressure over a bloody neck. His carotid artery had been punctured, a very serious wound. Several people were needed to carry him into the laboratory, where he was laid on a clean sheet on top of a table.

She kept hoping his neck would seal itself or at least slow the loss of blood. It was no use, if she took her hand away the blood just kept spurting. It was going to take a few stitches to close the wound. She looked him over searching for other wounds. He was punctured here and there but it was the neck wound that caused her worry. He could die right on the table, if something was not done soon.

If it involved Sarah, it involved Jake. He relieved her at the neck wound, so she could get organized. This was nothing she was trained to do; it just came naturally. She striped his clothing to get a better view of the mess that was Miguel. He had a sucking chest wound. That was an easy fix, if his lung was not too collapsed.

She stuffed a homemade Penrose drain into the lung cavity then covered it with gauze layered with petroleum jelly. Air could move out of the chest, but not into the wound.

A couple of broken bones an abrasion on his forehead. She ignored the implications of the forehead.

She was ready for the Carotid Artery. Right next to the artery was a facial vein and the Jugular. The longer she waited the more probability of brain damage. She hoped she knew what she was looking at, was the Carotid artery. It was hard to tell. Damn it, it was so hard to tell. She needed to buy some time, but there was no time remaining. Unless!

She went over to her supply of neurotoxin and drew a small quantity into a syringe. This better work. She injected the squirming patient and he fell instantly into a comma. His blood pressure was practically un-noticeable. The sucking chest wound barely moved. She checked his eyes and they were fixed and dilated. The neck wound trickled

She was not prepared for this sort of emergency. All she had was a common needle and thread. The only form of sterilization was a fresh bottle of Witch Hazel, to soak the instruments. Rubber gloves which she had in abundance were anything but sterile. She rinsed the gloves with the same disinfectant. She used a white bandana over her face.

A whole crowd of people gathered around as she started in on the procedure. First, she irrigated the wound with a combination of the Witch Hazel and fresh water. This was lucky for a small ball was within the area where she was working. This and other debris, was rinsed clear of the site in a stream of clean solution.

Sarah slowly closed the hole in the artery wall, with a long overlapping stitch. Her aim was to bring the jagged edges together. She did not want to puncture the artery, any more than she wanted to clamp it off. The stitches were just a suggestion of what the body should do for itself. She was helping the body do, what it had to do, under the circumstance. When satisfied, she laid another clean flexible rubber tube along the length of the artery. This was something she knew wound assist drainage in the area. It was not pretty to look at but it should work.

She closed the outer wound, using a few big stitches on the meaty part, then lots of little stitches on the epidermis. She let the rubber tube poke out of the bottom of the stitches. She covered it with sterile gauze. Sanguineous discharge trickled down the tube into the sterile gauze. Her hands were trembling by the time she was done.

He was still laying there moribund.

One of the old crones picked up a cloth, and was sponge bathing the body, as if for burial. Sarah poked around inside the chest cavity. The lung seemed inflated, to the best of her knowledge. She replaced the petroleum gauze. When the old lady was finished ministering the body, Sarah used plastic wrap around the torso as a chest binder. The same plastic wrap used to cover food. Miguel was now cleaner than he had been in months. The old lady even did his hair.

With his hair swept back the circular indent of a camera lens was clearly visible. Sarah had the presence of mind to snap a few shots of the corpse. She made a prodigious effort to include photos of the dent in his head. A dent made by a camera lens.

It is a cold cruel world, especially when a decision must be made. Every human contact has its meaning. Sarah looked around the room at all the faces. She knew they did not know anything. She could walk out of the room right now, and they still would never know anything. But she would have to live with herself. That is the difference between men and apes, the self awareness. She went over to the cabinet where she kept the antidote and prepared the injection. Who knows maybe the wound would still kill him. She administered the serum.

CHAPTER THIRTY-TWO

The mayor was among the crowd of onlookers. He saw for himself when the corpse became reanimated. Miguel began to stir and the color came back into his ruddy olive complection. He tried to sit up, when a throng of helpful hands held him in place on the table. He resisted for a moment then seemed to accept, they meant him no harm. So many people willing to help in an emergency showed how kind hearted they really were.

Miguel started blathering "Como, donde estoy yo?. Where es dis es..." he was making no sense. He rased his arms seeing both of them were broken just above the wrist. He crossed them over his chest. When he started shivering a blanket appeared out of the crowd.

The town never had a hospital, not even a clinic. Almost all the population relied on homeopathic medicine. Roots and herbs to cure anything from a headache to a heart attack. They were remarkably successful even to setting and splinting broken bones. Miguel lay there as two strong men, first set one arm, then the other. Wet linen was wrapped around each limb, over which a fine clay powder dusted the moisture. Working the powder into the linen a slick film developed. More linen, more powder. The bones were soon set in a plaster of Paris cast, as good as any modern hospital could perform. All without the benefit of X-rays.

There was the question of pain. Remarkably the unanimous decision of the crowd was; pain is good. Poor Miguel was going to have to tough it out. Sarah had aspirin, to check the swelling but this was the only pain reliever the people would allow.

A murmur among the crowd produced the opinion he may need a small measure of tequila. Just enough tequila to keep him from experiencing the delirium of being without the intoxicant.

As to where the poor man was to be quartered, during his recovery, was a topic of much discussion. Here is where the mayor shined like a diamond. He was curious of the strange mark on the man's head. That circular dent was scabbed over, it did not happen during the explosion.

He took Sarah aside to see what she knew of a dent resembling the lens of her camera. The story of an attempted rape, made the man furrow his brow. It seemed unusual a man would suffer such a serious accident the day after a rape attempt. For the present the wounded man would be moved to the jail pending further investigation.

The mayor knew all along, he would have to house the injured man. The only common building in town was the Jail. He searched for other ways to service the problem without success. There was no one willing to take Miguel into their home. On one hand, the Mayor had evidence of attempted rape. On the other hand, he had evidence of attempted murder. He needed more information. He left the crowded room going directly to the site of the injury.

His subordinate had done an excellent job keeping trespassers out of the rubble. Except for the effort to locate Miguel nothing had been changed. Of course, during the man's extraction the place was pretty well trampled. The mayor picked through the thatched roof trying to find the floor. He did not know what he was looking for, but he hoped it would not explode. He located a rifle, bent nearly at a right angle. It was loaded but it was never going to shoot again. He handed it to the other officer.

He located the cot where Miguel slept. To one side there was a hollow in the dirt floor. He tossed away the roofing rubbish to get a clearer look.

A strong odor of cordite assaulted his nostrils. With the area cleared he could see this was no accident. This hole was put here purposely. It had been here a long time and the owner could only be Miguel. The mayor checked angles and drew conclusions. He ordered a ball of string to be brought to the hole to confirm his judgments.

If the Gun in the hole belonged to Miguel, anything under the gun must belong to Miguel. The blast hit the gun bending it. Two broken arms showed Miguel was holding the rifle when the explosion occurred. According to eyewitness testimony, no one was in the area surrounding the explosion. The official record would indicate Miguel somehow blew himself up. There was no attempted murder.

As for the charge of attempted rape. The victim was reluctant to come forward. This was only important from the standpoint of whether or not to lock the door to Miguel's Cell. The jail was a small building. It would do to house the recovery of the man. It was a civil matter. As both the Mayor and Chief of police, he knew decisions must be made to restore public order. Miguel would feel right at home in the cell. He had visited it from time to time. Some of his best days resulted in him landing in the cell.

As he needed food and watered down tequila the town would simply pass the collection plate. It was the humane thing to do. Even a remote jungle has its humanity.

The mornings excitement came to an end. Miguel was carried away to recover in his own time. Sarah was exhausted. Thrown into the middle of such life and death situation, was more than she could handle. Yet she was in a state of ecstasy, over the not so clinical trial of the serum. Whatever possessed her to try the potion she could not fathom.

It was as if at the crucial moment everything came together dictating this course of action. Now that it was over, she was almost terrified of what she had done. She was not that kind of doctor. Even if she was that kind of doctor, what she did would have been wrong. She gambled with a man's life. She took a chance and it worked.

A report should be written, to explain what was done on behalf of the injured party. She was almost afraid to say anything. It was an emergency. If this had been the United States, she would be considered a Good Samaritan. A legal delineation of someone who used their training in a life-or-death situation. But she crossed over the line when she used the neurotoxin. She had only one trial with the substance. Monkey physiology is similar to human, but the brain is different.

She would have to check Miguel for signs of irrational behavior. This in itself was a losing proposition. Miguel was never one who spent much time on rational behavior. He went from home to the cockfights, to the cantina, and back home. Somewhere along the line he found enough nourishment to keep him alive. She could only wonder about the altar she found, what significance it may have played was a mystery.

"Oh God this is madness!" Sarah told Jake, "He is more a part of our lives now than he was before..."

"You did what you thought was right, quit beating yourself!" He held her in his arms, like a child being cradled by a parent.

"Yeah, but before he blew himself up, we could just ignore him."

Jake looked at her with a feeling of remorse. She had been thrust into an awareness of the vulgarity of war. She was a victim of the battlefield as much as anyone who ever served at the front. He felt responsible in a way, for the emotional distress she now endured. There was nothing to say, which would change anything.

Ernie looked on from across the room. He could sympathize but he could not enter into the consolation. He wished he had never forced his hand with Miguel that morning. This could all have been avoided. Maybe it was going to happen in any case, and they were all victims of fate. Unlike the others he felt Miguel had it coming to him.

Ceryle was a late comer to the events of that morning. His five-pound document kept him cut off from the world. It was only while taking a breather, he found out about the explosion. As he poked his head out of his hermit's hole, he encountered the return of the troop of men.

The squad was working their way back up river. They wandered into Bueno Rio unannounced. The surly demeanor of the men showed they were yet unsuccessful locating the shipment of money. The extended travel through the bush was breaking down unit integrity. They were no longer a squad they were a collection of bandits. Several of the troop showed signs of either malaria or dengue fever. They were all suffering, for the ones obviously infected.

The Cadre had an unusual curiosity into the details of the explosion. On the outbound journey, Miguel had distinguished himself as a worthy asset to the freedom fighters. They had hoped he would be helpful on the return trip. Soon they made their way to the jail, to pay respects to their fallen comrade.

Following close behind was Ceryle, with his five pounds of paper. He used it as a decoy for his true intention of keeping an eye on the intruders. The document served to gain access to a mayor, who's job as chief of police, kept him busy at the jail.

Even as an invalid Miguel was a problem. He complained of pain knowing watered down tequila was the only thing on hand. His visitors brought with them leaves of coca. Fortunately, the nature of his injury kept him from chewing the potent herb. He was confined to sucking on the leaves. He could sip soup; he just could not chew anything. But this did not keep him from talking. His jaw did not move but the words still came out. He babbled for the most part, as if this was anything new to him.

"Los Gringos...los gringos..." he kept repeating loud enough for Ceryle to hear.

The jail was too small, for all the men at once, so they came in two at a time. An elderly lady sat to one side, trying to feed the man soup. At a table sat the Mayor and Ceryle carefully going over the document. Ceryle kept his ears open for anything he could use. He knew there was bad blood between Miguel and the Gringos. He didn't have any idea how bad it would be. If Miguel kept babbling there was no harm. If he started making sense there was reason to worry. Those men had been out in the bush a long time. They might not still be interested in their original objective. They would not be the first squad to go outlaw. Especially with some of them suffering from malaria. Going home empty handed, was not going to look good, to whoever sent them.

The mayor was as concerned as Ceryle. These ten men were beyond the manpower of his quiet village. He reviews the document as he made phone calls on the antiquated telephone system. He knew many vaqueros from the ranches outside of town. Some were mucho loco when it came to defending the town. They rarely left the ranches, when they did; it was to visit Bueno Rio. Including the vaquero, the town was safe.

Unlike Ceryle, the mayor knew if it came right down to it, he would have to kill them. Kill them, and who ever sent them, would wonder what happened. When they came through town the last time, they were clean and orderly. The uniforms now were soiled and threadbare. They were out beyond their supply line. The prospects were good they were out of contact with their headquarters. But beyond all these civilities, the fact remained; they had no jurisdiction in the mayor's town. Enforcement of the law, could very well become a gruesome chore.

Miguel was tired from his ordeal as the parade of guests finally ended. The lady feeding him soup put down the spoon. Every one left except the mayor and Ceryle. Both men had lost interest in the document. The room took on an atmosphere of a storm center in a hurricane. Neither man spoke, but what was not verbalized hung in the air like smoke.

The silence ended when Sarah stopped in to check on the patient. Jake followed her, while Ernie waited outside. She did not wake the man, she just tended to the wounds. The drain in the neck wound was doing a good job. The chest drain could come out. Dozens of tiny superficial cuts and abrasions had scabbed over, in the few hours since the explosion.

She was not concerned about the broken bones. The folk medicine of the people always impressed her.

They left as a group, dragging Ceryle along. Everyone remained silent. Sarah asked Jake to spent the night. The others went away to drown their sorrows. The mood was as tense as a royal funeral.

"I shouldn't have done it." Sarah obsessed.

Jake had no words to comfort her. He just wrapped her in his arms hoping it would sooth her fears. This may have been the best way of quieting her racing thoughts. Instead of verbal exchange, making her mind race to argument, he remained silent. Slowly, she discovered for herself; she only did what she thought was right at the time. They stood there long moments until her rigid muscles relaxed in his arms.

"Well look at it this way; this time you don't have to clean up monkey shit!" he finally joked, hoping to lighten the moment. She started to chuckle and soon everything was normal again.

Ceryle and Ernie in the meantime were turning a black mood even darker with the aid of twelve year old Scotch. Two brooding cold war solders, each trying to astonish the other with murky storytelling. As the Scotch slid down their throats, the stories became more vivid. Ceryle was reticent, keeping his tales to details of cloak and dagger affairs. In sharp contrast, Ernie spoke of the gore and bullets, of a man keeping the cold war cold. What it amounted to; was an excuse to drink more Scotch.

The subject arose, covertly introduced by Ceryle, of a large sum of money. Ernie clammed up. Even with the Scotch, loosening his tongue, he was not inclined to enter upon that subject. He'd talk about helicopter rides and sniper assignments. But he was not going to talk about money.

Ceryle had no such restraint. He switched the subject to his business with the mayor. The golf course was coming along nicely. Town center would be preserved with a face lift. Surrounding the golf course would be a sports complex including soccer fields. Outside the sports complex a number of modern residential units including single and multi-family housing. A proposal for a small medical center was included in the plan. Just as if this was a business meeting; Ceryle laid out the five-, ten-, and fifteen-year plan. It was going to take some starter capital.

"Oh no, I see what you're doing...you're working me from a different angle" Ernie grinned with a two-finger grip of the scotch glass.

"My dear man, whatever gave you that impression?"

"Kitty said you could be devious..." Ernie continued to smile.

"Devious, how dare she say such a thing. That's the pot calling the kettle black."

"Speaking of niggardly, how about a refill their partner?" Emie offered his empty glass. His smile was now menacing. He was on the threshold of full disclosure and he knew it. Ceryle must have known it as well, for he made it a double.

"As I was saying... The potential comprehensive land use policy, paragraph C page 498, shows...." Ceryle launched into a presentation normally intended for a chairman or company president. He had been working really hard on his boat anchor of a document. He did not even turn the pages. It all unfolded verbatim without the slightest pause.

"You know the last time I saw a song and dance like that, it was a time share on a condominium." Ernie interrupted.

"Perhaps I was being a bit clinical..." Ceryle refilled the empty glass. He was stingy this time, not wanting to lose his audience.

"You know you're really going to have to save it for Jake. All I have is stuffed in a coffee can; he's the one you have to talk to."

Ceryle was feeling pretty good himself. He wanted to toy with the man now that he was primed. He reached over and withdrew a banana from a fruit bowl arrangement. Next, he snatched a knife from a nearby table setting. He proceeded to slice the banana right through the peel.

"See here Ernie. This is the whole project. Here is the Golf course. Here is the sports complex. Here is the housing, and here is the clinic. Of course, there will be schools and churches...."

"Of course!" Ernie pretended to be interested even though he was now only using one eye to focus. "What's a banana like that gonna cost?"

"It's hard to say...how much do you have to spend?"

"Didn't I just tell you, talk to Jake?" Ernie sounded mad.

It was a bitter disappointment for Ceryle to allow him off so easy. His talent was legendary. He had never come across one of the special force's types, and had no way of knowing their counterespionage training. He gave it a shot, more for the practice than to collect information. Still there was enough time in the universe to try again some other day. The last thing he wanted to do; was push the button, where the man went ape shit all over the lounge.

The bar tender came down wiping his territory with a towel, "You want me to put the banana on your tab?"

CHAPTER THIRTY-THREE

"Jake we gotta get out of this jungle." Ernie was serious. "Forget about the golf course. You can't play golf, with guerilla squads wandering in any time they want."

"What about Sarah, you ever think I have more invested in this community -than you do?"

"So, we'll take her with us, when we leave. Let's just pack everything up and hit the road." Ernie begged.

"I can't do it! I came here to get away from the crazy world. This is my home now."

"Well, there is a small army out there who says you're wrong. You ever think of that. What are you gonna do when they come busting in here armed and dangerous?" Ernie was making a whole lot of sense.

"I suppose, I'll have to defend myself." countered Jake.

"Aw shit, I don't like this at all. Now I have to stay! I can't just walk off and leave you outnumbered ten to one."

"If it makes you feel any better, I've been a hermit out here a long, long time." Jake offered, leaving Ernie plenty room to bail out.

"No, that's ok, they still don't know we have the money, or they would already be here." advised Ernie.

"Exactly, we're just a couple of crazy Americans with nothing to hide... Nothing at all! You got that?"

It was a bright sunny day as Sarah made her way to the jail. Miguel looked like Frankenstein with the tube sticking out of his neck. Sarah carefully tugged on it to see if it came loose. She extracted it when she found no resistance. The whole time keeping an eye on the man, to assure herself he was in no danger. She replaced the sterile gauze. Moving on to the chest wound she made a similar removal. Now that there was nothing left in the wounds, she felt more relieved. A few more days and she would be free of the responsibility. Not that anyone expected anything more from her than she had already done. She, herself, was the one demanding perfection. She even had a chart to monitor his progress.

There was something in his eyes. Some new light shining from within. The man had crossed over to the other side and returned. She saw it immediately, when she entered, but later paid no attention. Now she had time to explore the depth of his experience. He was sullen and unusually quiet. She eventually left the antiseptic smelling room.

The man rolled over to try a more comfortable position. His bandaged arms acted like flippers on a whale. Miguel was afraid to sleep for fear of crossing over to that other place. The glimpse of the other side was macabre. He had seen no light in a tunnel. No angels with wings came to greet his arrival. He was profoundly aware of everything going on around him, while he was under the effects of the injection. He could feel the needle pierce his skin. The amazing thing was he did not see it through his own eyes. It was as if he were viewing the event as a spectator. There was some kind of fold in the makeup of the universe, allowing the common dimension to view itself.

To Miguel it was terrifying. He did not think of it as a near death experience. He had no way to describe the ordeal. Right up to the moment when the antidote was administered, he was in a wondrous place. As soon as the antidote took hold, reality fragmented. Even now laying on his cot in the jail, he felt somehow connected with the other realm. There was nothing he could say to anyone to describe what he was feeling.

From the next room the mayor looked on. He was used to having his quiet little room to himself. He wondered how long before the injured man would be well enough to leave. It was disturbing to have someone in the cell without it being locked. He found himself getting up to close the door, only to remember he did not have a prisoner.

The guerilla band was making the most of the day. Camped at the same bivouac as the last time, the troop was packing up to leave. Miguel had acted the part of aide-de-camp on the earlier visit. Without his help there was no way to check out the town. There just wasn't anything remarkable about Bueno Rio. It was like a thousand other towns along the largest river in the world. They had failed in their mission, but given the size of the task it was to be expected. Now they were hurting for rest and relaxation. They would move on, pushing up stream, until night fall.

Jake and Ernie watched as they passed the compound. They look about as threatening as a wet puppy. Straining at the paddles of their boats they tried to look like a tight unit. Several of their members were just going through the motions, too ill to contribute real work. The last boat contained their commander. He did his best to look proud but he was as whipped at the rest of the crew. He raised his hand in a wave to men on the beach. Jake and Ernie waved back.

"There goes your army." Jake mentioned

"Nothing rattles you, does it?" Ernie smiled

"Aw hell why should it? The only one around here who has a clue is Ceryle, and he's gone promoter on us. You ever look at those plans he drew up?"

"Not seriously." Ernie responded.

"Well, you should. He's so meticulous, except for figuring out where the money's coming from."

"I thought we were supplying the money!" Ernie snapped.

"We wouldn't even scratch the surface on what he is planning. That gives me some reasons to question, if we even want to get involved."

"I don't know he was chopping up a banana last night, I guess should have paid attention. Seemed like he knew what he was talking about, except when he asked me how much we had to spend."

"He asked you that, huh" Jake smiled knowingly. "He still doesn't have any idea! That's great!"

"Oh, he has a general idea..." Ernie spoke deliberately "Kitty and Charlotte saw to that."

The boats disappeared over the horizon. Jake and Ernie could only hope they had seen the last of the jungle militia. Those men were too ill to present an offensive on the compound. If they had any business, they surely would have made it known as they were leaving. Instead, the commander made a friendly wave to the shore. Jake did not know exactly how to interpret the gesture. But then his mind was occupied with other matters.

"Ernie do you even know what kind of grass they use on a green?"

"Nope, not a clue."

"I mean if we were proper business men, we should know that!" Jake's furrowed forehead showed he was leading someplace. "How big is an area one hundred feet square?"

"Oh, that's easy, ten feet by ten feet." Ernie swelled with pride.

"OK so how many square feet is in a regulation Golf Green?"

"Aw Crap, you're getting hung up on the details and losing sight of the objective." Ernie announced. "All we want to do is turn over dirty money with a profit. When we build the golf course we can always sell out to investors and get our money back."

Jake was not as sure of the project as Ernie. He had a nagging suspicion fate would intervene any time now. He really did not worry too much as they were still working out of the money in the coffee tins. Soon they would be dipping into the real money. This worried him. Each brick was a decent amount of money. A year's salary to some folk. If they were not careful, they could spend all the money and still have nothing to show for all the hard work.

Just when he was about to call an end to the foolishness Emie showed up with a bushel basket of poison potato. The poison potatoes were rock hard averaging a fair approximation of the size of a golf ball. Ernie took his home-made driver and started pitching the vegetables as far as he could into the open country side. For the most part they just splintered, but some held together well enough to follow a path through the sky. Jake joined in, after all it was a bushel basket.

Within a few minutes the sensation of the sport was overtaking both of them. Golf has the feel of almost everything men crave. Hunting, fishing in the bushes, long walks through the countryside, golf is a perfect sport. It requires no ammunition but has a target range. A sphere passes though the atmosphere, requiring a measure of momentary attention. The player is required to hunt down his own mistake, then try desperately to correct the problem. Closer and closer to a goal and once arriving at a predetermined location, his efforts are rewarded with bragging rights. Or he is forced to suffer the humiliation of hearing the other fellow brag. Whichever the case may be; the player has wandered with an objective, through a familiar landscape.

Jake and Ernie could only imagine what it would be like, for they were only pulverizing poison potatoes. They soon were chasing the orbs, to see where they landed. The source of competition only heightened by each new challenge. On the western shoreline they aimed for a withered old tree. Ernie reached it in three potatoes. Jake took four shots only to land in the water. He took a mulligan to total five to the target tree. The victorious and the defeated, each able to return to the field of honor another day.

The experience was addictive. Not in the sense of over consumption, just from the aspect of a pleasurable experience. Whack and the ball go where ever it wants. Whack, and the ball seems to go in the intended direction. Whack, whack, Wack; violence focused into a club striking a one- and one-half inch sphere. A sphere who will never press charges. A sphere who only exists to be bludgeoned. The player soon learns; he defeats himself with his own equipment. That sphere will never change regardless of how violently struck. A man can get pretty beat up trying to smack a tiny little ball.

Slowly all the excuses fall away. The club is too long or too short. Jake and Ernie were using homemade clubs, a perfect excuse. A man may blame his foot wear, right down to the need for spikes. A better grip on the club. Maybe a glove will help. As long as there were excuses there was a market for golfing equipment. The irony was not lost on the two men. It was not about victory over an opponent. It was all about forcing a tiny ball to bend to the will of the player.

"You know that missionary spent twenty years trying to build a church down here." Jake mentioned as he swung away.

"Yeah, well?" Ernie creamed another potato.

"I just think a church is a lot more important than a golf course."

"Haven't you been talking to Ceryle Smyth. It is not about a golf course it's about grabbing a load of real estate, dirt cheap! We improve the land and move on. It can't fail!"

Somehow the practice range opened without a hitch. Four hundred yards deep by one hundred yards wide. Roughly eight acres of sports complex property. They only needed two and a half acres. Two hundred fifty yards was plenty deep. The plan was to whittle away at the side of the property to make room for a clubhouse. Someday a soccer field would stretch across the back of the property.

Ernie bought a ball picker, which like everything else, had come in boxes from the manufacturer. It hitched right up to the tractor. He was getting more equipment than a farmer; a mower, a grater, a plow blade and now a ball picker. He was spending enough time on the tractor to blister his backside. Ernie never complained, somehow, he felt perfectly at home bouncing over the fields.

Ceryle Smyth set up shop in the old general store renting buckets of balls and golf clubs to the engineers. He had been able to locate a company who sold him boxes of used balls from water traps. It was a real stroke of genius. He also brought in a fair shipment of new equipment, testing to see if the engineers were going to take the bait. He didn't waste his time on the top end line of products. He brought in affordable clubs, overstock from constantly evolving American equipment. His small pro shop took on the trappings of a gentleman's haberdashery. Hats, gloves, shoes, anything a well healed player would need at such a remote village.

The missionary had left the shelves filled with items the local population did not need. He made special deals with any of the players, who now sometimes felt inclined to come inside the spacious shop.

Some of the work the engineers had to do could just as well be accomplished on a golf course. The clientele was chomping at the bit waiting for the front nine holes. Ernie was a busy man. He spent most of his day mowing and grading the course. Plugs of Bermuda grass needed special attention on all the greens. Then to break up the monotony he had to plant miles of Banana trees along the fairways. He used banana because they were everywhere, and they never looked transplanted. Not that this was the only shrubbery he used. Anything that looked like it would survive without maintenance, lined the rough, outside the fairways.

Ernie was devious. He laid out the front nine from the top of the hill. The players worked their way down the slope. At the bottom was the driving range just begging the players to practice. The front of the range held a nine-hole putt-putt course to encourage people to play. The twenty odd acres came along in due time making a passable course. It looked as if it was Mayan agriculture. The graceful sweeping terraces dropping naturally into the next. Sarah had been right when she criticized the original design. The lay of the course was unique. It was in perfect harmony with the location.

Rentals was the name of the game. Ernie knew if the First hole was way up on top, he could rent more carts. Right now, the only cart in town belonged to the mayor but this was soon to change. Each time the Seaplane set down it brought a new cart.

Jake built ten carts before he had enough. He could do it in his sleep now. The seaplane pilot was grateful when he found the nonsense had come to an end. Soon a pedestrian was hard to find. It only encouraged business, to rent the carts for a few pesos. Even when they were not used for their intended purpose the carts were in constant motion. Prosperity was raising its ugly head in Bueno Rio.

People who had never been in an automobile were lining up to rent the golf carts. The precious few carts were the only thing preventing major traffic jams. People were even using them to collect firewood, transport chickens, and a number of other chores previously done by foot travel. Ceryle started renting them by the hour, only to find the renters loaned the carts when they were finished using them. Then they would haggle over how much of the hour they had used the cart. He spent more time chasing down carts than it was worth. He might even have to clean up pig poop before he could rent the cart again. Worse be could not find anyone to hire to keep track of the carts. The concept of an odd job was as foreign to the people as walking on the moon. They were all too intent on living life to be chained down to a job.

Thank God for the engineers. They were the backbone of the business. Ceryle got fifteen bucks greens fees for the nine holes. Three bucks a bucket for the balls on the driving range. More than one hundred men a day played the course. This was not just chicken scratch. With the notoriety beginning to get around, the ranchers and planters started coming into town. They needed equipment, and Ceryle saw to their every need. Ceryle went through his stock of equipment and ordered more. The poor seaplane pilot had something new to complain about. Luckily, he played a little golf himself, and was treated to a free game when his flights permitted. If he brought in new players he was also compensated with a dinner at the hotel. Word spread of the golfing oasis with the help of the pilot. He was quickly becoming the best promoter of the golf course.

The thriving business made way for more room by opening the back nine. Here Ernie arranged for the play to climb the hill so the front nine and the rear nine centered around the future club house, they would someday build. It was more skulduggery by Ernie. When the players had finished the front nine, they might have more business. The back nine sat there looking so innocent. Rising gracefully, it appeared no more challenging than the rest of the course. Even if the players had only paid for the front nine, they might be persuaded to lay down another fifteen dollars. The back nine was a wicked set of links. Pock marked with sand traps; it looked like a battlefield. Each green was as level as a billiard table. Getting to the green was like working your way through the jungle with a machete. You were going to use the same number of strokes. Ernie planed it like this, knowing it would only add to the notoriety.

Golf is a thirst business. A player has to remain hydrated. Even at the risk of offending the town's cantina owners, Ceryle kept a good quantity of cold beer on ice, in a huge galvanized tub. Clubs, balls, beer and accouterments he was raking it in hand and fist. He did not even stop to picture a yearend total; the money was moving so fast.

Every night he took three percent and placed it in an envelope. Each month he took the envelopes to the mayor and waited for the gregarious smile to appear.

It only made for good business to keep the town coffers full. Not that there was much pressing need for a town budget. Bueno Rio had always been an enigmatic place. The people did, whatever need to be done, not one ounce more. Having money in the bank meant nothing to anyone. In fact, there was no bank.

The Mayor was happy with a title. He did not need a salary. He was content with his other post, being Chief of police. Again, he needed only a small salary, it was as if his reward was the good will of the people. The thousand dollars a month he received as taxes from the golf course he put away for the future needs of the town.

In contrast to the pioneer town, the hotel was a state of the art; electronic transfer oriented, modern building. It was the closest thing to a bank in town. No one knew how much cash it kept on hand but it did thousands of credit card transactions each month. It held a small safe for the convenience of guests. Other than that, it was a financial entity to itself.

Ceryle started using the hotel financial services to wire money to creditors. He used cash without anyone rasing an eyebrow. Over the course of months, the transactions became so routine he was building up a surplus of electronic cash. This was his plan, to pay out in front of his expected expenditure. He developed a relationship with his suppliers, where the merchandise was already paid for, in advance of shipment. They liked that. So much so, they were always sending samples of new product lines, to reward his patronage.

The beauty of the plan made it possible to order Bermuda sod, in the middle of a jungle. The tropical equivalent to shipping snowballs to Siberia. More equipment followed the sod.

The pilot suggested they open a trucking company, for the freight charges they were squandering. He was only being practical. Every load he brought in had to be strapped down to keep the airplane level in flight. If they kept ordering sod, he was going to jack up the freight price.

Fortunately, in the humid climate the sod went a long way. All Ernie had to do was plug it into the rich soil where it spread like wild fire. A little chemical fertilizer, from a tank on the back of the Gravely tractor and he was in business. He even toyed with the idea of having the pilot use a crop duster on his precious fields.

The more the playing conditions improved the more players took to the links. The more players on the course, the more equipment they bought. Soon they were forced to ship heavy mowers over the barge route running up from Tucupita in the delta. The mowers were huge and expensive, making Jake scratch his head. If Ernie said they needed them, they must need them, so he mounted no opposition. Weeks went by as Ernie fretted over delivery. He was like a kid who ordered a baseball pendant. He ran to the shore every time a boat pulls up to the dock. Just like a kid, he never thought of where to put the machines until, they were already there.

With a bit of inspiration, he headed out to the four-hundred-yard mark on the driving range. Nobody ever hit four hundred yards. Here they built a shed for the equipment. Later they would move the shed to the side of the driving range where the club house was being erected. Little by little they learned from their mistakes, while the townsfolk simply whispered.

By now the dye was cast. The greens fees and rentals were keeping the golf course alive without any expenditure from Jake and Ernie. Ceryle was amazed. He never imagined it would work. For that matter neither did Jake. They were both looking to launder a load money as efficiently as possible. No one ever thought in their wildest dreams, the scope of the project would reach such dimensions.

"Jake, I got to talk to you..." Ceryle pulled him to one side. "We only have one problem...We've got to form a corporation."

"A Corporation, why a corporation?"

"Because if we keep going, like were going, we'll clear about three hundred thousand dollars a year."

"WHAT...."

"I know, I know, it sounds impossible. But that's the breakdown from only a few months of operation. I mean we haven't even had our grand opening. It's just remarkable."

"Three hundred grand gross?" Jake questioned.

Ceryle looked at Jake and just started to chuckle. "Gross ha! Three hundred grand- Net. After we hire grounds keepers, pay for equipment. Not to mention what we could earn hosting a tournament."

"Ok so explain about the Corporation, and keep it simple please."

"We've got to get insurance on this place in a hurry. Somebody gets struck by lightning and were out of business. I mean, this was just a farce up to now but it got serious in a heartbeat." Ceryle explained.

"Oh, I get it, a corporation to act as a insurance instrument, right?"

"Exactly my dear boy, I could not have said it better." Ceryle smiled which for him was a true effort. He was the serious sort.

"Here's what I have in mind, and I think you're going to like this. We fly up to the Cayman Islands with whatever remains of your loot and open not one, but two accounts. Tad da, holding company and corporate account."

"I don't follow you?" Jake looked lost.

"The holding company is to hide excess corporate account monies." Instructed Ceryle. "If we are ever sued for anything they will only be able to touch the corporate account."

"I don't know I'll have to talk it over with Ernie."

Ernie didn't seem to care one way or the other. He was so involved building the golf course, he had little time for anything else. He was his own boss and a fearsome taskmaster.

Half a day on Monday, was the only day the course was closed. He mowed all the fairways on that day. Tuesdays were slow so he mowed all the greens nice and close. The rest of the week he could spend mowing the rough, while players were on the course. It was a full-time job just maintaining the eighteen holes.

So far, he had not attracted a grounds crew. Even with the prospect of a full-time job, the townsfolk were reticent to labor. It was not they were bashful they just had better things to do. Quite a few of them were seasonal agricultural workers, they would not think of taking a job out of season. Gradually some of the men did show an interest, in hopping up on the machinery. It was more for the thrill than the prospect of a job. Ernie knew he could not trust them for a minute. He would ride along to make sure they did nothing to his well-manicured course.

Soon he identified a few good men who had a well-balanced appreciation for handling the equipment. He slowly grew to trust his equipment in the hands of employees. He hoped they would not carve up the course. Mistakes do happen. Every once in a while, he was forced to put in a new sand trap, in a unique location. He just played it off as routine. A golf course is supposed to change, to make it less predictable.

Bringing jobs to the otherwise sleepy village was more of a cultural event than originally foreseen. An agricultural economy thrives by providing the needs of the workers. Not just some of the needs, all of the needs. When the Spanish set up large plantations all over the new world, they knew this. Later when the Confederate states of America expatriated to South America, they knew this. Small villages like Bueno Rio only existed as a labor pool for the plantations during the off season. The population had modest needs, and lived in a modest village.

This had been going on for five hundred years, which in anyone's book is an exercise in tradition. Bluntly, if you hire someone you have to provide everything he needs. Jake, Ernie, and Ceryle walked into the middle of tradition, like babies in a bear trap. They were not prepared for the level of commitment they would entertain to hire a few grounds keepers. Uniforms, fine. Weekly paycheck without question.

Food and lodging? Wait a minute-wasn't that what a weekly paycheck was for? Evidently not, according to tradition!

Tradition dictated the employer provide everything, right down to a place to live. Bueno Rio was the living quarters of the planters and ranchers to the north of town. While these well healed agricultural communities had no problem sharing their labor force with the golf course, they risked a break in tradition. Even the modern hotel had to find this out for itself. That's why, no matter how often the hotel fired someone, they always hired the same individual again. The hotel could not risk the expense of catering to tradition.

"Aw Christ, we're running a company store!" Ernie exploded when the gravity of the situation finally sunk in.

Ceryle was as objective as usual. He pealed open his boat anchor of a document. There on page three hundred fifty was plans to build affordable housing out beyond the eighty acres of the golf course. "We have a contingency plan already on the books."

"That's great for you! I don't want to be some modern plantation owner." Snarled Ernie.

"If you would just calm down... It's all taken care of in the book. Look a clinic, and everything!" confided Ceryle.

"No! No way no how! I know how this story ends; they suck the life out of you with their problems. And while you solve their momentary needs, they go out looking for new thing to complain about. You'll never get beyond being a slave to the people."

"Aw come now, you're taking this all to seriously! It is only a matter of time before places like Bueno Rio modernize. We can at least choose to do things the correct way. Can you imagine what would happen in a place like this under the clutches of some egomaniac."

Jake had been sitting back taking it all in. He was just as concerned as Ernie and a whole lot more pessimistic than Ceryle. The whole reason he was living out here in the jungle was to get away from the petty squabbling of mankind. "Maybe it is the nature of man to never be contented. I mean we all want things to get better, but we don't want anything to change!"

"What the hell are you talking about?" snapped Ernie, "Choose a side I hate that middle of the road logic."

"Now listen to me! Most people need choices, but they rely on conformity, and they do not want conflict." Jake announced.

"All right I'll give you that." Ernie nervously agreed

"Well, it's simple we create these complex living arrangements, everyone trying to conform, anyone who doesn't is ridiculed as a heretic or worse." Jake was on a roll, "We've been hiding out in the jungle ignoring civilization, looking for a better way. What do we find?"

"Civilization chomping on our ass! That's what." Ernie replied.

"Exactly!" Smiled Jake. "I've been watching you. You are so happy and contented bouncing around on that tractor, cleverly changing the course every chance you get."

"Yeah, so what?"

"All you got to do, is -train your employees to be just as mischievous as you are, and you'll be a happy man. You let me and Ceryle worry about the rest."

"Ok fine! Just chew on this a while; You're going to have to hire carpenters and brick masons to build your utopia. They're going to want their own company store. Electricians are going to want they're own. Pretty soon were gonna run out of Jungle, to hide in." Ernie argued.

Jake turned to Ceryle, "You know we've got to get him a woman."

"Something that worries, more than he does. That's for sure." Ceryle laughed, "I think I'll give Kitty a call."

Worry, needless worry. A man spends more time conjuring up problems he is unable to control, he hardly has time to deal with the ones, that just pop up out of nowhere. Like when Ernie hires three men as caretakers. They gathered around at the end of the day expecting wages. He let it go the first day; explaining it was a onetime loan against their weekly salary. The next day they each brought a second man to share the work. No, defiantly not, he was not running a labor pool. So, one of the men quit on the spot leaving four men standing waiting on an answer. Ernie only had three jobs, barely three. He could get by with two people. As soon as he told the new comers to leave, they all went home. Predictably the same event was to play out over and over again. The first day they demanded wages, the second day they all brought a friend. At one time or another he had hired every able-bodied man in town.

He was reminded of Bakersfield, where the men congregate at a convenience store, waiting for trucks to pull up looking for labor. He had no patience for a bean picker work ethic.

He finally found three men who would show up every day, alone. He even was able to put together a schedule they all could follow without too much supervision. This was the beauty of having the same men every day. He didn't have to go chasing all over town in a golf cart to find his mower parked in a side yard. He still had to overlook the equipment being used for personal business by his crew.

He eventually got around to looking at it as a perk extended to his amigos. That was the other irritating aspect of being the boss. They would not let him be just an employer, he had to be their bosom buddy. They were gregarious, so full of life it made him weary sometimes to keep up with them. He often wished he had the nerve to screen them for contraband, except here in the jungle everything was legal. He himself never wished to pursue any of the copious herbal preparations shared among the inhabitants. He only wondered what it would be like to be happy all the time.

EPILOGUE

Jake and Ceryle sat in the sumptuous surroundings, of what an island paradise expects, of a bank lobby. Ferns, potted plants, deep leather sofas with wide ratan desks. Everywhere there was luxury right down to an espresso caddy making everyone welcome. Opulent, grandiose, every method imaginable; to make the customer feel his money was in good hands. Jake thought it over the top. He was used to small mid-western banks with linoleum floors. Ceryle made no comment.

Their personal banking representative, an elegant black woman, directed them into her private chambers. This was uncomfortable for Jake. She was dressed so well, he could take her from this spot, to the metropolitan opera. He, himself was dressed business style, but being Jake in a suit was still a rumpled affair. Ceryle on the other hand looked every bit the dandy. Without much debate on the subject, Ceryle was elected spokesman. From his smart leather briefcase, he pulled his five-pound document. It sat unopened on the corner of the spotless desk.

The document was only a theatrical prop at best. The elegant black woman was not interested in wherefores; she was here to bag and tag the money. She was not interested where the money came from, as a matter of fact, she would really rather not know. Name of the account and amount to be deposited, that was all she needed.

Business or private account? Her exquisite composure was snarled when she found herself tackling two business accounts and four personal accounts. They would also care for a safety deposit box with two keys. This was going to be a work out for her meticulously manicured nails. Knowing they were going to be here a while she showed interest in the boat anchor on the corner of the desk. Small talk and diligence got the paperwork done.

She was addled and breathless at the end of the business. "Here Gentlemen, is a business account for Bueno Rio Golf Ltd. with wire transfer instructions. A business account for Bueno Rio Housing and Development. A private account for each of the following: Ceryle Smyth, Ernest Copeland, Sarah Cross and James Durado. These are all pass book accounts, meaning to close them a pass book must be presented. Each account may be accessed electronically, with the codes provided."

Moving right along she instructed, "If you will follow me now, I will take you to the vault to use the safety deposit box. After which we will take deposit for the new accounts."

Ceryle had tried to persuade Jake to use a more dignified case than the old brown zippered bag. Jake refused. Just as he now shoved eight red bricks into the big metal drawer. He had his reasons which only God could figure out. The banking representative kept tapping the toe of her shoe as she waited politely a safe distance away. She was noticeably relieved when they were finished. There was still an enormous amount of work to be done to finish the accounts.

Ceryle furnished letters from the absent parties to confirm signatures on their accounts. Jake piled up a stack of cash still covered in plastic wrap with a strange orange dust cling to the wrapper. A grand total of one million seven hundred sixty thousand dollars -American.

The black woman immediately renewed her interest. Fortunate for her, because when they were finished, she was going to feel like a chew toy. Bueno Rio Golf Ltd. One thousand dollars. Bueno Rio Housing and Development One thousand dollars. Ceryle Smyth; Three hundred fifty-two thousand. Ernie Copeland; Seven hundred three thousand dollars. Sarah Cross; fifty thousand dollars. Jake Durado; Six hundred fifty-three thousand dollars. Thank you very much, have a nice day.

It was almost worth the trip to see the look on her face. They had to change planes four times, and taken two water taxis to get here. It was all worth it. The elegant black woman looked like Tina Turner after a gig. Her hair was all akimbo, her make up needed attention, and she was out of breath. Her immaculate desk was covered in dust and she needed the rest of the day off to recover.

The men felt sorry for her and took her to dinner. It turned into a lively affair when out of nowhere they were joined by two equally charming Red Heads.

Oh, they still had money they had a lot of money. They kept back all the earnings from the golf course, just as a cushion. Ernie had eight bricks still buried under the wood pile.

Sarah didn't even know she had any money. She thought she was just signing on as one of the partners of the golf course. Jake was not sure the gift would be proper. But what the hell, she could always give it back.

Milton Keynes UK
Ingram Content Group UK Ltd.
UKHW050924040324
438880UK00007B/24